KRAGNOS
AVATAR OF DESTRUCTION

Other great stories from Warhammer Age of Sigmar

• **GOTREK GURNISSON** •
Darius Hinks

GHOULSLAYER
GITSLAYER
SOULSLAYER

DOMINION
A novel by Darius Hinks

STORMVAULT
A novel by Andy Clark

THUNDERSTRIKE & OTHER STORIES
Various authors
An anthology of short stories

HARROWDEEP
Various authors
An anthology of novellas

A DYNASTY OF MONSTERS
A novel by David Annandale

CURSED CITY
A novel by C L Werner

THE END OF ENLIGHTENMENT
A novel by Richard Strachan

BEASTGRAVE
A novel by C L Werner

REALM-LORDS
A novel by Dale Lucas

HALLOWED GROUND
A novel by Richard Strachan

KRAGNOS: AVATAR OF DESTRUCTION
A novel by David Guymer

GODSBANE
Dale Lucas

• **HALLOWED KNIGHTS** •
Josh Reynolds

BOOK ONE: Plague Garden
BOOK TWO: Black Pyramid

• **KHARADRON OVERLORDS** •
C L Werner

BOOK ONE: Overlords of the Iron Dragon
BOOK TWO: Profit's Ruin

KRAGNOS
AVATAR OF DESTRUCTION

DAVID GUYMER

A BLACK LIBRARY PUBLICATION

First published in 2021.
This edition published in Great Britain in 2022 by
Black Library, Games Workshop Ltd., Willow Road,
Nottingham, NG7 2WS, UK.

Represented by: Games Workshop Limited – Irish branch,
Unit 3, Lower Liffey Street, Dublin 1,
D01 K199, Ireland.

10 9 8 7 6 5 4 3 2 1

Produced by Games Workshop in Nottingham.
Cover illustration by Igor Kieryluk.

Kragnos: Avatar of Destruction © Copyright Games Workshop Limited 2022. Kragnos: Avatar of Destruction, GW, Games Workshop, Black Library, Warhammer, Warhammer Age of Sigmar, Stormcast Eternals, and all associated logos, illustrations, images, names, creatures, races, vehicles, locations, weapons, characters, and the distinctive likenesses thereof, are either ® or TM, and/or © Games Workshop Limited, variably registered around the world.
All Rights Reserved.

A CIP record for this book is available from the British Library.

ISBN 13: 978 1 80026 233 1

No part of this publication may be reproduced, stored in a retrieval system, or transmitted in any form or by any means, electronic, mechanical, photocopying, recording or otherwise, without the prior permission of the publishers.

This is a work of fiction. All the characters and events portrayed in this book are fictional, and any resemblance to real people or incidents is purely coincidental.

See Black Library on the internet at

blacklibrary.com

Find out more about Games Workshop
and the worlds of Warhammer at

games-workshop.com

Printed and bound by CPI Group (UK) Ltd, Croydon, CR0 4YY

This book is dedicated to my childcare bubble. It was late, but it could have been a whole lot later.

I'll never again take school for granted, or complain about it in any way.

Promise.

CHAPTER ONE

Given how awfully the ogor had stunk as it had bulldozed through the Accari lines, it smelled surprisingly wonderful cooked.

There was no cooking pot or stove in the Freeguild's supply that was big enough and so they had done what Ghurites always did best: they had improvised. Roughly fashioned clay tandoors swung like clappers from bone frames, heated from below by fires that spat and popped under the drizzle of juices. Each contained an ogor recently slain in battle.

The hiss of roasting meat and the crackle of fat came with the creaking accompaniment of mechanical fans. There was no Accari in the regiment with the skill to work with moving parts or cogwheels, and the fan-towers were the work of Gunnery-Professor Arden Shay, who had been pressed upon to throw them together over the course of an afternoon. The humming blades wafted the cooking aromas away from the Freeguild positions massed in the hills overlooking the gluthold, and across the desolation that was known locally, and with good reason, as the Eaten Plain.

General Casius Braun of the Accari Hounds stood at the head of his company with his back to the sizzling tandoors, his arms crossed impatiently over his huge, bare chest, and watched.

The gluthold of the Bloodgullet Mawtribe was a belligerent jaw of rawhide and bone, jutting out of the Gnarlfast Mountain in challenge. Its grisly thirty-foot-high wall faced off against two full regiments of Freeguilders and all the firepower of the Excelsian Ironweld, bristling with crude armaments and trophies of its own. Its gate was shaped like a giant mouth, its upper lip decorated with flapping banners of human skin, and stubbornly closed. The fortress itself sank deep into the Gnarlfast. As far as Braun could determine, and Accari scouts were the best scouts in the Heartlands, he was looking at the only way in or out.

He could almost hear the grumbling bellies of those inside, forced to endure the sweet smells of roasted meat after the privations enforced on them by the siege.

The Freeguild had only been camped outside their gates for a week, but ogors were not like humans. They could not go a day without food. Their stores would dwindle quickly, then their slave-creatures, and their mounts, and then they would either turn on each other or they would come out from behind their walls and fight.

Braun preferred to encourage the latter. It had been a long week for him as well.

'Welcome to your new homes!' He spread his arms to encompass the span of the walls. 'This time tomorrow, all of this will be ours.'

The Hounds were the first Freeguild regiment to be officially raised from the city of Accar, itself barely fifty years old and sweltering under the haunted shadow of the Seraphon ziggurat-city of Mekitopsar. Accar had prospered under the aegis of far-Excelsis and now it was their turn to expand the dominion of Order into the Heartlands, to spread its faith, and its wars, to new and heathen peoples.

Braun relished both tasks equally.

He was a large man, built high and built broad, and made hard by the rigours of hard labour and countless battlefields. His face was sun-baked and blistered. An emerald-and-amber tattoo of the god-hammer, the great shatterer, cleft his face in three, the haft starting between his eyes and ending at the bone of his chin. The hammerhead, complete with excruciatingly intricate runic scrollwork, banded both eyes and had not spared the lids. He wore nothing but faded shorts and a pair of snake-leather boots with peeling soles and a hole in one of the heels. Lastly, he wore a belt for his weapons. Braun was easily strong enough to count himself amongst the Accari Greathammerers, the elite group of Hounds who could wield the holy bludgeoning instrument of Sigmar in battle, but Braun considered himself too pious to gird himself as the God-King. He bore two smaller hammers instead, one in each heavy fist.

His personal bodyguard formed a wall around him, as intent as he was on the fortress, anticipating the moment when its doors would open and the waiting would end, and the killing begin. They were known as the Dozen. Every one of the twelve had a story attached, but none of them ever got told around campfires and only Braun himself knew them all.

There was Jenk, the first amongst them under Braun – a thin, evil man with a prominent widow's peak and black eyes that disguised an appetite for pain. He carried only a knife. He claimed to need nothing else.

Then there was Ragn, Murdo, Slayk, Kemrit.

Efrim Taal in his feather cloak and his drakewood staff with the skull of a saurus warrior staring emptily from the top, his belt stuffed with shrivelled wands and his pouches of arcane powders and prophecy. Always beside Taal was Ferrgin, his one friend in the realms, whose wiry body was a constellation of pinprick dots assembled into the Heavenly patterns by the tattooist's needle.

Olgar.

Woan.

Kanta Grint was an enormously fat woman with whiskers on her wrinkled chin, but most of that excess weight was spread across her broad chest and packed into her upper arms. Braun had once seen Kanta lift a slain maw-krusha from the dead body of her eldest son. But that had been years ago. None of them were quite the heroes they had been back then. She wielded the greathammer as though *she* were doing *it* the honour.

Last of their number was Altin, an avowed cannibal, although the majority of the depravities ascribed to him were just rumour. It was a reputation he did little to discourage however, shaving his head, tending naturally towards pallor, and filing his teeth to points. He fought with a butcher's cleaver and a gutting knife, as though acknowledging Jenk's disdain for his enemies and deciding to go one further by disdaining his friends as well.

All of them were tattooed, scarred, clad in knobbled brown cuirass, vambraces, and cuisses made of maw-krusha leather. The very one that Kanta had once lifted, and that Braun himself had personally slain.

Twelve of them, including Braun himself. Sigmar's numeral.

They were unbeaten. Unbeatable. Untouchable so long as they held Sigmar's favour, and as they had held it for close to ten years, Braun saw no reason why they should lose it now. They were an undisciplined and almost chance union of thieves, murderers and eaters of human flesh, but there weren't twelve men in the realms, never mind the Heartlands, so blessed at not dying.

Braun signed himself with the twelve-pointed star, filled with his love for the God-King and the desire to fight his enemies in his name. He hoped the gates would open soon.

'I'm hungry,' said Altin.

'You're always hungry,' Jenk muttered, picking something from under his fingernails with his knife.

'If the ogres don't come out soon, I'm going to eat one of the Azyrites, I swear.'

There were chuckles at that.

'You'll be hungry again by midday,' said Kanta.

Altin's kohl-shaded eyes narrowed. 'Then I'll go back for another.'

Braun heard a deep sigh and turned his head towards it.

Gunnery-Professor Shay was looking up at one of the fan-towers she had helped to erect. She was an elderly woman with short white hair and thick-lensed glasses without which she could see almost nothing, inappropriately dressed for the humidity of Ymnog's Trample, or for battle, in a blueish gown embroidered with mathematurgical symbols. Going one further even than Altin and Jenk, she did not appear to be armed at all, but was rarely seen without a book. A typically heavy tome was lying open in her hands, leather bookmark drooping over its spine.

'I built cathedrals, you know,' she said, staring at her creation with disgust forming like cloud shapes in her rheumy white eyes. '*Cathedrals*. And the great lighthouse at Bilgeport. Have you seen it?'

Braun had. It was an impressive building.

'No,' he said.

Shay was the most renowned engineer in Excelsis. Even a layman like Braun had heard of her. She had taught three generations of artillerists and there wasn't a senior position in the Artillery School that wasn't held by one of her former proteges. She was said to have developed her own signature method of mixing gunpowder which had supposedly won many victories for the forces of Order and saved many lives. She had a lecture hall named after her in the Artillery School, as she was wont to mention occasionally, and had been assigned to lead the crusade's Ironweld contingent by High Arbiter Synor himself as an honour to their Azyrite allies: the most noble First Age Starhold Celestians.

Apparently, no other candidate was of sufficient esteem to be acceptable to the honour of either the Celestians, or the High Arbiter. That Shay's first love was for civil engineering, that she had not fired a real gun in the forty years she had spent teaching, and that she had protested the assignment even as her bags were being packed for her did not appear to have troubled anyone else but Braun.

A cheer went up from the watching ranks ranged across the broken plain, a beating of clubs and axes on leather shields and a stamping of banner poles on the rocky ground. Taal elbowed him in the ribs, and Braun turned back towards the glut hold. With a shriek of tortured iron, the huge gate-mouth began to grind open.

Grinning, Braun pulled his hammers from his belt. 'Tonight, we feast on ogor meat. And tomorrow we raise the God-King his new monument.' He clashed his hammers together and started forwards.

The Dozen followed.

Then his army.

Ellisior Seraphine Lisandr, general of the First Age Celestians, knelt as Mother-Superior Thassily Dispensa, warrior-pontiff of renown, blessed her.

'Heaven-made and Heaven-sent,' said the pontiff, scattering her bowed head with stardust and leaving her white hair glittering like a stellar nursery. 'With Heaven armed and in Heaven armoured.'

Lisandr signed the hammer and lifted her gaze.

The pontiff's eyes were as stern as sigmarite. Her armour was a full-plate harness of blued steel edged with gold, her open helm crowned with a laurel of teeth that were said to have been broken from the mouth of the great squig Gritztomper by the fist of the Celestant-Prime.

'To Heaven returned,' Lisandr finished.

Thassily nodded and moved on to bless Lisandr's squire.

Lydia Victoria Aubreitn was the daughter of a noble family with ambitions of adding the Aubreitn name to the prestigious rolls of Azyr's oldest regiment. She knelt to receive her blessing with the reins of Lisandr's demigryph still wound around her hand, armoured in midnight blue and starsilver, overlaid with the white tabard of her provisional rank with the regiment. In her right hand was a long spear that she leant her weight against, the multitude of heraldic devices that Lisandr had inherited or married into fluttering from the array of pennons tied around the haft.

The demigryph itself was a prince amongst its noble breed, proud enough that it would bear none but the scions of Azyr's oldest families to war on its back. Its shoulders were broader than the diamond carriages that conveyed even the lowest-ranking members of the Grand Conclave through the tiered colonnades of Starhold. Its plumage was as bright as a halo, its beak as sharp and elegant as stained glass. Its harness was silver, studded with blue spinels and sapphires, and caparisoned in heraldry older than gods.

Long before the first forging of the divine Stormhosts, there had been Celestians on the walls of Azyr's greatest cities.

As Thassily took Lydia through the Oath to Azyr, Lisandr stood and looked down the close-drawn ranks of her regiment with pride. Two thousand knights stood patiently beside their steeds and attended by their squires, unmoved by the rank horror of the gluthold before them, or of the Accari around them, each flying their own banners and personal heraldry. Some represented militant dynasties as old and gloried as Lisandr's. But not many.

For all the variation in iconography, however, every warrior was identically equipped and armed. A cuirass, fitted to each individual wearer by fusing together bands of meteoric iron and then studded with diamond rivets. Long, pleated skirts of silver rings that reached down to the knees to protect the thighs. In the right hand a long spear, sometimes referred to as a half-pike, more commonly a weapon of the aelves of Hysh, but proudly borne by the regiments of the First Age as a reminder of the ancient time when the god Tyrion had tutored the first of Sigmar's mortal legions in the conduct of war. At the left hip, ready to be drawn, was a scabbarded sabre, and across the back, a kite shield and a warhammer.

A Celestian was a lord, on the battlefield and off it, expected to be equally adept with any weapon and in any role, and to switch between them at the command of the moment.

As her forebears had marshalled the armies of Azyr for the purging of the Realm of Heaven in the Age of Myth, so would she now see this small piece of Gallet cleansed. She would oversee the establishment of the Accari's new settlement in the ruin of their enemies' former stronghold, and then by the order of Azyr she would be free to return to Starhold: a few precious months with her husband and daughter, and then on to the next crusade. She had won the God-King many victories in her thirty years of war, and lived only for the furtherance of the regiment's glory. She would never complain.

But she longed to be rid of this place.

It was the insect bites. The howls that filled each night. The insufferable humidity and heat, as if they fought not over a land of rock and earth but the hard-furred body of a fiery-tempered beast. It was the way the ground would tremble, at any time and without warning, severe enough on occasion to break bones and throw even demigryphs to the ground. Sometimes it felt as though that was the ground's intent.

After this crusade, a campaign in any other realm would seem preferable.

She looked up as the tramp of heavy-booted feet announced Braun's advance on her right. Another mob of Hounds, this one even larger, were marching more or less in time on her left. Lisandr was almost impressed. The Accari were organised, if one were to be charitable and call it that, along several parallel hierarchies of strength, each one tied together and in mutual competition through familial ties and bonds of marriage. Only Braun himself could get so many of them to go in the same direction at the same time.

They were as eager to see this battle through as she was.

As she turned, the sweet stench that Braun and Shay's infernal contraptions were blowing across her lines wrinkled her nose. She heard the jeers from Braun's troop as they marched past, Braun's shaman rattling his staff and making lewd gestures in the vague direction of Mother Thassily. His warriors, meanwhile, clearly encouraged by his less-than-worthy example, threw insults at the kneeling Celestians.

'If I knelt for every ogor I crossed I'd never stand up.'

'I wouldn't kiss this ground, it bites.'

'If the meat looks a bit tough, we'll soften it up for you.'

Lisandr's squire, Lydia, rose from the ground, going for her sabre, her young face flushed with offended nobility and sparkling with Heaven's blessing, before Lisandr's light touch on her sleeve restrained her.

'Inspire by example,' she said. '*Show* them Heaven.'

Sheepishly, Lydia slid her fingers from the grip of her weapon. 'Yes, my lady. Forgive me.'

'It is all right, Lydia. Ghur will make savages of us all, there is no shame in acknowledging that we are no more human than the Hounds, and strangers in a land that hates us.'

'Thank you, my lady.'

Smiling thinly, Lisandr put out her hand.

Lydia passed her spear.

Using the long pole as a punt, Lisandr eased her foot into her stirrup and guided herself up into the demigryph's high saddle. It issued an eager sound, something between a chirrup and a growl, but nothing so terrestrial or mundane: it was the whale song of one celestial body as it sang across the ceaseless void to another. She felt its movement under her, willing for her leave to charge. She restrained it.

One did not lightly command the beasts of Heaven.

Raising her spear aloft she cried out, 'Are there abominations such as the Bloodgullet to be found in Azyr?'

Half her warriors were still bowed and kneeling, awaiting their blessing, but the rest, fastidiously arming themselves and tending to their mounts, called back in fair voice, *'No!'*

'Why then do we tolerate them here?'

'We do not!'

'Show these Reclaimed savages Azyrite contempt.'

Lisandr pulled on her helmet, a silver barbute with a long plume and a vertical slit for eyes and mouth, but starsilver over both ears that muted her warriors' cheers. The face behind that vertical bar was gaunt and grim.

'Shall I sound the attack order, my lady?' Lydia asked, as the Accari Hounds continued to tramp by in seemingly endless ranks.

'No,' said Lisandr. 'I will not deny my soldiers their rightful blessings, nor cause a pontiff of Azyr to rush to meet the impulses of barbarians.' She nodded towards the glutfort where the gates were now fully wide, the first armoured gluttons stomping forth and forming into sweating ranks. 'If the Hounds are so keen to be the first into the fight, then I am not of a mind to deny them.'

Malec Grint should have been paying attention to the battle, but the Celestian woman who had volunteered to lead them across the Eaten Plain was so distractingly beautiful. Her hair was silver, her skin the flawless black of a night sky, her raiment and armour composed as though to frame that beauty in starmetal and jewels. Grint's mother, who also happened to be his chief and a noted authority on all things, and whose curmudgeonly utterances could be held as equal to Sigmar's law, had only contempt for the Azyrites. 'Wishbones', she called them, for the ease with which they would snap. But Grint had never seen anything so shimmering or wondrous outside of a reliquary or a dream. Her name was Ilsbet Glorica Angellin. He sighed. Even that was beautiful.

But he should have been paying attention to the battle.

The ogor cannonball whistled over his shoulder and turned his friend Abone into pink mist above the waist. Bad Luck Mikali, who had been running alongside him, screamed as bits of Abone splattered her face, and charged headlong into Grint's back, sending them tumbling down the shallow hill together. Grint landed on top of her, winding her. Mikali gawped around Grint's shoulder as pink lumps continued to rain over the hillside. Grint didn't feel any grief for his friend beyond the discomfort of Mikali's knee against his ribs. They were Heartlanders. Life was messy and short.

And he didn't blame himself so much as he blamed Mikali. The name 'Bad Luck' had started life as a joke but, like most people who spent too much time around her, that life had ended badly.

Grint had worked hard to bust himself down to the make-up mobs, those fighters who consistently fell short in some way or another, or struck the chieftains as somehow *off* and in need of 'toughening up', as they put it, with the most dangerous tasks. Like being first to meet the charge of starving ogors lured from their gluthold by the aroma of cooking meat. He'd done it because he'd heard that Angellin had volunteered – *volunteered!* – to lead them and, as Celestians and Hounds seldom mingled, it was a once-in-a-crusade opportunity to get close enough to impress.

Mikali, on the other hand, was already as tough as women got, and as hateful as a bullied grot with it. Her more-or-less permanent placement in the mobs was more as a deterrent to everyone else than as a punishment to her. Braun, Taal, Jenk and the other chiefs had long ago realised that Bad Luck could not be got rid of so easily, and had instead decided to make it work for them.

Cannon fire barked across the roof of the shallow defile that he'd just fallen into, more pink geysers erupting from the meagre cover on the Accari side, as several ogor leadbelchers came bellowing and belching over the lip. They were the first of their kind that Grint had seen up close and they made for an appalling spectacle. Twice the height and breadth of the biggest man, and ten times his weight. Their teeth were brown in leering grins. Their eyes were hungry. Their enormous, swinging guts were clapped in shields of iron or brass, bits of scrap plate and mail hanging off their shoulders. Each one hefted a full-size field cannon the way a human would wield a crossbow, their jowly chins streaked with red. Grint hadn't been as far ahead of the rest of the Hounds as he'd thought: the leadbelchers had eaten on the way.

'Warriors, to me!' Angellin shouted, her voice as high and clear as a hunting bugle through the Primeval Jungle. 'Scions of the First Age, show them Heaven!'

Leaping into the defile with her spear-point down and sparkling, the Celestian punched it through the shoulder of an ogor leadbelcher and bore him down, while the meanest and most misbegotten Hounds of Accar poured down the slope behind her and crashed into the gutbusters' over-eager line.

Gut plates crunched into leather shields. Warriors were hurled into their comrades, the leadbelchers setting about clubbing upraised shields and heads with the heavy butts of their cannons. The Hounds answered in kind with axes and knives, stabbing for throats, piercing blubber, the lowest creatures of Accar screaming as they pitted their collective strength against that of the ogors.

An ogor with a sticky goatee and a tattoo of a mouth inked badly around his own fat lips thrust his gut into an Accari shield. The warrior was launched well over the second and third ranks of warriors and crunched into the slope of the hill. A small avalanche buried him, and the ogor laughed, spraying the front rank with spittle, before Celestian Angellin thrust her spear up through the underside of his chin.

Breaks appeared in the Accari line. A sweaty mass of iron and blubber bullied its way far enough through to tower over Grint and Mikali where they still lay. The stench hit first and was overwhelming enough on its own. It was greasy armpits and sweating fat, bad breath and unwashed pockets stuffed with rancid meats. The ogor roared and swung up his cannon-club. His eyes swam with mad hunger, devouring Grint and Mikali even while they quavered before it.

Angellin ran her spear through the ogor's side.

It went in deep, the long blade sliding into the thick fat behind the heavy protection of his belly plate. The ogor threw his head back and howled in pain while fatty lumps slopped out of his side and heaped up on the ground about his boots. His legs wobbled and collapsed from under him, dropping the brute to the ground, where he began madly scooping up fistfuls of his own lost fat and stuffing it into his mouth. Grint stared at the tableau in horror, before the tip of Angellin's spear pierced the back of the ogor's skull and finally silenced his hunger.

The Celestian looked down on Grint and Mikali where they lay side by side in the muck and gore. She arched a silver eyebrow.

'Am I interrupting something?'

'No,' said Grint, so quickly that Mikali burst out laughing and Grint felt obligated to punch her in the chest with his elbow as he scrambled up to his feet. She curled onto her side and wheezed, still trying to laugh, as he dusted himself off.

In the ditch around them, the Accari were finishing off the last of the ogors, stabbing down with their javelins wherever an ogor still writhed or a grumbling belly betrayed one trying to play dead.

'Grint, isn't it?' said Angellin.

Grint pulled himself straight, looking to emphasise the breadth of his shoulders, the thickness of his brow, the many breaks of his nose and the scars on his chin. The Celestian did not appear to be particularly impressed. Grint looked at her, confused. She did not even seem to notice.

'Do you at least have a weapon?' said Angellin.

He drew his curved knife. All Accari carried one like it. It had three distinct cutting edges: the tip was for cutting the spice pod from the arraca plant that grew wild only in the jungles of Accar, the outside edge was for cutting through jungle vegetation, and the inside curve was for killing.

'I have this.'

Again, Grint noted a lack of impression.

'I understand that it is the Ghurite way to battle half-dressed, but did your masters in Accar not think it best to arm their soldiers before sending them on crusade?' Passing her spear across to her left hand, she drew her sabre and passed it to Grint. 'Take this. It belonged to my great-grandfather. He was a captain with the Eagles of Glimmerheim during the Realmgate Wars. His death in the storming of Gutwater Falls earned me this chance with the Celestians despite the minor nobility of my family.' Her grip on the weapon tightened before finally relinquishing it. 'So I want it back.'

'I understand,' Grint lied.

He had never known a grandparent. His father had died before he was born. All his mother had ever given him were broken bones. He clutched the starmetal sabre to his breast as though it had fallen from the sky with a note from Sigmar tied around its pommel.

'Sir,' Angellin reminded him.

'Yes, sir!'

Behind him, he could feel Mikali smirk.

Angellin turned away, and Grint felt the light go out of him, the sabre turning suddenly into a weight many times greater than he was used to wielding and sagging on his arm. Inwardly, he cursed himself for offering so little during the fight beyond the chance for the Celestian to save his life. He glared at Mikali. This was almost certainly her fault. He should have known better than to try to win a woman like Ilsbet Glorica Angellin with Bad Luck around.

'You have fought well,' Angellin announced to the mob now gathered up with her in the offal pit at the base of the hill they had just charged down. 'I will tell your commanders as much when the day is won.'

A few ragged cheers went up, most of them cheerfully ironic because, as everyone here had cause to know, there was no pleasing an Accari chief who had got it into their head to dislike you. That was why Grint had had to work so hard to get this punishment, given who his mother was, and it had actually never occurred to him that he might have just as hard a time getting out again. Of course, it hadn't been quite as intentional as he liked to pretend.

'Generals Lisandr and Braun have tasked us with distracting the defenders on the walls while the main force follows behind us to assault the gate.'

She turned and pointed with her spear towards the gluthold.

The Eaten Plain was a no-man's-land for a thousand miles in every direction from the Gnarlfast. The bottomless appetites of the ogors had stripped it barren, nothing growing there now but a few cacti that had learned to live off the drops spilled from butchers' wagons. The Accari's siege had not been a long one, but mortars, rockets and cannons had gouged great defiles, such as the one they stood in now, through which brackish streams trickled. Bits of junk, launched from the gluthold by gnoblar scrap catapults, stuck up out of the landscape like weird sculptures.

'We can go crater to crater, and take shelter from the ogors' guns for at least part of the way.'

She moved, picking up those Hounds who had busied themselves during her speech looting the dead for pretty stones and metals, one hopeful individual pulling off an ogor's coat, and started into a run. Grint pushed his way to the front as they zigzagged around pulverised hills and scrambled over bloody rivulets on hands and knees.

Their mob numbered about a hundred and thirty men. Aside from the blood-coloured leather tunics that a few of them hadn't lost or gambled away, there was no such thing as standard kit amongst the Hounds. Their uniforms were a patchwork of what they could borrow, steal, peel off a corpse, or make for themselves from the land. In terms of equipment, most bore only what they had joined with, which for the most part meant spicing knives. Small hammers and hatchets were also common, with many Accari liking the feel of one of each in either hand.

With the gluthold's walls looming, Celestian Angellin led the mob into a shallow defile. It looked to have been a natural feature through the landscape once, before the ogors had stripped the entire country bare. A week of Ironweld bombardment had subsequently flooded and expanded it. The broken bodies of another mob that must have got here before them polluted the dirty puddles: bits of kit and the occasional half-chewed limb poked through the mess.

A gnoblar looked up from where it was crouched over the body of a Hound, something shiny in its grasping fingers reflecting the inhuman malice in its eyes.

Grint roared as he charged and swung his sabre at it. He was unfamiliar with the sword's design, but he knew a cutting edge when he saw one and the starmetal that the Azyrite weapons were forged from was almost magically sharp. The blade cut through the greenskin's large, flappy ear and went deep into its shoulder. The child-sized monster went down with a piteous scream. Grint stepped on it, almost tearing the gnoblar in half as he fought to pull the sabre out of its shoulder.

The rest of Angellin's mob surged ahead, shrieking like gryph-hounds at the kill as the remaining gnoblars who had been picking through the loot that the ogors had left behind them threw up their arms and scattered.

Grint howled like a feral loon, running down one as it broke for the side wall. He hurled himself for it at full stretch, tackling the little horror to the ground and rolling with it to the revetment. The gnoblar was a quarter his size but wiry, with sharp teeth and strong hands, and he was bleeding from a score of scratches and bites before he finally got his hands around the thing's throat and throttled it at arm's length.

The creature kicked. Its eyes bugged, its face turning a deeper shade of green.

Gnoblars were smaller than their grot cousins. And meaner, if that were possible. They were rumoured to taste so terrible that even the ogors preferred not to eat them. Even so, Grint doubted that a week of starvation rations in the gluthold had gone well on the gnoblar population. This one died as though grateful that Grint had made it so quick.

Flushed with success, he held it up like a wrung chicken by the neck, offering up the kill he had made with his bare hands as a testament to his strength and his courage. And also, to the recklessness that promised a troublesome man would not be around long enough to trouble his intended into old age. The tradition was time-honoured, inherited from the original jungle tribes from whom the likes of Taal were descended, who had hunted the lizards of the Primeval Jungle before the coming of the trade pioneers and early settlers from Excelsis.

Angellin looked at it. She looked at him.

'Well done,' she said uncertainly, and then splashed away through the flooded defile, rallying her easily distracted fighters to her.

Deflated, Grint lowered his dead gnoblar to the ground.

'I'll take it,' said Mikali.

Grint looked at his spurned bride price. 'You?'

'I know. You're not much to look at. But I'd be a fool to pass up the chance at winning Kanta for a mother-in-law.'

'You've been at the shroom bread.'

Mikali grinned nastily. 'What did you do to get down to my level anyway?'

Grint sighed. 'I gave Mother Thassily lip.'

'You're lucky it wasn't Braun who caught you. If he heard you back-talk a priest he'd have cut that lip off.'

'This is it!' Angellin yelled. 'The final stretch.' She went over the top of the ditch, the Hounds sufficiently keyed up from fighting to follow her without question and sweeping Grint along, up out of the defile, just a few hundred yards from the gluthold's monstrous walls.

Other make-up mobs, led by minor chiefs who had offended the more important leaders somehow or, more rarely, a Celestian officer like Angellin with something to prove, surged over the rocks, the dull roar of the main horde behind them. Ahead, the walls' stupendous upper heights were strung with an abundance of grisly trophies and totems to the Bloodgullets' gluttonous god. Or it might just have been rubbish. Grint did not know how to tell the difference between what an ogor would call art and what it would throw away. The ogors were not as stupid as they looked, however; nothing draped the parapet that hung far enough to the bottom for a man to reach and climb up. And all the while, leadbelchers fired down from platforms into the mad scrum of fighters, some getting carried away and throwing down their cannons, or screaming gnoblars, instead of remembering to reload.

Men died in droves and they didn't care. The battle madness was on them, kill or be killed, and neither Braun nor Lisandr was its master.

Angellin charged headlong into the random blasts of gunfire.

Three fighters burst as an ogor cannonball ploughed through them. Their leader ran recklessly on and the rest followed her.

'Grenadiers!' she yelled, as they came within fifty feet of the thirty-foot-high walls.

There was a breed of lizard living in the Primeval Jungle that, despite its uncharacteristically peaceable and placid nature, lived largely predation-free due to its spectacular natural defence of exploding when slain. The tribesmen had mastered the delicate feat of exsanguinating the lizard safely, of storing its volatile fluids separately in the chambers of desiccated kara nuts to be hurled in battle as deadly alchemical grenades.

There were no archers or crossbowmen amongst the Accari. Most ranged-weapon users carried a javelin or two. Only the oldest and bravest carried kara grenades.

Well within range now, the grenadiers tore the palm-sized nuts from bandoliers and hurled them towards the ogors' wall. On impact, the dried shells cracked open and the carefully separated fluids explosively recombined. Fireballs rippled along the wall in pink, yellow and green – the exact alchemical properties of the explosive compound varying from lizard to lizard – ripping through its grislier adornments and torching the rawhide hangings. The underlying defences, though, were thick as well as high, built of ironoak, and as the initial explosions burned themselves out, they left behind a wall that was denuded and scarred but otherwise intact.

The leadbelchers jeered from their platforms, but what they had not accounted for was what generations of cooking fat and tallow would do to a wall. The guttering alchemical fires caught in just enough places, and a second later the entire stretch of wall went up with a *whoosh* of irresistible hunger that turned the ogors' mockery into screams as they were burned alive to sate it.

Angellin grinned, her face coming alive in the dance of multi-coloured flames and the death throes of monsters.

Her warriors cheered, and Grint cheered with them, and ignored her completely when she tried to make them withdraw.

The war-chiefs of the Accari howled as their enemy's house went up in flames, and they redoubled their efforts to get across the Eaten Plain and amongst them, their troops following with handmade or purloined banners, blasting on horns of bone, banging on cymbals and beating drums.

The full strength of the Accari Hounds had never been properly accounted. According to the rolls of the trade pioneers and spice barons who had sponsored the recruitment, and the muster that had been inscribed on a celestium tablet to be held in perpetuity in the library of the High Arbiter in Excelsis, it stood at twenty-five thousand men.

That, of course, was a wild overestimate.

At least half the men had volunteered themselves two or three times over in order to pocket the extra glimmerings, while Braun had himself fielded two entirely fictitious clans onto the regimental lists. One of those had even performed with valour in forcing the crossing at Glutton's Gorge, and earned every non-existent fighting man a handsome bonus in Excelsian coin.

There had been the usual losses. Truancy. In-fighting. Attrition.

A reasonable estimate would have put their strength at fifteen thousand. Still seven times what the warriors from Starhold could field, and three-quarters of which was now pouring across the half-mile desolation between the Freeguild camp and the Gnarlfast.

Braun crested the last hillock of consequence before the gluthold's walls and planted his foot on the rock as though claiming it for the God-King. He tapped the cardinal points of the hammer tattoo on his face, then pumped both fists in the air, giving a wordless howl as his soldiers thundered beneath his vantage. It was a rapturous experience. Like being borne aloft on Sigmar's tempest. The Dozen made a ring of maw-krusha skin and mean-faced steel about him as Braun shook in an ecstatic rage, beating his hammers together above his head and foaming at the mouth as he charged.

The gates to the ogor gluthold were thirty feet high, plates of bone and great sheets of rawhide drilled with iron into thick, dark oak. They held, even where the flames from the burning section licked at the frame.

The ogors had thrown them wide in their eagerness to taste the meat that Braun had offered them. A handful of ravenous gutbusters had charged headlong onto the plain and been tied up by the make-up mobs, but a glut of reasonably well-disciplined ogor warriors armoured with gut shields and stiff leather bracers were forming up in front of the gate. They were sweating profusely in the heat of the Ghurish day, thumping mauls and metal tenderisers into their waiting fists.

A desultory crackle of fire from the handful of leadbelchers still perched on their groaning platforms punched human soldiers from their feet. Bouncing cannonballs scythed through their comrades by the score. But still the rabid Hounds ran on. The first wave slammed into the ogor gluttons like a fist into a huge, fat gut.

The line bowed for a moment, rippled, and then snapped back hard. Ogors roared and bellowed as the swings of their weapons sent broken men flying. More Hounds piled in, frenzied beyond rational fear or any sense of pain. For each man that threw himself onto an ogor's swinging mallet, a hundred or two hundred more slammed bodily into the huge, sheer posts of the burning stockade in an attempt to scale them.

'Sigmar!' Braun howled, running like a steam tank at the head of the second wave, and flung himself at the glutton line.

Two quick blows from his hammers caved in an ogor's chest. Jenk leapt on another, the leader of the Dozen stabbing it frenziedly in the eye until Kanta came up, spitting on her palms, and threw them both as though tossing a tree trunk. Efrim Taal muttered an incantation, reaching into one of his many pouches and tossing its contents across the glutton ranks. Ogors howled, dropping to their knees and scratching as the sparkling dust transformed into living mites that burrowed into their skin.

Braun whooped as he fought his way towards the gates. Both his hammers were stringy with ogor pulp. Blood smeared his arms to the shoulder and he could feel the fire that burned through every vein in his body, force-feeding a heart that hammered like a maniac in the throes of a religious fit.

The gluttons, though, were going strong yet, everywhere but where Braun and the Dozen fought, butchering and laughing at the same time. They were taking the fight to the Hounds as the Accari lost the impetus of the charge. The line advanced steadily from the gate, the slow swell of a mighty gut with the release of its belt. It was almost a game to them. An ogor could kill ten men with contemptuous ease. For that same number of men to bring down a single ogor, on the other hand, was a heroic feat, one that would be rightly celebrated with feasting and prayer.

'I know you, small human.'

The voice was deep and breathy, damp from pushing its way through so much wobbling meat on its way up from the brute's chest and out of his fat mouth. His broad, bullet head was wedged into a metal skullcap. The rest of his mountainous bulk was clapped in iron plate, draped in fur, mail and leather, and topped by a rack of trophies bolted to his shoulders. The skulls of humans, duardin, aelves, saurus and the battle helm of a Stormcast Eternal swayed, as though from a washing line, above his head. In a blood-smeared hand wider than Braun's chest he wielded a blunt spear longer than Braun was tall.

'Braun,' said the ogor. 'The man who beat Rukka Bosskilla and took his favourite pet's skin.' He looked Braun down and further down. 'I thought you'd be bigger.'

Braun scowled. The defeat of the Ironjawz megaboss and his 'Big Rukk' should have been his defining moment, the triumph to cement his reputation as the brightest young general in the Heartlands outside of Excelsis. He could have eaten free for the rest of his life.

Should have. Could have.

For reasons only his Dozen understood, it was one tale he never liked to tell.

'Yeah, well,' he said. 'I don't know you.'

'Grob Bloodgullet's my name.'

Braun raised a hammer to signal his Dozen. 'Get over here and show some respect. We've got the Tyrant himself here.' He turned back with a mock flourish of a bloody hammer and a bow. 'I didn't recognise you without a giant great wall in front of you.'

Grob's ironclad belly jangled as he laughed. 'Good, small human. Good. Grob hates meat that will not chew back.'

'I'm going to eat you myself.' Braun bared his teeth. He licked his lips theatrically. 'Every. Last. Bit.'

The Tyrant's expression firmed into something serious. 'You feel it too? I should've known. The one who beat Rukka...'

'Feel what?'

Grob beat vaguely on his chest, as though sounding out a

rhythm, like a drumbeat through stone. His fat-slack face managed to look both ecstatic and fearful. 'It.'

Braun allowed his hammers to lower as he listened, and despite the tumult around him he *could* almost feel the heavy drums of Ghur that the Tyrant described. He felt something close to a kinship between himself and the ogor in that moment; closer, certainly, than anything he shared with Ellisior and her joyless soldiers. Were they not both creatures of Ghur, the general and the Tyrant? Was it no longer enough for them to knock down each other's castles and make trophies of their bones without needing to make more of their conquest than that?

Did they really have to settle and build and raise crops? Ghur would only tear it all down, in the end.

Grob's slobbery bellow snapped him out of his reverie. The Tyrant clobbered towards him on fat legs that pulverised the ground with his passing. Braun backed towards his Dozen, twirling his leading hammer as both a goad and a distraction. Grob narrowed his eyes and snorted, and thrust his spear for the spinning blade. Braun swept one hammer out from the jab and struck over the top with the other. The weapon rang off the Tyrant's iron rerebrace and knocked the spear aside, but sheer bulk forced him to give ground or be trampled.

The Tyrant heaved his gut around and the rest of his body followed with impressive agility. He slapped the upper haft of his hunting spear into his off-hand palm, shortening the reach, and jabbed it towards Braun's chest. Braun bent around it, then shoulder-slammed the haft to throw it wide and force an opening to the ogor's gut.

The Tyrant laughed and kneed him in the face.

Braun's head snapped back, arms flying out. It felt as though he had just dived backwards off a cliff, the weightless sensation lasting for a two-count until he hit the ground and skidded, the rocks cutting his bare back to bloody ribbons.

Grob banged his fist on his iron breastplate and strode unstoppably towards him.

Two of the Dozen came running in. Ragn and Jenk. If Braun outlived the day then he'd be *damned* sure to have words with the other nine. Jenk went down with the butt of Grob's spear in his stomach and puked his guts over his knees. Ragn caught the reverse swing as an uppercut, shattering every bone in his jaw and tossing him fifteen feet through the air.

'Braun likes to fight dirty,' said Grob. 'Like a nasty gnoblar, I heard.'

'Says who?' Braun snarled from the ground.

'Says everyone. You've got a reputation.'

The Tyrant bent down, grabbed Braun by the belt of his shorts, and lifted him off the ground as though he weighed no more than a bushel of hay. Braun milled his arms and his legs, but the Tyrant's arm was too long and nothing connected.

A shadow passed over the Tyrant's face. Braun felt a wind across his chest.

He looked up.

The griffon shrieked its challenge, trailing blue-white sparks as it bore Mother-Superior Thassily Dispensa, warrior-pontiff of blessed Azyr, over the slaughter. She shone like a comet, blazing its magicks as it crossed the sky. Her favoured weapon was a two-headed monster of a hammer that Braun was too pious to wield himself but would never begrudge a priestess. Lightning haloed its head as she chanted. She was yelling every word but, over the roar of the battle, Braun could not make out a single one. Energy fulminated down the weapon's haft and writhed around her forearm.

Grob bellowed impotently at the nascent storm.

'Sigmar is the storm and the hammer,' Braun growled.

Lightning flashed. Thunder rolled across the sky.

'He is the anvil and the–'

A bloody and unexpectedly lengthy life flashed across Braun's eyes as the lightning bolt struck the Tyrant's iron helmet, the ensuing *crack* hurling the Accari general aside like just another piece of steaming ogor in a storm of meat and electricity.

When he was next able to peel open his eyes, corposant crackled from his eyelashes. Every nerve in his body sang with pain and he rejoiced at having felt the fierce slap of Sigmar and lived to tell of it. He laughed hoarsely, the echoing peals of the thunder-crack rolling out across the battlefield.

The mother-superior and her griffon sailed righteously on.

Braun sat upright, stiff as a piece of crisped bacon, and watched dazedly as the ground beneath him trembled and the desolation behind him turned silver.

The knights of the First Age Celestians thundered towards the gluthold. They came mounted on their demigryphs, huge warbeasts with the sharp beak and long neck of a bald eagle and the hind quarters of a leonine monster, lesser relations of the war-priestess' griffon, but flightless, and draped in silver barding.

The heavy cavalry swept around the gluttons' flanks with their spear-points lowered, and where a mob of human fighters would struggle hard and still fail against one ogor the demigryph knights tore them down by the score and thundered through. Braun watched as the surviving Hounds, no longer fighting for their lives and forsaken by the temporary insanity that had given them courage in battle, broke and ran for their tents on the plain.

The Hounds were on this crusade to supply human shields for the Celestians.

It wasn't written down anywhere, no one had ever spoken it aloud, the gluthold was supposed to become *their* city, but there wasn't an Accari who didn't know that it was true. Braun had always known it, but seeing it first-hand made his blood simmer anew and his hackles rise.

'General Braun.'

He looked up over his shoulder. He knew from the disrespect loaded into the speaking of his rank that it would be a Celestian. And it was. The high, gaunt face of a Celestian male, framed by a tall helmet with the visor open, peered down at him. His monstrous mount bristled, as though sensing the mutual bad feeling, and raised a talon paw as if to pin Braun, in the manner that an eagle would trap a mouse, before the Celestian reined it in.

'General Ellisior Seraphine Lisandr commands you attend her at once.'

Braun grunted. 'I'm a bit busy right now.'

The knight idly gestured with his spear to where the Celestian cavalry was thundering through the open gates and taking the last of the fight inside. 'By the time you get to her, you won't be.'

The Mortal Realms have been despoiled. Ravaged by the followers of the Chaos Gods, they stand on the brink of utter destruction.

The fortress-cities of Sigmar are islands of light in a sea of darkness. Constantly besieged, their walls are assailed by maniacal hordes and monstrous beasts. The bones of good men are littered thick outside the gates. These bulwarks of Order are embattled within as well as without, for the lure of Chaos beguiles the citizens with promises of power.

Still the champions of Order fight on. At the break of dawn, the Crusader's Bell rings and a new expedition departs. Storm-forged knights march shoulder to shoulder with resolute militia, stoic duardin and slender aelves. Bedecked in the splendour of war, the Dawnbringer Crusades venture out to found civilisations anew. These grim pioneers take with them the fires of hope. Yet they go forth into a hellish wasteland.

Out in the wilds, hardy colonists restore order to a crumbling world. Haunted eyes scan the horizon for tyrannical reavers as they build upon the bones of ancient empires, eking out a meagre existence from cursed soil and ice-cold seas. By their valour, the fate of the Mortal Realms will be decided.

The ravening terrors that prey upon these settlers take a thousand forms. Cannibal barbarians and deranged murderers crawl from hidden lairs. Martial hosts clad in black steel march from skull-strewn castles. The savage hordes of Destruction batter the frontier towns until no stone stands atop another. In the dead of night come howling throngs of the undead, hungry to feast upon the living.

Against such foes, courage is the truest defence and the most effective weapon. It is something that Sigmar's chosen do not lack. But they are not always strong enough to prevail, and even in victory, each new battle saps their souls a little more.

This is the time of turmoil. This is the era of war.

This is the Age of Sigmar.

CHAPTER TWO

Vagria Farstrike swung her boot out of the stirrup and jumped down from the saddle. Her gryph-charger, Starsid, scuffed anxiously at the thick cattail grasses that grew in the valleys of the Morruk Hills with the long talons of his aquiline forepaws, his golden eyes like half-moons in the radiant gloom of dusk. With a threatening caw, he turned his snowy-white neck back towards the predacious tree-herds that had stalked them all the way across the Carcasse Donse. Hungry wood groaned, shivering in the warm air, as the trees withdrew to a safer distance.

Content that the things that would hunt her were not yet frustrated or numerous enough to challenge a Stormcast Eternal, Vagria laid her gauntleted hand flat upon the ground. It trembled like an animal.

Not with fear. At least, not with any fear of her.

She pushed her fingers through the surface litter and into the topsoil. The earth was dense and moist, like a heavy clay but warmer, as though an animal had worked it through its mouth before spitting it out and smearing it over the subsoil. Insects beyond any rational number wriggled out from her hand as she lifted the clod of soil she had pulled away. A threadworm with a leech-like mouth launched itself at her in an attempt to sucker her little finger. It left a bright salivary trail down the sigmarite. She laughed, commending its valour, before splatting it between forefinger and thumb and licking off the syrupy yellow paste.

She winced at the unexpectedly intense flavour, and smeared the dirt from her gauntlets on the golden stoles that draped her armoured shoulders. Lowering herself to her chest, she put her ear to the ground and listened.

A faint tremor ran through the earth.

THUD-THUD, THUD-THUD.

Worms and beetles writhed against the cheek of her mask, trying to eat the metal, seeking out the eye slits and mouth holes, as though in the throes of some desperate predatory drive. It was hungry, even for Ghur.

'This is *his* doing,' she murmured.

She did not know yet who '*he*' was.

This was a nuisance for her, but it was not a problem.

She had tracked endless spells that could slide seamlessly between the realms. She had hunted shape-shifters escaped from the gallows of Druchiroth, who could pass as human before even a Judicator's scrying eyes. She had entered Stormvaults whose very existence had been forgotten by the gods who built them.

The prophesiers of Excelsis had glimpsed visions of trogg-herds on the march, of gargants gathering once more into tribes under the leadership of would-be heirs to the World Titan, of grots spilling up from every dank and neglected hole to choke the fragile civilisations of the Coast of Tusks, of great orruk war-chiefs rising to the head of armies a million strong. A new star had appeared in the Constellation of Minatlacaq, swelling the constellation's belly day by day before falling as a comet and obliterating entirely the temple-city that the Coalesced had raised in its honour. In the aelven freeport of Lún'Qesh, in a pelagic hinterland connected by whirlways that ran through the realms of Chamon and Ulgu, it had rained frogspawn for a hundred nights until there was nothing left of the sub-realm but slime. In parts of Ghyran, two or sometimes three moons at a time had started to prowl the night sky in place of the usual one, and its days had shortened as its suns hastened from the sky to flee them.

These were omens of rebirth and a new cycle of destruction.

Somewhere in the untamed wilds of Ghur, something stirred. Even the dead, a plague on the Coast of Tusks since the upheavals of the Necroquake, had inexplicably withdrawn to their crypts and their citadels with the onset of the omens and had not risen again since. Another slumbering godbeast was what Vagria's intuition told her, made restless by the Arcanum Optimar, and Lord-Veritant Sentanus, the White Reaper of Excelsis, had petitioned the Templia Beasthall for its foremost hunter to find the awakening creature and destroy it.

Before the doom it heralded could come to pass.

Pushing herself back up into a crouch she took up another handful of soil and, with some reluctance, pulled her helmet from her head. Her face tingled as though numb as she stuffed the entire lump of soil and wildlife into her mouth and chewed thoughtfully. She tasted bitterness, aggression, rage; something else that she had never tasted in the earth and did not know how to name. She swallowed and grimaced, wiping her mouth on the back of her hand, her lips numb and feeling nothing, and turned back to her warriors.

Two-score Vanguard-Palladors of her Vanguard Auxiliary Chamber, the Farstrike Hunters, waited impatiently in their saddles, the amethyst and gold of their battledress dulled with earth and strung with totems and trophies. Many of them bore faded tattoos from their savage mortal lives, or bright new ones etched into their skin not with ink or woad, but with the lightning of Reforging. There was intensity to their fierceness, and for the moment at least they were silent. From all over the Eight Realms they hailed, but every one of them was a hunter and they took a hunter's pride in their work. The gryph-chargers they rode, beasts of the infinite Celestial Plains, shared their riders' temperament.

Knight-Azyros Horac touched the end of his tongue to a grain of soil, and then immediately spat it out. His bearded face screwed up in disgust.

'It tastes vile.'

'The silver tongue of the Azyros temple,' laughed Kildabrae, sitting straight-backed in her saddle. The rippling banner that she carried was brashly large, bearing a motif of a stag impaled upon a great spear.

The Knight-Vexillor was rumoured to be the tallest warrior ever forged under the Astral Templars' storm: eight and a half feet, and as bald as the Sidereal Mountains where star eagles vied for their roosts. Her war-name was the Heavenscar, for the scar across her lips that was the mirror of that which Gorkamorka had put across the Constellation of Dracothion.

The Farstrike Hunters had taken her to their hearts as a good luck charm. The blessings of three gods in one most fearsome warrior.

'Speak more poetry to me, you Ghurite fox.'

Horac glared dolefully at the Knight-Vexillor while the Vanguard-Palladors laughed. The Knight-Azyros was a fierce but frail thing, like a model of a bird built from silver wires. There was some darkness in the warrior's spirit that used up his years too quickly, almost in spite of his supposed immortality.

Vagria quickly donned her helmet. Many Astral Templars

preferred to fight without, including some of its most famous sons, to the extent that the bare-headed, huge-bearded warrior had become almost synonymous with the Stormhost's name. But Vagria had always been more comfortable with the Mask Impassive than without. Her own face discomforted her, surprised her even, sometimes, when she caught it reflected back at her from a polished surface, and she felt no sense of touch when she fitted the mask back into place.

Comfortably masked again, she drew her boltstorm pistol while she worked that foul part of the taste that she *did* recognise from her mouth with her tongue.

It tasted of orruk.

CHAPTER THREE

Casius Braun knew that he was dreaming. He knew because he had had this dream, or dreams very much like it, so many times before. The place was the Izalmaw. The time was ten years ago, the last decisive battle against Waaagh! Bosskilla before it had grown large enough to threaten the cities of Izalend or Bilgeport. Orruks bellowed in the snow, the heavy tread of troggoths and warbeasts reverberating through the deep drifts. Even the fighters closest to him were wraiths, grey and hazy, outlines without faces and with faraway screams that he could not make out. The Dozen were out there somewhere. He felt them there with him, but he could not seem to remember what they looked like.

But, of course, they had not been the Dozen then. They were just eleven nameless warriors. Eleven, from the twelve Tuskan Wildmen who would not die that day.

Braun could not remember now if the snow had really been so thick, the enemy so numerous, the air so cold that he could not breathe, or if that was just how it was in his dream. He had dreamed it so many times now that the dream had become his memory.

But the massacre of his nightmares was not what he remembered. He knew that. It was what should have happened, what *would* have happened if any one of a hundred desperate gambits in the days leading up to the battle had failed to come off. What if Woan had failed to slow them with his guerrilla raids in the frozen swamps? What if the preceding season had been wetter and the stakes that he had cut to ward the river crossing had been too soft? What if the eleventh-hour raid that he had led himself, to poison the feedstuffs of the Ironjawz cavalry, had been thwarted? What if he had not strangled Captain Usapien in his sleep to prevent him from taking the Ice Barons and their veteran winter fighters back to Izalend?

What if?

What if?

What if?

'Braun!'

The voice rumbled through the snow like a gathering avalanche.

'Braun!'

He sought to back away but the drift had become too thick behind his legs. A shadow wavered through the billowing snow, horned and monstrous, THUD, THUD, THUD the sound it made as it approached, growing impossibly huge as it drew near, until it loomed like a mega-gargant clad in spiked iron.

'Braun!'

The fighters who had surrounded him a moment before were gone, vanished like hope with the sunset. No one rushed to his defence. He was armed, but the thought of defending himself never even occurred.

What if Rukka Bosskilla had not died that day? His body had not been found with his maw-krusha, and Braun had been forced to find the next largest head to cut off and present to the then High Arbiter Vermyre of Excelsis as proof of the deed.

What if?

What if?

What if?

'I is comin' for you, Braun...'

Braun woke with a start, his head tangling with the layered tepee of bug nets that had been set up over the vast, smelly bed he had claimed for his own. He fought his way free of both, swinging his feet off the mattress and scuffing the heel of his toes on roughly ground stone. As soon as he was upright, his belly clenched and he bent over his knees with a groan.

It was possible he had indulged a little too hard. Slightly.

Shivering in spite of the early morning heat, he got up and wandered towards the window, small bones crunching under his bare feet. The window was enormous, too high off the ground even for a man of Braun's stature, forcing him to go up onto tiptoes like a child in order to peer out.

The ogor longhouse had belonged to Grob Bloodgullet. Braun had been able to deduce that much from the throne that stood at the head of the hall, fashioned from scrap wood and animal carcasses with blunt tooth marks still in the ivory, and from the large personal cook pot that hung suspended over a pit in the middle of the floor.

The view from the window encompassed the majority of the former gluthold, smaller longhouses joined by viaducts and causeways and linked to larders that had been extended from the natural cave systems of the Gnarlfast. Several of these larders led into a maze of tunnels that the ogors' gnoblar servants had used to get about under the noses of their hungry masters, and which had still not been wholly cleared.

The whole stronghold formed the shape of a mouth, with the

longhouses arrayed on flat-topped plateaus becoming its teeth. And in the centre of it all, on a straight road that ran symbolically down from the gate, was an oily bowl-shaped depression that Taal had dubbed the Butchers' Quarter. It was a place of fire-pits and shallow graves, a greasy stain of ash and suffering in the heart of the new city despite the best efforts of Mother Thassily to exorcise the shades of those whose souls had been devoured by the gluttonous god.

Looking east, across the Eaten Plain towards Ymnog's Trample and the jungles of home, he saw a sky still leathery and dark, trembling like a doomed animal as the rising of Hysh pierced it with its teeth. The living hills that dotted the plain, known as the Cuspid Mesas, trumpeted to one another, shuddering with distemper and loosing the occasional rockslide as their rocky skin warmed under the dawn.

In spite of the unlikely hour, the sounds of construction were everywhere. Arden Shay had been excited to begin what she had called 'the real work' while most of the Accari were still celebrating the victory. A skeleton of timber scaffolding surrounded the burnt-out section of the ogor's curtain wall. Wells had been dug, along with drainage ditches and latrines, neither of which the ogors had concerned themselves with during their stewardship of the Gnarlfast. Proper storehouses had been made out of the caves. Longhouses had been converted into barracks. Level promontories had been marked with flags to be turned into gyro-pads. On another peak, slightly higher than the one that claimed the Tyrant's longhouse and that the ogors had never reached for, quarrying was underway to clear the foundations for what would eventually become a permanent castle. Lisandr's white pavilion and flags fluttered there in the alpine winds, as though claiming the spot for the warriors of Starhold. The outline of a pair of temples, one Ghurite in design and one Azyrite, had been staked out and stared one another down from opposite sides of the otherwise deserted Butchers' Quarter.

Braun drew his forearms into his belly and groaned. His mouth tasted of sick. His stomach felt as though he had swallowed a bell weight. He had eaten far too much. No wonder it was giving him nightmares. He traced the hammer tattoo across his face, made the tracing hand into a fist and lowered his forehead to it in prayer.

He had not been a faithful man before the Battle of Izalmaw. But a slaughter like that had a way of making a man reassess his importance in Sigmar's great order. So many had fallen on the mouth of the Izal that day. Afterwards Braun had been forced to acknowledge, perhaps for the first time, that his own life, too, was fragile. He could be killed, just like anyone. One arrow, one spear, one bad day would be all it took. That he had survived a battle that had taken thousands of others was nothing short of miraculous. Sigmar had obviously preserved him for a purpose, for the waging of his wars and the crushing of his enemies.

He tightened his fist and prayed harder. *Please, Sigmar, let Rukka be rotting at the bottom of the Clawing Sea.*

But he prayed that some other menace would arise soon enough. Peace did not suit him. It left him too much time for thinking.

There was a creak as the huge, round, ogor-built door opened and a gust of warmer air blew in from the outside. Braun turned towards it as Murdo and Jenk pushed inside, and no sooner had they set eyes on him than Jenk was cackling with laughter.

'Sigmar, you look like death.'

Braun opened his fist and brought it to his face, wiping the sweat from his brow. He was still shivering.

'Meat sweats, chief?' said Murdo.

'Yeah,' said Braun, unwilling to confide in his warriors that he still had nightmares of the Izal. 'Must be.'

'You didn't really eat him all, did you?' said Jenk.

Braun gave a wavery grin. 'I promised him I would, and everyone heard me say so.'

Jenk nodded sagely, understanding. 'Yeah, chief. They all heard, and that's what they'll all think.'

'So. What is it?' Braun shuffled back to his bed. 'Must be something to get either of you up before dawn.'

'Who says we've been to bed?' said Murdo.

'You're an old man now, Murdo. Stop pretending to be an angry young pup, it's embarrassing to us both.'

The fighter bared his teeth, but shut up.

'Scouts have been coming back in,' said Jenk. 'The ones we had still out on the plains before the battle. They weren't thrilled to have missed the sack, but so it goes, and they did bring back talk of greenskins moving about beyond the Gnarlfast. Of Spiderfang rising up out of their crannies to the east, and Ironjawz marching to the south. A few even sighted gargants, moving together across the Trample. My gut tells me there's something going on, something *they* know about but that we haven't quite felt yet.'

'You want to send out a patrol,' said Braun.

'Just a little one. And just us Hounds.'

'Any reason you don't want to trouble the Celestians? They'd be fresher. I didn't see any of them celebrating last night.'

Murdo and Jenk shared a look. 'There was a bit of trouble overnight,' said the former.

Braun raised an eyebrow. It was a phenomenal effort of stamina and grit.

'Nothing out of the ordinary,' said Jenk, quickly. 'No one lost any eyes. You know how it is. But still…' He shrugged. 'I can't promise it'll stay that way in the future. Probably best for everyone if the Azyrites keep their eyes to themselves.'

'Fine,' said Braun. 'I'm sure you know who to send.'

Jenk dipped his head. 'Of course.'

At the foot of Grob's old bed, Braun opened up the small wooden chest that contained his belongings and looked inside. 'Let me know if they find an army out there and I'll lead the Hounds out myself. I'm sick of this place already.' He reached into the chest and drew out a skin-wrapped pouch. It jangled in his hand as though it were filled with broken glass.

'Are you sure you want to be starting on that stuff, chief?' said Murdo. 'It's barely dawn.'

Tossing the skin-pouch up and down in his hand, Braun beckoned Murdo over. The old fighter glanced at Jenk, then shrugged and came over.

He never saw it coming.

Braun's headbutt cracked his forehead and dropped him to the floor by the foot of the bed without so much as a cry. Jenk winced theatrically, and then chuckled.

'Don't question me,' Braun growled, loosening the skin-pouch's drawstrings and pulling out a thumbnail-sized piece of glass.

Clear prophecy, freshly cut and minted from the Spear of Mallus that rose out of Excelsis Harbour, looked like mercury. The object in Braun's hand was ashen and used, grey with uncertain possibilities. It was the best he could still afford. No one, probably not even the apprentices of the Prophesiers Guild, started dabbling in prophecy because they wanted to see the future. No. They did it because their past was that terrible.

'And don't abuse Sigmar's name for your curses,' he added over Murdo's supine lump.

Jenk coughed and raised a hand. 'Actually, chief, that was me. Sorry.'

Braun threw his arm around his second and crushed him in for a hug, drawing a gasp of day-old meat breath that brought tears to the eyes. 'You were there for me against Grob Bloodgullet.' He shoved the man from under him, and Jenk stumbled away. 'And now we're even. Get out of here.' He stared into the prophecy shard. 'I've got thinking to do.'

'Make way!' Malec Grint charged through the ankle-deep slop of the main spoke-road from the Gnarlfast down towards the Butchers' Quarter. He clutched the message roll in one hand, the shrill urgency of the great hawk that had entrusted it to him still ringing in his ears. A blob of silver wax, impressed with aelven characters and the eagle-wing emblem of the Swifthawk, sealed the roll. 'Make way!' He knocked over cooking stoves, burnt his shin on a kettle, went through a clothes line on which sleeveless leather tunics steamed dry in the heat. 'Message from Excelsis for the general! Make way!'

Someone flicked a nut at him, somehow hitting Grint plumb in the eye even as he hurtled by the nest of tents that clustered in the armpits of the intersecting ogor roads. He yowled, slapping his hand to his eye as laughter rolled after him down the street. He slowed, his first and last instinct to turn and punch the ringleader in the mouth, but the seal in his hand convinced him to grit his teeth and run on.

Make-up duty wasn't as much of an adventure when there were no battles to be fought and no Celestian women to impress. As a matter of fact, it was an awful lot like the sort of actual toil he had left Accar to escape.

Around the borders of the Butchers' Quarter there was a circular path that went through the heart of the hold, and from which the so called spoke-roads fed off towards the longhouses of the Gnarlfast and the gate in the east. Grint didn't intend to run that far when he didn't have to. Short stretches of tunnel and surface alleyways cut through perilous-looking gnoblar shanties and the bare rock at irregular but frequent intervals. Taal, who had taken charge of the settlement while General Braun made good on his vow to eat his beaten foe and then slept off the consequences, had forbidden the Hounds from using them until Jenk had figured out where they all went and cleared them of whatever pets the ogors had left behind. However, Grint didn't know anyone in his mob who hadn't slipped into one for a quiet chew on his arraca stem or a shortcut to the latrines.

He darted through a side tunnel, pulling up short at a cupola formation that the gnoblars must have used for hiding food from their master, and where a twenty-man brawl was currently in progress. Accari men and a couple of women rolled around in the thick mud like boars. Grint slowed long enough to look for the mob chief, and found him standing over the melee and to one side of it, red-faced from screaming obscenities and kicking one of his fighters over the head.

Grint blinked, and turned away. It was really none of his business.

Mikali had told him that there had been some fighting between a mob of Hounds and one of the Celestian units, something to do with the temples that were going up around the Butchers' Quarter, but then, it had been a celebration. Grint was sorry to say that he'd missed out on that too, stuck running errands and waiting on messages. Make-up duty was the worst.

He left the side tunnel and re-emerged onto the next spoke-road counterclockwise, took a hard right and pushed his burning thighs for the last uphill stretch, back towards the middle heights of the Gnarlfast.

The Tyrant's longhouse was a castle of fire-darkened wood and old bone, crouching on a flat berm of rock that stuck out from the mountain face like a bulb nose. A cluster of grand, semi-permanent tents belonging to the big chiefs and the Dozen encircled it, uprights crowned with skulls of orruks and ogors, scraped by skinning knives and branded with the hammer of the God-King. Pennants flying the scarlet and tan of the Accari

Hounds flapped at the ends of their poles, like horse tails swatting lazily at flies. If there was one thing that did still live on the Eaten Plain then it was the flies. Any creature that lived off sweat, blood or ordure and which was too small to be eaten in turn had prospered well under the reign of the Bloodgullet.

Jenk stood watch outside the longhouse's covered portico. At least nominally. He was pissing noisily up against the side wall and singing a song about a chameleon skink.

'Grunt,' he called cheerfully.

It didn't matter who his mother was, there wasn't a man above a certain rank who didn't find that nickname hilarious. But Jenk was the first lieutenant of the Dozen, and so Grint bit his tongue. Unlike most of the Hounds with their mismatched gear, Jenk wore a complete set of livery and wore it with apparent pride. The leather was oiled and cared for. His receding hair had been combed. He even wore armour. The plates of knobbed leather practically marked him out as a king by the sparsely outfitted standards of the Hounds.

Shaking himself off, Jenk nodded Grint through. Feeling slightly offended at being below even cursory suspicion, Grint drew aside the bug screen that had been put up over the doorway and stepped inside.

He coughed. The air inside the tent was syrupy thick, heavy with arraca smoke and incense, and other aromas he didn't even recognise. Just breathing it in seemed to pull him a second into his own future and, when he turned around, he almost caught himself coming in through the door and staring back at himself in alarm. He coughed, deliberately this time, and covered his mouth with his hand, blinking his eyes until the visions passed.

General Braun was spread out on the giant bed, naked from the waist up and slick with fever sweat, his belly still distended from its efforts of the night before. His eyes were open, but they were as vacant as the smoke that wreathed him. Drool trickled from a half-rictus.

'Rukka.' His expression became fearful before settling again. 'Kragnos. No...'

Murdo, another of the Dozen, bulkier than Jenk and with a full head of long brown hair but similarly dressed, sat against the wall nearest the bed, where he nursed a cracked forehead, a vicious scowl and a burning arraca stem that was producing most of the smoke now filling the longhouse. In Excelsis, Grint had heard, you needed the wealth of a prince to pay for an arraca habit. In Accar, where the flowers it came from grew wild, it was so abundant that the locals chewed on the raw stems.

Murdo, though, preferred to smoke it. He told everyone it made him feel like a king. The old fighter looked up as Grint entered and, with a grunt, offered up his arraca stem.

Grint mumbled his apologies and backed out. He looked over the great sprawl of the former gluthold, message roll in hand, until his gaze settled on the white pavilion that fought against the wind atop the next peak. An unwanted resolve settled over him. He didn't want to be a message boy – he wanted fighting, and adventure, and to impress – but he'd be damned if he wouldn't do it right.

Cursing under his breath, he started off up the hill.

Ellisior Seraphine Lisandr wiped a tear from the corner of her eye. The last bars of 'The Song of the Broken World' drifted through the Jewel of Ohlicoatl that she held in her outstretched palm, and Lisandr sniffed, remembering at the last moment to clap, tapping her fingers against the inside of her wrist. There were two Ohlicoatl Jewels in existence and her family was in possession of both of them. They enabled their bearers to communicate with one another, instantaneously, regardless of the distances that might separate them. As a girl, it had been a plaything for her and her siblings to tell one another jokes and stories from the far wings of the palace. Here and now, she was not sure she could have endured so many months abroad in Ghur without it.

'Well done, Honoria,' she said, addressing the aetheric projection of the small girl that hovered under the white canvas ceiling of her tent, lowering the argentimer from her lips and glowing in a cool, cosmic facsimile of a daughter's pride. 'Your playing is improved much since the last time I was in Starhold.'

'It has been forever, mother. See...' Honoria leant into the priceless arcana, causing her mouth to balloon in a manner that made Lisandr want to laugh whilst simultaneously breaking her heart. The little girl smiled. 'I lost another tooth.'

'I hope you bathed it in silver to keep the Gloomspite from stealing it.'

'Of course,' said Honoria, as though dealing with a child. 'Will you be back again soon?'

'I will,' said Lisandr. 'I took the Bloodgullet gluthold only yesterday. With all being well the Accari will settle themselves in a week or two and my regiment will be free to return to Excelsis. I will be back in Starhold to hear you perform to the galleria for the Reconquest Night feast.' The projected image went wavery with the girl's delight. 'But I need to speak with your father alone for a moment. Is he there?'

The girl nodded obediently. The image fractured into beams as the second Jewel of Ohlicoatl was passed from hand to hand.

It coalesced again, this time around the handsome, patrician face of her husband, Tornan Lisandr. He was dressed in a formal samite gown, and though the Jewels transmitted little colour, she could make out the elaborate celestial imagery in the pattern's weft and the lustre of the cloth-of-gold stole draped over his shoulders. His eyes looked tired, his face weary from a day of debates and motions on the floor of the Grand Conclave. It must have been evening there. The differences in the flow of time between Starhold and the Ghurish Heartlands never failed to confound her attempts at synchronising their communications. Ghur delighted in working to the opposite rules of most cosmological puzzles: not only did it cease to be measurable only once the effort was made to measure it, but it seemed to actively change said measurements to spite the measurer. It was infuriating.

'Don't make promises that you cannot keep,' he said. 'She follows after fifty generations of Sigmar's soldiers. She will understand if you are unable to be home in time for the feast, but a broken promise is another matter.'

'The crusade is over, Tornan. If it were up to me, I would be standing my soldiers down ready to leave. Really, we are just waiting for word of the conquest to make it back to Excelsis and the withdrawal order to return. Five or six weeks, and we will be marching back into civilisation.'

'Then why haven't you? I thought you were in charge.'

Lisandr snorted. 'So did I, but... wait, is Honoria still there?'

The projection flickered as her husband glanced to one side. 'She has gone out onto the balcony to watch the dance of the stars.'

'The Accari attacked a temple last night.'

'What?' Tornan looked rightly shocked.

'High spirits, they tell me. Honestly, the Reclaimed are worse than animals. I swear they have only grown worse on the march from Accar. There is something in the air in this part of Gallet, I am sure of it.'

Tornan smiled like the career diplomat he was. Lisandr found herself wondering at how very easy it was to be that enlightened when you looked down on the Mortal Realms from a chancel in Azyr.

'Inspire by example,' he said. 'And show them Heaven.'

'I said something similar to young Aubreitn just yesterday.'

'Sage advice.'

'Easier to give, I think, when you are not living amongst them. Their soldiers are congenitally disobedient. Their officers are worse. General Braun actually presented the ogor Tyrant at the victory feast and swore to eat him. To *eat* him.'

'Sigmar, was he cooked?'

'Yes, I think so… How is that the first question on your mind?'

'I…' The image shrugged helplessly.

Lisandr scowled and went on. 'The only person I've ever seen Braun actually listen to is Mother Thassily.'

'The pontiff?'

'He is a very pious man,' said Lisandr, with pursed lips. 'One of his few redeeming qualities.'

'Then he cannot be entirely bad,' said Tornan dutifully.

'He has already lost one regiment, so I hear, but good luck learning anything about the Tuskan Wildmen from him.' She sighed in weariness and frustration. All she wanted now was to be heading home. 'The Accari look at me as though I am an angel sent to walk amongst them. As if I might glitter and vanish like a Seraphon if they approach too closely, and… What is so funny?'

Her husband smoothed away his smile. 'Nothing.'

'Never mind,' said Lisandr, suddenly riled. 'I have work to do. And it looks as though I caught you late. I will try to contact you at a better time tomorrow.'

'Wait, Ellisior, I didn't mean to–'

She closed her fingers over the sapphire-blue scale and the aetheric projection flickered as the linkage between it and its twin was broken. The foreign stars that the Jewel had mapped across the ceiling of the tent faded, leaving the ruddy light coming through the canvas to shoulder the burden of illumination. As an afterthought, she blew a kiss towards the silent stone, thinking a prayer that it find its way to Honoria, only to be interrupted by a shout from outside.

'Forgive the intrusion, sir, but I have one of the Accari here. He claims to bring a couriered message from Excelsis.'

Lisandr frowned, returning the Jewel of Ohlicoatl to its bespoke strongbox and closing the lid. It was far too early for Excelsis to have learned of their success. 'Very well, Halon. Let them in.'

She straightened, making the transition from homesick mother and wife to general of the First Age in one deep breath, as the tent flap was thrown back and Lydia Aubreitn entered. She was still dressed in her white tabard and armour, although both had been well washed since the battle of the previous day, and was casting distasteful looks back at the Ghurite who shuffled in behind her like a pig-hand invited unexpectedly into an empress' palanquin. His unwashed body was clad in a stitched leather vest while his hands – fingers grubby, nails cracked – clutched a message roll bearing the Swifthawk seal as though it were a token to appease a covetous dragon. Wide-eyed, he took in the regimented clutter of Lisandr's personal quarters.

'Has your curiosity been duly sated?' she asked sharply.

The man swallowed nervously and made a rough meal of a Celestian salute. 'Grint… er… sir.'

'If I wanted your name, I would have asked for it.'

'Yes. Yes, sir.'

'You may give your message to my squire.'

'Your–?'

Realisation dawned on the young idiot, who, with a nod, passed the cylinder to Lydia. She, in turn, crossed to Lisandr's desk and handed it over with a smart salute and a smile at the Ghurite's expense. Then she stepped back to give her general room.

Grint fidgeted on his own.

'Stay there in case I need to send any messages of my own,' said

Lisandr. The boy looked disappointed, but did as he was told. 'And fetch me a glass of water,' she called after Lydia. 'There are days I long for the dry heat of the Vandium campaign.'

'Yes, sir.'

With another clipped salute, the Azyrite moved to the back of the tent, where the servants supplied them both with food and water. While she did so, Lisandr examined the seal on the side of the cylinder. It was impressed with a miniaturised aelven script that the Swifthawk employed to encode their formal communications. Lisandr had studied the root language at the War College in Starhold and, though she lacked the keener eyes of her aelven tutors, she could read it well enough.

With a disappointed sigh, she raised her gaze to address the boy. 'You have come to the wrong place. This is addressed to General Braun.'

The boy took on a cornered look. 'The general, well, the general is...'

Lisandr cut him short, flicking the message roll back towards him and rapping his knuckles with the parchment. 'I am well acquainted with Casius' vices, believe me.'

'Yes, sir.'

Lisandr smiled, discovering, in the boy's glum look, an unexpected sympathy in herself. 'Nevertheless, it would be improper of me to open a fellow officer's private correspondence. I would suggest you find one of your own superiors and have them throw a bucket of cold water over Casius' head.'

The Ghurite looked mortified by the idea.

Lydia returned bearing a tall glass filled with clear water. Lisandr took it and turned to the boy, somewhat irked to find that he was still there.

'Go on,' she said, taking a sip. 'Shoo.'

* * *

Efrim Taal had not slept all night, although not for the same reasons as his men.

Elsewhere, bedded down in the pebble-bone and ash that bordered the Butchers' Quarter, Taal's mob stirred under their nets. The fighters muttered, growled, fought the monsters that plagued their sleep. A handful of pre-dawn risers nursed woody arraca stems, smoking them in the Excelsian style or chewing them raw. Others sharpened javelin-points and axe-blades, shaved beards using spice knives as both a mirror and a blade, or beat their bare chests and howled their morning prayers. In the nearest bug-tent along, Ezra and Karze, distant cousins on his grandmother's side, arm-wrestled over an upturned box for the entertainment of a small crowd. A few yards along, Mawgren and Kadd appeared to have cornered a lone gnoblar while Brodd rolled around in the mud trying to bag it, to the uproarious laughter of those watching on, and the equally vital curses of those only now retiring to their tents.

Taal sat cross-legged on a rubbish mound on the outskirts of the Butchers' Quarter, looking in, obeying the general command to stay out of that area while thumbing his nose at it in spirit. The tough leather cuisses of maw-krusha leather dug into the inside of his thighs, his heavy robes bundled up in his lap. The garment's random weave, altered and repaired over many generations, conjured patterns that migrated over the wild terrain of folds and patches with the rise of Hysh over the eastern wall. With his staff, he unconsciously struck out the tempo that had lodged itself in his mind. *THUD. THUD. THUD.* He had been hearing it all night, but it was stronger here, a rhythm that he could feel running through him from the ground and speaking to him through the faces of the clouds.

He looked up. The skull at the top of his staff gleamed in the new dawn. He had found it atop a column of white stones within the ruins of a Seraphon outpost, while undergoing the traditional shamanic pilgrimage into the Primeval Jungle, to seek out the source of the Slannstongue River and the ziggurat of Mekitopsar. As soon as he had reached out to lift it down, he had heard the cold, dead voice in his head.

He would do one great deed in his life, it had said, and he would save the people of the Heartlands from the tyranny of the returned god.

From that moment, he had believed that the god he was destined to defy was the god to whom he gave praise. Sigmar had bested Gorkamorka, whom his farthest forefathers had once worshipped, and conquered the Realm of Beasts. Through right of might, he had earned Taal's devotion and Taal gave it willingly. But the Azyrites who spilled through the Realmgates to supplant and uproot the cultures of the Heartlands were not the God-King. He ruled from his distant throne of stars, as a God-King should, and expected his followers to fight out their differences amongst themselves.

THUD, THUD, THUD, the skull said to him now.

Braun was the only member of the Dozen who actually hailed from Accar. The rest of them came originally from the Azyrite cities on the Coast of Tusks, with the exception of Taal himself, and his nephew, Ferrgin. They were the only men of Braun's council who had blood descent to the original peoples, men with a nose for the words of the gods and a talent for magic. Their skin had an amber hue, demonstrating their bond to the spirit of the realm. Their muscles were heavier, their backs broader, their legs long, for a true Accari could run down a stonehorn without tiring.

If there was one man in the regiment that Casius Braun would not dare to cross then it was Efrim Taal. No one else could treat the Azyrites with such open disdain, or exhort a handful of drunken fighters to vandalise their temple, without fear of serious censure.

The God-King could not be bound in stone or displayed with jewels.

He closed his eyes, head back, shoulders rocking to the rhythm of his staff.

THUD.

THUD.

THUD.

This was sacred ground; he was sure of it. Sigmar had guided the Hounds to this spot so that he might be worshipped in the proper manner. Taal just needed to understand what that manner was.

'What ate you in the night?' said Ferrgin.

His nephew was bent over a tin pot, stirring a thick broth and cackling every time one of the ubiquitous winged bugs flew into it and died, thickening the broth a little further. The steam rising off it made Taal's stomach growl. Ferrgin was an unlikeable wretch with almost no worthy qualities whatsoever, for which even a relationship to Taal and the ear of the gods could only forgive so far, but he got away with it on account of being a remarkably gifted cook.

'You don't hear it?' said Taal.

Ferrgin cocked his shaved head, then shrugged, using his free hand to draw his spice knife from its half-moon sheath on his hip and draw it down his arm to dislodge the sweat-beetle grubs that had hatched there overnight. Left to mature they would burrow into the sweat glands and leave a man in agony for a week until they re-emerged to breed. They didn't kill. They just made you wish they did. Ferrgin plopped them into his broth.

Taal counted thirty. Not even close to a regimental best. Crodden had once combed one hundred and ninety from both arms. Taal had shelled them and made them into a prayer string that he still wore around his neck.

'You need to train your intuition,' Taal snapped. 'You have to listen for the gods, rather than wait for them to speak to you.'

He had stopped beating out the rhythm with his staff while he spoke with Ferrgin, though he could still hear it. The entirety of the Eaten Plain and the Gnarlfast was alive with it, agitated by it, the vastness of the sky trembling in counterpoint like vibrations in a drum skin or a pool of water. Ferrgin's ladle, he noticed, stirred around the inside of the tin pot to the exact same tempo.

THUD. SCRAPE.

THUD. SCRAPE.

Taal was pleased to see that his nephew was not entirely deaf to what the Heartlands were telling him. Perhaps there was some hope for humanity in Ghur. He felt it, even though he professed to be unaware of it.

'The aftershock of some violent act has marked this place,' Taal muttered. 'The ground carries its echoes.' Could this be why the Bloodgullet settled here in the first place, and why their gnoblar slaves refused to give it up? Was this why the nearby greenskin tribes had become active only now that this place had been conquered? 'This could be the very ground where Ymnog fell! Or one of the twelve craters across Gallet and Andtor where Sigmar smashed Gorkamorka's face into the ground of the realm.'

Ferrgin nodded disinterestedly, concentrating on his stew. 'Yeah. Maybe.'

Taal gripped his staff. Regular beatings throughout his misbegotten childhood had not improved Ferrgin's character any, but Taal lived in hope.

The sound of clamour from the outskirts of his mob's camp drew his attention from his nephew, and he looked up to see Kanta's youngest stumble out from behind the scaffold of the half-started church and into half a dozen men who were slowly spit-roasting an ogor leg over a fire. Ignoring their insults, and the cooking fire he had just walked through, Grint held a message tube over his head and panted, red-faced.

'I'm... looking... for... my mother.'

Taal grunted and jerked his head towards the heights of the Gnarlfast. 'She went with Kemrit and Ragn to speak with Braun.'

Grint cursed. 'I'm not going up that damned hill one more time.' He walked up and handed the message to Taal. 'I'm done.'

Taal examined the tube, breaking the seal with a shrug before Grint could protest and drizzling his forearms with stardust, indelibly marking him to those with the sight, which out here meant himself and his nephew, as one who had improperly opened a Swifthawk message. In civilised places, the punishment for that was a life of hard labour in the prophecy mines of the Mallus Spear. But Taal had no interest in civilised places.

He slid out the rolled parchment that was inside, unfurled it and scowled. 'Why does Synor have to write his orders in High Azyri? Are Thondian characters not good enough for him? It's Braun he's writing to, isn't it? Who's he trying to impress?'

Ferrgin tasted his broth and shrugged. Taal made a non-committal sound and held the scroll up to the dawn light.

General Braun, it read. *It is with regret... that I must order your immediate withdrawal from the Bloodgullet Crusade. Henceforth, you are to march with all haste to Accar. The greenskins are on the march everywhere along the coast, Izalend and Bilgeport are already besieged and there have been troubles here that I will not commit to parchment even under the safekeeping of a Swifthawk seal.*

The White Reaper has sworn to hold Excelsis or perish, never to be reborn, in the attempt, but even so I have been forced to draw every Freeguild garrison from the Trade Road and the principalities to concentrate on the defence of the city. I arranged for this order to be addressed to you, rather than to General Lisandr, in the hopes, Ghurite to Ghurite, that you will understand.

Excelsis must stand. Anything else may be sacrificed.
March swiftly, general.
High Arbiter Synor.

'It seems that Excelsis is in some kind of peril,' Taal surmised.

'Excelsis is always in peril,' said Ferrgin. 'Last time I was there, there were so many prophecies going round they were actually taking bets on which doom was going to be the one that did for them.'

'I heard its Freeguild has half a million men,' said Grint.

'No one here cares about Excelsis,' Taal murmured, looking over the top of the parchment at Kanta's boy. 'Can you read High Azyri, boy?'

'Can't read,' Grint answered proudly.

Feeling a shiver of predestiny, as if he were striking a blow that had been sanctioned decades before – when he had first set out on his path, and plucked a skull from a tree that had itself been set there millennia before that – he leant forwards and tossed the parchment in Ferrgin's fire.

'It was nothing for us,' said Taal, in response to Grint's startled look, and resumed tapping his staff.

THUD. THUD. THUD.

This was holy ground. A new home for the true Accari, far from the false civilisations of Azyr. This was where Sigmar wanted them to be.

They weren't going anywhere.

CHAPTER FOUR

Brendel Starsighted, Knight-Venator in command of the Farstrike's Angelos retinues, had always had an affinity for the air and an understanding with its creatures. In a mortal life that he could now only dimly recall, he remembered building himself a flying harness of leather straps and brass – as a forfeit on a lost wager, more than likely, or perhaps simply as a dare. Nor could he recall the exact manner of his death, though suffice to say he had his suspicions.

Now, his flying harness was made of sigmarite and lightning, and he sailed over a restless landscape of great hills and forests of serrated pines. His keen eyes picked out every sharp-edged leaf and poisonous berry, while the senses of his soulmate, the star-eagle Eliara, overlaid his sight with her own. It was as though a silver dye had been poured over the terrain, running into every blemish in the landscape to provide heightened definition and depth.

The Serpent River dominated every viewpoint for a thousand

miles. The foaming torrent carved its way across the Morruk Hills, bounding from rock to rock with an energetic roar that was deafening even at Brendel's altitude. The mass of vapour it threw off left the air sultry and hot, begging for the deliverance of a storm.

Brendel adjusted the angle of his wings. The narrow beams of focused starlight projected by his wing harness to form 'feathers' sputtered as they caught on the cloying air and lifted him above a furious swarm of carnivorous insects that had gathered to strip a screaming megadactyl of its flesh.

This was Ghur, and Brendel adored its savagery.

With a *crack* of his wings, he levelled out at his new altitude. Eliara swooped nimbly below, snapping at a buzzing aether-tic that had become separated from the swarm and swallowing it with apparent relish. Brendel frowned. Not that he disapproved, but it was unlike the star-eagle to hunt so openly by day. She chattered away, oblivious, even as she hiked her neck to force down the still-struggling tic, excitedly describing to him all that she could see.

Brendel nodded with her. He saw it too.

The savage orruks moving across the Morruk Hills below them were less than ants. They were thin hair trails made up from the thousands of indivisible migrating specks that he and his Prosecutors retinue had been shadowing for the last fifteen days, like plainspeople following the migrating herds. The notion stirred in him a memory, but it was as high and thin as cirrus clouds, impossible to grasp at even with Sigmar's wings, and he gave it little thought other than to recognise it and guess at its shape.

The tragic Stormcast Eternal. He chuckled hollowly behind his impassive mask. *Forever tormented by my faltering memory and ever-loosening grip on humanity. When did I become a cliché?*

'Finally,' came a metallic voice from behind. 'They come to a destination.' The Prosecutor-Prime, Artros, flew twenty yards off

Brendel's shoulder, but did not need to raise his voice to address the Knight-Venator: they spoke through the gift of the storm and the power of Sigmar saw to the rest. 'I have never seen so many on the move at one time, and to think… This is but one of a thousand hordes migrating across Thondia.'

'The orruks are tomorrow's quarry,' said Brendel, holding his altitude. The chances of being spotted from the ground were vanishingly remote, but the Bonesplitterz were not without their own cunning. Brendel had died too many times to mistake greenskin savagery for stupidity now. 'They merely hunt the same prey.'

The gryph-chargers scrambled down the wooded slope, agile as hunting cats at play and swift as the winds of the Storm Eternal. Trees flashed by to either side. The landscape blurred. The chargers' feathered bodies flickered, energised to the brink of breaking apart.

Vagria Farstrike thrust her starbound blade in the air and whooped, the riders thundering after her answering with barks and catcalls of their own: the ululating war cries of as many lost chiefdoms of the Mortal Realms as there were Astral Templars in the Farstrike Hunters. Every warrior competed to shout the loudest, to strike the hardest, and to be first upon their quarry. Martial prowess and hunting skills were considered the ultimate leadership quality amongst the Astral Templars.

The Bonesplitterz coming the other way on their boars were so numerous it was as though the ground heaved itself up to roll them forwards, an avalanche thrown uphill by tectonic belligerence and the sheer power of the orruks' will. Spray from the Serpent River spumed up over the boar-riders' backs and stabbed impotently after them with a million rainbows.

Vagria narrowed her eyes. The wind force coming in through her mask's eye slits would have beheaded a mortal woman. It was making her eyes water.

'Raukos! Columna! Kildabrae! You know what to do.'

From one hectic charge the Vanguard-Palladors split smoothly into their four retinues, breaking every which way and galloping away at speed.

The orruks bellowed in consternation, ploughing their war boars into one another as they attempted to pursue every breaking rider at once. Vagria laughed as they flailed and trampled one another. An enemy soundly beaten through strength of arms was an enemy beaten, and nothing pleased the God-King more. But an enemy beaten through guile, who was beaten in spirit as well as body: that was the sweetest victory of all.

Shrugging off their confusion impressively quickly, the Bonesplitterz broke themselves instinctively into four groups and gave chase, two hundred boars to every fleeing Vanguard-Pallador.

Vagria shouted 'Yah!' and urged her retinue to continue forward, as though determined to meet the Bonesplitterz charge head-on. The fear of death beat in her immortal heart and she rejoiced in it. The Bonesplitterz responded as though they felt the same, bawling and yelling, frothing at the mouth, sitting so far forward on their boars that their broad green knees were resting on the backs of the animals' tusks.

Amongst the Stormhosts, the Vanguard-Palladors of the Auxiliary Chambers were classed as a versatile skirmish cavalry: compared directly to their awesomely armed counterparts from the Extremis Conclaves this was certainly so. But they were still Stormcast Eternals. Only the heaviest troops in the Mortal Realms could stand before a Pallador charge.

Shaking off the near-indescribable urge to carry the charge to its conclusion and lose herself to the glory, she yanked once on the reins and turned, until Starsid was galloping parallel to the Bonesplitterz boar-riders. Her retinue flocked behind her like a formation of birds, the Bonesplitterz swallowing up the distance left between them. With senses that were superhumanly keen, sharp even for a Stormcast Eternal, Vagria could almost pick out individual bellows from the mob, hear the excited, laboured breathing of the boars, the slapping of long, matted hair on their flanks.

Starsid continued to gain speed.

Vagria raised her starbound blade, a mockery of a farewell salute, even as the pressure of her raw speed built against her chest and yielded with a *crack*.

The gryph-chargers took to the winds aetheric, the tide of orruks stretching out towards an imagined singularity at the end of a long, infinitely flat smear of green. The trees, too thinly spaced and slender to be made out at all at such speeds, simply vanished from view altogether and the gryph-chargers swept right through them. Vagria did not even attempt to guide Starsid to where she wanted him to be. It would have been like steering a comet. She trusted him to know that better than she did and enjoyed the ride.

There was another loud *clap*, and then a lurch that snapped the world back into place around her. The sky continued to spin for a few seconds afterwards, as if to suggest that Starsid had not, in fact, moved at all, but had rather performed the paradoxically simpler feat of spinning the Realmsphere around him.

The Palladors formed up around her. After a journey as unnatural as that one, even a Stormcast Eternal needed a moment to gather themselves and catch their breath.

They appeared to have flown several miles and the Bonesplitterz boar cavalry were well out of the way behind them. The Serpent River was close enough to be visible, a white-bodied force of nature savaging its way northwards through the Morruk Hills on its way towards the Clawing Sea.

The Pallador-Prime, Raukos, and his retinue danced amongst the sawing pines that bristled its near bank, baiting a small mob of spear-armed orruks that, with their own cavalry now indisposed, had no hope in any of Shyish's many hells of laying a finger on the Vanguard-Palladors and their steeds. Boltstorm pistols erupted from the forest with silent puffs, the Serpent so incandescently loud as to devour even sound, orruks flailing and dropping as though startled to death by the blue smoke disgorged from the Stormcasts' guns.

'The first to die is the first to beat down the walls of the Heldenhall!' Vagria yelled, not even caring, in the heat of the moment, how untrue that boast had lately become, and spurred Starsid into a charge.

Caught between Prime Raukos' teasing cavalry and Vagria's headlong charge, the savage orruks went down under the heavy bills of angered gryph-chargers and the starmetal swords of their riders. It was over before it began.

Raukos thumped his breastplate in greeting as Vagria drew in alongside. She returned the gesture, turning away even as she did so to fish in the haversack strung across her saddle bow for her astral compass and draw it forth. It was an ornate disc of gold and embellished amethyst that fit neatly into her armoured palm. Within it, under a crystal shield, a celestium needle floated on a bed of neutral aether.

She studied the wobbling needle for a moment.

'Ride on,' she barked, and indicated the desired direction with an expansive gesture of her arm. 'Upriver. Draw the boars further that way and run off as many of their infantry as you can.'

'Yes, Lord-Aquilor.' He saluted her with his boltstorm pistol and wheeled away.

Vagria drew a keen breath, battling to keep Starsid from chasing after the Pallador-Prime, which he loudly protested, hating to be still.

She consulted the compass again and shook it. 'Blasted thing.'

'Tell me at least that we are close, Lord-Aquilor.'

Horac stalked towards her, his wings partially furled and crackling behind him, leaving an arcing trail to show exactly where and how he had descended to join her. The stigmata of the storm lay differently on every warrior. Whether it was a thunderous rumble in the voice or the tendency to leave glowing after-images behind them where they walked, every warrior bore its mark to some degree.

Vagria wondered if hers would be the last generation of Stormcast Eternals to bear such marks. Would the legacy of Be'lakor's Cursed Skies be that every warrior bearing the name *Eternal* be new forged from heroes as yet unborn? Given what all now knew, even if no one openly spoke of it, of the flaws in Sigmar's process of Reforging, might that not be preferable?

After century after century of war and endless hunts, was the real possibility of death at long last not something to stir the heart?

'Then I will, Knight-Azyros!' Vagria declared. 'We are close.'

'I understand you have a reputation to protect, Farstrike, but must we battle every greenskin in the Morruk Hills to find the resting place of the sleeping godbeast?'

'A hunter must sometimes rely on her hawks and her hounds as well as her own senses,' Vagria replied. 'The Bonesplitterz have an intuition that you and I lack, and have already guided us better than the auguries of the Consecralium.' She scoffed. 'Lord-Ordinator Dolus would have had us digging in the mud a thousand leagues from here in the Carcass Donse. I for one do not mind letting the orruks drive out my prey. So long as they learn to let go when I bloody their mouths.'

'*Orruk* blood is no concern of mine either.'

The Knight-Azyros looked dolefully at her. The eyes behind his Mask Impassive were pure and startlingly white, but his appearance otherwise was so much like that of a tired old man in a hero's armour that Vagria could not help but pity him for a moment.

'How many centuries would we have been dead already if not for Sigmar's wars?' she asked him. 'Did we fight all these years because we were immortal, and because our sacrifices meant nothing? Or did we fight because we are his Stormcast Eternals?'

'Immortality is not some inconsequential feature of the Striking, like the colour of a Stormhost's regalia or a Paladin's war-name. It was fundamental to Sigmar's plan for us. It is what we are. It may have been no gift, but it was arguably the greatest weapon he ever bestowed upon us. It troubles me that you continue to fight as though the God-King's foe has not seen us disarmed.' The Knight-Azyros threw back his wings and lifted himself powerfully off the ground.

Vagria watched him go. Whatever was stirring in the Heartlands, it was not only the greenskins that it was beginning to affect. Horac's was a troubled soul, with a tendency to dwell in dark places and to wax poetical about the fate he saw ahead for the Mortal Realms, but it was not like him to despair.

Vagria swept up her sword to signal for her retinue. If the godbeast they sought could break the spirit of a Stormcast Eternal, then truly nothing in Ghur was safe.

Kildabrae Heavenscar was, by her own stern measure, the mightiest of Vagria Farstrike's warriors. Mightier than Farstrike herself, some whispered, although never Kildabrae. She thought it, of course, but was content for the question to remain as a matter of speculation, because even immortals – especially immortals – needed an imponderable to chew on around a campfire. Vagria was the guided spear that always found the prey-beast's heart. Kildabrae was the hammer that followed to put it from its misery and end its twitching.

Surrounded on all sides by boar-riders, buttressed on one flank by the enormous haft of the Lord-Aquilor's flag, Kildabrae gave a roar and put all her strength into a blow that would have decapitated a statue.

The Weirdnob parried the hammer with his head. Fulminating green lightning sheeted outwards from the point of impact and across the Weirdnob's head like the visor plate of an arcane suit of armour. With an unintelligible bark, he headbutted the stalled hammer, the implosive shattering that resulted hurling Kildabrae's weapon from her grip and blasting them both from their respective mounts. The Weirdnob bounced to his feet as though even the bones in his body dared not defy him. Garish energies caused his eyes to glow and his muscles to swell and his tattoos to swim like eels around his green skin.

Kildabrae was not so agile. Had she couched herself properly she might have landed with less fierce an impact, but there was no outcome to this day that would end with Kildabrae Heavenscar relinquishing the Farstrike banner from her grip.

The Weirdnob leapt on her, bone staff high in both hands.

She raised her knee. The staff cracked across her shin. Pain flared to her ankle and hip, but the armour spared her worse than a bruise. She struck out the leg, kicking the orruk hard in the groin and lifting him a foot into the air.

The Weirdnob swayed like a drunk who felt no pain. His tongue lolled from his mouth. His glowing eyes rolled about in their sockets like unmarked dice. Kildabrae scissored her legs from under her and, bracing the standard between them, swung herself back onto her feet.

The Weirdnob threw a jab at her shoulder before she had a chance to find her footing. Then again at her stomach. She parried the first with the haft of her standard, gave ground before the second. The Weirdnob gave a manic cackle that Kildabrae wiped from his face with a roundhouse punch that struck flickering green motes of corposant phlegm from the orruk's mouth. The

Weirdnob staggered back, heavy limbs swinging, and then unexpectedly vomited up a fist.

The punch passed straight through the golden cloth of Vagria's standard and hit Kildabrae's mask. She went down, still holding onto the standard, as though struck by a club.

The temptation was to lie down forever, but a careless boar-rider would kill her as surely as a Waaagh!-empowered maniac if she stayed down. Wiping green slime from her eye slits, she made herself sit.

She found the Weirdnob facing her on his knees, his eyes wide, the green glow in them much diminished as he retched on the muscular bicep stuck in his throat. Shaking her ringing head, half a mind on the orruk boar-riders and Vanguard-Palladors doing battle around her, she got her feet under her and stumbled towards the shaking Weirdnob. There, and without further ado, she brained the orruk with the heavy banner pole, and then struck him four times more while he was down for good measure.

Gasping for breath, Kildabrae pulled off her gunge-splattered helmet and let it fall, spitting until she was certain there was nothing of the orruk and his green sorcery left on her lips.

The Weirdnob and his boars had been circling a rugged outcropping of orange-coloured rock that rose like a bicep between a sharp bend in the river. Whatever it was that Excelsis had set Vagria hunting, Kildabrae was certain that the Bonesplitterz had found it for them here. Why else would their shaman have been here, when the other boar-riders had been drawn out by Vagria's false charge and his foot-soldiers were rushing to engage the Vanguard-Palladors amongst the trees?

Turning her bare face upwards, she hoisted Vagria's standard three times, signalling Horac or Brendel to attend. She lowered her gaze from the sky, intending to find her lost mount and rejoin her retinue in battle, when a swaying movement from the pine woods downriver from the outcropping caught her eye.

The Serpent River crashed on in a north-easterly direction, running sometimes uphill and sometimes down as it bit and gouged its way through the Morruk Hills. The slender trees clustered close to the frothing channel in misted gullies throughout the hills. They were tall enough to conceal almost anything. Her first fear, watching as the swaying canopies turned to a sudden thrashing, was that the greater strength of the Bonesplitterz horde had evaded Raukos and Columna and returned to fight the Astral Templars for their prey.

But Vagria had quite deliberately sent them south, not north.

She wished, afterwards, for ten thousand orruk boar-riders.

The hundred-foot-tall mega-gargant pushed through the treeline the way a human would a grass thicket. In the process it uprooted a tree that was only slightly taller than the sunburned crown of its head and used it as an impromptu club to smack a savage orruk to jelly. Gargants had been known to shadow armies in the hopes of interrupting a battle in progress and garnering a free meal from one or either side, but they had been bold of late.

In the moments it took for the behemoth to emerge, the shape of the battle changed, and Kildabrae Heavenscar did absolutely nothing. The only right response to the unlooked-for appearance of a mega-gargant was complete and paralysing terror.

A single stride carried the child of the World Titan over a pair of Vanguard-Palladors and two-score savage orruk boar-riders. Nobody was fighting each other now. Everyone was running. Both the Stormhosts and the Bonesplitterz had the methods and the weapons, and in many cases the desire, to bring down such godly prey, but on the wrong side of an ambush the only tactic available to either side was flight.

The mega-gargant's sandaled foot thudded into the base of the outcropping and sent several dozen combatants tumbling down its side. Its foot was longer than Kildabrae was tall. If it were to land on her, there would be no part of her body long enough to escape crushing.

Giving every appearance of enjoying itself enormously, the mega-gargant stamped an orruk into green paste and sent a long arm swooping lazily out to snatch a Vanguard-Pallador from the saddle. Her gryph-charger was fleet as the wind, but there was no escaping the gargant's reach. The mega-gargant licked its lips as it brought the struggling warrior to them. Blunt teeth cracked thrice-blessed sigmarite.

Her screams were appalling.

The warrior's body and raiment broke down into lightning, blasting free of the mega-gargant's mouth in a spray of teeth. Kildabrae looked up with hope, but rather than bolt back to Azyrheim and the Forge Eternal, the Pallador's disembodied soul arced and forked across the sky like a bird that had forgotten the way home.

No matter how many times Kildabrae witnessed the legacy of Be'lakor's Cursed Skies and Sigmar's failure to overcome the daemon prince's sorcery, she still found another dent to threaten her faith.

How many more blows before it broke?

Merrily swinging a boot while it licked its fingers, the mega-gargant punted a howling orruk from the back of its boar and into the river. The Serpent frothed over the thrashing greenskin, bearing him downriver to be devoured at leisure. The mega-gargant belched, peering amusedly down at the tiny warriors trying desperately to scatter before it.

The only one holding their ground was Kildabrae Heavenscar.

She was not sure if it was out of valour or terror.

The little shelf of rock on which she stood lifted her almost to the level of the mega-gargant's chest, but went no way at all towards convincing her that she could best it in battle. She still had no hammer, but she held Vagria's standard and she gripped it tightly. The golden cloth hung limply from the crossbar and it was only then she noticed that it, and her – and the mega-gargant as well, in fact – had become thoroughly drenched.

Out of nowhere, it had started raining, but there wasn't a real cloud in the tortured sky.

She dared herself to look up, and knew in an instant that she would never be awed by a mega-gargant again.

The first thought in Vagria's mind, on seeing the entirety of the Serpent River rise up out of its bed, was awe that something so gigantic could possibly live. Her second was a burning desire to kill it.

The river began to bubble, then to boil, its banks trembling as though with the footsteps of something godlike and terrible. From the seething waters four spouts appeared, two way downriver and two way, *way* up, small at first but rapidly growing. At about the height of a mounted Stormcast the rear spouts ceased growing, but the forward pair continued until they were ten or eleven times Vagria's height. With a roar like a great river crashing around an obstacle, the forward spouts *bent* outwards, water streaming down what were definitely now limbs gouging channels for reptilian claws out of the rock. Its overall form was that of a gigantic alligator, four hundred feet long and twice the height of the mega-gargant that stood dwarfed under its dripping body. Teeth of white froth filled its long mouth, dark spots and whorls armoured its back.

There was an explosion of feathers and claws and colour as every thing that had been living on the banks of the river evacuated its vicinity while the Bonesplitterz, with equal clamour, turned around and started sprinting towards it.

A deluge dropped over Vagria Farstrike and her retinue, and for the first time since departing the Templia Beasthall her purple armour and golden heraldry gleamed unblemished.

'Is this it?' yelled Pallador Oldro, who rode beside her, in her ear and yet near impossible to hear all the same. 'Is this the godbeast from the Excelsian prophecy?'

'I don't know,' Vagria cried back. 'Kill it now and read its entrails later.'

'How do you kill a river?'

As they spoke, the Serpent struck.

Its jaws closed around the mega-gargant's waist and, with the power of a million tons of water plunging into the Clawing Sea, lifted it up into the air and shook the son of Behemat viciously from side to side until it snapped. Vagria just managed to catch a glimpse of Kildabrae, a zephyr mote of purple and gold, before the Serpent stepped on her, a column of water more massive than the Prophesiers' Guildhall of Excelsis obliterating her, and the rock she had been standing on.

Vagria's retinue cried out in despair and anger at seeing the Heavenscar, their standard-bearer and twice-blessed totem, so inconsequentially slain. Vagria herself felt a curious elation: the thrill of the illicit and the dangerous that came with an immortal warrior's fear of death. There were times she wondered… if there was a death in her past to remember, would she chase one of her own so eagerly now?

'You ask how we slay a river?' she yelled, raising her starbound blade high. 'We slay it as the Astral Templars have always slain such beasts. For Sigmar!' She urged Starsid forward, but the rocks had become slippery and the best the animal could maintain was a tentative canter.

The Bonesplitterz, on the other hand, were already swarming ahead of them, largely ignoring the handful of Astral Templars now, in favour of the beast. Those of them who remembered they were carrying bows lobbed arrows at the watery monstrosity, while orruks operating in pairs to wield impractically enormous wooden spears ran dementedly to ram its haunches and belly. To Vagria's surprise, the weapons proved remarkably effective, spilling river water from numerous wounds in the Serpent's liquid skin before it could adjust to the tattooed irritants prancing around under its belly and crush them.

As far as Vagria understood the Bonesplitterz's form of worship, which – given she was neither green nor mad – was not well, they praised the Great Green God, Gorkamorka, by hunting down the great spirits of the realms and then taking their power: either by eating them, wearing them, turning them into a weapon, or some combination of all three. It was one of the great ironies of the realms that, in so doing, they inadvertently performed the same service that Gorkamorka himself had grown bitter of millennia ago, and which the Astral Templars now performed about half as well: eliminating such beasts as might threaten the bastions of Order.

There was method to their apparent madness, however. When the Bonesplitterz pierced their bodies with the finger bones of a ghyrlach to bestow themselves with great strength, or tattooed themselves in the toxic ink of a colossipede to ward off an enemy's blows, they seemed to receive exactly the boons they desired.

'We should wait on Raukos and Columna,' Oldro cried. 'We need their numbers.'

Ignoring the Pallador, Vagria drew her boltstorm pistol from its gold-embellished holster. She had no idea of knowing how big the Serpent was going to get, or if the savage orruks were capable of killing it without help.

They rode directly underneath and between the Serpent's hind limbs. The air there was thick enough to clog the mouth. The roar was so great that she could no longer actually hear it; instead it became a vibration that ran under her skin and through her armour, as if from the inside out. Her pistol discharged in relative silence, and but for the kick against her arm, she might have thought it had not fired at all. The volley of sigmarite shot punched through the Serpent's belly.

If she had opened fire on an actual river, she doubted she could have caused it less injury. Oldro screamed a warning. The Serpent arched its back ponderously to address them, and raised one foot. The Palladors swerved as it came down, galloping clear drenched and shaken, but unscathed.

Vagria reloaded as Horac swept overhead. The shutters of his celestial lantern were drawn wide, the light of every star in Azyr blazing from its glass. Steam hissed off the Serpent's back and it arched as though in pain. Vagria sprayed the monster with shot, her riders continuing to fill its underbelly with sigmarite as they swerved again to avoid its agonised thrashing.

'That is how you kill a river!' Vagria roared, shaking her head to get rid of the water flooding the mouth and nose holes of her mask. 'Burn it with starlight and lightning!'

Following in the Knight-Azyros' wake came the Prosecutor retinue of Brendel Starsighted. Their javelins transmuted into bolts of lightning as they were cast from the warriors' hands and strafed the wounded monster's back. Brendel himself swept in low amongst the stabbing bolts, pinning the Serpent with arrows while Eliara looped in behind. With a shriek of challenge, the star-eagle banked towards the Serpent and dropped as though on a suicide attack, her body bursting into one of living lightning and plunging into the Serpent's back.

The monster thrashed and writhed, steam rising off it as divine electricity arced and spasmed through its body.

Vagria called out a warning to fall back as the Serpent rolled onto its side in a bid to dislodge the creature that was inside it, drowning several hundred orruks in an instant.

Circling a thousand feet above the Serpent's writhing belly, the coolness of the hunter exemplified, Brendel reached into his bottomless quiver for the single star-fated arrow it contained.

Eliara burst free of the Serpent's chest, transforming back into flesh and blood, and with a roar of pain the supine river snapped its jaws for her.

Brendel loosed.

The beast-slaying shaft plunged into the roof of the Serpent's mouth and snapped its head violently back. It fell away from the fleeing star-eagle and died, its body bursting into a thousand raging channels, daughter rivers to the great Serpent, each competing with and consuming one another in their quest for the swiftest course through the newly ruined landscape.

For a long while the Morruk Hills were still: silent but for the gurgling of water over broken rock.

Vagria holstered her pistol and signalled wearily for Horac and Brendel. They had to work quickly.

CHAPTER FIVE

Excelsis was two months east towards the Perimeter Inimical, across Ymnog's Trample and through Glutton's Gorge, and over the broken continent of Donse where the dead still walked and grot warlords scavenged kingdoms from the bones of empires. From her post atop the eastern wall, still a mess of scaffold turrets and casemates even after twelve weeks of restoration work, Ilsbet Glorica Angellin tried to imagine that she could see it.

The Thondian Free City was parochial, to say the least, and a recent movement opposed to conspicuous wealth had made it an awkward staging ground for the First Age Celestians, but it was one of the crown jewels of Sigmar's ever-growing kingdom nonetheless.

The boundaries of its influence extended far beyond the six occulum fulgurest that channelled the storm energies of the Mallus Spear through its outer bastions. Through wealth, might and political patronage it supported a constellation of satellite colonies and dependent states. These stretched the length of the Trade Road from Hyesca to Quallifae, and across the gulfs of the Clawing Sea to the distant ports of I'meth Falls. Its influence even stretched, albeit uncertainly, as if wary of having its hand bitten or stung, inland into the true wilderness of the Ghurite Heartlands. The sweltering jungles of Mekitopsar marked its westward extremity, and the city's influence extended even to the thick steel walls of Fort Abraxicon, raised in prehistory by mason-priests of Grungni the Maker as a gateway to the Realm of Metal. The Realmgate had been won back only recently, and at tremendous cost, from the orruks of the Shattered Shin. The death of Warboss Grukka at the hands of the White Reaper, Lord-Veritant of the Knights-Excelsior and dread protector of Excelsis, had been celebrated as a terrible blow to the greenskin menace and the dawning of a new age of Order on the Coast of Tusks.

The crusade to destroy the Bloodgullet gluthold had been called by Excelsis' Grand Conclave shortly afterwards, and signed off as a mere formality by its high counterpart in Azyrheim.

Another bold step in the civilising of the Heartlands. Another great push of Excelsis' influence, and by extension Sigmar's, into the more habitable climes of the realm's core. Or so it had been said at the time.

The twelve weeks in which no word at all had emerged from Excelsis had put General Lisandr into a noticeably volatile mood, and a restive commander made for anxious troops. The Accari war-priests, Ferrgin and Taal, had taken to prophesying that a second Time of Omens was upon them all. That period of darkness had wracked the realms of her grandfather's time with portents and foreshadowed the Shyishan Necroquake, whose aftershocks they all still battled today. Predicting a second coming was the raving of a bored, superstitious, angry and often very drunk man, Angellin was certain. The Tribulations had disturbed even the cemeteries of Azyr and, so it was rumoured, disrupted the sacred processes of the Forge Eternal itself. What were a few greenskin armies and gargant stomps roving the Ghurish Heartlands to compare with that?

And it had to be said that neither she, nor any of the Celestians prepared to set aside the vast disparities in social status to talk to her, had experienced any of the so-called 'omens' that the Accari complained of: the persistent growling of beasts in the night, the trembling of the earth like the skin of a beaten drum, or that Hysh had suddenly grown teeth and turned the sky around it red.

From above the stockade, Angellin could hear the late-night revels emanating from the Accari side of the stronghold. The occasional barked laugh or animal whimper made itself heard above the hammering and sawing and smelting of reconstruction, and only then because the stronghold did not boast a huge surfeit of space to create much of a buffer between them.

Without an enemy to fight, other than the annoyingly persistent gnoblars, the Accari had grown dissolute and sullen and, after one skirmish too many, Lisandr had commanded that the two regiments be strictly segregated except for the joint patrols that still went out in the Eaten Plain every day. Braun called his southern half of the city Goreham, while Lisandr had named the eastern wards under her control Fort Honoria. For her daughter. The First Age Celestians had so much history that it was customary to name their monuments in honour of future heroes.

It was rumoured that Lisandr and Braun had not spoken to one another in days.

Angellin sighed, swatting idly at a needlewasp, and tried to appear properly attentive whilst watching over the stark emptiness of the Eaten Plain. The once verdant savannahs were cracked desolation as far as the eye could see. The ever-widening Bloodgullet Mawpath had stripped it of the mega-herds that had once migrated across it, of its vegetation, and even most of its insects except for those uniquely adapted to surviving amongst ogors.

The city, as it had existed under the Bloodgullet, had been host to a startlingly impressive burgh of wooden longhouses. Each had been massive, and solidly built, and linked to one another by a system of soundly engineered, almost beautiful viaducts and natural tunnels. The level of nous on display had been eye-opening. Ogors destroyed and consumed: they were not supposed to build. Angellin had confessed these doubts to Mother Thassily and been duly chastened for them.

The ward directly behind her, encompassing just a few hundred yards of gently sloping ground between the wall and the abrupt, bowl-shaped depression of the Butchers' Quarter, was the thinnest part of the former gluthold. It was host now to a busy village of lean-tos and enclosures, adapted from Celestian tents strung along the buttressing beams, and home to a lively new community of Azyrite servants, Accari labourers and Ironweld engineers. For all their rough edges the Accari were skilled and hard-working. Their Azyrite counterparts, she admitted, were not quite so willing to tolerate physical labour.

Angellin could smell Azyrite dishes being prepared with Ghurish spices, and hear familiar songs accompanied by the primitive sounds of local instruments. She regretted that she could not head down at the end of her watch and see the tent village for herself first-hand without having to disobey the general's orders.

She looked up, scratching compulsively at her itching scalp. She understood now why the great majority of the Accari cut their hair short or went bald. The High Star of Azyr, Sigendil, twinkled in the firmament from afar. Just as it did over the night sky of every realm in the Cosmos Arcane. She watched it for several minutes, the sight of its watchful permanence reassuring her troubled spirit.

A bestial shout arose from somewhere amidst the leaning

wooden shanties of Goreham and she returned her gaze quickly to her watch.

'There will be some sore heads tomorrow,' Artem Vitus Carnelian, her less-than-willing companion on the graveyard shift, observed, leaning boredly on his spear.

Angellin nodded, but offered no opinion. Field Marshal Garviel Ernest Jayko, the Celestians' second officer, had once casually mentioned that her comrades found her unsolicited attempts at conversation boorish. Not to be discouraged, however, Carnelian went on, deciding perhaps that a few hours of charitable discourse beat a lonely watch on the Eaten Plain.

'What are you being punished for?'

'Oh, nothing,' said Angellin. 'I volunteered.'

The other Celestian frowned at her. Angellin noticed that he had a black eye and a split lip, both of which had been poorly concealed with make-up.

'What did you do?' Angellin asked.

'Nothing,' he said, turning away, apparently deciding on the lonely watch after all. 'I volunteered too.'

The Ironweld had promised that the Grand Cathedral of Fort Honoria would take thirteen years to complete, requiring the import of a rare blue marble from Azyr and the commissioning of a master glazier from Excelsis, whereupon, they assured, it would be recognised far and wide as one of the marvels of the Ghurish Heartlands. Malec Grint had watched the Hounds put theirs up in three months, adding a sizeable outbuilding that had since been converted into an alehouse. Because, as it was with most common activities, a person prayed better with a drink or two inside them.

Four-score large fighters with nothing better to do packed the common room, twice as many again spilling boisterously into the courtyard it shared with the temple. They guzzled the Tyrants' ale as it sloshed out of the barrels or arm-wrestled over rough-hewn tables, engaged in headbutting contests, or rolled knucklebones for forfeits. Many simply sat with their heads in their hands, muttering, chewing on their arraca stems, tapping out a *THUD-THUD* rhythm on the tabletops until someone put an ale in their hands, and occasionally pronouncing the doom of all civilised men.

The air hummed, inside and out, with spider-moths and flies, drawn by the spilled ale and the warm bodies, and by the oil lamps that flickered dangerously from the cordwood walls. Every so often, the infectious laughter of Chief Lusten, better known as Blind Lusten for his unerring aim, drifted out through the din from inside.

In the yard looking out onto the Butchers' Quarter, Kanta Grint held court. The woman was so huge that no ordinary stool could encompass her, and so she had been provided with a bench, which she filled on her own, sat at the head of a large table and surrounded by children, step-children, children-in-law, half-cousins and nephews and nieces. By virtue of Kanta's fertility, long life, many marriages and famed brutality, the Grint clan was larger than any other two in the Hounds, making her second only to Jenk in the convoluted hierarchy of the Dozen. In all, close to a hundred men and women had found a way to cram themselves around that table, jostling and snarling, as though proximity to Kanta Grint was synonymous with proximity to Braun.

Malec Grint sat at an overspill table in between a third cousin called Kursh and his half-sister, Debrevn, and opposite a wild-eyed mess of scars and crazy that he had never met before but who was presumably a distant relation.

I'm going to ask her, he thought. *I'm going to walk right on over there, and ask her.* He glanced across to the head of the main table.

Grinning broadly, her eyes glazed by Bloodgullet ale, his mother was launching into yet another poorly remembered and incoherent tale of the old days with the Tuskan Wildmen. Kanta was not, by nature, a garrulous woman. She preferred to speak with her fists, as the splintered bits of memory from Malec's childhood would attest if they dared, but brute size and bloody reputation enforced a respectful hush, even on close relatives, that a little drink then encouraged the old woman to fill.

'...*not been this bored since Izalmaw and, of course, despite what Braun'll tell you, we technically lost that battle*...'

Malec coughed and turned away. *Maybe after a few cousins have left.*

Picking up a wooden spoon, he looked down at the earthenware laid out in front of him: a chipped bowl containing a pair of wood-hard wheat-cakes and a small jug half-filled with sow's milk. With a sigh, not feeling terrifically hungry, he picked up the jug and splashed milk over the two cakes.

He was aware of Debrevn and Kursh leaning in from either side.

The relation opposite banged his fist on the table and gave a cheer as the first wriggly black speck emerged from the drowned cakes and rose slowly to the top. The weevil floated upside down on the surface of the milk, kicking its tiny black legs as it died. Another followed it, then another, until thirteen of the drowned insects were bobbing in his milk.

'Lucky in some parts,' said Debrevn.

Grint looked at her sourly.

Kursh passed Grint the sieve, which he then used to scoop the thirteen weevils from the bowl. Shaking off the carry-over milk, he tipped them onto the table. Thirteen wasn't bad. Nowhere near close to Torric's thirty-eight, while also being comfortably clear of Mikali's all-time record worst of zero.

'...*and then Altin killed her dog and Olgar burnt his house down!*'

The Grints howled with laughter.

Malec wished he'd heard the start of the story. *I'm going to ask her*, he reminded himself. *I'm going to ask her permission to pursue Ilsbet right now.*

Malec had fought his way down the pecking order because he'd heard that Celestian Angellin had a tendency to volunteer for the kinds of duties that the Accari preferred to pass down the command chain as punishments. But with only a handful of patrols going out onto the Eaten Plain these days, and most of those segregated along regimental lines, Malec had found opportunities to get close to her harder to come by since the night of the sacking. He sighed, wondering what it was about Angellin that made her worth it. But that was the way of the Heartlands. A person saw a thing they wanted and they went to get it. Stopping to think was the surest way to lose your prey to a larger predator, or to get eaten yourself. He was just getting impatient, he decided, and the impatience was making him restive. The make-up shifts had long ceased to be the amusing anecdote that he'd thought he might one day tell his grandchildren when asked about the long, ultimately triumphant courtship of their grandmother.

He'd rather face his mother's wrath and the mockery of his family than run another damned message.

'*...you'd better believe they found the general another troop to command pretty damn quick after that night...*'

Grint dunked his fingers into the bowl and picked up the moistened cake. He stared at it as if it were deliberately and maliciously detaining him from getting up and walking over to his mother's table.

He bit in. The wheat-cake was still hard in the centre. Excess liquid that could not penetrate that far streamed off its rounded edges and down Grint's fingers. On the two-week march from Accar they had practically lived off them and, so long as there was something to soften them with, Grint couldn't care less that they were almost entirely without taste.

One cake. Then I'll ask her.

Grint opened his mouth to take a bite, only to pause as he noticed the sudden quiet that was emanating from the alehouse doorway and spreading across the courtyard to touch even the Grint clan table at its far edge.

'Don't mind me,' said Jenk, with a reptilian smile once everybody was good and quiet. He walked into the courtyard, the thumb of one hand tucked in his belt, and slapped the head of the first fighter he came to, which just happened, of course, to be Mikali, who had been drinking alone near the engineers around the threshold of the alehouse. 'Bad luck, Mikali,' he said. 'You've volunteered for an excursion. Well done.' He wandered the courtyard, poking and slapping soldiers at random while at the same time, most unerringly, sparing Kanta and those closest to her. 'Gnoblar hunt!' he declared, once his promenade around the courtyard was done, to the deep groans of those selected and the relieved cheers of those who had escaped this time.

The gnoblars that still infested parts of Goreham may not have been threatening to look at but they were reviled more deeply by the Accari than their ogor masters had ever been. Braun, Lisandr and Arden Shay were in rare agreement that there were probably several hundred of the creatures still at large, and that this was a number which would become several thousand very soon if they were allowed to continue pilfering from their dwindling supplies unchecked. They were small enough to hide themselves in the tightest and most hard-to-reach of crannies, had a natural inclination towards the dank and, worst of all in Grint's mind, an intuitive love of traps that more than made up for the more warlike traits that they lacked. It did not help the already strained relationship between the regiments that most of their holes seemed to come out in parts of the city claimed by the Accari.

More than a few of the lesser chiefs, men like Lusten and Stavn, who could lead a few close relatives under the command of the Dozen, argued that the task of extermination wasn't worth the bother. Easier to build another castle, they said, and leave this one to them. They'd start killing each other as soon as they were numerous enough, and save the Accari the bother.

Grint allowed himself to relax as the chosen men filed out under Jenk's grim smile. He set the cake back in the bowl and slapped his hands to the table, resolved to go over and ask his mother's permission to pursue Ilsbet's hand before she started on another blasted story, just as the leader of the Dozen's cold hand fell on his shoulder.

'Did you think we'd forgotten you, blasphemer?' Jenk tutted loudly. 'Braun's a pious man, you know. Mother Thassily told him all about what you said to her, and he asked for you *personally*.' He spoke just loudly enough for absolutely everyone in the courtyard, in the common room it adjoined, or praying in the temple next door to hear. 'Don't mind if I borrow your son for a day or two, do you, Kanta?'

His mother squinted down the large table towards him. 'Is he one of mine? After the eighth they all start to look alike.'

His older brothers laughed along, Sigmar damn them. Grint hoped it was only a joke.

Mikali slid her arm through his. She looked at him smugly. Grint would have throttled her if he hadn't seen another fighter try it once and accidentally slip and break all the fingers in his right hand.

She shrugged. 'Some people are just born unlucky.'

'Once the building work is completed, General Lisandr, this will all look very different.'

Gunnery-Professor Shay waved the slim leather-bound treatise, *Principia Optika*, that she had been carrying throughout the city without ever once referring to, as though she was a lecturer drawing a class' attention to an equation on a board. She gestured enthusiastically across the torchlit building site that presently described the lower ward of Fort Honoria. Corn doll's houses, unfinished and slightly ominous, teetered over ground that the ogors had stripped even of soil. Rope outlines, fencing, or even just holes in the ground marked out where new shops and houses would eventually rise. One short spoke on the growing twelve-point-plan that would become a new Free City of Order.

Here was uniformity, Lisandr thought. Here was order. Every fence post and paving stone laid in accordance to a plan. Lisandr found it all passably pleasing to see. She was accustomed to being well on her way to the next battlefield before any conquest in which she had participated reached this stage of its development. Her orders from Excelsis were already worryingly overdue, but what could she do except wait? The Coast of Tusks was months away on foot, and she did not wholly resent this opportunity to see for herself what the blood of Celestian warriors had borne.

'I can see it, professor,' she said, the torches carried by Shay's servants dancing like starlight across the diamond rivets and silver mail of her guards. The revels of neighbouring Goreham on the other hand, lamplit and wild, were a flicker at the corners of her eyes, and a susurrant growl at the edge of hearing, like the snores of restless hills. 'I can see what it will become.'

Shay spread her arms, as though making a measuring triangle of her body with which to assay the dimensions of the city's wall. 'There is only one way in and out of Goreham and Honoria, and so *this* is where migrants and traders will enter. They will take this road that we are standing on now. Their goods will fill the warehouses that will be built in this ward, they will buy and sell from its shops, find accommodation in its houses and seek work in its enterprises.'

'And when will the walls be finished?'

'Pfft.' Shay looked over the heavy frame of her glasses. 'I expected grander vision from you, general.'

'Walls are important. That is why every city I have ever visited has them.'

Shay brushed the critique away. 'Rest assured, general, Fort Honoria will have its walls.'

The white-haired engineer performed a one-hundred-and-eighty-degree turn, long robes scuffing the road that descended from the Butchers' Quarter circular to the gate. It was not quite a dirt road, having been levelled flat and bedded with pebbles and coarse sand, but it had yet to be properly paved. She pushed her spectacles up her nose and brandished the *Principia* towards the Gnarlfast. Eyots of construction grew about the old longhouses, the seeds of what would one day become districts and burghs with characters of their own, shrugging off Shay's benign attempts at standardisation and being the stronger for it. Flags flew in clusters, red and tan, silver and blue, depending on whose viaducts or causeways they fluttered over.

'And this is the first thing that our new settlers will see when they come through them.'

Lisandr followed her gaze, across the empty bowl of the Butchers' Quarter where the Azyrite and Ghurite temples to the God-King faced one another from opposite sides, framing a breathtakingly open view of the Gnarlfast.

'Now, imagine this view with the castle completed,' said Shay, growing increasingly breathless as she laid out her vision. 'Its floorplan will be that of a blessed dodecahedron, twelve-fold towers cut into the side of the Gnarlfast itself, the white gleam of celemnite in stark contrast to the brown of the mountain, visible to the naked eye from the far edges of the Eaten Plain. One day, a Grand Conclave will rule from that castle, and in place of a general like yourself or Braun there will be a High Arbiter elected to sit at the table's head, and all will know that good order has come at last to Gallet.'

'I did not take you for an idealist, professor.'

Tucking her book securely under her arm, Shay appeared to diminish into herself as all that her imagination had built returned to dreams and the mass of outline sketches covering the walls in her quarters.

'One does not get it into their head to build cities, general, without having something of the dreamer about them.' She looked meekly up at the Gnarlfast, as though it had bested her this time, and sighed. 'Give me two hundred years, general. I would build you a citadel out of this mountain to rival the Palatine Keep of Excelsis.'

Lisandr felt a tug on her own lips. Nothing was so infectious as an old woman enthused, particularly when one was a middle-aged woman determined for so long to be aloof.

The professor, she knew, had not asked for this last adventure and had strenuously protested the 'honour' being given to her, even after they had picked up the Accari Hounds and departed Accar for the final leg of the crusade. On the road, and even during the siege itself, she had complained of every malady of old age known to humankind, but since exchanging a tent for four walls and a bed, and the tools of war for her beloved blueprints and books, she was a woman reborn. In Excelsis, Arden Shay was a celebrated, even revered figure, but her fame went little further, and her life's achievements were not so great that they would outlast her grandchildren's generation. Here, she was beginning to realise, was the unlooked-for chance at a crowning act, to be present for the founding of a Free City, and to live forever in the minds of millions as the architect who had built Goreham and Honoria.

'I don't believe either of us has another two hundred years left in us, professor.'

For some reason, Shay smiled at that. 'A shame… At the very least, I would wish for the chance to see the city when it's finished, even if I were too senile and frail to oversee all the work myself.' She sighed again. 'Such is the fate of the architect.'

'And of the soldier, professor.'

The engineer fashioned another, somewhat warmer smile. 'Do you think you might call me Arden, general, if I were to call you Ellisior? All of this *general* this and *professor* that – it makes me feel as though we're back at the Artillery School. So stiff and formal, don't you think?'

Lisandr smiled thinly. She favoured stiff and formal. They were synonyms for *orderly*.

'If you are certain that I cannot stop you.'

'Thank you.' She saw the old woman's teeth, their golden crowns flashing in the torchlight. 'Ellisior.'

Lisandr cleared her throat, unsure whether she liked the sound of her given name in that low-born, faintly Thondian accent, but there was little hope of rescinding the invitation to use it now. 'What else did you wish to show me?'

'I thought you might be interested in the common stables we're building in a square by the gate. Given the variety of beasts used as mounts here in the Heartlands, they are going to be grander than the ogor longhouse that General Braun has been living in.'

Lisandr gestured for Shay to lead the way. 'Then by all means, I would love to see them.'

The Celestians headed the march down what would become the city's main thoroughfare, stamping their footprints into the sand and gravel, Lydia Victoria holding Lisandr's banner aloft so all would have warning to show the proper deference to a general of Azyr. The torches of Shay's servants followed after them, picking out the silver thread, quartz and moonstones of Lydia's standard, making them dance like a dilettante scattering jewels to the street.

Even in the middle of the night, work did not stop. Rowdy work songs roared out of the timber frames, like beasts disturbed in their caves. Oil lamps, strung higgledy-piggledy over scaffolds, threw bars of light and weird shadows everywhere. Hammers barked. Saws growled. Draught animals bleated. The soldiers and their entourage tramped through, the occasional bowed head or wild grin appearing out of the shadows of the roadside as the torchlight found them, but more often eliciting a sneer or a hawk of phlegm. The Ironweld had drawn up the designs and supervised the construction. The engineers were respectful and educated, as Ghurites went, but it was the Accari who provided most of the labour.

'There's something I've been meaning to ask,' said Shay.

Lisandr pulled her gaze from a scaffold full of hungry, glaring men. Shay hobbled on, unconcerned.

'Ask it,' said Lisandr.

'Celestians' names. You all have three. Do you not find it a bit of a mouthful?'

Lisandr frowned, unsure if she was being mocked. 'They are given name, exemplary name and family name.'

'Exemplary?'

'They are given to us by our first unit commander when we become Celestians. It can be considered a testament to our character, something our commander saw in us or a trait they hope to inspire by naming.'

'What a beautiful idea. So, Seraphine?'

'It means... godly, or holy guardian.'

'Wonderful.' Shay glanced towards her squire. 'And Victoria?'

'I'm sure you can work it out,' said Lisandr, irritably now, although not entirely sure why, looking up at what sounded like raised voices coming from the cluster of Ironweld storage tents that had been pitched under the gate. The lights there were bobbing a little too violently to be accounted for by the occasional ground tremor or the panting, breath-like gusts of wind off the Eaten Plains, while the voices were too out of time for even an Accari working sound.

Fighting, she realised. It was the sound of Accari fighting.

One of her Celestians called a warning, but Lisandr was already pushing past him, sabre drawn, toes crunching into the sand underfoot as she broke into a run. 'Weapons down!' she yelled. 'By order of General Lisandr!'

A dozen or so bulky, dark-disguised figures broke and ran at the sound of her voice, scattering into the maze of tents and scaffolding. A six-man unit of bloodied Celestians and a couple of dead Accari were all that was left by the time Lisandr reached them, Lydia and her escort arriving on her heels. The warriors lowered their shields so the pointed bases rested on the ground, turning spear-points and swords blade down. There was no condition, not even a command from a superior officer, that would provoke a First Age Celestian to voluntarily disarm themselves.

A Celestian was battle-ready at all times.

This unit had been stationed, at Shay's request, to protect the Ironweld's supplies, as well as to supervise the comings and goings through the gate. Sorties were heading out into the Eaten Plain and Cuspid Mesas every day, venturing increasingly, dangerously, further afield in search of forage, for the Bloodgullet had stripped the land clean for miles around.

Starris Valoris Mestrade, a corporal, was the commanding officer. The Celestians were a small, elite regiment, and Lisandr knew every line officer under her command. She had always considered Mestrade to be solid and dependable, committed to the regiment and with a rare talent for an inspiring turn of phrase. His family was rumoured to possess a first-edition print of the verses of Theraclese, the Bard of Glimmerhall, and he was well known for favouring the uplifting poems of the Bard when reading to his unit on the march.

His nose was broken and he swayed slightly as he stood to attention. A large purpling bruise mauled his ruggedly aristocratic features around one foggy blue eye.

Lisandr shoved her sword back into its sheath. 'What in Nagash's blackest hells is this?'

The Celestian met her gaze solidly. The lip swelling under his bushy moustache made him appear deliberately sullen and Lisandr resisted the urge to strike him. There was a place for corporal punishment, but there were proper formalities and procedures to be observed. She was not sure what, exactly, goaded her towards summary violence now.

'They attacked us, sir,' said Mestrade.

'Who did?'

The corporal shrugged, nodding towards one of the two bodies on the ground. 'The Accari.'

'I want names!'

'I don't know any of their names, sir. Not one of their leaders, that is for sure.'

Lisandr took a deep breath. Her hand ached from resisting its desire to make a fist. Sigmar, what was wrong with her? It was this place. She remembered something she had said to Lydia. *Ghur will make savages of us all.* Enclosing her fist in the other palm, she forced it back to her side.

At the sound of crunching sand and wheezing, Lisandr turned, gratefully, as Gunnery-Professor Shay, helped along by her servants, finally caught up.

'Good heavens,' said Shay, shaking off an attendant's arm and staring at the bodies on the road. She looked up, fixing Mestrade with an expression that was suddenly as stern as anything Lisandr might have mustered. 'Did they take anything, young man?'

'No, sir.'

One of Mestrade's battered soldiers flashed a grim smile.

Lisandr rounded on her. 'Are you proud of your work here, Celestian?'

The soldier's smile vanished in an instant. She shook her head vigorously. 'No, sir!'

'I should hope not. What do you suppose General Braun will make of this when he finds out? Two of his men dead? And over what?' Lisandr forced herself to take a step back. She pushed her fist behind her back and gripped it tightly there in the other hand. 'The usual punitive details are considerably oversubscribed at the moment. Wait here for Mother Thassily. We will see if she cannot come up with something creative for the six of you.'

'But–' the unsmiling woman began.

'Sir!' Mestrade barked, cutting the soldier off and silencing her protest with a sideways glare.

Lisandr nodded. She turned away just as a boy, about fifteen years old but already heavily muscled and broad in the Ghurite way, stumbled blinking into the Ironweld's torchlight. There was a moment in which they stared at one another, the Accari lad squinting in the light, before the Celestians levelled their spears towards him. The boy screamed, turning his head aside and shutting his eyes, and thrusting out a leather tube as if to ward off the bristling of starsilver. Lisandr noticed the silver gleam of the Swifthawk seal along its side, her heart growing wings and fluttering, and she stepped through her escorts' spears to snatch the message tube from the boy's hand.

The first word from Excelsis in months.

She tore the seal, upended the tube to slide the message into her waiting hand, and then threw the tube away to unfurl the scroll and held it up to the torchlight.

General Lisandr, it read. *We expected your return four weeks ago. Izalend has fallen. The greenskins responsible for its sacking march now to reinforce the horde laying siege to Bilgeport, and when it falls Excelsis will be assailed from all sides. The Waylord of the Excelsis Eyrie is adamant that, since you have not returned already, you must be dead, and if our need for soldiers was less acute then I would not have risked another courier to the greenskin menace to reach you. I do not care what you are doing. I do not care how far away you are. If you are holding this message in your hand then you are to waste no further time in returning to Excelsis. Four weeks ago, general, that is when I want you here.*

It was signed *High Arbiter Synor*.

Lisandr made to re-roll the message, but her hand was shaking with such fury that she scrunched it flat between her knuckles. Her mind turned back, recalling in sudden, startling clarity the other, older boy, who had brought her a message that he had been unable to deliver to Casius Braun. When had that been? Twelve weeks ago?

'Grint,' she snarled. 'Malec Grint.'

'No, sir,' the boy stammered, taking a step back until the look in Lisandr's eye pinned him where he was. 'My name's Leon.'

'Where is Grint?'

He shook his head. 'Don't know, sir.'

Lisandr brandished the scrunched parchment like a pair of hot pliers under his nose. The boy's eyes crossed, and he swallowed hard.

'If you had a message for Braun but could not get it to him, who would you give it to?'

'Jenk for sure. Or Kanta or Taal if I couldn't find him.'

'Where are they now?'

'The Dozen are all in with Braun, except for Jenk, but–'

'Mestrade!' she barked.

'Sir.'

'Do you want to kill some more Accari?'

'Sir?' he said, not sure if she was joking. Right then, there, she was not sure herself.

She snatched a torch from one of Shay's attendants, and turned towards Goreham. Her sword was already back in her hand. She did not remember drawing it, but nor was she especially inclined towards putting it away.

'All of you, come with me.'

CHAPTER SIX

THUD.

The Bonesplitterz had been gathering at the foot of the Twinhorn, biggest and hardest of all mountains in Ursricht's Kill, for longer than Uturk could remember. Not that Uturk could remember much. He couldn't remember, for instance, when the sound of the Waaagh! had first moved into his head. It'd made him want to scratch his eyes and hit things. There'd been other orruks with him back then, but all the scratching and the hitting had driven them off, and he'd been alone.

THUD.

He'd spent hours staring into the campfire, to burn the Waaagh! out of his head, but it had made it hammer and wail more loudly. In the end, the campfire burned down and he'd forgotten how to make a new one, and so he'd sat alone, laughing out loud when the Bad Moon leant in right close as though he was the only one around thinking what it was thinking.

He wasn't mad. His old mob had been the mad ones. They could have been here with him now–

THUD.

The Trampla beat at the walls of his prison. Uturk felt the reverberations through the tough rocks of Ursricht's Kill. The green song had roused him. Uturk felt that too, in amongst the savage bestial howling that passed around his head in place of real thoughts. It had stirred the trees that grew atop the Twinhorn to grow tall, sending their roots down deep, deep enough to break the harder rock that had held the Trampla in the mountain's heart for ages, unremembered by anyone save the realm-touched and those mad enough to listen to their ravings. It was an alien song, not like the howls of the Waaagh!, sung by the goddess of a foreign realm, but it strengthened sluggish muscles and filled the jaggedy edges of Uturk's 'thoughts' with a red-misted fury.

THUD.

In his slumber, the Trampla had dreamed of the havoc he would wreak once free, and through him, in a way, Uturk and his kind had dreamt it too. He would smash the cities of the draconith and the Seraphon and the vile shaggoth. He did not know what these things were, but he intended to smash them. His mouth watered at the thought. These were the dreams that had brought the earthquakes that wracked Ursricht's Kill.

THUD.

But now he was awake. The Trampla was awake, and his wrath would not be limited by his dreams.

THUD.

To smash one's way out of a mountain was a feat worthy of Gorkamorka, his strength equal to the sum of every orruk in the Mortal Realms, but the Trampla had been working tirelessly at the challenge for years. An age. Longer than Uturk could know, and he had been one of the first, here almost from the beginning, welcoming those others that had come after. The Trampla's strength – lessened by confinement, maybe, and by his forgetting, perhaps – was as tireless as the ground under Uturk's feet still.

THUD.

THUD.

THUD.

The side of the mountain broke.

Uturk saw the head of a mace break through the rock, and a great clamouring went up from the thousands of savage orruks now gathered around the foothills, sensing the Great Waaagh! of their fevered visions was at hand. They were dancing, feasting, fighting, spontaneously daubing one another's green bodies with orange paint and hollering at the top of their lungs now that the drumbeat of Ghur had reached its crescendo.

Uturk of the Wavy Eye, self-anointed Big Prophet of Da Boss Trampla, raised his hands in praise. The man-gods, the Chaos-gods, the dead-gods: they'd all had their go. The orruks' time was coming.

He held his breath. A thousand savage orruks paused in their wild celebrations and held theirs. The ancient god of the Heartlands bared his teeth and bunched his muscles.

One more blow…

A river that was newly young crashed through a series of energetic rushes and short bounds into a shallow basin at the foot of a craggy bluff. The water swirled and frothed, aggressive as a dracoth pup working its still-growing teeth on its handler's wrist, wearing away at the faint shimmer of amber under the water and carrying it away downstream. Vagria had found the half-buried amberbone deposit while searching the devastation left by the Serpent River for any sign of Kildabrae's remains. She had found nothing of her Knight-Vexillor – even the mega-gargant she had died battling had been swept away in the river's death throes – but even in death, it seemed, the Heavenscar brought the Farstrikes only good luck. Heaven.

Vagria crouched at the edge of the basin and stared down, hypnotised by the way the realm's magic glimmered through the water from the pool's bottom. Like a piece of amber would look, if held up between finger and thumb and positioned directly in front of a light.

'Is it coincidence, do you think?' said Artros, the Prosecutor-Prime, who knelt on a rock shelf fifteen feet above her. His search, too, had come up with nothing.

'A seam of amberbone?' Vagria asked. 'Not a stone's throw from where Lord-Ordinator Dolus believed the disturbance in the realm to lie? No, Artros, it is not a coincidence. Find Brendel Starsighted and send him to me.'

'He hunts the last of the Bonesplitterz.'

'Take his place. Tell him the task I have for him is more urgent.'

'He will be far over the Morruk Hills by now.'

Vagria bared her teeth behind her mask. 'Then by all means fly *quickly*, Artros.'

His own expression equally hidden, but bristling in his demeanour, the Prosecutor-Prime threw out his wings and launched himself into the air.

Rather than watch him go, Vagria returned her attention to the basin's edge. The noise of the falls was astounding. The tingle of apprehension she felt at approaching the great river so soon after it had slain her greatest warrior and closest companion brought a guilty shiver. But this was not the same river that Brendel's star-fated arrow had brought low. It was newborn, with a puppyish aggression that did not yet know the fullness of its strength. Her mount, Starsid, wandered downriver unattended, lowering his beak to the runout to root for fish eggs or amphibians that might have re-emerged into the shallows with the return of tamer waters.

With great deliberation and care she removed her gauntlets and set them on the rock beside her. With hands free, she then set about pulling off her vambraces, her rerebraces, detaching the besagews with their beastmarks commemorating the creatures she had personally slain, and removing her pauldrons. From there, she got to the real business of unbuckling her breastplate and plackart and stepping out of what was left of her armour. Most warriors would have begun at the helmet. Removing it gave a warrior's fingers easier access to the chin and shoulder straps before moving onto the arms, but Vagria always, almost subconsciously, kept her face covered until last. Somehow, she just knew: it wasn't her face.

Shrugging off the creeping shiver that threatened more serious unease if she were to think about it too deeply, she set the helmet down beside her with the other pieces and, clad only in her arming jacket and thin furs, stepped into the basin.

The water foamed around her toes. It was restless and warm, hungry but uncertain what to do about that hunger. In time it would relearn the lessons of its parent, how to ravage and how to kill, remembering perhaps that warriors in amethyst and gold made for dangerous prey.

For now, however, there was an opportunity to be taken.

She waded out into deeper water. The water closed over her head, the playful fury of the falls hammering against her back. The basin was only shallow, the falls having had no time yet to eat away at the rock, but it was deep enough that she had to go fully under and then some to touch the bottom. Unencumbered by the burden of her armour, she paddled down, turning herself belly down in the water, and reached out for the amberbone.

Six rib-like growths protruded an arm's length from the floor of the pool, but there was no way of knowing how deep into the rock they might go. Superficially they looked like bone, albeit abnormally large and amber-coloured, mottled with darker patches as though aged by untold millennia.

She grasped one.

THUD.

She recoiled as the sound went through her, as though physically struck by whatever had caused it, bubbles escaping through her lips as she tried to cry out. Even as she did so, however, the shard twisted in her grip, edges that had previously appeared smooth turning serrated and digging into the bare flesh of her hands. She made a snarl that was nine parts pleasure to one of pain.

If it's a fight you want…

Blood from her torn hand plumed the water. A lightning storm brewed within the expanding red cloud as her body bled more of itself into the water than just the contents of her veins. Her mouth twisted in frustration as she tightened her grip on the amberbone, wrapping her second hand around the first and bracing her feet against the bottom of the pool.

The amberbone was buried deep.

She heaved against it, bubbles streaming from her mouth as she screamed, her last breath burning a hole in the walls of her chest, memories coming up like pockets of stale air.

A child. Running through a forest. Hunter or hunted? She couldn't tell.

Excited shrieks. Blood. Death.

Lightning.

She thrashed her head from side to side, a growl letting out another flume of bubbles.

It took an enormous amount to kill a Stormcast Eternal. They were not human, and even in the wake of the Cursed Skies they were still more than mortal. Even with that being true, most things that were deadly to a human woman would, given enough time and extraordinary persistence, prove fatal to a Stormcast as well. They could starve, for instance, though it would take many months. They could freeze to death, or drown.

And wouldn't that be something?

She could not say she was not a little tempted. More than once, she had been slain in Sigmar's service. Eight times, by her count, although every time the memory faded and the years of battle blended together a little more.

But she had never *died*.

For the first time since Sigmar had taken her up, the Cursed Skies made a real death possible. She was curious to know how that would feel. And given that she remembered less than nothing of her own culture and mortal life, she could only wonder at the new lands in the Realm of Death to which her spirit might roam if it were to break free of the Cursed Skies, and who or what would be waiting for her when she arrived.

Her restless spirit craved that one last adventure, whatever the consequences, but deep in her heart she knew that she was Sigmar's warrior still. She had been reforged as an Astral Templar: stubborn as a dog with a bone, even when it was in her own best interests to give it up and fight another day, in some other way.

In the end, however, it was the amberbone's dogged determination, as much as her own, that saw her prevail. The back-serrated teeth dug into the skin of her palm, tougher by far than mortal flesh, and so stuck there without tearing. The pain was incandescent, but Vagria pushed herself through it.

The extra purchase was exactly what she needed. Feeling the bone finally begin to slide free of the rock, she pulled, kicking off the bottom with the amberbone in her hand, and swam hard for the surface. She emerged with a gasp, bringing up the hand that was still skewered to the amberbone, and spluttered for breath. Spitting out tepid water, she splashed for the shore.

Horac was there waiting for her. Armoured but unmasked, there was no discernible expression on his long, grey-bearded face – beyond the general sense of weariness that one usually took away from too long in the Knight-Azyros' presence. He offered his hand to help her out, but she shook her head and climbed up onto the shore without help.

The amberbone refused to let go of her hand, forcing her to press it to the ground and stand on it, and rip her hand away. She grimaced, half her palm staying behind on the bone. The serrations quivered, a definite chewing motion, and the blood and flesh sank into the amberbone's internal structure. With a curse, she clenched her dripping hand into a fist and drew it to her chest. The amberbone, meanwhile, had reverted to an inanimate thing, innocent as a ghyrlach chick and pulsing softly to the faint heartbeat of Ghur.

'That was foolish,' said Horac.

'Nobody was ever thankful for an *I told you so*, Knight-Azyros.'

'Only because those who receive them are those in need of hearing them most often.'

'You have an answer for everything, don't you?'

Horac shrugged. 'Ask me again when I have experienced everything, and I will tell you.'

She produced a dripping wet fist and threw a playful punch at his arm. Her bare knuckles crunched into his gardbrace and drove him a slippery step back over the rocks. He cursed her in inventive terms, and she laughed at his poetry, her near drowning already forgotten.

Turning away from him, she dropped to her haunches and crouched again by the basin. The water was too restless to cast anything more than an outline reflection of her face, and she quickly broke even that by plunging her injured hand into the pool. To her surprise, the water was warm and oddly soothing, like having a wound licked clean by a beloved pet. She flexed her hand and watched the current carry the flow of blood away, taking the glints of amber still in the wound along with it.

Vagria knew of many Bonesplitterz tribes, and even a few naturalised human populations here in Ghur, who crafted weapons from amberbone. She had seen what they could do, and would not have wanted her wound to heal with any of the Ghurish realmstone still inside her.

'You should have waited for aid,' said Horac.

'And made someone else go down in my place?' Vagria snapped over her shoulder.

'You are our leader. You should not have gone in yourself, and certainly not alone.'

'I am not afraid of a little nibble, Horac.'

'*And* you should have worn gauntlets.'

'This is my hunt.' Vagria drew her hand from the water, tentatively clenching it into a fist and then flicking it dry. The wound was already on its way to closing. Stormcasts healed fast. All the more reason for her to cleanse the wound as quickly as she had.

Horac was silent a moment, lost in reverie of the falls. Behind his old eyes, he was composing a maudlin song, or seeing the doom of all existence foretold in the play of water over rock. Sometimes, Vagria wondered what drove him to rise each morning and fight at all.

'I, too, grieve for the Heavenscar,' he said at last. 'Do not give up hope that she may yet return. Who among us knows what becomes of those wayward souls, scattered from their rightful path to Sigmaron by Be'lakor's Cursed Skies? Not I. None of us are wise enough to be in Sigmar's counsel, or mighty enough to aid him in his own wars.'

Vagria shook her head and made to turn away, but Horac caught her by the arm and held her. She had never seen him regard anything with such passion.

'Do not be so keen to hunt death. It lies in ambush for us all.'

Vagria regarded him levelly. 'It will not find me unready.'

Horac threw up his hands in mock despair. 'Sometimes, Lord-Aquilor, you are impossible to talk sense to.'

'I hope so.'

They both glanced up, heightened senses alerting both warriors at the same time to the appearance of a twinkle in the sky. At first it resembled a shooting star, one of the omens of Azyr, but it came on a looping course and grew quickly into Eliara, the star-eagle soulmate of Knight-Venator Brendel Starsighted. She descended to the foot of the waterfall with a squall of greeting. Vagria could not converse with the star creature the way Brendel did, but she sensed that the eagle was genuinely pleased to see her.

Eliara circled, showering both warriors with stardust from her long tail and tapering wings, making Horac scowl as she came in to land on the Knight-Azyros' shoulder. She dug her talons into the deep purple sigmarite of his pauldron and ruffled her plumage primly. Horac looked down his nose at her. The look on his grey face made the entire expedition seem worthwhile. Vagria's explosion of laughter rang from the Morruk Hills.

'Why always my shoulder?' Horac complained.

'I heard that a star-eagle will always pick out the one who likes them least,' said Vagria, wiping a tear from her eye and barely noticing the numb tingle she felt where her finger pressed against her cheek.

'I do not dislike her,' said Horac, adding after a lengthy pause, 'I dislike everyone.'

Brendel Starsighted landed just as Vagria broke into fresh gales of laughter, alighting with a resounding *clump* that cared nothing for the feelings of the rock or for whatever anybody else had been attending on that was not him.

'What is so funny?' he said.

Vagria sighed, her laughter drying up. 'Apparently nothing.'

'I have been hunting savage orruks for hours. I have seen more than one mega-gargant attempting to move stealthily under the tree cover in the valleys and rockgut troggoths lurking in many of the caves, waiting on nightfall. None, thankfully, have returned this way as yet. Something seems to draw their attention north and westward, but they are there, and the Morruk Hills have an evil reputation as the home of orruks of unusual cunning. They will not remain passive, so long as we remain. So, I would say that we are in complete agreement, Lord-Aquilor. This is not funny.'

'I sense you are in a bad mood,' said Vagria.

'As keen a sense as a starving gryph-hound, as ever, Lord-Aquilor.'

She took the compliment as though it was one. 'Do I take it that your hunt was unsuccessful?'

'You can take from it that I do not believe the Serpent to have been our true quarry.'

Vagria lifted her face as though sampling the taste of the wind or swearing a binding oath on a star. 'You heard it though, didn't you, Brendel, the heartbeat in the ground when the Serpent was slain?'

'And in the air. Yes.'

'As did I,' said Horac, softly. 'But I thought it more a beating drum, a marching beat for the doom of this place.'

Vagria snorted. 'Of course you did.'

'I felt the rhythm pause for a moment when I shot the creature,' said Brendel, showing an admirable lack of shame in reminding all present that it was he who had landed the killing blow. 'But only for a moment.' He glanced at the amberbone, dripping on the rocks amidst a heap of purple and gold plate. 'You found this here?'

Vagria pointed to the plunge pool at the base of the falls. 'There.'

Brendel turned at her gesture, then followed the downstream run-off with his eyes. 'I would not allow Starsid to drink from that water.'

Vagria swore, and whistled for her steed to back off from the water's edge. The gryph-charger raised his long neck from the water and went to lie down regally on the rocks.

Brendel, meanwhile, crouched by the amberbone shard and reached into one of his many bags. Out from it came a silvery square of fleece that he flicked out to unfold and then draped over the glowing amberbone. Suddenly, it was as though a nagging belligerence from just below the level of conscious perception was no longer there. The amberbone struggled and growled, its aggressive properties smothered in the innate tranquillity of the Azyri fleece.

'The beat *was* stilled when I slew the river,' said Brendel.

'It was,' said Vagria. 'As though something felt it through a shared connection to the amberbone and was given pause.'

She joined Brendel, kneeling down by her pile of gear and picking out the astral compass. Around the ornate gold bezel were a number of adjustable dials, also in gold. Rotating them one way or the other enabled the hunter to track various cosmological phenomena, be it the light of Sigendil, the pull of the Shyish Nadir, or the cosmic lodestone of the Allpoints. It had even once guided her in pursuit of an ogroid thaumaturge who had thought himself completely concealed against all forms of arcane scrying, tracking the powerful anti-magical forces of the nullstone talisman he had been wearing around his neck.

Under her adjustments something within the arcane mechanism clicked, and an image constructed from beams of starlight blew out from the compass crystal. Horac and Brendel gathered around her, gazing up at the astral chart that had been contained within the myriad devices of her compass.

The map depicted the regions of Andtor, Thondia and Gallet, the uncivilised and occasionally warring subcontinents that together made up the Ghurish Heartlands. Topography appeared in relief, but corresponded to no hills or ranges that Vagria and her hunters had ever traversed. Rather, it was a map of geomantic forces assembled through divination and prophecy. They stood now over one such peak in the map, one of the largest and the nearest to Excelsis, which had seemed reasonable at the time as it had been the origin of the prophecy and this quest.

Vagria tilted her head.

'Does anyone else see that?'

'I'll be damned...' Horac muttered.

Viewed together the peaks took on a quite obvious pattern, a huge and curving horn, like that of a charging bull, running directly from the Ursricht's Kill Mountains in Gallet to Excelsis in the south-western corner of Thondia.

Brendel made the sign of the God-Bear, Ursricht, the bloody-mouthed patron deity of the Astral Templars Stormhost, as it dawned on him as well. 'If an amberbone deposit was the source of one of these geomantic upheavals–'

'Then an amberbone deposit may be behind them all,' said Vagria.

'I have used my star-fated arrow, and we have lost the Heavenscar,' said Brendel. 'I would not want to face another Serpent River so soon.'

'You can always fly back to the Templia Beasthall and drink ale with the old men and the servants.'

'You know what I mean.'

Vagria grinned fiercely. She was not sure she did. Was she really the only Stormcast here who would gladly run, and run, and run, until her quarry revealed itself or every one of her warriors was dead? 'What if we were to secure the deposits and dig them up, one by one? The amberbone could be bound in fleece' – she pointed at the one in Brendel's keeping – 'and made safe, perhaps even removed from Ghur entirely by the nearest Realmgate. Pull the beast's teeth and it will learn not to bite. Excelsis' doom can be averted once and for all.'

'There are too many ifs, buts and maybes in your plan for my liking,' said Brendel.

'You are starting to sound like Horac,' said Vagria. 'Who would have thought that wings would make a warrior so timid.'

The Knight-Venator took a sharp stride towards her, until Horac positioned himself in between.

'We are essentially agreed,' said the Knight-Azyros. 'In any case there is no road back to the Beasthall now that is easier than the one ahead of us. We can only go on. If the Lord-Aquilor's plan is successful, then so be it. If not, then we are bound to fight and slay the godbeast in any case, and this map is still our clearest path to finding it.'

Brendel crossed his arms and nodded. Vagria dipped her head to him in turn.

Horac pointed to a node on the map. It rose above a flat region known as the Eaten Plain. 'This is the nearest node of Ghurish energy to us. This is where we must go next, although if we are forced to make pilgrimage all the way to Ursricht's Kill, then I will not be wholly displeased. I have always longed to lay eyes on the hunting grounds of our patron god.'

'There is my Knight-Azyros.' Vagria smiled.

'That said…' Horac warned, reverting to his more customary demeanour, 'the Breakface and the Brokenjarl are on the mawpath.' He tapped his finger through the projected image. 'This geomantic node will send us right upon the gluthold of the Bloodgullet Mawtribe. It will not fall easily.'

Brendel snapped his fingers. 'Did you say *Bloodgullet?*'

'What of it?' said Horac, rarely moved by drama.

'If either of you ever drank ale with the old men and the servants then you might remember that Excelsis recently launched a crusade to conquer that gluthold.'

'It would be useful to have allies,' said Vagria. 'I have forgotten what it feels like.'

'The entire realm is alive with enemies,' said Horac. 'What chance is there that they even made it to the Bloodgullet gluthold alive?'

'Sigmar,' Vagria despaired. 'You are so gloomy, Horac.'

'I would be less concerned about the possibility that they failed and more about the possibility that they may have succeeded,' said Brendel. He looked at the shimmering stars of Vagria's map. 'Because if they have, then they are sitting on top of the largest deposit of amberbone in the Heartlands.'

THUD.

The roof of the world shook. It was a tambourine the size of the sky with an oily brown skin and a mountainous rim of jagged teeth and bone, beaten with the boundless enthusiasm of the Great Green Fist in the Sky.

Gorkamorka cheered, and he was right to.

Rukka Bosskilla, megaboss of Da Choppas and the biggest thing that was green from the Thunderscorn Peaks to the Krakensea, smashed in a stump of wall with the flat bit of his choppa. It had been a duardin wall. A house maybe. He couldn't be sure, and hadn't properly cared even when it had been standing. He stamped on the rubble until the piles started to infuriate him less.

The drumbeat from the sky rolled over him. It rang through his heavy armour, painted in blue and white checks, through his tough green skin, his thick bones, and down, deep, into the small and brutally contented thing that, if he had ever stopped long enough to dwell on it, he might have called a soul.

A celebration of destruction.

The boyz of his Big Rukk, several thousand strong and the best of the biggest, spread over what was left of the Sigmarite town, paused in the serious work of breaking stuff to look up at the uncommonly belligerent sky and roar right back at it.

'*Gork!*' they yelled. '*Gork! Gork! Gork!*'

An altogether different sort of brute might have wondered at the fact that the realm had never seen fit to stand and applaud his work before now, but Rukka was nothing if not entirely the sort of brute that he was, and thought nothing of it at all but a vague tingling of excitement. As though somewhere nearby there was a fight happening, and he'd be hearing about it soon. With a roar of pure, exuberant savagery Rukka thumped his pig-iron choppa – beaten into shape with his own fist and sharpened on his tusks – on his chestplate.

Guntstag, one of Rukka's bigger bosses, climbed halfway up the glassy stone column that still stood in the middle of the town. It had been so tough to break that Rukka had demanded his boyz save it for last. According to Weird Wurgbuz, the humies had used it to look at the future. Even after Wurgbuz had explained to him what this 'future' thing was all about, Rukka wasn't sure he understood the point.

He'd been looking forward to smashing it all day.

With the height advantage it granted, Guntstag waved his choppa up at the big sky and hollered. Rukka punched him in the small of the back and pulled him down. Then he stood up on the Ironjawz boss' backplate and yelled all the louder.

The shaking of the sky-drum didn't ease. If anything, it got louder.

THUD. THUD.

The ground shivered. It was the great web of the Spider-God quivering with the struggles of tiny, tiny flies. Earbug Glibspittle, self-styled Shady King of the Glossom Crevasse grots, gave his sceptre a convincing jiggle and cleared his throat before pronouncing on this obvious portent. Ordinarily, the Clammy Hand was a lot more obtuse: it disguised its omens in the weird drift of a spore cloud across the Deepenglade, or the dance of a grotgobbler spider that spun the same web thrice, depending on Earbug's clever know-wotz to properly untangle their meaning and guide the tribe to the Everdank.

Frankly, he found this latest showing offensive. A scraggly yoof could have picked up on it. The Clammy Hand was getting right lazy.

'Listen up, you ungrateful gitz!' His shrill voice echoed way into the up'n'up, around crooked bowers heavy with webby nets and gloaming fungi, the danksome forest that made up the Deepenglade, the capital of the Little Kingdom that Earbug ruled with wisdom and benevolence and of which he was rightly proud. 'Anyone wot doesn't stop fightin' and start payin' attention dis zoggin' instant is gettin' fed to da Glossom Queen.'

The bloody carry-on continued despite his threats. Grots in their millions, clad in glossy armour and stalkspider silk webbing, feathered headdresses and turbans of bright yellow fungus, brawled over the roots and branchways and the burrow holes that led into twisty tunnels down to the troggholes.

Earbug planted his hands on his hips.

'Dis just ain't good enough.'

The scrap had started out of nothing. The usual disagreement over who got first dibs on the feed trough or whose swag was shinier, but it had soon got right out of hand.

'Dey isn't listenin', boss,' said Goonsplat, his chief shaman, hunched under the weight of a seriously impressive hat and muttering sourly.

'I sees dat.'

'Gloomspite's on 'em,' said Fubsickle.

Earbug nodded.

The grots were a cunning and clever race, but when the madness known as the Gloomspite came on them, brought on by the meanderings of the Bad Moon, it triggered in them a violent need to rise up from their dank and lovely hollows and ring in the despoliation of the Mortal Realms. It was the worst of times, and Earbug hated it. Everything worth nabbing ended up getting smashed up, and even properly spider-fearing grots stopped listening to their Webspinners in favour of rushing after the biggest, baddest orruks to follow.

'*He's* comin',' he mumbled.

'Wot?' said Goonsplat.

Earbug shook his head, shivering the weird premonition off him, and waved his sceptre towards his gitz. 'If dey carries on like dis dey is gonna break everyfing.'

'What should we do, boss?' said Fubsickle.

Earbug gave a deep, long-suffering sigh. 'Only fing we can do when da Gloomspite's up.'

Somewhere, deep in the Realmweb, something many-legged and malicious was about to break out of its egg. Earbug felt it. He could *see* it. He could follow the trembling of the thread-stuff to where it lay in the north and west and, worse, he had a good sense of what *it* was even if he had no true name for *it* just yet.

'Da Boss Trampla,' he breathed.

Goonsplat stuck a long finger in his ear down to the knuckle and twisted it around to clear it out. 'Wot?'

The strongest orruk in Ghur couldn't outfight what was coming. But perhaps, just perhaps, the most cunningest of grots might be able to outwit it. And when all the hateful little stars in the night sky had been gobbled up and Frazzlegit himself was gone, when the orruks were smashed and the humie cities broken, then the Shady King of the Deepenglade would be the last voice laughing.

'We rise up,' said Earbug. 'We takes it all for da deep'n'dark. While dere's still anyfing left up dere to take.'

THUD. THUD. THUD!

The final shattering blow broke the mountain's flank in half.

Its death knell rang between earth and sky, and Uturk and his followers hooted in celebration as the rubble of the Twinhorn tumbled from their exhumed god's shoulders. With sweeping antlers and stomping hooves, Da Boss Trampla cleared himself a passage down to the mountainside. He lifted his shaggy head, great body smeared in godsblood and the dust of those who'd sought to hold him, and turned his gaze east. He took his first breath of Ghur…

And expelled it in a roar of such fury that it shattered one half of the Twinhorn's summit, and sent avalanches cascading down the slopes of Ursricht's Kill.

The stars swarmed across the bowl of the sky, as though his bellow had broken them loose, and more than one savage orruk pointed excitedly up at the sky even as rock slid down the slope of the Twinhorn towards them. Only the familiar point of Sigendil shone with its usual defiance, but even the Man Star was partially eclipsed by a large and ugly-looking moon that glared down on Ursricht's Kill with a sickly yellow grin that put a fire in Uturk's belly and made him want to dance.

'Da Bad Moon! Da Bad Moon!' he sang, jumping up and down and flapping his arms.

The hordes of Bonesplitterz, their bare green bodies painted like Uturk's with crude renditions of antlered heads, trampling hooves and centauroid gods, banged on skin drums and howled in manic fervour. They gave off a kind of wild energy, as all orruks do when gathered together in great number, but few were so excitable as the Bonesplitterz of the Heartlands.

'Trampla!' the ecstatic greenskins chanted. *'Trampla! Trampla!'*

The roar grew in the Trampla's chest. The mountains of Ursricht's Kill quaked in terror of it, and as it erupted from his throat, Uturk could feel all the Ghurish Heartlands and beyond shaken from end to end.

It would all be torn down.

The god shook the rubble of the mountain from his mace, and reaffirmed his grip. It was called the Dread Mace. Its head had once been the biggest and densest source of magic in Ghur. This, in his manic excitement, Uturk, as the Trampla's self-anointed prophet, knew and understood. Then the Trampla unlimbered his shield. It was called Tuskbreaker, and the Trampla had crafted it aeons ago from a piece of metal that Gorkamorka had spat out after finding it too hard to chew. This, too, Uturk knew. The Trampla strapped the shield to his forearm, pulling the bands in tight with his teeth and then, properly armed for the first time in many ages, made his way down the mountainside.

The Bonesplitterz's fervour grew more raucous. The dancing became more energetic, the singing louder and faster, until it was just a thousand voices gabbling gibberish at the top of their lungs. Uturk jigged forwards, uphill, leaving his boyz behind. As the first to hear the call and the first to find the mountain, it was only right that he be the one to greet the Boss Trampla as he made his way down.

Uturk spread his arms, looking up, a grin of huge and childlike devotion softening his rugged face as the giant centaur picked his way down the mountainside towards him. He was bigger than any orruk ever, bigger than a mega-gargant. There was dust all over his fur, the smell of the mountain clinging to him like a coat. The mountain he had just killed. At the thought of the gigantic things that the Bonesplitterz would be able to hit with the Boss Trampla returned to lead them, Uturk felt positively light-headed.

'Trampla!' he yelled.

Like most Bonesplitterz, his mind was too full of blood and noise to manage even short sentences. That he could fashion whole words at all marked him as a natural leader and something of a savant amongst his kind, and he put all the excitement and joy that he felt into that one, savage bark.

The Trampla gave no answer, nor acknowledged Uturk in any way. But Uturk didn't care. The Trampla could do what he liked. He was *the Trampla!*

Uturk's heart filled with wild excitement as the Trampla drew near, near enough to feel the god's titanic heartbeat going *THUD-THUD-THUD* through the ground, beating uncannily in time to the Bonesplitterz drums. Uturk felt as though his own would explode out of raw devotion.

He stood and waited while the Trampla's hoof came up. He turned his head back and stared up at it, awed by this rare glimpse of god, of his god, the god that was going to shake the Mortal Realms to pieces.

'Trampla–' he began but did not quite finish, as the hoof came down and flattened him.

CHAPTER SEVEN

The gnoblar tunnels spread through the Gnarlfast like the roots of a weed. How deep they went, how far from the fighting lands of the Cuspid Mesas they extended, who or what had first made them: these were mysteries to which no one had answers.

Unlike the glutfort itself, the tunnels teemed with every kind of life, safe from the fat and grasping fingers of ogor Tyrants. The light from Jenk's oil lamp returned a myriad of colours from the rustling shells of insects both small and frighteningly massive. The walls and ceiling rippled like a living, breathing thing and Grint could even feel its angry beating heart. *THUD-THUD*, it seemed to go, echoing out, *THUD-THUD*. Lizards turned tail and scurried into the darkness. Mothlike things dropped from above to attack the light and the men carrying it, only to be batted away by Malec Grint, who, naturally of course, had been given point.

The passage narrowed. Grint shuffled around to approach it side-on, leading with his right arm and the glinting edge of his knife. He was wearing only a pair of scuffed leather shorts. His tunic was tied around his waist. The rock rubbed across his chest and back like something's tongue: gritty, clammy and faintly warm. The sense of claustrophobia was not dissimilar to what he had known a hundred times over in the Primeval Jungles, where kapok and xate trees grew so close together that a spice-trailer had to crawl between their trunks to get through.

The light trickled into the stones as his body plugged the gap. It was as though it had been made for him. Or him for it. For the first time since he had lost sight of the sky he began to sweat. His breathing barely brought stale air into his lungs before expelling it staler.

The thought that some unknowable design had planted the idea of freedom and adventure into his impressionable young head so that he might die in this exact place, and in this exact way, for reasons too great for him to fathom, was impossible to shrug off. The Accari liked to think themselves wiser than the Azyrite settlers, and those Ghurites that Excelsis had tamed through city living. But a man could deny the predestination that humans worshipped in that city, yet still fear it. It was a monster, one that those reaching adulthood could not say, with complete surety, was make-believe.

Shaving off enough skin to make room, he wormed his way through the narrowing tunnel. The space widened on the other side. Enough to breathe more comfortably, to roll his shoulder a fraction and turn his neck back.

Sorl and Petrec were immediately behind him. Both, like him, were from Kanta's mob, huffing and scowling as they manoeuvred their heavier frames through the narrows. After them came Jenk and their lantern, because nothing ever happened to the man in the middle. He was trailed by Gorman and Varden, both Blind Lusten's men, who himself was lesser chief to a score of men under Altin's command. The most popular Hound in the company of the most loathed of Braun's Dozen: there was a story in there, but Grint didn't know it. Bad Luck Mikali took up the rear. Now he thought of it, Grint wasn't sure who Mikali's chief was. Or if she even had one.

Shuffling and twisting until he was again facing forwards, he saw that the tunnel ahead narrowed even further.

He hated gnoblars. There wasn't a man there who wouldn't have taken an entire ogor glut over a pack of gnoblars.

'It should be the Celestians with their skinny hands down here,' someone complained. Grint didn't know who it was, but agreed wholeheartedly. All of their voices sounded the same in the tunnels. Distant, dank, crushed by stone. Absorbed by that powerfully beating heart that set their spirits on edge. *THUD-THUD*. All, that was, except for Jenk. He, somehow, came across as he always did: like the most reasonable man in the Eight Realms, drawing no pleasure at all from the knife that happened to be in your back.

'Braun likes to do it,' said the voice that was definitely Jenk's. 'It makes him feel special.'

'I don't see his special self here now.' Someone, again.

Jenk chuckled. 'Where are we now, blasphemer? Any sign?'

'Not yet,' said Grint. 'Maybe we trailed them down a wrong turn.'

'Well, I don't like the idea of turning back just yet. We'll head on a bit further, see if there's an easier way out ahead.'

They continued on, Grint in the lead. His eyes adapted to the occasional glimmers of light that leaked around the bodies between himself and Jenk's lantern, like a man who'd grown accustomed to gruel and would throw up anything richer if it was offered to him now.

Occasionally the passage widened, never quite enough to let him squeeze through at full height or without giving a bit more of himself to the scraping rock, but more often it grew narrower.

At times the ceiling descended so low he had to walk through on bent legs, or wriggle like a worm on his belly. On these occasions he became so focused on threading his body through the latest obstruction that, when he was finally past it, he would panic, fearing he had left his comrades behind and that he was alone. But Sorl and Petrec were never more than a few seconds behind him, wriggling and cursing and waiting for him to continue.

Sometimes he had the definite sense of moving upwards. At others, down. That was where the gnoblar caves differed from the jungles. There, at least, there had always been some sense of direction. He had understood it, as he had understood the ghurlion and ghyreraptor, even as he had feared them. This underground world was alien. He could have been crawling towards the centre of the Realmsphere, or crossed through a secret Realmgate into an oubliette dimension, and never been aware of it.

Every once in a while, the drip of water or a damp breath of air would reach him from *somewhere*, suggesting that the tunnels did end before Realm's Edge, but in the end only teasing him with what they promised. He felt certain that if someone, some Ironweld cartographer perhaps, who could read and add numbers, had taken him aside and shown him just how far he had actually gone then he would have been embarrassed with himself, and probably more than a little angry at having worked up so much sweat for so little gain.

Not that anyone would really notice.

They were all angry here. That strange rhythm, just like Taal liked to preach about hearing, getting into their heads, and so much stronger now that they were underground with it. It worked at their tempers. *THUD-THUD*. Ghur taught its children how to cope with their darker instincts. It taught them well or they tore one another apart, or died trying to murder a carnosaur with their bare hands. They drank, they fought, they picked on the weakest with violent games. Occasionally someone got hurt, sometimes people died, but more often than not the animal inside was exorcised for a little while, and they could all revert to being half-civilised men afterwards.

Most of the time it worked. They were not orruks, for all that they shared a primal feeling for their home and the disdain of Azyrite settlers.

Without realising he was doing it, Grint tapped out the drumbeat with the flat of his knife on the stone. *THUD-THUD. Tap-tap. THUD-THUD. Tap-tap.*

The sound echoed into the deep, sweaty darkness. And still: no gnoblars.

At a cavern just about spacious enough for all seven to bunch in together, Jenk suggested they rest. Braun's man rarely gave orders. He had a way of winning others round to his point of view.

Grint blew at a beetle that was crawling over his nose. He could not reposition his arms far enough to flick it off.

'Leave it,' said Sorl. 'Once it's bitten, the others will leave you alone.'

He bit his lip, holding still, then jerked with a quiet grunt as the beetle sank its mandibles into his nose.

Sorl chuckled softly. 'I can't believe you fell for that.' His tattoos were a faint shimmer in the darkness, as though Sigmar himself shone down through the constellations picked out there. But it was only Jenk's lantern and the metals in the cheap ink.

Grint didn't know the older man well. Another cousin. He was a name and a face and a clutch of stories not dissimilar from a hundred other men. Wedged shoulder to shoulder in the dark, they seemed more important for some reason, and Grint felt a pang of regret for not knowing them better.

'Can you reach your waterskin?' Grint asked.

'No. You?'

'No.'

'I hate gnoblars,' Sorl opined.

'I hear gnoblar hides make the best waterskins in Ghur,' said Mikali, her voice coming thinly from the back of the group.

'Shut up, Mikali,' said someone else.

'No one wants to drink gnoblar water.'

There was some muffled laughter, some mild scuffling with Mikali appearing to come off the worse from it, and the company fell mostly silent.

'The first gnoblar I see I'm going to skin alive and Mikali can do what she likes with the rest,' said Grint.

'The first gnoblar you see'll be the one coming *after* you've put your foot in its trap,' said Sorl, matter-of-factly. 'Then I'll have the skin and make a start on that new set of boots I've been thinking about. Mikali can dream on.'

Grint sighed. No woman in the Mortal Realms was worth this.

'I wish I knew what I needed to do to get out of make-up duty. Braun thinks I don't have enough love for Sigmar.'

Sorl shrugged. 'Do you?'

'I don't know. How much is enough?'

'Now *there's* a question.'

Grint wriggled himself into something like a comfortable position to stew in as Jenk's voice came back at them from the silence: 'I never knew you made boots.'

'That's right,' said Sorl.

'I figured you were born with a hammer in your hand.'

'Twenty years a cobbler.'

'You think you know a man...'

Jenk got them up again shortly after that.

The going felt easier for the rest. The tunnels seemed to be widening, as though they had entered the belly of the mountains and, though they had dared it to trap them, it had declined to do so, and now they emerged tired but triumphant on the other side. How long had they been underground? He didn't know. He might have asked Jenk. The man had a golden timepiece that he had undoubtedly slipped from some duardin's pocket. But he wasn't sure he dared.

And still nothing: not so much as a stain on the wall from a gnoblar's greasy fingers. He might have wondered whether this was all not an elaborate punishment that Braun had devised for Grint's sole benefit if not for the sounds that began to mumble through the tunnel walls.

He crouched down to listen and waved for the others to follow suit. For all that they were older and bigger and stronger, they all did so. They knew when to be animals and when they needed to be soldiers and this was the latter. He strained his ears, waiting for the sound to return. It sounded like voices.

'Look lively,' Jenk breathed, although they all had knives in hand and Grint was so alert he felt as though his head might crack under the tension. Jenk tightened the aperture on his lantern, easing the choking flame down towards a quiet gasp of bloody light.

There was a grille in the floor. It was more obvious with the lantern shuttered, a dim light of its own filtering up into the tunnel from the other side. The iron looked as though it had been made by the ogors and was absurdly dense, built to deter whatever subterranean nuisance that gave an ogor butcher sleepless nights. Skaven, perhaps. Or the shroomy fingers of Moonclan grots in their stews. The metal was slick with crimson algae. As heavy as it looked, it probably wouldn't stand up to one solid kick.

The voices were coming through it.

Grint peered down. Jenk sidled up to join him, leaving his lantern on the ground, pressing his finger meaningfully to his lips. They were directly above a wagon that had been parked in a bay made up of piled-high sacks of grain, its rear covered with a sheet. Two soldiers in light grey meteoric metals moved around it, trading a word or two as they passed before separating again, which accounted for the sporadic voices Grint had heard from the tunnels.

'Celestians,' Sorl whispered, appearing between Grint and Jenk's shoulders. 'You've had us crawl under half of the Gnarlfast to get us two hundred yards closer to the east wall.'

'What's going on here?' said Grint.

'Payback.' Jenk grinned. 'Word is, the Celestians have been hoarding supplies, and taking the bigger share of what the foraging parties bring in through their gate. We're just going to take our share. Fair's fair.'

Sorl lifted himself a little higher to peer over Grint's shoulder. 'Is that an Ironweld wagon?'

'Maybe?'

'Yeah... Yeah, I think it is.'

'Fancy that.'

'Does Braun even know about this?' Grint hissed.

Grint saw a flash of teeth in the dark. 'Do you even need to ask?'

'So, we're just... we're just going to kill these two?'

'Why not? They're not ours.'

Grint swallowed, watching the two Celestians moving about below him. He thought about Angellin, the flat of his knife ringing lightly off the tunnel wall, *tap-tap*, and only then did he notice that the underlying beat he had been unconsciously aping was gone. He felt a sudden anger, as though something he'd never even known was his had been taken. His heart beat harder, as though to step up and take its place, but it was too small, too fast, his body tingling with the aggression building up under his skin.

He felt... brutal.

He wanted to do this. He wanted to fight the entire realms.

'Yeah,' he murmured. 'Why not?'

He raised his boot and kicked in the rotten grille.

Lisandr pushed through the huge gnarlwood door, and strode into the Tyrant's longhouse.

A burly Hound with tattoos crawling around his naked, barrel chest was sitting inside by the door, on a three-legged stool. He rose with a growl, drawing one of the Accari's signature spice knives from his belt, until Lisandr planted her boot heel in his chest. Caught halfway between sitting and standing, squatting with a stool between his legs, the bigger man went over with just the littlest of pushes.

Lisandr stepped over him. Lydia Victoria was next inside. The ogor doorway was easily wide enough to admit both women at once, and her spear sang as it came to rest point down against the supine Hound's throat. The brute opened his palms, the knife clattering to the stone floor, and creased his constellation tattoos as he attempted to make a friendly smile.

The rest of her ten Celestians, led by Corporal Mestrade, swept inside after them.

The gathering of scarred old warriors at the far end of the hall before the Tyrant's throne turned slowly around. Hard eyes glinted like splinters of glass, shaved heads, scarred faces and animal tattoos all turning under the torchlight. Efrim Taal leant on his staff, made a fist around the fetish that hung from his neck and shook it like a war-priest with a rosary. Altin, the so-called Izalmaw Cannibal, bared his dagger teeth, his narrow face waxen and sweaty in the warmth of the hall. The rest bore expressions that Lisandr would only describe as fearful, worn down by worry to the instinctual aggression that all Ghurites kept under their civilised masks.

About six feet away from them, she stopped. Her Celestians gathered up behind her.

Braun himself sat hunched on the bottom step up to the dais. In spite of the thick heat and spitting torches, he was shivering. His bare shoulders were draped in a flathorn pelt, a haze of prophecy crossing his brown eyes. He squinted, uncrossing his eyes to focus on her.

'Lisandr...' he muttered, shaking his head and raising a hand in warding as though he had just been visited by a spectre, leaning back onto the steps. 'You were there!' His eyes widened in terror, pupils dilating to such an extent that they swallowed his irises to the whites.

Lisandr felt nothing but disgust for him then. He wanted to gaze into the eyes of the Heavens, like the seers and the prophets, but look at him: wrapped in a blanket and shivering, stinking of burnt arraca and animal dung.

'Snap out of it.' She took another step towards the Tyrant's dais. Braun pushed himself another step up to get away.

'You were there!' he insisted. 'I saw us both together, fighting Rukka Bosskilla before the gates of a city. You were charging on your demigryph and I was carrying a Celestian spear with an amberbone point. And I saw... I saw...' His eyes appeared to tear up. 'Something I've never seen before. It had four legs, like a bull, and the body of a... of a beastman... I think. It was leading the orruks towards us, and Rukka... and Rukka...'

'Rukka is dead,' Lisandr snapped. 'You killed him ten years ago.'

Braun shook his head but did not answer, making a fist and pressing his knuckles to his lips. Eyes glistening, he looked away from Lisandr and her torches.

'A most powerful vision,' Taal murmured.

Whatever terror had inveigled its way into Braun's heart appeared to snap in him, and he rounded on his war-priest with a snarl. 'Don't patronise me, you–'

'Enough!' Lisandr screamed. 'Enough. I am not here to talk

about your witless attempts at prophecy.' She foisted her torch on Mestrade, who shouldered his shield in order to take it. The rest of his soldiers kept theirs fully addressed, spears and sabres turned towards the lounging Hounds, who eyed the weapons pointed at them with the nonchalance of beasts in their own lair. Lisandr fished in her cloak pocket and drew out the rolled message. She held it aloft. 'Twelve weeks ago, the very day after the conquest, we received orders to abandon this city and withdraw. Excelsis itself is in peril.'

'Excelsis is always in peril,' Ferrgin and Taal answered at the same time. A few of the Dozen chuckled.

Braun only looked confused. Lisandr could not be sure if it was genuine or if it was the prophecy he was obviously still coming down from, making past or present harder for him to fix upon than the future.

'Why are we still here?' She drew the tightly rolled parchment back as though she meant to strike the nearest of the Hounds with it, a hugely muscled and lump-faced brute called Ragn, she believed. He blinked massively, and did not move. 'Why were these instructions never passed to me?'

Braun shook his head, looking to his warriors, who shrugged, all with the exception of Taal, who pursed his bone-pierced lips and would not meet his general's questioning look. Lisandr turned to him.

'The boy who brought me this.' She brandished the parchment roll. 'He told me that if he had a message that he could not deliver to Braun then he would take it to you, Taal, or to Kanta or Jenk. Did Grint take our orders to you?'

The Accari war-priest ran the bones of his fetish between forefinger and thumb, his pursed lips relaxing into a grin. 'Yes. I saw them. And I burnt them.'

A flash of anger propelled Lisandr another step towards the Tyrant's dais. Mestrade and her guards tried to follow, but they could not get any closer without being physically on top of the Hounds. She was surrounded by Braun's Dozen. The air bristled with spear-points. But she did not care. She barely saw them except for Taal.

'You destroyed orders from the High Arbiter,' she said. 'You *opened* orders from the High Arbiter. I would be within my rights to summarily execute you right here if your own commander won't do it himself.'

With a growl, Braun sat forward, the flathorn pelt sliding from his shoulders to bare the animal enormity of his torso. 'Don't ever question me.'

'Who do you think you are talking to, Braun?' Lisandr cried, her voice shrill with rage.

'Don't *ever* question me.'

With the pad of his shaking thumb, the Accari general traced the heavy amber-and-green head of the hammer tattooed across his eyes. Lisandr had once seen the real thing, Ghal Maraz, borne by the Celestant-Prime in the panoply of the Hammers of Sigmar during a parade of the First-Forged Hosts through the wards of Sigmaron. Whomever Braun had paid to affect this likeness in his skin had not captured it at all. It might just as well have been Grimnir's axe, or Gorkamorka's club.

'I command this crusade,' said Lisandr.

'I outnumber you five to one.'

'My warriors are better.'

'We'll see about that.'

'I have seniority, you oaf, and written orders from High Arbiter Synor.'

Braun ran a hand over his bald head as if to reassure himself that it was where he had left it. In spite of the airs he put on, or whatever the reverse quality of 'airs' might be, Braun had never been entirely uncivilised. He had been expensively schooled in

Excelsis, or so Lisandr had heard, had commanded a regiment of civilised men from the northern Coast of Tusks, and been celebrated as a hero up and down the Great Trade Road. He was a brute, yes, and a bully, absolutely, but Lisandr had never seen him lose his temper completely.

He rose to his feet, shrugging into his full, Ghurish height.

Lisandr stared up at him from a lower step, the absolute certainty that she was a better swordswoman than anyone else here cloaking her in armour tougher than meteoric iron.

'We have to stay here,' he said. 'Greenskins are everywhere in the Heartlands now. And ogors. And gargants. Or will be soon. That's what I saw in the prophecy.' His voice became angry. 'And if we leave, then Rukka will still find us.'

'Rukka is dead, damn it!'

'We have to hold this place. Fortify it, and weather the Waaagh! that's coming.'

Taal laughed, a mad cackle, the butt of his staff beating a THUD-THUD metronome to his mirth. 'That's the cities of the coast talking. The Heartlands were never meant to be defended. They're there to be bled on, and fought over, torn down and rebuilt, over and over. That's how the men of Ghur sing their praises to the God-King. Not by hiding and growing fat behind our walls.' He sneered at his general and for a moment, in the wavering light of the torches, the saurus mounted on the top of his staff seemed to share the expression. 'No wonder the ground has stopped beating.'

'Stopped beating,' Ferrgin echoed, his eyes dull in the torchlight and ringed by dark hollows.

'This was sacred ground,' Taal went on. 'I felt it. The spirits of the realm and the gods of old guided me here so I could guide *you*.' He jabbed at Braun with a blunt-nailed finger. 'I wasn't going to let the Azyrites or the High Arbiter take it away, not when this is where Sigmar commanded us to be.'

'This is what I saw...' said Braun, wide-eyed, too easily won by an appeal to his god or to his vanity, as Taal had to know as well as Lisandr. 'We have to hold this place.'

'We are far from their civilisation here,' said Taal. 'We can be strong on our own terms, and save the Heartlands from the returned god and his people.'

'He told you all of this?' said Lisandr.

Taal turned his head away and spat. 'True gods don't speak, and true believers don't need what their hearts already know spelled out for them in words. I knew it. I felt it. This was our place, but now it's gone. We're being tested.' He whirled and thrust his staff towards Lisandr. 'It's because of y–'

His eyes widened, growing so huge in their sockets that Lisandr wondered if they would pop out of his head. Drool built up behind his bottom lip, dribbling over as he tilted his head to look down. He tried to mumble something.

Lisandr followed his gaze down. To her hand, pressed against his belly. Her sword, driven through his gut.

The moment he had rounded on her with a weapon, she had reacted instinctively. Even as she thought it, she knew it was no excuse. A Celestian should be better.

Ghur will make savages of us all.

She snatched her hand back from her sword's wet grip, and brought the blood-sticky fingers to her open mouth. Taal groaned with the removal of her hand's pressure and stumbled like a disconsolate stranger into her arms, her own sword pommel poking her in the ribs. In a state of shock, she stared over Taal's shoulder, suddenly, acutely aware of the fact that she had not only marched ten warriors and her squire into the company of eleven Hounds. She had marched them into the house of the Dozen, the heroes of Izalmaw, and the toughest group of warriors to have waged Sigmar's war across the Heartlands this last ten years without tasting defeat.

Ferrgin shrieked in rage at the attack on his uncle, driving a six-inch-long spice knife so deep into a Celestian's breast that his wrist disappeared in the soldier's ribcage. The Ghurite howled like a dog as blood sprayed his face red, and Lisandr felt the confidence that had earlier seemed unshatterable falter and flee, as though it had been a mirage all along, created by her anger at the Hounds' betrayal.

She fell from the Tyrant's dais, dragging Taal's moaning body with her. For some reason the thought of dropping him never occurred to her as an option. It was possible that she was still in shock and not yet thinking clearly, or that she felt some responsibility for the war-priest's injury and a Celestian's honour would not allow her to leave a fellow soldier behind.

It was equally possible that it was because her family's heirloom sword was still trapped in his guts.

Mestrade started belting orders, and with crisply practised manoeuvres, the warriors of Starhold locked shields around their general and surrounded her with a bristling wall of spears. Lisandr looked up to see the giant woman, Kanta, pull a warrior out of the formation by the shield and hurl him across the hall. Altin the Cannibal stood over the still-groaning Celestian that Ferrgin had stabbed, licking his knife with the most inhumanly ghastly look on his face. Mestrade kept on shouting, as though it was his contest with Ferrgin's grieving howl alone that would hold the Dozen at bay. Behind her, Lisandr heard the breath bubbling out of a man's body as Lydia drove her spear through the door guard's throat. The Bloodgullet Crusade had been the young woman's first war. She had never killed a man before. Lisandr was appalled to hear her giggle.

In the middle of it all, Braun just looked confused.

Sigmar, Lisandr thought as her warriors shepherded her out, still clutching the Accari war-priest to her breast. *What have I done?*

Ilsbet Glorica Angellin and Artem Vitus Carnelian ran down the half-cut granite causeway that traced the face of the Gnarlfast to the site of Shay and Lisandr's 'castle', and exited into the westernmost quarter of the town of Goreham. They had been assigned to protect the workers there in case of gnoblar attacks, when Angellin had seen General Lisandr and Mestrade fleeing from Braun's longhouse. Even under the circumstances, she had been conflicted about leaving the Ironweld's workers unguarded, but she hoped that Field Marshal Jayko would be sympathetic enough to settle for a reprimand.

'This way!'

Her stride lengthened, leaving Carnelian a yard off her pace and gasping. Her armoured boots crunched on the bone chips and pea gravel with which the Hounds had paved some of their own roads. She drew her sword.

One of the Celestians, retreating up the sloping road with General Lisandr and, she now saw, a wounded Accari dressed in a heavy red robe and leather armour, glanced back and spotted Angellin racing to relieve them. She shouted something to her commander, Mestrade, who glanced back himself before putting his eyes forwards again.

A mob of Hounds was boiling up out of the tents and shacks, charging up the hill to throw themselves on the Celestian shields. They were led by a tremendously tall warrior whose wiry body was a sprawling constellation of vividly coloured tattoos, the foam of a slow-building frenzy flecking his chin. Mestrade barked an order and the rearguard formed into a shield wall, stabbing the weighted points of their kite shields into the road and bracing, while Mestrade and another soldier grabbed hold of Lisandr and the injured Hound and dragged them on up the hill.

Angellin sprinted past them, feeling a weight lift from her for knowing that her general was safely away. A second behind her,

Carnelian did the same. Ahead, the thin line of starsilver and blue fought to hold back the tide.

Taking her sword two-handed, she gave voice to a wordless cry.

She had come of age in the years and wars that had come after the Necroquake. Like most soldiers of her generation, she had earned her glory fighting the nighthaunt and deathrattle legions of the Undying King. And then had come the deployment to Ghur, and the Accari's crusade against the Bloodgullet ogors. Angellin had never fought another human before. She did not know why this fight was happening now, had not yet thought about it long enough for the enormity of it to sink through, but the prospect of *a test* thrilled her in a way that muddied her exultation with shame.

She surged into the shield wall just as it was beginning to buckle under the strain. One of the Hounds pushing against it looked up as she bore down. He was armed with a knife and a hatchet, neither exactly a weapon, but both perfectly capable of killing when handled by a man so large.

The Hound threw a fierce, across-the-belly slash. If his intention had been to hack through jungle vegetation it would have been a fine stroke, but against a swordswoman who had consistently topped the duelling classes at the War College he might as well have been throwing knives with his eyes in a blindfold.

She checked onto her back foot, allowing the sickle-curve of the spice knife's leading edge to tinkle across her silver aventail, slid her left hand down her sword's grip to power a backhand, then launched an inch-perfect crosswise riposte towards the warrior's chest.

He put his axe in the way, parrying with tremendous strength but no discernible skill. They spun apart, throwing each other into a thicket of stabbing spear shafts and howling bodies, the *clang* ringing in her ears.

But Angellin had fought hand-to-hand with orruks, she had battled ogors, and put the sword to mordant abominations with the strength of many men. The artifice that went into the making of a Celestian weapon, even for a line soldier of little independent wealth such as herself, went a long way towards mitigating against that kind of mismatch, and robbing such foes of their advantage. The starmetal sang off the vibrations of the impact before they had the chance to reach her grip and deaden her arm.

A twist of her sword blade nudged the Hound's axe aside, and she turned under an Accari javelin to shoulder-barge his chest. Of the two of them, he was by far the heavier, but it was a question of technique and timing.

Angellin was flawless in both.

The Hound stumbled back, her flashing sabre opening him up across the middle, and putting him on his back in the road. He looked up at her in shock. She looked down at him with an identical expression. The battle lust that had made his brown eyes bestial and glassy was gone, and in its place was a pure and human terror of death that empathy could not ignore.

The senselessness of it all suddenly hit her. She thought she might be sick. The Celestians and the Accari had rubbed along for months without coming to serious blows. What had happened?

Taking a human life, it seemed, was not as easy as she had hoped.

Even as she hesitated over the killing blow, Carnelian arrived at her side. The time it had taken her between arrival and putting a dying man on the ground had been measured in seconds. The other Celestian's bladework lured his own opponent into a frenzied rush that ended with the *bang* of his chin against Carnelian's shield.

Forcing herself to leave her opponent to die in the road, Angellin back-pedalled towards the re-forming shield wall, sweeping her sword up into a high guard and then neatly sidestepping the first clumsy lunge thrown her way. She whirled around it, dancing, her sword crunching into her attacker's spine. He flapped with his arms as he fell, failing to fly, but crashing face first into the gravel and screaming that he could not feel his legs. Two men came at her together. She spun, hardly moving off the spot, deflecting knife and axe blows that came at her faster than she could see until one of the men gurgled and Carnelian withdrew his spear from the throat of the second.

He had sheathed his sabre between opponents.

Angellin nodded her thanks. He nodded back that none were needed.

With a strangled yowl, the leader of the Hounds hurled himself at her. He was leaner than the average Accari, made up of sinew and gristle, all the bits that no butcher wanted, put together in the shape of a man. He came in hard with a daemon-may-care whirl of axe-blade and blunt-force hammer. Angellin parried with every ounce of instinctual desperation and skill that she could muster. He was good. Perhaps too good. She nicked his cheek. He gashed her collar. She cut a line through the constellation tattoo that circled his left eye and he then snarled and spat in her face.

If she had been thinking properly, she might have retreated to her comrades' shields and let the man go. An hour ago he had been an ally, even if she could never have imagined being able to call him a friend. But she was barely thinking at all. Martial instincts ruled her now.

Kill or be killed. Was that not the first law of Ghur?

With a howl, the Accari threw his axe at her. She ducked to the side and it flew across her shoulder. For the brief moment she was distracted, the man flicked his now empty hand in her direction, as though he was flicking water in her face. An amber light flashed in her eyes, her ears filled with the buzzing of a million tiny wings, and she reeled, deaf and blind, with a cry that she could not hear.

In the split second before she had lost her sight, the Accari had been darting left with his hammer. *Feint*, her instincts screamed at her. She had trained every day of her life against the best warriors of Azyr. She had sparred with the swordmasters of the War College and even, once or twice, with Lisandr herself. Everything about the Accari's stance, the way he had stacked his body, the shape of his two-handed grip around his hammer, told her that he would be coming at her from the right. She saw it from start to end.

At least if she was wrong, she would probably never know about it. She stabbed to the right. She could not see, could not hear it, but she *felt* the impact of a starmetal blade against a ludicrously tough leather chest piece, the suction of flesh as it penetrated, as though pulling in the very blade that was killing it. Her relief was brilliant, but fleeting, lasting until the moment that strong hands pulled on her from behind. She struggled, hard enough to crack someone's jaw, before recovering enough of her senses from the Accari's cantrip to recognise Carnelian's voice yelling urgently in her ear.

'Do you have any idea who that was?' Angellin could not tell whether he was appalled or impressed, and it was possible that he was both. 'That was Ferrgin. Gods among us, Ilsbet, you just killed one of Braun's Dozen.'

She should probably have felt proud of herself. The Dozen were notoriously resistant to being killed. But all she felt was cold.

As though she had just done something that should never, ever have been done.

The two Celestians standing guard over the storehouse both turned as one as the grille crashed in and first Grint, then Jenk, dropped to the floor. Grint had seen the Azyrites fight. He knew very well that seven against two were not bad odds for the Celestians, but Jenk was the leader of the Dozen: they were both dead before Sorl was out of the tunnel. Jenk wiped his spice knife on Sorl's sleeve, grinning all the while as though this was a moment the bigger man could tell his grandchildren about. Grint made to step over the dead Celestians, managed to trip over an unnaturally angled leg, and stumbled the rest of the way towards the mouth of the cave.

Petrec and Varden, meanwhile, clambered into the back of a covered wagon and shouted back that it was full of gunpowder.

'Quiet,' Jenk hissed, holding his knife up to the torchlight and finding it to his satisfaction. 'Fill your boots, boys.'

'We're stealing the Ironweld's gunpowder?' said Grint, glancing back while the two men set to work shovelling powder into the pockets of their shorts. Gorman was helping Mikali back to her feet, the younger woman having snagged her tunic on her way through the grille and landed badly.

Jenk patted Sorl on the back with the flat of his knife, indicating that he was now free to get lost. 'The Excelsian Ironweld are known to mix a little used prophecy in with their powder, to make their guns fire true and their shots count. Let's just say that the general's running short and withdrawal is a bitch of a thing.'

'There must be almost nothing in there.'

'Luckily, I didn't misspend my youth on *school* and just do as Braun tells me. All I know is that the Azyrites and the Ironweld have been holding out and now they're gonna learn to share.' Jenk waved his knife towards the entrance. 'Go keep watch or something, but do it over there.'

The tunnel from the old gnoblar cave through to Fort Honoria was a narrow slash in the rock, just wide enough for one of the Ironweld's small wagons, but about three times as high. Grint put his hand to the warm, sweaty rock and shuffled down the passage on a shallow decline. After half a minute he emerged into clean starlight and coughed, his lungs protesting after the stodgier fare to which they'd become accustomed. The clash of steel and bone and the screams of men rang off the hard flanks of the Gnarlfast and funnelled down through the mouth of the cave.

Grint stared out over Goreham and Honoria, his mouth hanging open.

Jenk appeared behind him. 'Shut your trap, blasphemer. You know what the flies are like here. If they get in they'll get out by eating their way out.'

Grint shut his mouth. 'What in the Twelve Stars happened while we were gone?' he said.

Braun's man shrugged. 'Convenient, isn't it.'

'Convenient?'

Jenk whistled for the rest of the men, and started down the narrow causeway towards the fight.

General Lisandr stood on the embankment that had been heaped around the site of the future castle from quarry spoil, watching through a pair of crystal-lensed binoculars as the Hounds mustered outside Braun's house, and fighting slowly spread across the whole of the city.

Sigmar, she cursed herself again, *what have I done?*

This was her doing. For just one little moment she had lost control and caused this. But how had it got out of hand and spread so quickly? It was as though the ground had been angry, waiting for any excuse to lash out, and she had given it one. She wondered if the greenskins that the patrols were reporting on the Eaten Plain felt it too.

She lowered the binoculars. No point compounding guilt with impotence. She turned from the ledge and climbed down the ladder.

Taal was laid out on the campaign desk that had been installed under a pavilion outside her tent, crystal ewers and silver platters of fine food swept unceremoniously aside to make room for the giant man. Blood trickled out along the tabletop and *pit-pattered* to the stone floor. Gunnery-Professor Shay, who had fortunately returned straight here when Lisandr had cut short their tour of the gatehouse ward, was standing over him with her long sleeves rolled up, issuing rambling instructions for fresh towels, boiled water, a jar of iodine, more wine and an actual doctor if one could conceivably be found, without once checking whether anyone was listening.

Lydia hurried off into the circle of gawkers. Lisandr waved them away, conscious that at least three-quarters of them were day labourers from the Accari side.

Mother Thassily laid her large hand across Taal's forehead. The Accari war-priest shuddered as though some evil were being forced out of him.

Shay spread her hands across the table and leant in. 'A marvellous piece of work.'

'You're not… too bad to look at… yourself,' Taal growled, a bloody gash for a grin.

The professor sniffed. 'I was talking about the sword in your stomach.' She turned to Lisandr. 'I assume you want it back.'

'And the man, if at all possible.'

Shay sucked in through her teeth and tutted. 'It's a nasty wound. Deep.'

Taal gave her a wan show of teeth. 'You should see… the other guy.'

Lydia returned. Shay uncorked the bottle of sparkling white that she'd brought, held onto it for a moment and then with a sigh of resignation handed it to Taal.

Corporal Mestrade cleared his throat. The Celestian and his bloodied unit, along with Angellin and Carnelian, whose timely intervention had bought them the seconds they had needed to escape Braun's house, stood to one side of the impromptu theatre.

They were dishevelled and tired, but also the largest single complement of warriors she had available. The rest of her warriors were out on patrol or scattered throughout the city, on account of the Hounds being too distractable to be trusted with even simple guard duties unsupervised. But she would count on ten Celestians to hold a walled motte against ten thousand Hounds, even if Braun decided to storm it in person.

She did not want to consider the possibility.

'Shall I saddle the demigryphs, sir?' the corporal asked. 'I could have that rabble on the causeway sent packing to their caves in Goreham with a single charge.'

'No!' Lisandr snapped. 'I'll not compound everything by ordering slaughter.'

'Are our lives not preferable to theirs?'

Lisandr looked at him sharply. 'I will pretend that I did not hear that, corporal.'

Mestrade fell silent.

'We hold our ground,' said Lisandr. 'We beat the Hounds to a stalemate if we have to, but I will not let my mistake be the death sentence for every soldier out there.'

'Do we have another choice?' Mestrade asked quietly.

Lisandr glanced towards Taal. Lydia and Thassily together were both struggling to pin the beast of a man down while Shay cleaned around the wound with silk handkerchiefs that she had found in one of the desk drawers.

'I am hoping that he might talk them down. If Shay can save his life.'

'I can't believe they're willing to murder us all over this,' said Mestrade.

'It's not just over this.'

'*He's* coming,' Taal growled, as though addressing the conversation, but his eyes were wide and staring in a way that made Lisandr shudder.

'Who?' said Lisandr.

'He's drunk,' said Shay.

'Or he's caught Braun's second-hand prophecy,' said Mestrade.

'He's coming,' Taal said again, starting to struggle under Shay's hands. 'That's why I had to destroy your orders. He's coming.'

'Hold him still,' Shay snapped. 'Any time now.' Lydia, Angellin and Mestrade came in and took a limb apiece. Lisandr squeezed Taal's hand. Shay adjusted her spectacles and stepped back. 'I should probably warn you, I've never done this on a living person before.'

'Wait,' said Lydia. 'What?'

'It'll all work out fine, I'm sure.' The gunnery-professor smiled crisply. 'I've practised on cadavers dozens of times. Almost a dozen times.'

While Shay prepared, Lisandr leant over Taal, seeking out his wild gaze with hers. 'Who is coming?'

'*Him*,' said Taal. 'I feel him. Can't you?'

Mestrade shook his head. 'He's raving, sir.'

Lisandr wished she could believe that he was. 'Don't die, Efrim,' she said. 'That is an order.'

Taal growled, dribbling blood down his chin. 'You know what I make of... Azyrite orders.'

'And I have not forgotten, but I thought you might make an exception for this one.'

Lisandr nodded to Shay, who leant in with both hands for the sword. Taal gritted his teeth and tensed, but at a touch from Mother Thassily the gunnery-professor released her grip around the hilt. Taal gasped, a small tear running down his cheek to the tabletop.

'I can pray with you before we begin,' she said. 'If you will accept the blessings of Azyr.'

Taal spat on her hand.

'Very well.' The pontiff pushed down on Taal's shoulder, hard enough to turn his fingers white. 'By all means, professor, begin.'

Shay glanced to Lisandr, who nodded, and then, with a deep breath and a bright smile, took a hold of the sword.

Taal screwed his mouth shut.

The screams burst out of him anyway.

The breath of the Eaten Plain was hot and moist. Above a certain altitude, where all but the dominant bulls of the Cuspid Mesas fell away, it congealed into fatty clouds, rain like sweat and lightning the colour and odour of twice-baked leather lashing the sky. In ordinary times, a morsel the size of a Knight-Azyros would have been of no interest to a prowling hill, but the convulsions that had gripped the Heartlands since his decision to fly ahead of the Farstrikes had made a nonsense of his older lore. Patient hunters were now ravenous, pack animals turned cannibal, while territorial beasts went on thousand-mile rampages before perishing from accumulated wounds and exhaustion.

Horac was staying high, taking no chances until he had to. Slow and sure, that was how the Anvil of the Apotheosis burned. Not the hottest fire in the Cosmos Arcane, for sure, but it would last forever.

Steering himself well clear of the rumbling, flat-topped Mesas, he left them behind and made his final descent towards the gluthold. Ghurish energies chewed at the Azyrite frame of his wings, growling as if in insatiable hunger. The wings guttered, occasionally responding to the goading with a warning *snap*, and flooding his flight path with a burnt-hair stench. *Azyr and Ghur*, he thought, *they mix like gryph-hounds and frost sabres*.

Horac had flown at greater heights than this and been unafraid. He had flown over country that had no ground at all. His wings did not permit him to fly so much as they enforced Sigmar's will that he not fall. But as he wobbled through the clammy thermals and the ground beneath him rumbled and his own stomach lurched, Horac was driven to address the fact that Sigmar's will in the Heartlands had been markedly ambiguous of late. Was the calamity that all the seers foretold already upon them? Or was this merely a warning tremor? Would the true apocalypse promise worse?

Horac found that he hoped so. He was an old man and a barbarian, and he had so little to measure the passing of the years but the disasters that came and went to mark the end of one age and the beginning of the next. And there was the small matter of being proven right, but Horac did not concern himself with that. No one had ever been made to look a fool by prophesying the end of the world. Not in his lifetime.

As his descent brought him down through the clouds, Horac saw a horde, several hordes, moving through the Cuspid Mesas. Bat squigs – giant mouths, essentially, with leathery wings attached – flapped furiously up to intercept him. Horac sent them back down to the masses with short work from his sword

He flew on. The horde, or hordes, fell away behind him, but continued to follow in his wake. A day or two from the gluthold at most.

The jutting jawline of a fortress emerged from the flab of the Gnarlfast Mountain. Its essential symmetry was that of a mouth: curtain walls for lips; blunt, weathered towers for teeth; a deep pit in the centre for a throat. But he could also already make out where maw-effigies had been pulled down and replaced with hammers, the scaffold scars of recent building, and the nascent twelve-pointed plan of a Sigmarite Free City.

So, Brendel Starsighted had called this one correctly. The Bloodgullet Crusade had been successful.

Time alone would tell whether Horac had been wrong.

The Accari Hounds were mustering in the street outside Braun's front porch, about fifteen hundred of them waving javelins and torches, but with more spilling in from the surrounding labour camps and shack-villages all the time. From the vantage of his top step, built to an ogor's scale, Braun could see the signs of fighting creep into every ward of the new city. Azyrites and Accari duelled in doorways, tussled over street corners, blocks of Celestians hiding behind their tall shields as they retreated under a hail of fire bombs and javelins towards their mountaintop bastion. Their temple was burning. Again. The fighters in the street, meanwhile, were cheering, chanting, working themselves up to something and calling for Braun, whose predominant emotion was confusion.

Azyrites and Reclaimed had found reasons to hate one another for as long as the latter had been forced to put up with the former. Perhaps, if Braun had come down harder on Taal's mob for vandalising the Azyrite temple that first night, then things would not have spiralled this far out of hand. But then Azyrites couldn't take a joke. That was their problem. The Accari gnawed, they pushed, they tested boundaries; it was how the Hounds let off steam when cooped up for too long in one place.

And then Lisandr had had to go and kidnap Efrim Taal.

Braun didn't want to have to fight Lisandr, and certainly not over Taal. They were all on roughly the same side, although Efrim had more of a tendency to skirt that line. But he was also a war-priest of Sigmar, an elder of the old people and one of the Dozen. Insults had to be answered, unless Braun wanted all of Goreham to believe that their leader was too weak to stand up for his own.

The problem was, he still wasn't entirely sure what had happened or why. The Lisandr who had marched into the longhouse and stabbed Taal in the gut was impossibly wrapped up in the Lisandr with whom he had seen himself fighting side by side to save this city in a prophetic vision.

He shuddered, still only half-dressed, and stepped out into the street to a roar of acclaim that was as comforting as white noise to a newborn. He took prophecy deliberately so as *not* to see Rukka Bosskilla. The Ironjawz megaboss was not supposed to be in his future as well as his past.

Unless… What if getting rid of Lisandr was the way to cheat this prophecy?

Surrounded by fighters, Braun pumped his fists in the air with a howl, the Hounds responding in deafening fashion as though he had a gargant bellowing in each ear. He turned towards the Celestian encampment. It stood at the end of a long, narrow and immensely defensible causeway, for all that it was still under construction, behind a steep embankment of earth, stubbled with broken spears and cannons. The Azyrites were continuing to withdraw towards the fluttering banners and the shield wall that stood at the top of the earth bridge in lieu of a gate, retreating from the increasingly reckless Accari under the *crackle-pop* reports of the Ironweld guns.

It seemed as though Shay had picked her side. Braun was not wholly surprised, but he was disappointed. He shared every Ghurite's fascination and love of loud bangs and big guns. But this was what city living did to Ghurish folk, and he should know, having been brought up in the greatest city in Ghur.

He marched on the causeway, drawing fighters to him like ghurmites drawn to a poking stick.

'Now, chief?'

The warrior beside him was called Kadd, one of Taal's senior men, and shared a distant familial appearance, but without the grey hairs and the air of cunning. Muscles bulged in a tight vest, and a greathammer rested against one shoulder.

'Now.'

Braun beat his chest with the butt of his axe and gave a roar, raised his axe above his head, and started running towards the Celestians' keep. A sizeable fraction of the Hounds' strength in Goreham howled and hollered, and charged with him.

Handgun fire crackled along the embankment. The guns punched running men from their feet, lead slugs making bloody messes of leather shields and unarmoured bodies, but the Hounds leapt over their dead and shouted down the noise.

The Ironweld guns were powerful: a warning volley was often enough to startle off a Stalkspider hunting party or a Bonesplitterz warband, particularly the further one ventured from Excelsis, but they were difficult to keep in condition, and painfully slow to reload. No match for a good man with a javelin or a grenade, and the Celestians, for reasons of tradition and pride, carried no missile weapons of their own.

As if the gunpowder barrage had been an audible range marker of some kind, Hounds started to drop out of the charge and hurl their own missiles towards the embankment. Explosions rippled along the barriers, throwing up clods of spoil and bits of spear, six-foot-long javelins sticking up out of the earth wall and vastly outnumbering the defensive stakes that the Azyrites had set there. Hardly any found a human target, but sheer volume had the Ironweld keeping their heads down. Gunfire petered away.

The Hounds clamoured to push forwards.

Two shield-armed Celestians who were serving as a rearguard for the rest gave a sudden shout, pulling away from their comrades, and charging back down the causeway towards Braun and the Hounds.

The first thrust with her spear, her room for manoeuvre limited by the mass of bodies, and Braun turned his body under the shaft. There was a shout of pain from behind as Brodd, another of Taal's mob, took the point in the shoulder. Braun swung his hammers, an uppercut that cleft an aristocratic chin and dimmed the brilliant topaz of the woman's eyes. The second fell back with Mawgren and Karze pulling at his shield. The two Accari eventually succeeded in wresting it from his arm and dragging him down. Karze stabbed him twenty times, the Celestian still trying to breathe through the red holes in his chest while Ezra crouched over him and ripped off his earring. He was still admiring the bloody silver as Braun sprinted past.

A clarion sounded from inside the keep and two disciplined blocks of Celestians, twenty soldiers with spears and shields, marched to reinforce their comrades on the causeway. Braun recognised the officer who led them, though his moustaches were longer and more tousled than he remembered, his armour in a shoddier state.

'Mestra–!' he began.

The twenty men immediately behind him disappeared in a crimson pulp and, even buffered by the bodies, the exploding mortar shell lifted Braun off the ground and threw him face down onto the causeway. He coughed, the breath in his lungs turning to fire as bits of his own men mixed up with pea gravel rained over his back.

With a ruthlessness that Braun had never seen the Azyrites employ before, masked by shiny armour and dusty traditions, Mestrade and his Celestians pushed into the scrum of injured men that the artillery had left strewn over the causeway. Their counter-charge rolled over the stunned Hounds with a sound not dissimilar to that of a metal rolling pin softening meat, an automated Azyrite machine working a particularly coarse bit of marbling.

Braun staggered upright with a yell he could not actually hear, punched his hammer into a Celestian's helmet and dented the cheek guard. The Azyrite staggered back, dazed, easy pickings for another of Taal's men to drive his knife up under the chinstrap. The knife-wielder himself fell in short order with a Celestian spear in his chest. The spearwoman went on to spit six more Accari fighters with neat, precise thrusts despite being swarmed on all sides. Her armour resisted blows that would have killed eight men before finally giving way under Braun's hammer.

Sigmar, they were going to massacre one another here. If they carried on this way then the only ones who would cheer the outcome would be the Guild of Spicers and Waggoners, who had put up for the Hounds' founding and would not be forced to welcome home the newly battle-hardened band of petty-crooks, thugs and malcontents they had only just foisted onto Braun. For some reason, more than any amount of brutality and senseless killing, the thought of making the money men happy made him pause for just long enough to think.

He lowered his hammers.

'What in the eight hells are we doing?'

A missile, purple and gold, but so fast that Braun barely registered the movement, flashed down from the sky like a rocket and hit the midpoint of the causeway rise. There was no explosion, but the impact of its landing was enough to throw several dozen warriors of both sides flat.

A seven-foot-tall warrior-king encased in purple and gold plate and chased with lightning stepped out of the crater he had just made and shook out his wings. Braun went weak at the knees.

A Stormcast Eternal.

But the champion was already moving. Striking low, and with the flat of his sword, he took a Hound's legs out from under him and, in the same efficient moment, delivered a punch that beat a Celestian's shield in two and knocked the warrior behind her to the ground. A flex of his wings knocked two Celestians and nine

Hounds back, while a casual backhand broke Kadd's jaw and sent him tumbling and screaming down the steep bluff of the causeway's flank.

The warrior loomed over Braun.

He was too stunned to defend himself. To even consider it. A Stormcast Eternal was so far beyond his experience, and even his imagination, that he might as well still have been dreaming.

The Stormcast plucked the axe straight out of his hand, then punted him onto his back with the toe of his boot. It was not a hard kick. A hard kick, from that warrior, would have driven Braun's ribs out through his spine. It was a gentle shove, such as a man might give to push over a small dog who had got carried away barking and ignored every command to stop.

Braun looked up from the ground in awe.

'In the name of Sigmar,' the warrior demanded, 'this madness will cease.'

In the giant's left hand was an ornate object that Braun had initially taken to be the head of some kind of mace, mercifully unused, but when he raised it above his helmet the shutter fell away and revealed itself as a lantern. What blasted out of it was not *light* as Braun had ever known it, but as though a star had been roped down from High Azyr and detonated over the Gnarlfast. Fighters screamed and, Braun included, threw their hands to their faces as Sigmar's fury burned the red mist of Ghur from their eyes.

When it was done and the worst of the pain had passed, replaced by a not-unpleasant numbness all over, Braun lay on his back, looking up at the clear sky and panting, blinking away tears and wondering how in Heaven's name it had come to this.

Mestrade put up his spear and walked hesitantly to where Braun lay. He offered his hand.

'Forgive me.'

Braun grunted and, after a moment's thought, allowed the Celestian officer to pull him up.

'My name is Horac Long-Winter,' the Stormcast declared, his deep voice booming from his featureless amethyst mask and ringing over the mountainside like words beaten in lead. 'Knight-Azyros of the Astral Templars, bearer of Sigmar's beacon, and emissary of Lord-Aquilor Vagria Farstrike. By the grace of the God-King, this insanity has been purged from you. For a time, at least. But tell me…'

The Knight-Azyros sheathed his sword, dousing its brilliance in a golden scabbard.

'What fool's idea was it to build a city over the biggest deposit of amberbone this side of the Beastgrave?'

CHAPTER EIGHT

The two hordes started fighting as soon as they spilled out of the Cuspid Mesas and met one another on the Eaten Plain.

There were other armies already out there on the vast plains, gathered around their colossal campfires and their effigies to Gork and Mork. Furtive Moonclan scurried about like hooded ants. Dankhold bosses and their troggherds squatted in the holes and ditches that the humans had dug out of the hills, picking the bones of those they had found there. Orruks of a hundred tribes warred across the plain. Biggest and brashest amongst them were the Shinners, shiny-armoured nobz led by Mug Fisteater, the last surviving boss of Warboss Grukka, who'd terrorised the Coast of Tusks before the White Reaper had got him. Maneater mercenaries from the Holdbrawl Kingdoms of the far west gathered all and sundry for garrulous feasts and tales of plenty, and only occasionally gobbled up those who showed less than willing. Bonesplitterz gathered into anarchic mobs to race one another up and down the plain, as if theirs was the kind of energy that could be burned off by exertion.

It was the mightiest horde to have darkened the Heartlands of Ghur in a hundred generations, united in the common cause of appearing to be headed in the same direction.

A fight was coming. A real fight.

And *he* was right behind them.

No one could say with certainty who *he* was, but from the most devious grot shaman to the thickest trogboss, they felt it with the same all-powerful certainty. He needed to be worshipped. He needed to be impressed with destruction. And the old Bloodgullet gluthold, now the squat of humie warriors, was in his path.

But, of all the Fists, Skraps, Stalktribes and Rukks staking out their positions on the plain for the coming fight, it was clear to all that these two latecomers from the Mesas were the biggest, and every other boss instinctively got his lads out of their way lest they be caught in the middle of something they couldn't finish.

Rukka Bosskilla glowered over the sea of chittering bodies and rustling, scuttling legs. He could not count, but even if he could have, he would not have been able to estimate how many Spiderfang grots there were spilling down out of the opposite valley.

'Loads o' the little beggars,' grunted Weird Wurgbuz, the shaman.

'Loads,' Rukka agreed, before stomping slowly to face their leader.

Rukka stomped everywhere slowly. Walking infuriated him, and it seemed he was always doing it after his maw-krusha had gone and got itself killed. Doing it slowly, though, seemed to help him store the anger up better for when he finally got wherever he was going. A lot of his boys took it for a cunning affectation to make himself look good. *Dere goes a boss wiv all da time in da realm for krumpin' stuff,* they would admiringly growl.

When he was the proper distance from his opposite number,

generally recognised amongst all greenskins as the distance of a punch in the face, he stopped.

He looked up, trying and spectacularly failing to keep a pig-iron lid on his rage.

The biggest and baddest bosses went on foot. Gorkamorka had gone on foot. Mostly. Anyone who rolled along like he was the Fist of Gork himself on a monster bigger even than the legendary Bigteef was just deliberately setting out to zog him off.

'I is Earbug Glibspittle,' came the tiny voice from way up on the top of the enormous spider. 'Da Shady King.' The grot was swaddled in black spider silk from throat to ankles, his head stuffed into a tall hat of bright red and yellow feathers. His gaunt face and long, strangler's arms were similarly decorated with little dots and jags of colour. Beady red eyes peered down through an elaborate mask of paint.

'I knows who you is,' Rukka grunted back.

The grot shaman turned his head away and cupped a hand to his large, flapping ear. 'Wot's dat? I can't 'ear you from all dat way down there.'

'Come on down then,' Rukka growled, stroking his choppa. The arachnarok war-spider regarded him more closely, its glittering black eye cluster at his own eye level. Its armour was yellow and black, daubed all over with grot handprints in red paint. Its hairy body chittered, never still, sounding like voices but all of them whispering behind his back. Rukka longed to stick his choppa in it. 'Don't reckon you'd look half so shady down 'ere.'

'Temptin', but nah. I knows who you is too, Rukka. I knows why dey calls you da Bosskilla.'

For a while the two warbosses, both of them great kings by their own unruly reckoning, afforded each other a grudging mutual respect. A friend was only an enemy you weren't yet fighting. An enemy was just a friend you were fighting for now.

Rukka turned away first. 'Let's get started then.'

'I reckon we'd better.'

'But I'm goin' first.'

A moment's pause. 'All right.'

Rukka nodded and gripped his choppa. Two titans of statecraft had battled here and come away with a bloody mouth and a draw. 'All right.'

Braun's ascent to the top of the east wall brought a ragged cheer. He gave the warriors a wave, and the sort of grin that a fearless leader of men and the Hero of Izalmaw might be expected to wear. The entire strength of the Accari Hounds, a number he now knew to be close on eleven thousand men, since one of Shay's assistants had got it into her head to count, were spread out along the parapet. The Celestians had been mounted and relegated to reserves, all with the notable exception of Mother Thassily, whose griffon swooped the length of the stockade, lifting Braun's spirits, albeit briefly, with every soaring pass over his head.

It felt good to have the pontiff on his side again.

Taking a deep breath of the wind off the Eaten Plains, he looked along the length of the wall. To the Bloodgullet, the wall had been a mighty barrier. To a human considering assaulting it, thirty feet high and solid wood, it looked impregnable. To that same human standing behind a seven-foot-high crenellation, unable even to see their attacker from behind it, it might have felt invincible, if the memory of sacking it had been more than three months old.

In many places the wall was little more than a vertical barrier with no walkway for a defender to stand upon. In others, a warrior tasked with defending it needed to perch on a rudimentary platform with no battlement to protect them from an attacker's fire. These, the Ironweld had spent the days since Knight-Azyros Horac's arrival converting into artillery casemates, setting up davits and cranes to install cannons and construct the new defences. But there had not been enough time. Shay's initial priorities had been the building of churches and the laying down of roads and, as of that moment, most of the artillery casemates were ensconced within barricades of rubble or recycled boxes stuffed with brambles.

More guns had been hastily redeployed from the Celestians' encampment into the gatehouse ward, behind the wall. Shay herself, feeling mainly responsible for the gaps in their defences perhaps, because Braun hadn't yet heard her complaining about it, had overseen the deployment of rocket and mortar batteries. Spotters, specially kitted out in bright clothes and with an array of signal flags, stood out like dyed hairs amongst the earthy colours of the Hounds wherever there was a battlement for them to stand on.

Pushing through his men to a gap in the rampart, Braun frowned across the Eaten Plain. Hordes of greenskins were coming across the plain, covering the ground like a fungal mat as far as the trumpeting masses of the Cuspid Mesas, and presumably into them as well. Tens upon tens of thousands, predominantly grots, but with the bulkier silhouettes of orruk mobs more than abundant enough for Braun's tastes, and interspersed with the even larger forms of troggoths, ogors and grot engineering. Singing and dancing, or that was what it sounded like to Braun, marching under a cacophony of horns and gongs and waving flags, they marched towards Goreham and Honoria.

'A dawn attack. At least they're traditional.'

With a grimace, feeling the shrapnel wound in his back that there had not been the time to get looked at, Braun reached into his pocket. His fingers ran through the fine-grained black powder, picking up the faintest impressions of prophecy that sat within like the dregs at the bottom of a beer mug. The images they put into his head were so vague they could have been of anything, and anybody. But this was where Sigmar wanted him to be. He was sure of it. He drew his hand from his pocket and licked his finger, making it look as though he were chewing on his nails.

He was good at disguising his habit. Nevertheless, Jenk looked at him distastefully.

Most of them were there. Ragn, with his head looking like a boiled potato after Grob Bloodgullet had smashed it in. Murdo. Slayk. Kemrit. Olgar. Woan. Altin the Cannibal with his ridiculous little knife and butcher's cleaver. He'd given Taal a command of his own, right out on the edge where the fighting was likely to be lightest, what with having a Celestian sword pulled out of his gut the night before last. Kanta Grint with her large mob he'd put out where he needed numbers. He could see her tatty flags flying all along the left flank.

Ferrgin was missing. Obviously.

The thought of losing one of his Dozen chilled him. If they were not twelve, then they no longer had Sigmar's numeral to protect them. And if the God-King had withdrawn his blessings... He put his hand back in his pocket, fingers hunting for fresh signs amidst the scraps of prophecy.

'They're Ironjawz out there,' he said.

'Yeah,' said Jenk.

'Blue and white.'

Jenk nodded. 'Rukka's colours.'

His vision from the earlier night had shaken him. He'd never known a fight harder than the Izalmaw. It wasn't just that the Ironjawz were tough. It was that they were tough and that they never *ever* gave up. They always wanted more, and they enjoyed it. The harder you fought to beat them off, the harder they came back at you. They were worse than the ogors. So much worse.

'But Rukka's dead, chief. You know he's dead. You *saw* him dead.'

'Yeah...'

Braun shivered. He ached for a real prophecy. Then he remembered what his last prophecy had showed him and pulled his hand back out of his pocket, laying it instead on the plate of maw-krusha leather that covered his belly.

He was fully dressed and he was wearing armour. That was how seriously he was taking the prospect of facing the Ironjawz in battle once again.

'You all heard the Knight-Azyros.' He made the sign of the Shatterer across his tattooed face. 'An army of Astral Templars races here even now. We've only got to hold this city until they get here.'

Jenk bit his lip, looking out. Saying nothing.

Excitement almost pushed out the nagging voice of Braun's fear. He had never fought alongside the Stormcast Eternals. He had never seen one until one had fallen out of the sky and put him on his back. The behaviour of gods if ever Braun had seen it. As far as he knew none of the Accari had. They were just second-hand stories of the founding of Excelsis and the Realmgate Wards. But if the Stormhosts could wrest control of creation itself from the invictunite grip of Chaos, and hold back the legions of the Undying King, then they could save this day.

Throwing one arm around Jenk's shoulder and another around Woan's, Braun drew them in close and shook them.

'We will hold them here, with our blood and our strength, and then the might of Sigmar will annihilate them. Praise Sigmar!'

Another half-hearted cheer rippled along the walls.

'We're not fated to die here,' said Braun, more softly, almost to himself. 'I saw Lisandr and I fighting the Bosskilla. I didn't see us fall.'

Jenk scratched the side of his head, sounding mildly annoyed by the inconvenience of what he was witnessing as the approaching greenskins broke into a run. Several mobs were hoisting up ladders. 'They're coming.'

'Yeah, I see that.'

'Is there a plan?'

'Course there's a plan.'

'You know how I hate to pester, chief...'

Braun clapped him on the back. 'Pray, Jenk. Pray.'

Efrim Taal sat on an old man's stool, set way back on one of the leadbelcher firing platforms, head bent, and watched destruction come.

Ironjawz daubed in blue and white checks threw ramshackle ladders against the wall as though daring one or the other to break, the metal side rails bowing under the weight of the hulking brutes as they climbed. Moonclan wheeled up wobbly siege towers that disgorged hordes of cave squigs and looncap fanatics, sometimes even after they'd crashed them into the wall. A pair of mancrusher gargants, identical twins by the look of them, staggered drunkenly in the vague direction of the gate, pushing and shoving at each other, as though there just happened to be a battle going on nearby, taking an occasional break from their brotherly feud to scoop up an unfortunate orruk and eat them or boot a grot towards the defenders on the walls.

The Hounds screamed to the God-King and the old gods of Accar as they tipped over buckets of heated pitch and followed up with grenades. Rockets corkscrewed wildly over the walls, loop-the-looping, leapfrogging, trails crossing and criss-crossing before detonating, seemingly at random, amidst the oncoming hordes.

Black-robed bodies flew apart and high into the air. Siege towers burned. Mushrooms shrivelled and burst, coughing out billowing plumes that burnt men's faces and had yellowcaps popping up out of the woodwork where they touched. One of the gargants theatrically pinched his nose and wafted his hand in front of his face while his twin brother guffawed and accidentally backed into another Moonclan tower that was still being heaved into the wall, knocking it over and instantly killing every mad grot inside.

It all seemed woefully indiscriminate, but for the furious semaphore being passed between the spotter on the parapet and the battery crews below.

Taal regarded the signalman suspiciously. His feelings towards him were mixed. He didn't trust a man beside him who wasn't there with an axe or a hammer in his hand. He hated that a man who'd stood beside his nephew's killers, the kin he'd groomed as the next shaman to the Accari, could stand so close without fearing a knife in his back. He loathed his guns. But Shay had saved his life. And Sigmar, how he hated her for that.

A trio of mortars ensconced directly behind his bit of wall fired all at once, their reports rolling together into one awful sound. Taal flinched from the noise just as he did every time, and just as he did every time, he swore that next time he'd be ready for them.

'Are you sure all your bits are going to hold together?' asked Brodd – his second, now that Ferrgin had gone back to Ghur. He was a good enough fighter, even in spite of the flesh wound that had put his arm in a grubby sling, but the Hounds were filled with good enough fighters with two good arms. He wasn't the sharpest tooth in the mouth, and he hadn't a glimmer of Ferrgin's talent for magic.

Taal scowled at nothing at all, despite the great deal of something pummelling the wall scant yards away. Ignoring his idiot half-cousin, he turned slightly aside and tilted his head back to look at the top of his staff. The skull of the saurus observed the battle as dispassionately as its current keeper.

'I brought the Hounds here from Accar,' he hissed at it. 'I

followed the drumbeat of Ghur, far from the false civilisations of your people, and I kept my faith even when the drumming ceased. You didn't mention anything about the death of my heir when I picked you out of the Primeval Jungle. Did you miss that one? Or did you think it wouldn't matter?'

'Not to worry, chief,' Brodd mumbled, looking out across the writhing sea of green. 'I heard that General Braun had a vision.'

Taal snorted irritably, shifting his discomfort forward on his stool. 'Prophecy only shows what prophecy shows. It isn't perfect.'

'Prophecy comes from the Mallus.' Brodd dutifully traced the sign of the Shatterer.

'*We* aren't perfect. We interpret our prophecies with every bias we've been bred to hold.' Taal put his hands in his pockets, and drew out an arraca stem. He didn't bite it straight away, but holding it seemed to focus his bitterness for a moment. 'You ever hear of the Vermyre Prophecy?' He scowled at Brodd's baffled look, leant into his staff as though to get up to give a proper lecture, only to think better of it as the stitches in his belly gave their verdict on his plans, and eased himself back down. 'It famously foretold the doom of Excelsis, mere days before the city was beset by daemons and High Arbiter Vermyre exposed as a slave of Chaos.' He flinched again as shells roared over his head, cursing them as he bit down on the arraca stem in his fingers. 'But who says the events of a prophecy are going to happen tomorrow? Or the next day? Or at any point in your lifetime? My father, who was shaman before me, taught me that the future's set in amber. Real prophecy is inviolate, and since Vermyre's attack on Excelsis was thwarted, then the doom that was foreseen is still coming.' He looked around. 'Perhaps soon.'

'And the general's vision?'

'He saw himself and the Azyrite fighting. He didn't see them winning. And he didn't say anything about what happens to the rest of us.'

A panicked cry swept across the platform as a heavy Ironjawz ladder smashed through the temporary Ironweld fascine that stood in place of a battlement and dug in.

An enormous head appeared over the top, grilled in iron, followed by an equally monstrous body. The Ironjaw grabbed the first defender and threw him screaming over the wall. He crushed another soldier's skull with a squeeze of his hand and, with a rattling laugh, tossed the limp body aside. Another man dented his breastplate with a greathammer. The Ironjaw cut him in half with a slice of his choppa.

The greenskin was almost the size of an ogor and far heavier in his clanking iron plate. He smelled of pig dung, stressed metal and burnt rubber. Men smashed feverishly at the ladder with axes and hammers, but it was made of solid pig iron and resisted every blow. The signalman waved his flags determinedly, right up to the moment that an Ironjaw jumped over the low parapet and struck its choppa into the back of his skull.

A brave lad, Taal conceded. There was some honest Ghurish fight in these Excelsians, after all.

Three strong men roared at the top of their lungs and wrestled the second Ironjaw back. The brute bellowed with laughter as though the Accari were being unexpectedly great sports, as it toppled back off the parapet, clutching one of those men to its huge chest in each arm.

More climbed up to take its place.

'Chief!' Brodd yelled.

Taal spat on the back of his hand and muttered a guttural incantation.

The muggy breath of Ghurish magic rose in a cloud of evaporating spit, and Taal blew it towards the backs of the fighters wrestling the Ironjawz for the parapet. Where it touched the orruks, bite marks and slashes appeared across their tough green skin. Where it brushed across Hounds a more hideous effect by far took hold. Their limbs snapped and lengthened. Their jaws, wide with agony, dislocated to accommodate the mass of growing teeth. Muscle weighed down their broadening shoulders until they stood hunched and panting, fur sprouting from their backs, the cries of beasts that had once been men emerging instead as wild, slavering howls.

By the time the arcane breath had dispersed itself into the air, every man and woman for ten feet around had been transformed into a slobbering, bearlike beast.

Taal slumped back in his stool, exhausted, as his Hounds tore the Ironjawz apart.

Grint wanted a bigger knife. He wanted a sword like one of those the Celestians carried or, gods help him, even a spear. And a shield. He definitely wanted a shield. He charged towards the Ironjawz that had made it onto the battlement at the far left end of the wall in a group of about forty and with a two-inch-long spice knife in his fist. He had no idea what he was going to do to them when he got there. Part of him hoped that some miracle would stop him from ever getting there. The Ironjawz were too big to fight, too hard to kill.

The Accari ran into the Ironjawz with a sound like a mailed fist hitting a steel plate. Men swung hammers. Orruks built like steam tanks laughed them off.

Mikali slipped on a piece of flesh and went down.

'Bad luck, Mi–' Sorl began, before a battle-maddened Ironjaw cut Grint's distant cousin in half and proceeded to blitz through the rest of his mob. Half of them were dead before Grint realised what was happening.

Plastered in blood, staring up at a monster, Grint felt only dumb shock.

The Ironjaw swung up his choppa and bellowed, then staggered back a pace as a javelin sprouted from its chest.

Kanta Grint swept in like a Scourge galleon at full sail, gigantic ankles overflowing the collars of her boots, which squelched in turn over the body parts of her men, as she punched a hissing kara grenade down the Ironjaw's throat. She clamped its mouth shut with a huge hand, holding its head under her arm in a lock as though she were wrestling down a boisterous dog. There was a muted *boom*. The iron plates around the orruk's throat buckled outwards, smoke rising from its flat nose. It made a plaintive noise and Kanta let it flop, dead, to the ground. She dusted her palms.

'Weren't running away, were you?' she asked, as Grint and Mikali unstuck themselves from the ruin of their unit. Grint picked up Sorl's large axe, surreptitiously wiping Sorl off it on his shorts.

'No, mother.'

'Good. I'd hate to have to send a son of mine back to the make-up mobs.'

Grint shuddered at the thought. He didn't want to imagine what *they* were doing right now.

Lisandr would have preferred to be anywhere but the Butchers' Quarter.

The battle for the east wall was a distant grumble, a single drawn-out scream over a susurrus of clattering steel and barking guns, like one soldier dying very, very far away. Pebbles worked loose from the Gnarlfast by the commotion skittered down the rock face. Her demigryph crowed, sensing her anxiety, feathers bristling, clawing at the forbidden earth and even in that idle act of excavation bringing up the baked, broken bones of a dozen dead things.

She tightened her grip on the leather strapping of her shield.

She shouldn't have been here at all, but given that she was left with no choice now she would have given anything, anything, to be dying on the wall with the Accari.

But perhaps the Butchers' Quarter was exactly what she deserved. How much more would the distrust and the loss of life that she had done so much to bring about cost the Freeguild, beyond her own sense of uselessness?

'General?'

Lydia Victoria Aubreitn stood beside Lisandr's demigryph, armoured in midnight blue and starsilver, and overlaid with the clear white square of a squire's tabard. In her right hand she carried a long half-pike, Lisandr's sigils fluttering with unearned pride from the array of pennons tied around its haft. Two-score of demigryph-mounted knights led by Corporal Mestrade, attended by as many squires again on foot, clanked and chirruped alongside their general.

'It is nothing, Lydia.' She stretched her jaw, the muscles tense from grinding. 'Dark thoughts.'

'If there is anything I can do, my lady. Anything I can bring?'

Lisandr smiled tiredly and shook her head. 'There is no anguish of the heart that one small victory cannot assuage.'

Lydia's young face frowned as she thought back to her War College lessons. 'Hersbetter?'

'Meristiles, *Lessons from the Wars of Death*.' Lisandr was feeling unusually forgiving this day. 'Their styles are very similar.'

She turned in the saddle, alerted by the scuff of metal and rock to the emergence of Knight-Azyros Horac Long-Winter from the shallow grave-pit he had been exploring. In spite of the army at the gates, he had insisted that the role he had to play was here, and been adamant that one Stormcast Eternal would make no difference at all to the outcome. The Stormcast's exquisite warplate was smeared in the mud and ash of his toil, and his face, seeming at once haggard by time and preternaturally ageless, was flushed with the effort.

Lisandr's position had brought her some familiarity with the Stormcast Eternals. As much as any mortal, however prominent, privileged or wealthy, could expect to attain. The gold of the Hammers of Sigmar had been an infrequent, but unexceptional sight around the twelve-fold campuses of the War College, lecturing on subjects as varied as military history, theology, and the languages of dead civilisations. They had often led officer cadets in drills, to prepare them for the day when they would support the Stormhosts in battle, and there was no thrill in the realms like witnessing one Stormcast Eternal intent upon combat with another. In Excelsis too, parochial as the city was, her status had accorded her an invitation to dine at Lord-Veritant Sentanus' table. Even in the shadow of an unsought for battle, she shivered at the recollection.

While the Hammers of Sigmar were the manifest justice and majesty of the God-King, and the Knights-Excelsior were imperial to the very brink of evoking outright terror, Knight-Azyros Horac had a manner that felt almost… human. At least until he moved, or spoke, or bared his teeth to smile, or did anything to reveal himself as an eight-foot-tall war god, a stalking bear in human shape and Heaven's armour.

He wiped old soot and not-so-old grease from his brow. 'You say that no one has ventured into this part of the city since the conquest?'

Lisandr nodded.

Gunnery-Professor Shay, Efrim Taal and even Mother Thassily had all expressed an interest of one kind or another in exploring the ogors' holy place, but declaring it off-limits had been the one thing that Lisandr and Braun had agreed on in a long time.

'I cannot vouch for every individual, but no.'

'Good. That is probably the one intelligent decision you have made since deciding to occupy this place.'

Lisandr had a prepared response about orders, and the virtue of a good soldier in obeying them, but bit it back. One did not argue with an avatar of their god, and she had doubts whether this one would be impressed by the commands of a politician from faraway Excelsis. 'We did what we thought was best with what we knew at the time.'

Horac grunted, apparently not so impressed with that answer either. 'There is a deep seam of amberbone here. If I were to judge it on first instincts alone, I would say that it is larger than the deposit that Lord-Aquilor Farstrike extracted from beneath the Morruk Hills.' The Stormcast appeared almost to shudder. 'I will not go into what it roused from the hills there. Save that I would not care to meet its like again, not here, without a full chamber of my brothers alongside me.'

He looked up at her. She had heard that the Knights-Azyros, as well as serving as envoys, ambassadors and the shining tips of the God-King's spear, were often employed to sit in judgement of crimes too heinous for mortal deliberation. In their brief moment of eye contact, Lisandr had some inkling of how it must feel to stand so accused.

'Your feud with the Accari pre-existed your arrival here, I would guess, but the amberbone, over time, will have fuelled it. That is why I say you are fortunate.' He gestured around him with a grimy gauntlet. 'Had you attempted to colonise this ground along with the rest of the gluthold then you would have murdered one another long before I arrived to save you.'

The revelation that she was not entirely to blame for triggering the short-lived war between the Celestians and the Accari should have brought her some comfort. It did not. Perhaps it was the way the Knight-Azyros said it. There was no succour at all in his voice.

'Do you think the Bloodgullet knew it was here?' she asked.

'Undoubtedly,' said Horac. 'The ogres are no fools. They will have been drawing on the power of the site in their ritual cookery for many years. Perhaps even centuries.'

'But you believe that the greenskins attack because of the amberbone?'

Again, that look, another measure on the cosmic scales in her favour or disfavour. 'The Lord-Aquilor believes it, and that is enough for me.' He paused as though considering something afresh, having spoken it aloud. 'But do not tell her I said so.'

'And you think that removing it will end the attack?'

The Knight-Azyros shook his head. 'Nothing but their destruction will end the attack now. But we might buy your city some time. Time for Vagria Farstrike to come to our aid. Then we may properly bind the amberbone to dampen the effects of its magic and remove it from the city.'

Lisandr fought down a shudder. 'Respectfully, and I know we have had this argument already, but even if my Celestians and I are best placed here, you at least should be on the wall.' Even if she had only seen Stormcast Eternals in practice war, it was an experience that one never forgot. If there was a single warrior in all of Fort Honoria who could hold a line against troggoths and gargants and stand toe to toe with the champions of the Ironjawz then it was Knight-Azyros Horac Long-Winter.

'I am the only one who can do this,' said Horac. 'No one but me can handle the amberbone in safety until I have had a chance to bind it.'

Lisandr's attention snapped to the Gnarlfast as a trickle of rubble cascaded down the rock face. A demigryph warbled in reply, and as Lisandr's eyes adjusted to the change in perspective a yellow-bodied spider the size of a pony unfolded its limbs from a tiny crack in the high bluff and scuttled out onto the rock.

A spear-armed grot festooned in brightly coloured silks and a feather headdress sat bestride its back; it spotted the Celestian knights down below and threw them a rude gesture.

'Spiderfang!' Lydia shouted. 'How did the Hounds let them pass?'

'The gnoblar tunnels,' Mestrade returned, pointing with his half-pike. 'Look! They are coming in through the tunnels.'

Lisandr turned to Horac, her demeanour suddenly turning hard now that there was action to be taken. 'How long do you need, Knight-Azyros?'

'Until the Farstrike rides across the Eaten Plain.'

Lisandr clicked her tongue, wheeling her demigryph around and tilting her spear. 'Then you will have it.'

Horac smiled faintly before returning to his labours in the pit. 'Mortals fighting to defend a Stormcast Eternal – will the ironies of the age never cease?'

Braun and his Dozen held the centre by the red tips of their broken fingernails.

Massive Ironjawz waded through all but the biggest and toughest of the Accari Hounds, laughing off hits from hatchets and great-hammers alike and butchering a score for every one of their own that the Hounds were able to pull down. If the brutes had put half as much energy and thought into simply killing the defenders as they gave towards smashing up the wall itself then the Dozen would have been driven back to the Celestians' castle hours ago.

With the back of his hammer, Braun traced the twelve points of Sigendil across his chest, and threw himself back into the fighting with a roar.

The roar was mainly for show. It impressed the orruks and it impressed his men. But he'd learned in the hardest possible way that an Ironjaw would not be put down by pitting strength against strength. He fought defensively, delivering sharp, concussive blows to upper arms and elbows only when the battle's flow presented him with the opportunity. As fearsome as Ironjawz armour looked, it was almost always lighter there. It was a rare greenskin who understood the idea of joints, and so they tended to scrimp on armour in those areas. Even rarer was the Ironjaw who didn't want to flaunt its muscles to impress friends and enemies alike while it fought.

He bared his teeth as an extended swing crushed an orruk's bicep. The brute bellowed. With laughter, Braun thought, as orruks did not feel pain, and flexed his fingers. The Ironjaw bulled on into the Dozen with the arm hanging limp by its side, where Jenk then proceeded to carve it up with his knife. Braun headbutted another, sent it staggering back and knocking a lighter orruk off the parapet, then caught an incoming blow on crossed hammers and shoved the Ironjaw into Altin and Ragn, who pulled the brute down like a pair of ravenous dogs. With another savage roar, he swung with both hammers at the same time, beating an orruk so hard in the head that it twisted halfway around its trunk-thick neck. Woan stabbed the brute in the mouth to finally kill it.

They were a hard crew, his Dozen, and they knew better than most how to fight things bigger than they were. Using the dead orruk's chestplate as a step, Braun raised himself above the brawl and pumped both hammers in the air.

'For Sigmar!'

'*Braun!*' came the inhumanly deep rumble in reply, as though an old cave or a malevolent cliff had been touched by a god and granted speech. '*I is comin' for you, Braun!*'

Braun felt a chill like a head-first plunge into the River Izal. He wondered if he was dreaming.

Because he'd had this dream, or dreams very much like it, so many times before.

CHAPTER NINE

In Braun's memories, his visions, and in all his nightmares, Rukka Bosskilla had not changed at all in the ten years since their last battle on the Izalmaw. Braun had aged in those ten years. He was carrying a little weight that he hadn't been back then. He was a little slower, not quite as tough or as strong. The reality was a shock to his nerve. Orruks only grew more monstrous with age. They were rightly feared for it. They didn't ever stop until someone or something even bigger finally succeeded in killing them. The more fighting an orruk did, the bigger they grew.

And Rukka Bosskilla looked as though he'd been doing a lot of fighting.

The Ironjaw's armour was as Braun remembered it, monstrously thick, checked blue and white, the paint carrying over onto leathery green hide where whoever had wielded the paintbrush had got careless or carried away. The occasional ding or dent spoke of the years between Izalmaw and now, but it was the brute inside that had inflicted most of the changes, buckling the great heap of iron plate with his ever-expanding bulk.

Braun signed the hammer and backed as far away as the mob behind him would allow. This wasn't right. He'd seen the future and this wasn't it. If he was going to fight Rukka then Lisandr had to be here. That was part of the reason, the guilty part, that he had argued so hard that her place was in reserve.

'Kill him!' Braun roared, finding the space for one more step back as a horde of men charged past him.

Moments later they were all dead, decorating the snarling megaboss' armour.

Every Ironjaw that Braun had ever faced lived for the fight. They enjoyed it, celebrated it, praised the brutal half of their twin god, Gork, through it. When they weren't fighting, they were migrating to where their next fight would be, and fighting whoever was too stupid or too slow to get out of their way. Braun understood them. A part of him almost liked them. But it was what made them such monsters in battle. An ogor mawtribe or gargant stomp could be bought off. A Moonclan uprising could be discouraged, with enough soldiers and guns, but even total, overwhelming force wasn't enough to dissuade an Ironjaw from fighting, for the simple reason that they weren't trying to win anything from the fight beyond the satisfaction of the fight itself.

It meant you had to kill them all, and you *always* had to fight.

Rukka had been that way, back before Braun had killed his beloved maw-krusha, Facekikker, and broken his Waaagh! Now, there was a madness glowering from behind his wrought iron grille that Braun couldn't remember seeing there before.

Rukka wasn't here to have fun. He was *angry*.

'Fight me, 'umie!' the megaboss roared. His choppa clove another half-dozen men to pieces. All the Hounds in Goreham would not slow him down. 'Fight me like you woz too scared to fight me before.'

'Kill him!'

Braun backed up again, but there was nowhere left for him to go. The battlement walk was too crowded for him to get any further. 'Fifty thousand glimmerings and Ferrgin's place on the Dozen to whoever kills Rukka Bosskilla!'

There was nothing left in Rukka's way now but the Dozen.

Murdo was the first to meet him and the first to die. The megaboss' choppa clove through his neck and sent his body tumbling thirty feet to the bottom of the gatehouse ward. Braun swore. Jenk cursed the dead man's ghost and darted into the gap he'd left behind, looking to evade by keeping low, keeping close and keeping moving. The rest of the Dozen flowed after him, ducking, whirling, cutting, exhibiting an almost supernatural level of understanding to allow every comrade the room to land a blow or sidle away from the megaboss' ripostes.

Braun steeled himself, and then threw himself into the fight alongside them.

His hammer clanged into Rukka's breastplate. The Ironjaw didn't so much as stagger. Braun grimaced and followed through with the left-hand weapon. Rukka fought some flexibility into his knee joint to lower himself and watched the hammer pass over his shoulder and crunch into the wooden rampart. Pulp and splinters rattled across the orruk's spiked pauldron like grapeshot from tiny guns.

Rukka rose up from the ground, ramming Braun's open chest with his spiked pauldron. Braun beat the megaboss savagely about the head with the pommels of his hammers, only stopping when the charging Ironjaw slammed him against the rampart. The breath exploded from his lungs and he stumbled aside as Rukka stepped back. He wheezed, reeling away, feeling blood trickling, unseen beneath his armour, but the tough maw-krusha plate seemed to have held.

'I's gonna pull you outta dat armour,' Rukka growled. 'And then I'm gonna kick this castle down wiv all your boyz still in it.'

'Sigmar breaks,' Braun panted, clutching at his chest as he struggled to draw in a breath. 'And Sigmar rebuilds.'

Jenk cut in with his knife.

Rukka blocked with the broad edge of his choppa, then made a quick follow-up with the immense shieldlike plate of his forearm. Slayk piled in, landing a blow on the megaboss' helmet grille that knocked his head back. Rukka returned a blind swing that Jenk daintily slipped under, but which obliterated every bone in Slayk's jaw. The Ironjaw turned and kicked the reeling fighter in the shin. His leg snapped in two and the veteran fell, screaming, into an impotent heap at Rukka's feet.

The megaboss casually stamped on his stomach.

And then twelve, already made eleven, and then ten, became nine.

'Sigmar can get down 'ere and rebuild dat if he dares,' Rukka sneered.

'He's done it before,' said Braun, trying and failing to sound as though he believed it.

'He ain't doin' it now.'

'There's an army of his Stormcasts coming here.'

Rukka barked a mirthless laugh. 'Good.'

The megaboss shouldered his way through Jenk and Ragn, the diminished Dozen powerless to stop him, and sent his choppa looping towards Braun's head. Braun gave more ground, inadvertently backing into a man he never saw and sending him flailing from the battlement walk. The outsized orruk axe crunched deep into the woodwork, the Ironjaw grumbling as he paused to pull it out. Altin jumped in to stick his blunt knife into Rukka's knee-pit. The megaboss grunted and shrugged him off, the knife still sticking out of the back of his leg, and then idly toe-punted Kemrit over the edge.

Eight. The unholiest of all numbers.

Braun retreated, openly throwing glances over his shoulder for a way back off the wall. He had fought Grob Bloodgullet in single combat, and faced down worse over the years. But the thought of facing Rukka Bosskilla a second time made his muscles turn to water.

'Thinkin' of runnin'? Hah! You can run from me, but there ain't no runnin' from *him*.'

The megaboss delivered a low swing for the belly that, for all its unstoppable power, came in slow enough for Braun to dodge and counter. He swatted the choppa's blunt edge with his hammer and knocked the orruk weapon into the rampart. Then he stepped up, following in with an uppercut to the chin that would have crushed a man's neck, but which merely brought a gob of spit from the Ironjaw's mouth. The megaboss took a stumbling step back, startling Jenk, who'd been coming in from behind, and tramping on the man's foot.

The leader of the Dozen screamed as though he'd never felt pain before and didn't like it. For one little moment he wasn't paying attention, and that was the moment in which Rukka grunted, picked him up by the crown of the head, and idly tossed him over the parapet.

The expression on Jenk's face was, at first, disbelieving, then terrified, hands grasping at nothing as though he could *insist* the walls be nearer. He seemed to hang, eyes wide, mid-scream, fingers spread, before he finally fell, his despairing wail and final impact lost to the iron churn of greenskins below.

Braun gawped, numb.

Seven.

'Braun!' Rukka rolled out his shoulder and flexed the neck joint. 'I hasn't got all day. Anyfin' still 'ere when he gets 'ere is gettin' krumped and I want wot's mine.'

'Who?' Braun breathed, hardly daring to ask it aloud. 'Who's coming?'

Rukka's cracked lips split wide, but whatever it was that had so briefly amused him was forgotten mere seconds later.

With a piercing shriek and a snarl of lightning, Mother Thassily descended. The griffon sank its talons into the hardwood parapet as though claiming it for Azyr, lifted its long, kingly neck and reprised its ear-shattering challenge in even more strident fashion. Braun felt his heart soar even as blood trickled from his ears and he lost his balance, stumbling sideways into the high rampart. The warrior-pontiff held aloft her warhammer, energies summoning a lightning-blue halo that brought a tear to Braun's straining eyes, sporadic arcs of power turning towering Ironjawz into small heaps of molten slag.

'Rukka Bosskilla!' the pontiff's voice boomed. 'Sigmar passes judgement upon you. Prepare yourself to face sentence.'

Braun could almost see the red mist that descended over Rukka's eyes. The megaboss had always, even in the old days, harboured a violent hatred of everyone and everything that was bigger than him.

That was how he'd earned the name *Bosskilla*.

Braun launched himself at Rukka's back, a desperate lunge intended to simply wrestle the megaboss to the ground, before he could round on the pontiff, but the megaboss shrugged him off like an old coat, rounded on the pontiff anyway, then lowered his head like an enraged doombull and charged.

Mother Thassily swung underarm, discharging a lightning bolt that ripped through Rukka Bosskilla's ironclad torso. Every muscle in his gigantic body went rigid, dark green smoke boiling around the rivets in his armour, but through the sheer belligerence of his will he somehow forced his stiffened muscles to keep him moving through it.

The griffon squawked in surprise, and reared, raking its foretalons across Rukka's chest and snapping for the Ironjaw's head. Braun could only imagine that surprise stole from the killer instinct behind the warbeast's blows as its beak merely glanced off the top of the orruk's helmet. Its huge claws gouged deep into the megaboss' armour and dragged him in, whereupon Rukka, instead of allowing himself to be rent limb from limb, took the griffon's feathered neck in a headlock and roared.

The monster shrieked, beak clacking gamely, pounding its wings in a panic. Mother Thassily smote the Ironjaw's helmet with a lightning-imbued blow from her greathammer. Rukka shook his head and bellowed angrily back. The warrior-pontiff called down curses unbeknownst to lesser clergy upon the megaboss' stricken brow, and a halo of celestial lightning crackled into being around her while her griffon continued in its attempt to take wing. But Rukka had it by the neck like an iron collar with a grudge. Their struggle carried them backwards.

And then the three of them went over the rampart, the griffon's last desperate scrabbling tearing the battlement walk to shreds, dropping together like a rock.

Braun blinked.

The battlement was empty. Blood and human wreckage lay everywhere, matted with feathers. Rukka and Thassily had done a better job of clearing the wall than Braun ever could have, but it had cost him.

When Braun fought Rukka, it always cost him.

With trembling arm, he lifted his hammer above his head, barely able to breathe fast enough to keep up with his beating heart, never mind lift a weapon. He looked guiltily over the corpses of his Hounds, and found the strength to shout, 'Sigmar! We hold for Sigmar!'

'SIGMAR!' his Hounds returned.

Braun prayed for his forgiveness.

Earbug Glibspittle grimaced as a plume of bright orange shrooms billowed across the Bloodgullet wall and turned the wood black. His eyelid flickered as a band of Maneaters threw a rope between a projecting turret and one of the Bilgestomper Brothers and, goading the gargant back with meat and ale, gave a drunken cheer as the turret was wrenched from the wall. The stringy muscle of his jaw twitched as he watched the Bosskilla fall, trying to throttle a griffon like a right pillock, but his amusement dampened more than a bit when the griffon managed to take most of the parapet with it on the way down.

Years he'd spent, casting his covetous little red eye over Grob's place from across the Trample, dreaming of the day he'd be able to add to his Little Kingdom. Assuming he'd be able to get rid of the stink of gnoblar. Mork, but he hated the filthy friggin' gnoblars. Their fingers got in everything and they reeked.

But first chance this lot gets at the place and what do they go and do?

'Dey's gonna smash up da whole place,' he muttered.

Earbug saw nothing else for it. He was going to have to go in there and save the ungrateful lot of them from themselves. Stood up on tiptoes, on the rickety palanquin that distant, spider-worshipping ancestors had built across the enormous back of the Glossom Queen, he shaded his eyes from Frazzlegit and read the signs.

A horrible kind of ecstasy shivered through his bones as the enthusiastic Waaagh! of thousands of orruks and tens of thousands of screaming grots sent the fingers of the Clammy Hand running along his crooked spine. The swarm of lesser spiders that attended the Glossom Queen jiggled their bottoms and sang in reedy high voices. Even the Glossom Queen herself, a stately old lady above that kind of silliness, rhythmically flexed her limbs, colossal mouthparts chittering in tune to the Waaagh!

He was coming. *He* was almost here.

Earbug was touched by the Clammy Hand of the Everdank. As a yoof he'd been visited by the Spider-God in his dreams and been bitten. He could see the sticky threads of the realm web by which his god, cunningest and most brutal of all gods, would, when it was good and hungry, trap and devour all things.

He longed to turn, just for a peek: the avatar of the realms' destruction would be a magnificent sight, he was sure.

'I sees… a sign,' he said at length.

'Boss?'

Goonsplat, mounted on his own little spider, looked up at his boss from under his towering hat. Earbug pointed his sceptre towards the castle's walls.

'Now or never. It's time ta show dis lot 'ow it's done.'

Stretching himself up tall, a fine and impressive-looking grot, he gave the signal. And with a sound like the furtive rustling of sheets, the Spiderfang of the Deepenglade in their many thousands scuttled across the Eaten Plain.

The demigryphs tore up the cliffs that ran behind the Butchers' Quarter, clawed feet gouging deep into hardscrabble ground and over inclines that would have condemned even the lightest horse-mounted cavalryman to a steep fall and an early grave. The rocks reverberated to fierce shrieks and eager hunting caws.

The spider-riders higher up scrambled with ease over rock faces that would outfox even the sure feet of a demigryph, the grots straddling their backs loosing arrows from crooked bows as they went. One bent shaft struck the broad peytral plate that guarded the chest of Lisandr's mount, and snapped. Another hit her shield, the barbed head scratching her jaw as it broke off, the rest of the shaft skipping across her armour.

With a scowl she couched her spear.

The demigryph approached a jumble of impassable terrain and leapt, a chasm opening up in Lisandr's stomach as the monster soared, landing with a crunch onto a rock ledge that a spider-rider had been attempting to scurry around.

The celestial warbeast caught the spider by its hindmost leg and dragged it in towards it. The grot rider leapt clear with a screech, only for the demigryph to release the spider's leg, and with bird-like reflexes catch him in its beak. A savage jerk ripped the grot in half and sprayed Lisandr's half-plate swamp-green with its blood. At the same time, ignoring the distraction, she angled her spear down and thrust, impaling the giant spider through its back.

Three more scuttled in.

Reversing her grip on her spear, holding it in a flat palm over the shoulder like an Accari javelin, she launched it at the nearest rider. The spear took him through the chest, and he fell with a pathetic wail. Suddenly free, his spider bit through his leg at the knee and scurried back up the near-vertical cliff with its prize.

Lisandr drew her warhammer from its backplate mount. The remaining two broke off and circled her, one going left, the other right, stabbing low with their short spears. The demigryph kept moving.

A cavalry battle was never static: even for demigryph knights, tanks of flesh and blood and feathers, their momentum was their greatest strength.

Sheer mass and bristling aquiline presence forced one of the spiders to scramble out of the way. The spider was far too low to the ground, relative to Lisandr's high saddle, and she ignored the beast this time and swung for the rider. The grot capered nimbly to the other side of the spider's back, hooking the toe of his boot into a gap in the carapace, sticking out his tongue and throwing a rude gesture as the hammer sailed harmlessly wide, then laughing shrilly as the spider scuttled up the cliff face out of reach.

With his mount perched at a near-perfect right angle to Lisandr, the grot looked down and pulled a face.

Lisandr reined sharply in. There was no pursuing that particular grot and she would not be goaded. She looked around quickly and took stock.

A pair of knights were taking their demigryphs up the slope by the longer route, looking to circle the steepest part of the cliff and come at the Spiderfang from the other side. A dozen more, under Corporal Mestrade, rampaged on past where Lisandr had been before leaping the gap, scattering the spider-riders that had ventured that far down from the gnoblar tunnels and managing to run down and slay a handful of the slowest.

Back at the foot of the ascent, still within the Butchers' Quarter, Lydia marshalled the lower-ranking squires in a defensive cordon around the old cook pit where the Knight-Azyros still laboured, their tall shields bristling with grot arrows. Lisandr resolved that if either she, or her squire, survived long enough to cheer the arrival of Lord-Aquilor Farstrike to Fort Honoria and finally make their return to Excelsis as ordered, then she would see to Lydia Victoria's promotion to Celestian. The girl had more than earned it.

Just surviving that long would be a feat all on its own. Regardless of the number of grots that the Celestians were able to run off or kill, more kept pouring out of the gnoblar tunnels in the cliff face. If they were going to have any hope of stemming the flow, then they had to deal with those tunnels. And to do that they had to reach them.

Before she was able to do any more than frown at the impossibly steep ascent, she felt what she could only describe as an existential chill settling deep into her bones. There was a tremor, as though beneath the ground she was standing on was a mirror landscape in which something anathema to her existence scuttled towards her, and then past, the vibrations receding towards the Butchers' Quarter. She grimaced, the scent of dead spiders and long-decaying silks seeping out of the air, as she turned about in her saddle.

Screams rang out from the base of the cliff.

As Lisandr watched, something chitinous and black spun out its own existence, right in the midst of the squires' formation. Translucent spinnerets rippled and bulged, spewing out flesh and exoskeleton from the raw stuff of the cosmic aether, manifesting a segmented limb fused in glassy black carapace that shot out, skewered a boy's chest, and pinned him to the ground. The squire howled and struggled to pull the thing out of his lung, like a ghost trying to uproot its own gravestone. Lydia jabbed her half-pike at the sac of grave-dull eyes buried in the monster's head. It knocked the shaft aside on another rapidly forming limb, then punched her shield and knocked her down with another. A third limb impaled the woman through her hip bone, dragging her screaming up towards its snapping mouthparts, before hurling her contemptuously to one side.

Lisandr felt a small part of her heart break as the remainder of the squires broke and fled. She could not find it in her to blame them. Hauling her demigryph back around, she gave the beast its spurs. Mestrade and the others were already further up the cliff face than her. They could deal with the gnoblar tunnels. She would deal with this.

Ghur will make savages of us all, she thought, before pushing the intrusion aside. This was not for Lydia. This was not about vengeance.

She told herself that.

The demigryph issued a warbling shriek, then launched itself into a thunderous downhill gallop, Lisandr holding grimly on with her thighs as she gripped her warhammer with both hands.

The enormous spider scuttled about to face her. It was like no creature that lived, not even in the dankest and most misbegotten hollows of this realm. Its eyes were blank, dull as the black marble of a sarcophagus lid, and eerily unreflective. Lisandr saw nothing in them but myriad glimpses of herself: an old woman, tired and homesick, and well past due an honourable death in battle.

She screamed, barely coherent, and swung her warhammer right towards those eyes.

The power of a charging demigryph lent enough power to the blow to split the monster's carapace, several eyes bursting open and shedding what looked like mould. The monster issued a high-pitched squeal, like rusted nails being dragged across a pane of glass, and reared in pain. Lisandr recoiled, clapping her forearms to her ears, while her demigryph clamped its beak over the spider's upper foreleg. Chitin crunched under the demigryph's powerful bite, the spider sinking to its belly on that side as the demigryph partially mounted its back for better purchase. The spider stabbed and thrashed in a bid to wrestle itself free, two monsters pitting their strength against one another while Lisandr tilted the scales as best she could with another carapace-splitting *crack* from her hammer.

The spider gave another long shriek and wrenched its body away, leaving its torn leg to flop loose in the demigryph's beak. The celestial beast delivered a hoot of triumph, and rammed the reeling spider.

It fell back towards the Butchers' pit that Lydia and her warriors had been guarding, limbs tangling as it struggled to adapt to seven legs and resist the demigryph's attack. Lisandr saw the partially unearthed amberbone spike that erupted from the lip of the pit, directly in the spider's path. There was a *crunch* of ruptured armour, a wheeze of depressurising innards, and the spider screamed. High, loud, strangely feral. Not hurt so much as angry. Hungry. A berserk light fumed from its many eyes and, shaking itself aggressively loose of the amberbone spear, tearing open its abdomen and spilling floods of dust in the process, it threw itself bodily at Lisandr and her mount.

Her warhammer split the chitin armouring its head, snapping off one sword-length fang, but this time it ignored the injury, knocking her from the saddle and landing on the demigryph's back. The spider's weight drove the warbeast to the ground on its side, the monster sinking its remaining fang between the articulated starmetal lames that armoured the demigryph's neck.

Almost at once, the prince amongst beasts began to convulse, a river of poisonous-looking foam pouring from the nares in its beak and pooling in the oil-slicked rocks underneath it. It jerked, drowning. Its eyes rolled back into its head.

It was still.

'Die!' Lisandr screamed, dropping the warhammer as the spider abandoned its kill, as though unsure what to do with it now the life was gone from it, and scurried towards her. The hammer was a cavalry weapon, too unwieldy for a warrior of her stature to wield on foot. She drew her sabre, and shrugged the kite shield from her shoulder down onto her wrist.

The spider went through her like a Juggernaut of Khorne through a wall of sand, throwing her hard to the ground and winding her. Dazed, she hurriedly drew her shield back up and over her, hunkering behind it as the berserk monster hammered into it. In between the rain of blows, the wobbling shield, she saw the rabid frenzy in its eyes, the poisonous saliva dribbling from its mouth, the tuft of white feathers glued to its fang. Something in her arm went snap and she screamed as the next blow against the shield turned her whole body to fire. It would have been easier to drop the shield and just die, rather than endure, but the thought never made it through the gauntlet of pain, as though her own body did her that one terrible favour, better than the irredeemable act of shame that was the alternative.

Suddenly, and for no reason of her own doing, the blows stopped falling. The smell of burnt insect and ozone drifted around the bent rim of her shield.

With a moan, and the aid of her uninjured arm, she managed to heave the dented shield away from her and look up.

Knight-Azyros Horac stood over her, wreathed in snow and lightning, both of which seemed to emanate from his own long mane and beard, one sigmarite boot on the spider's side. He wrenched his starblade out of the monster's head.

'The skitterstrand arachnarok are being lured from the Graveyard of all Spiders in Shyish to the magic of the amberbone,' he said. 'Or possibly to the magic in me. Or maybe… *it*.' He looked east towards the wall. 'Maybe they are being drawn to him.'

'I'm just glad you came when you did.'

'I was finished,' said Horac, then bent down to claim the amberbone shard embedded in the skitterstrand's carapace. It came out with a crunch of chitin and a squelching of soft innards. 'And I came for this.'

Without waiting for a response, he ignited his wings and leapt. Lisandr could only scream after him, struggling to push the colossal dead weight off her shield with her broken arm as the tremble of insubstantial legs skittered ever closer.

The Eaten Plain looked as though it was moving, heaving like the Clawing Sea all the way out to the Cuspid Mesas. Not that Arden Shay had ever been on the Clawing Sea. She'd gone part way up the Mallus Spear, to the drilling platform she had helped design and build, had a hand in rebuilding the sea wall after the Vermyre business, and even overnighted in the lighthouse once or twice while sketching out the one she would construct for Bilgeport, but it occurred to her that she had never gone further out than the marina. She adjusted her spectacles on her nose with the old six-barrelled service revolver that she'd pulled out of storage.

This wasn't what she'd come out of retirement for. But here she was, watching spider-riding grots flood towards her like the sea she'd never seen up close. They covered the barren, thrice-pulverised landscape in chittering yellow bodies. They smothered the smouldering siege equipment left abandoned by their orruk and Moonclan kin, burying the corpses of grots and gargants alike with their numbers. The desultory crackle of gunfire and the occasional bloom of an Accari firebomb brought out the bitter yellow of their carapaces, the black segments coming to dominance as the fires guttered, drawing the creatures back into the shadow and nightmare to which such horrors rightly belonged.

Her throat ached with the cruellest thirst she could remember. The air was fire to breathe. Smoke stung her eyes. Her face was raw. Her clothing stank of sulphur and saltpetre and the tiny amounts of prophecy that the Excelsian Ironweld blended with their powder. Her ears bled. She was deaf but for the belching of the guns.

Bitterly, she rubbed at the back of her right hand with the fingers of her left. She did not know why. A phantom pain from a wound she did not have. The taste of prophecy tickled the back of her mouth.

Did not *yet* have.

The long line of handgunners spread out along the middle section of the east wall, with Chief Grint's troops and the gate to her left, and Chief Taal's band of horrors to the right. They reloaded in ragged sequence and fired, pops, crackles and bursts of smoke spreading along the parapet. A greatcannon boomed. Shay gritted her teeth. A moment later, a geyser of mud and spider-legs exploded from the plains. Several lighter pieces then opened up, taking Shay's numb ears and doing their utmost to concuss them. Rockets. Demi-cannons. Mortars. Shay could name them all. She had written books about them. Master gunners screamed into the din. Shay wondered who heard them, because she did not. Tapers fizzled. Everything was sound and a terrible chaos.

Where in the name of Grungni's Forge was Lisandr?

They couldn't hold against this. It was surely time to withdraw into the Gnarlfast. She thought about giving the order herself. With Braun and Lisandr missing, that probably left her with overall command, and she'd certainly seen more battle than either of those two combined. Even if the bulk of her experience had been over forty years ago.

Her lips froze over the 'R' of *retreat*, pincered around that consonant sound.

The Cuspid Mesas were trembling. The great hills were moving.

They were *getting out of the way.*

'Hammer and tongs…' she mouthed, as she laid eyes on the stag-like thing that came galloping through the new valley that the hastily withdrawing hills were in the accelerated process of carving between them. 'What in Grungni's blazes is that?'

Gesticulating as though the frantic spirit of a six-armed coward possessed her, battling simultaneously against a raging stitch up her side, she hobbled behind the thin line of handgunners to where a six-gun battery had been embedded in a temporary casemate at the end of the battlement. The master gunner was screaming at the crew of a volley gun, who in turn were struggling to dismantle the hot barrels of their piece. Shay pushed her way in to assist and scalded her fingers.

She swore, resisting the urge to blow on her hands. It would only make them sting more. The master gunner turned and screamed at her. He was three feet away and Shay did not hear a word. He might as well have been screaming down a well.

And then, all of a sudden, he stopped. His eyes rolled up, as though something had just unexpectedly landed on his head. They turned glassy, and the man slumped forward into the battlement. Shay gasped, noticing the crooked arrow sticking out of the side of his neck.

She swore.

Now it was the rest of the volley gun crew yelling at her. Shay could not figure out what they were saying, but she could deduce intention behind their words.

What is that thing?

'Kill it!' she screamed back, hoping that they understood, even if they could not hear. 'Fire!' Some of the smaller guns boomed. She saw a cannonball ring off the monster's shield. Another bashed the muscle of its shoulder, bruising it, and killing a large orruk outright when the rebound landed on its head.

If it could be bruised then it could be hurt. If it could be hurt then the Ironweld could hurt it.

'Feed it iron!' She bent down, pain splitting through her knees, hips and spine like hot needles, as she took up the taper rod that the gunnery commander had been holding in his hand. She lit it, and turned to the volley gun.

'The Hounds spoiled the reserves in the fighting,' one of the gun crew shouted in her ear. 'There's almost no prophecy left and we've been cutting the gunpowder too fine.'

She smiled reassuringly. She had built *cathedrals*. Tearing something down was invariably easier.

'All nine barrels,' she snapped. 'Bring that nightmare down.'

Barking out angles of adjustment, gauged purely by eye, she

brought the smouldering slow-match to the touch hole under the volley gun's side.

And never even felt the explosion that ripped the gun apart.

Horac raised his arm to shield his eyes. The explosion from the Ironweld positions ripped a twenty-foot-wide hole out of the thirty-foot-high walls, bits of wood and iron shrapnel spraying high into the air and dinging off the Knight-Azyros' armour, bursting into blue-burning motes of flame where they struck his wings. Spiderfang were already swarming the entire span of wall en masse, spilling only slightly faster through the recently blown-out section and scattering the Freeguild and Ironweld soldiers before them. The cries of men and women who had battled like heroes to deny the Ironjawz became screams as the charge of the grots finally broke them.

Horac swooped low, the clamour of hand-to-hand combat, of massacre, of rout, rising precipitously and then falling equally sharply as he punched through the pall of smoke that hung over the blasted wall, and out the other side. He yearned to stop there, to stand and fight and hold that breach, to save but one mortal life at the cost of his own. Such was the mettle from which the Astral Templars were forged. But he knew that the greater doom lay beyond the walls.

Colossally huge, the beast stampeded across the plain on four hoofed feet, crushing Spiderfang grots too slow in getting out of its way to ichorous paste and heedlessly barging aside anything larger. Similar, albeit on a godly scale, to something like a Kurnothi centaur or a shaggoth, its body above the waist became manlike, but with a bestial physique that existed nowhere in the human race. Its face was a fierce thing of prominent ridges and deep furrows, that of a great, antlered primate, and crowned by a mane of shaggy red fur. Fat rings pierced its ears and lips. Bracelets bedecked its arms. In one hand was a large round shield that dripped magicks as though it had been wrested from the bottom of an ensorcelled pool. In the other was a mace with a lump of beaten metal for its head.

A riotous cavalcade of beasts and monstrosities followed it out from the Mesas like an unruly train. A troop of Bonesplitterz shamans mounted on war boars led a great migration of troggoths, gargants, blinking cave squigs and other, rarer fauna of the Ghurish Heartlands that had overcome their phobia of open spaces and their mutual animosity towards one another for the instinctual need to follow *this thing* to wherever it intended to go.

As a Knight-Azyros, Horac had travelled more widely even than most Stormcast Eternals. He had stood in the presence of kings and queens and demigods. He recognised an exceptional power when he felt it.

This thing before him was a god.

The realisation brought a calm to his inner storm. Here, then, was the calamity that the seers of Excelsis had foreseen when they had called on Vagria Farstrike. For some reason, there was peace to be had in recognising his destroyer, and knowing that it was mighty.

Goreham and Honoria boasted but a fraction of Excelsis' strength. It was doomed. Horac could not save it. But it would be a glorious and heroic failure. One that would ensure the Six Smiths of Sigmaron worked doubly hard to reforge the broken pieces of Horac and the Farstrike Hunters if and when they finally broke free of the Cursed Skies.

Holding his sword aloft, the light of his wings and of his celestial beacon playing across the long blade, like flames trapped in molten silver, with a cry of challenge Horac dropped down to attack.

* * *

The Stormcast Eternal went down in flames.

He fell like a piece of metal from Azyr, burning up in Ghur's thick, moist air before hitting the ground, ripping a lightning-snarled crater out of the mobs of savage orruks and painted grots that swarmed around the Titan's fetlocks.

The beast did not even slow.

'The Trampler,' Taal breathed, digging into the oldest lore in his deepest memory, hazy recollections of old visions, the faded cliff-face drawings of his nomadic jungle ancestors, and the second-hand descriptions of children's stories. 'The End of Empires.'

Karze was dead. And Mawgren. And Kadd.

And Crodden, whose arms had yielded more sweat-beetles in a night than any man in Taal's mob, gutted by a grot spear. Chief Stavn had been netted and clubbed to death while his cousins broke for the stairs. Brodd was alive, just, but slumped on the ground and panting like a rabid thing in its last hours as Taal's lycanthropic magic failed his dying body.

Shay was dead and the Ironweld she had been commanding in the centre were broken and fleeing. Even as Taal watched, chewing on arraca-stained fingernails, he saw a horde of spiders surging through the breached wall to run them down. To their right, towards Taal's position, over the gate, Kanta's huge mob was crumbling too, fleeing before the oncoming Titan.

Even the Celestians were running.

Braun's flag was somewhere towards the opposite end of the wall, but Taal couldn't see it any more through the gunpowder smoke and the thick clouds of mushroom spores. He had no way of knowing if the general was still alive, and even less success caring. He wiped the sweat from his face on the heavy fold of his sleeve and banged his staff on the ground.

'This is holy ground.' The saurus skull chattered on its pole.

Spittle flew from his mouth as he screamed at it. 'Holy ground! The new home of the Accari!'

It didn't need a prophecy to know that the Farstrike wasn't going to be getting here in time to save them.

'Ezra!'

An amber-hued, intricately tattooed face turned from the crush at the parapet. A silver Celestian earring inset with a blue topaz winked in the bloody sunset, lending him a piratical bent that wasn't wholly out of keeping with his character.

'Just you and me now, chief.'

The Titan galloped on through the cannons and the lightning. It reached the gate and did not stop. It went through.

The gates exploded as though kicked in by the God-King. The neighbouring lengths of wall and platforms listed into the breach. The ground was shaking, an earthquake brewing. The whole city was coming apart.

'Chief?' Ezra asked.

Taal shook his head. This wasn't happening.

'Run,' he hissed.

CHAPTER TEN

Malec Grint found himself suddenly, and unexpectedly, glad for all the messages he had been made to run up and down the Gnarlfast. It had made him *fast*.

The gates were down. The walls were breached. Orruks were pouring through the Ironweld's reserve lines and into the city. A mega-gargant armed with half a ship and wearing what looked to be an entire whale as a cloak was striding purposefully up the main spoke-road towards the Butchers' Quarter. Men were dying everywhere. Grint took off down one of the branch roads heading north into Goreham, and he had no intention of doing it slowly.

'Malec!' someone called from behind him. 'Wait!'

There were eleven of them left. In addition to the half a dozen Hounds that his mother had pulled off the wall and succeeded in keeping alive, that number included two Celestians that they had adopted in the fighting and a bloody-headed signalman that they'd found wandering dazed through one of the tunnels. In no order whatsoever other than that Grint was well in the lead, they footed it along the scrambling, uphill trail.

In Goreham, perhaps, camouflaged by a thousand suspect odours and shepherded away by the barking of dogs, they could lose their pursuers and go to ground. But the Azyrites had already started remaking their half of the city according to Shay's neatly ordered plan. The roads were wide, and laid, and ready to be paved.

They were for cavalry.

'Grint!'

He glanced over his shoulder and cried out in alarm. A mob of savage orruks pursued them, thundering up the avenue on heavy boars, whirling bone clubs and stone choppas over their heads, the tattoos on their bodies glowing brighter and brighter as their excitement grew.

'We're not going to make it!'

Grint spun away, digging out an extra burst of speed. Ahead of them, grot spider-riders scuttled over unfinished rooftops, dancing agilely along beams and dropping into the road. A few with bows twanged arrows towards the fleeing soldiers. Grint screamed a curse. Somehow, the Spiderfang had got into the heart of the city even before the gates had been breached and the walls taken. That must have been why the Celestian reserves had never come, and why the survivors of Kanta's mob had been fighting running battles with them all the way through Honoria.

His legs wobbled at the thought of fighting them again now, and he almost let himself fall. He was sick to death of the whole battle. He just wanted it to be over.

'There!' Kanta barked.

Most of the buildings in the Celestians' side were unfinished, grand skeletons with maybe a wall or two and a roof. The one his mother pointed to had both, with a white-daubed exterior and a door. Grint spun back and crashed through the door. He held it open, gasping his breath back, while the others piled in behind him. Mikali was last. The woman turned and slammed it, ramming her shoulder into it and groping for the locking bar or bolt.

There was neither.

'Bastard Celestians,' she said.

Grint grinned on habit. 'Bad luck, Mikali.'

Mikali glared. 'Get me something to brace it, or shut up.'

Grint turned into the room. Kanta swore. The room was unfurnished, the smell of sawdust from newly cut floorboards hanging in the air.

'Did you think Azyrheim was built in a day?' one of the Celestians offered wearily. She did not look or sound the least bit offended. A shared and imminent doom seemed to have bonded Azyrite and Reclaimed, even Kanta, who would have broken the arm of anyone who used the word *Reclaimed* in relation to her, better than either of their commanders had achieved.

'There's no way out!' Grint wailed.

Kanta beckoned for her Greathammerer.

The big man called Gart hurried over. He was of average height, but with a powerful build, his upper torso rippling with muscles under an unsleeved vest. He'd not wielded the greathammer for long, but claimed to have always wanted to, and had taken the first opportunity that came along to lift one from a corpse in the street as they'd fled.

Something beat hard against the door.

Half the soldiers yelled. Grint screamed. Mikali was driven half an inch along the floorboards, her back still pressed to the door, and a long, hairy black leg forced its way inside. Without thinking, Grint slashed it with Sorl's axe. *His* axe. The spider shrieked and withdrew its limb, Mikali shoving the door hard back into its frame. The pressure on the door relented, supplanted by a light pattering that ran quickly up the wall and onto the roof.

They all looked up.

'We need to get out of here now!' said Grint.

'Gart,' said Kanta.

'Chief,' Gart grinned.

'Make me another door.'

Gart looked delighted. He spat on the hammerhead for luck, then sent it through the back wall. Levering the long haft vigorously he wrenched away the wooden lathes and kicked in anything lower than waist height. He cradled the weapon to his chest.

'I'm calling you Melis.'

The spider dropped on him from above.

Its black carapace was slashed with stripes of poisonous yellow, its rider bound in a burnoose wrap of shining silk. The grot's small red eyes burned with a passion, an aggression that went past what should've been normal for so cowardly a creature. As though he was drunk on breaking and killing. Would he wake up in the morning, Grint wondered, and look back on the rampage he'd run the night before with embarrassment and horror?

The spider bit through Gart's neck, arterial spray turning the back wall red, the dead man spasming as the spider struggled to swallow his head. Kanta roared, spitting out blood, blind with it, and swung her own greathammer. The blow stove in one of the spider's legs and dropped it, squealing, onto its side. The Celestian she had just spoken with earlier followed in behind, better protected from the spray by her helmet, and drove her spear through Gart's half-chewed head and into the spider's mouth.

It spasmed violently, flipped onto its back and died.

Grint ran out after the grot, but it fled and disappeared behind the rubble heap that the labourers had left at the back of the yard.

'Via Fortis Pyranon,' the Celestian panted, wiping her spear tip on the spider's belly, and flicking a spot of blood from the end of her nose, where it showed through the vertical slit of her helmet. 'An honour to fight alongside you, Chief Grint.'

A giddy shriek pealed out from above before Kanta could answer. Grint looked up, heart sinking towards his stomach at the rotund shape of the cave squig dropping out of the sky. A grot in flapping black robes clung to its gnarled hide, a huge grin cutting its narrow face in two.

'Squigalanche!' someone yelled.

The squig crashed through the roof of the house, everyone throwing themselves flat as dozens of the bouncing horrors hit the roof like a rain of cannonballs. Grint saw the confused signalman, still standing, take a flying beam through the back as the house collapsed around him. A shrill voice rang out *'Yeeeeeeee!'* and the lead grot launched his squig through the back wall and clear over the cowering Freeguild's heads. Grint scrambled away, overcome by terror, as squigs bounced in all directions. One of the Celestians lost an arm to gnashing jaws. Kanta herself got her ankle looped in a trailing lasso and was dragged, bellowing and cursing, into the air to the outrageous mirth of the Moonclan riders.

'Mother!' Grint screamed, scrambling up onto all fours to charge after her, even as he watched the squig herd crash through the roof of another building a hundred yards further up the hill.

Mikali yanked on his arm. Her face, showing a stunned despair that had gone through fear and way out the other side, must have mirrored Grint's own.

'She's gone!'

The woman tugged him the other way and, hunched under the ongoing barrage of splinters and bounding squigs, they left their comrades behind and ran.

They vaulted a fence, skirted the back of another unfinished building, found themselves back approaching the main east-west concourse from another angle – the mega-gargant kicking in a storehouse and laughing – then left it again at the last minute, skidding down a rocky revetment and landing in a heap in the Butchers' Quarter. This time it was Mikali who pulled him upright, and they fetched up together against the side wall of an old compost heap. Mikali threw up. Grint wasn't sure if it was the near escape or the old reek of the heap. It could have been either. When she was done, and could breathe again, she looked up at Grint.

'Do you think anyone else made it?'

Grint shook his head. Not because he thought nobody had, but because he didn't know. He thought of his mother and felt his eyes start to water. Sigmar, he'd hated that woman. He sniffed.

Mikali pushed herself up and looked around. 'Is this near to where Jenk took us on his gnoblar hunt?'

Grint shrugged. It felt like forever ago, and all the holes in the ground looked the same to him. He sat there against the compost heap, staring at nothing.

Mikali shook him. 'We need to move.'

'Move where?' said Grint.

'The tunnels,' said Mikali, gripping his arm tightly, as though cutting the blood off there would spare more for his head.

'The tunnels...' he echoed, thoughts bouncing off him rather than coming from anywhere within.

Before Mikali could make another attempt to shake him out of it, he was looking up as a unit of Celestians, six in all, clattered into view through the weird terrain of pits and mounds. Those at the front had their spears and shields up, those at the rear casting fearful glances over their shoulders as though expecting pursuit. At the sight of Grint and Mikali, sat down with their knees drawn up as though just sitting this one out, their leader pulled them up short. He was a thin, older man, with one weak eye and a grey pencil moustache. Grint dredged his memory.

Reregard. Corporal Reregard.

The man spluttered briefly, but before he had a chance to add words, one of his Celestians lowered their shield from their face. A confused jumble of feelings pulled away at some of the debris cluttering his head. A little light got in.

'Angellin?'

She squinted over her shield at him, and for a moment he had the awful certainty that she wouldn't recognise him. Wouldn't that just cap the day off?

'It's all right, sir,' she said. 'I know these two.'

'They look like deserters,' said Reregard, in no mood to be disabused of his first impressions.

'I'll vouch for them.' She wisely made no mention of the fact that she knew them from the punishment mobs.

'She knows me,' Grint murmured to himself.

'She knows me too,' Mikali hissed back.

'They are coming!'

The Celestians spun around, just as a giant spider came scuttling over an earth mound and slid down the near side into a warrior's shield. The impact knocked the warrior down, the spider rearing for the kill only to be fended off by a thicket of his comrade's spears. Arrows wittered down from above. A Celestian gurgled and fell, clutching at the arrow sticking out of the slit in her helm. Grint shaded his eyes as if a raised hand would stop an arrow, and saw a small group of grot riders squatting on a mid-sized heap topped with chalky mould, chortling to one another in high voices as they loosed arrows from wobbly bows.

Mikali scrambled round the compost heap for cover, while Grint scooped up what he thought was a large stone but which turned out to be a bit of hip bone, and hurled it back. The improvised missile cracked the side of a spider's shell. Its rider gabbled something furious and brandished its middle finger.

Then its head exploded.

Grint gawped as the headless corpse slid off the back of its mount, the startled spider scurrying away over the rooftop.

Efrim Taal limped up the path, favouring his unwounded right side, with his tall staff in one hand and a wand made from braided bone and bothered by hungry flies in the other. There was a look of determined hatred on his face – as though, if he were to let it go, he'd be letting go of life – as he hurried as fast as he could towards the other warriors. A group of Ironweld handgunners in padded jackets with iron plates sewn into the chests and backs followed him in, pausing to drop and aim, firepower ripping through the shallow gulleys and pasting the sides with chitin chips and yellow ichor.

The Ironweld, Grint could take or leave, but the appearance of one of Braun's Dozen left him feeling better than he had in hours. He thought guiltily of his mother, and pinched something from the corner of his eye.

Meanwhile, half the handgunners busied themselves setting up a perimeter, crouching, reloading, organising themselves impressively with Reregard's Celestians, while the rest bustled back the way they'd come. To get more guns, Grint hoped, or bigger guns.

'What are you Azyrites doing here?' Taal demanded of Reregard, by way of a welcome.

The Celestian seemed to debate inwardly over whether to salute and evidently settled against it. 'General Lisandr ordered us to sweep the Butchers' Quarter for the gnoblar tunnels that the Spiderfang have been using to get into the city.'

Mikali elbowed Grint in the ribs. 'The tunnels. I told you they were our way out.'

'What is this?' said Angellin.

'If that's the way they're coming in then that's the way we can get out,' said Mikali.

'But you aren't going to like it,' Grint added.

A distasteful look crossed Reregard's face. 'You would have us *run?*'

As if on cue, a terrific bellow shook the flank of the Gnarlfast, a cascade of gravel rattling down from above to hail over the rubbish heaps and the soldiers' helms. Somewhere not so very far away, something large and sturdy – the Accari's temple, perhaps – was being comprehensively destroyed.

'The city's finished,' said Taal, not arguing, just giving facts. 'The wall didn't stop that thing. The embankment you've got around Lisandr's tent isn't going to slow it down. The mightier has won its fight today. It's time for us to go, and fight again some other time.'

'Celestians,' Reregard announced, moustache stiffening. 'Do not retreat.'

A dangerous grin began to open Taal's face, but he caught it quickly and put it away. 'Have you seen it?' he said instead.

'Have I seen wh–?'

'It.'

The Celestian hesitated. Grint wagered he hadn't. If he had then he wouldn't have stopped to think about how to answer, but he'd have felt it. He had to. They all had now.

Taal turned to Grint and Mikali, the matter now settled to his satisfaction. 'You can find these tunnels?'

'Maybe,' said Grint.

'Yes,' said Mikali at the same time.

Grint looked at her.

'I was apprenticed to a tracker, back in Accar. I can find my way back, and if there's a way out, I'll find it.'

Grint realised how little he had ever cared to ask the woman about her past. In Accar, good trackers were as highly prized as

Greathammerers. It was their job to find where the arraca grew, mark out the safer routes through the jungle, and trap or drive off the more dangerous saurids before the picker gangs followed come morning. A good tracker was the difference between life and death. The best ate at the chief's right hand, and even the mediocre never had to pay for their own drinks.

He wondered how she had ended up in the make-up mobs. She really was bad luck.

'Then what are we still doing here?' said Taal.

'Wait,' said Angellin. 'What are *you* doing here? Weren't you on the wall when it fell?'

As she spoke, the departed Ironweld troopers returned, stretchering between them a horrifically injured woman. She was missing her right arm, and half of her face, along with most of her clothing, had been burnt off.

'Sigmar protect us all,' Grint muttered, and made the sign of the Shatterer across his chest. Like most Accari, piety had been beaten into him young.

It was Gunnery-Professor Shay. She was still breathing. From the look of her, Grint didn't expect that to stay true for long.

'Strength in numbers,' said Taal.

And behind him, a city died.

CHAPTER ELEVEN

The Farstrike Hunters formed up in a single file along the ridgeline.

Vagria had pushed them all day and all night, flying across the Thondian border country as if on wings. Regardless, the Palladors sat eagerly in their saddles, their exhausted mounts snapping irritably at buzzing flies or the merest suggestion of inattentive handling. It killed them to wait, but Vagria wanted the moment, to see the battlefield for herself before committing her brothers to die upon it. A hunter understood the virtues of patience. Even if she hated it. Kildabrae Heavenscar had always been the patient one. Her rock.

The ridge they had mustered along overlooked a shallow descent, one of the lower Mesas that faced west onto the Eaten Plain, too small to battle its way into the centre of the formation. The plain was littered with debris and dead, all the way to the gates of the ogor gluthold, which had been smashed open, the walls breached, burning, or so riddled with fungal mycelia that they had collapsed in upon themselves. Most of the greenskin force was still fighting inside the doomed stronghold, but handfuls of spider-riders pursued mortal soldiers across the plain, blowing them in the direction of the Mesas like brown leaves before a wind. A little further up the slope, a more coherent host had gathered together to fend off the Spiderfang harrying their rear. Handgunners and artillery crew were scattering as fast-moving spider-riders scurried around the mortals' formations, bugles sounding off in panic.

Vagria took her moment. She was by inclination a hunter first and foremost, not a battlefield commander, but her mind was sharp, bright as a lightning bolt, and she feared neither death nor pain. Nor defeat, provided it was glorious.

Her gaze lingered over the wreckage of the former glutfort and the contours of the plain: both possessed of a certain familiarity of aspect that she could not explain. As though she had been here before.

'Where is Knight-Azyros Horac?' said Pallador Oldro, beside her as always. 'I would have expected to find him with the larger group, marshalling their withdrawal until our arrival.'

Vagria nodded, but there were too many ways for a hero to fall in battle to account for them all. She had even conceded the possibility that Horac may not even have made it to the gluthold at all.

Brendel Starsighted and the Prosecutors of Prime Artros' retinue crunched down onto a jutting promontory, ridged like an enormous eyebrow, that overlooked the Palladors' position on their right. The Knight-Venator raised a hand and waved to Vagria. His long hair, dark and worn in braids, chattered with the voice of bone ringlets on his armour. His face was painted in a pair of vertical, purple stripes, and bore its usual ill-tempered grin.

'Head back into the Mesas and round up the rest of the mortal host.' Vagria had passed several small bands of mortal soldiers, crawling out of concealed foxholes and fleeing into the hills, stinking like an ogor's discards. There must have been thousands, all told, but scattered, and she did not have the time to rally them all. 'Bring them back here. We may yet have need of them if we mean to retake the city and slay the godbeast within.'

'That can wait until after the battle.'

'Battle?' Vagria gave a laugh, struggling now to restrain Starsid, who had been still for all of five minutes and was chomping at the bit to run. 'This is not going to be a battle. Fly, Starsighted, and rest assured that you are missing nothing of note.'

'Do not battle the godbeast without me.'

Vagria threw the Knight-Venator a gruff salute as, with little snaps of lightning, he and Artros' Prosecutors took to the skies. She watched them climb, separating like fingers uncurling from an electric fist and disappearing into the Mesas.

They had all spent far too long on this hunt already. The Astral Templars were great warriors, but with a natural proclivity to get on one another's nerves.

'Good hunting,' she murmured.

The mountainous stump that her map called the Gnarlfast, a hunched castaway of the Krondspine Range to the north-east, brooded over the pall of destruction cloaking its feet. The sounds rumbling through it reminded her of the storm quarries that orbited the Mallus, or their lesser cousins in the prophecy mines of Excelsis, the preternatural roar of smashed and obliterated stone. Vagria shivered as though something were calling to her, challenging her. Her body moved as though it understood and answered.

She gave a sudden, rising yell.

There had not been a prearranged signal, but every Pallador in her chamber recognised it as one. Starsid shrieked, and leapt from the ridgeline as though he could fly. Vagria's stomach took off with him, coming back to ground with a lurch as the gryph-charger's long talons touched down, digging deep into the loose slope, and swept them downhill. The Vanguard-Palladors of the Farstrike Hunters gave chase, running so swiftly that they rode at the crest of the avalanche that their own charge had triggered.

Mortals in the red and grey of the Excelsian Ironweld flashed past them. The keen-eyed chargers bounded agilely between the fleeing groups, passing through them before even the Palladors became aware of the innocent obstacles in their path. Others were still running the other way, downhill, to join in the fight at the foot of the slope, and were swiftly overtaken and in many cases blown right off their feet by the charging Palladors, as if by the wind itself.

Vagria leant forward, teeth bared, relishing the sensation of careening down a hillside and into danger at breakneck speed. A fierce wind blustered through the eyeholes of her Mask Impassive and numbed her face. Corposant lightning crackled around the flutes of her armour as Starsid gathered charge from the winds.

The battle lines drew close.

The Freeguild never even saw their saviours coming. There was a *crack*, as reality surrendered to raw speed, and the Vanguard-Palladors took to the winds aetheric. The human soldiers became smoke. To the mortals themselves it must have appeared as though a sheet of lightning had just rippled across them, warrior-shaped after-images flickering across their vision perhaps, before the Farstrikes lurched back into the physical constraints of Ghur on the other side of the line.

A gigantic yellow-and-black spider reared up in Vagria's face. She cried out, pulling dazedly on the reins as Starsid jinked at the last minute from under the spider's fangs. Half-blind, tears of speed still glazing her eyes, she fired her boltstorm pistol, winged the spider's carapace and blasted the grot from the creature's back. There was a reason that Palladors did not routinely charge straight into battle from the winds aetheric. The sudden shifts were disorienting, to both the mount for whom they were second nature, and the rider for whom they were not, and the effort was particularly daunting for the beast. But it had been a long chase, and Vagria was feeling particularly reckless about getting to its conclusion. She whooped and reloaded.

The rest of her chamber were breaking from the winds aetheric behind her and careening into the greenskin line, shots going off with staccato *bangs*, barks of blue smoke and muted snarls of lightning. The grots' hasty return of bow fire clattered off sigmarite warplate that was as good as inviolate when set against such low-grade projectiles, or were bitten straight out of the air by the lightning-quick jaws of the gryph-chargers themselves.

Vagria took a big, joyous lungful of that rancorous air. Thirty seconds of contact with the Farstrike Hunters, and the all-conquering hordes of the Spiderfang had been put to rout. It felt good to be doing what she had been made to do, killing foes that mortal forces lacked the means to kill, dying if need be so that they did not have to.

She reined in. With much straining at the bit and, after failing to twist around far enough to nip at her hands, Starsid deigned to be slowed. Vanguard-Palladors continued to flash ahead of her, loosely marshalled into retinues under Raukos and Columna. The soldiers of the Freeguild broke eagerly from their battle lines to support the rout, as mortal soldiers always did when Stormcast Eternals took to the field beside them.

By every right she should have been an absolute terror to mortal eyes. Half again the size of the largest man, baroquely armoured and hung with pelts, masked and faceless, ribboned by otherworldly energies and blessed with uncanny powers of perception. And yet she found that she did not terrify, but inspire. She wished she understood it.

The bulk of the rabble – and a rabble they were, though Vagria did not disapprove – were outfitted in sleeveless leather tunics, painted with red slashes to impart a sort of order, and armed with a rough collection of hunting tools. A second group, smaller in number and tighter in formation, looked almost as well equipped as Stormcast Eternals. Their armour and weaponry glittered with meteoric metals and precious gems, and with the faintest of brushes with the same powers of the Storm Eternal that imbued Vagria and her kin with their gifts.

Vagria knew which of these warriors she would rather have beside her in battle, and she knew which she would rather celebrate victory with afterwards. And they were not the same.

A thick-necked mortal male with the attitude of a leader approached her with a group of four large, but shaken-looking men close behind him. He was impressively proportioned for a human, bald-headed, muscular, matted with hair and scarred by war. A tattoo that was a fair enough representation of Ghal-Maraz for one who had never seen it lent his brutish appearance the slight uplift into zealotry. His torso was sheathed in maw-krusha leather, which impressed Vagria even more. It was a hard material to get hold of, for obvious reasons, and there were not many armourers in the Mortal Realms with the skills needed to cure and work it. He looked up at her, chest heaving from his recent exertions and, though respectful, did not appear quite as overawed by the encounter as Vagria was accustomed to expecting.

Her eyes narrowed behind her mask. 'I am not the first Stormcast Eternal you have seen.'

The mortal shook his head. 'Two days ago, another came. He told us you were coming.' He jutted his chin out.

Vagria felt the stranger whose face she wore smile. She loved the mortals when they were angry. There was something adorable about their passions.

'You're late.'

'I would like to have seen you cross all the country between here and the Morruk Hills in less than a week,' said Vagria. 'Now tell me, where can I find the Knight-Azyros. I would speak with him before I ride to slay the beast.'

'He's dead,' the man grunted.

The words pierced her. She had imagined that Horac's demise was possible, but had not considered that it would move her. Not after she had shed no tears for Kildabrae. Her hand moved to her mask, as though purple sigmarite might weep. She prayed for their safe return and eventual Reforging – or if not, grand new adventures in the underworld of their desire. The Mortal Realms would not see more heroes like them in this age.

Turning away from the mortal, she faced the hulk of the Gnarlfast once more. The sight brought a tingle through her bones.

An anticipation. A prophecy of doom.

'Then I suppose I will just have to speak with you.'

By the time Knight-Venator Brendel Starsighted returned with three mortals in tow to where Vagria had been waiting for him on the Mesa it was almost dawn again, the sun bleeding like a sacrificial heart into the dust haze of the Eaten Plain. The air had become clammy, the crash and grind of destruction continuing to ring out of the city and sink, unremarked, into hills that had themselves fallen quiet.

Bidding the humans to wait, Brendel walked towards her. His unlit wings were a skeleton strung across his back, rattling out a dead note with every stamp of his boots on the rock. The eagle, Eliara, was nowhere to be seen. It was possible she was taking advantage of the lull to hunt, though Vagria fancied it more likely that she was scouting the east wall of the city with Prime Artros and his Prosecutors, loaning the Knight-Venator her eyes even if

Vagria insisted that he be physically present here. A small act of rebellion that Vagria thought it best not to discourage.

It was the small acts that kept them all sane.

'I have been here for hours,' she said.

'They took some finding,' he grunted, which was all he had by way of an apology, then turned away from her, unfolding his arms from his breastplate and beckoning for the mortals to approach. 'Ellisior Seraphine Lisandr,' he said, indicating a tall, severe-looking woman.

Her long white hair was held tight in a ponytail with filigreed hair claws, the blessings engraved into her blued armour managing to shine through in spite of its recent travails. She had a dazed look, as though Lisandr was no longer entirely at home. Her arm was in a sling.

'General of the First Age Starhold Celestians,' Brendel finished, already waving his hand disinterestedly towards the next. 'Casius Braun, you know. General of the Accari Hounds.'

Vagria inclined her head slightly. The Accari general had wiped his face, but otherwise looked as unashamedly barbaric as he had on the battlefield.

'The Casius Braun who halted Waaagh! Bosskilla at Izalmaw. I should have recognised you, but when you live for as long as the Starsighted and I, you expect the heroes you have heard of to be dead.'

Braun gave a non-committal shrug, looking anywhere but at her expressionless mask.

Brendel signalled impatiently for the next, all too aware of the beast still at large in the city before them. This was a much older woman, bird-thin and wan, and missing half of her face. The other half was scaly with burnt, black skin. Her right arm was a shredded bit of sleeve. From the way her right shoulder periodically tensed, moments before her left hand rose to do something, it seemed to have been her favoured one.

'Gunnery-Professor Arden Shay of the Excelsian Ironweld,' said Brendel.

'Damn it, Brendel, this woman is dead on her feet. Get her a chair to sit on.'

'What am I?' The Knight-Venator performed a perfunctory shrug in his massive armour. 'An inn?'

'Just do it. And be quick.'

Brendel bowed, with exaggerated courtliness which he had no doubt read about in a book, and stalked off in the direction of the Freeguild camp.

A quarter of an hour later, during which Vagria pressed the three on the small details of their time in the gluthold that they had renamed Goreham and Honoria, the Knight-Venator returned. He bore an ordinary oil lantern, which he set on a rock and, as though the Labours of Behemat had never been so stern, saw the mortals seated on upturned boxes and supplied with refreshment. Then he retreated to the edge of the light, arms crossed like a winged ghoul.

For herself, Vagria squatted down on the bare rock. Over a standing mortal she would loom. Before a seated one she would have towered like a demigod.

She decided to get right to it. They had all been waiting long enough.

'I am here to kill the godbeast. I aim to do it before he leaves your city and his scattered host rallies to him. I hope to have your help.'

Braun watched her warily, chewing on something pungent that stained his teeth brown and waiting for someone else to speak first. Lisandr merely looked through her. Even Shay appeared more focused, and she looked half a step from unconsciousness.

The engineer licked her dry lips. 'How can we help you?'

Vagria thought where to begin. Where, but at the beginning?

'It is rare for the Astral Templars to come together in a force as great as this one,' said Vagria. 'Rarer still for us to remain together for as long as we have been, hunting this new thing across Thondia and Gallet. The White Reaper himself sent messages to the Templia Beasthall, begging that I find and kill the doom that has been foreseen for his city. The gods war for the Mortal Realms. Nagash has been vanquished in Hysh. The goddess Alarielle spreads her bowers across the wider realms. Morathi advances long-held schemes and the daemon-king Be'lakor burns the skies. Stars perish and new, hungry constellations are being born. Even in Azyr, the dragon ogors stir again in their mountain fastness.' Lisandr roused herself at that, but her eyes were dead and she said nothing. 'The rise of a new god in Ghur is the least surprising news I have heard of late.'

'It would be my honour to fight alongside the Astral Templars,' Braun growled, thumping his leather breastplate with the meat of his fist.

'Do you have a plan?' said Shay.

Vagria shrugged. 'I fight it. Then I kill it.'

Braun looked as though he wanted to laugh but didn't quite dare.

Lisandr stared at her glassily, as though addressing a ghost. 'Our orders were to withdraw to Excelsis.'

'Who gave you those orders?' Vagria asked.

'High Arbiter Synor.'

'I am not sure if I outrank a High Arbiter or not, but I doubt this Synor would dare countermand me if he were here.'

'We are needed in Excelsis.'

'*I* need you *here*.'

'It can't be killed,' said Lisandr, her voice cracking as it rose to a shout.

'You're talking to a Stormcast Eternal,' Braun reminded her quietly.

'It killed Knight-Azyros Horac,' Lisandr replied. The Accari hung his head and did not argue.

'There are not many things in the Mortal Realms that I have not hunted,' said Vagria. 'Do you believe, General Lisandr, that I cannot defeat this monster? I ask honestly, so answer truthfully.'

Lisandr thought a moment. 'No. No, I do not believe you can.'

'And yet I can see for myself that the godbeast has already dismissed or broken most of its horde,' said Vagria. 'My plan, such as it is, is to lead my chamber into the city and strike at the beast. We can be in quickly, and at its throat before any creature currently at large on the plain can react. But if the monster is half as powerful as you claim it is–'

'It is,' said Lisandr.

'If it is that powerful, then I will need someone to hold the greenskins' attention while we slay the beast.'

'You want… a distraction?' said Lisandr.

With one arm on his heavy thigh, Braun turned towards the Celestian commander. It looked as though he wanted to say something, but the presence of a Stormcast Eternal made him settle for a look. The Celestian shrugged and said no more. She looked defeated already. That was not good.

Vagria wished for Horac, or even for Kildabrae. Either of those two would have drawn the mortals out and had them eating from their hands. The Knight-Azyros had had the divine gifts for it and, more importantly, the patience. The Knight-Vexillor had simply had that rare love of people. Vagria did not have the knack.

'What she means,' said Shay, her voice frail, 'is that you ask a lot from us. More, perhaps, than one of the God-King's immortals could understand.'

Vagria threw a glance at Brendel, but the Knight-Venator was already looking at her.

What to tell them? How much to withhold?

Vagria sighed. She hated secrets. If she kept them better than most it was because she could go so long without seeing anyone. 'I cannot promise you a Reforging, it is true. No one can. Perhaps not even Sigmar himself.' Vagria frowned, holding her hand up in front of her mask and losing her track, for a moment, in an appreciation of how solid it appeared, how strong, and yet ultimately how impermanent. A thing of lightning and aether, without past and without future. A creature of the raging present. 'No fallen Stormcast has found their way back to Sigmaron since Be'lakor's cursing of the skies.'

Lisandr blinked, the revelation as effective a purgative as a bucket of ice water. 'What?'

'Horac advised me to take the threat of a real death as a lesson. To adapt. It is advice I am delighted to see he ignored in facing his own end, and I intend to do the same. Because I am an Astral Templar, and I will throw away all that I have for the sake of the cause, in whatever foolhardy manner that *I* choose.' She beat her hand against her breastplate to enunciate her conviction. 'So if we ride now – and with or without your warriors, rest assured that we ride now – it will be under the same shadow of death as you. I will slay this monster. I will slay it because it is what Sigmar long ago called me to his hall to do. And because better heroes than I have already sacrificed their immortality to give me this chance.'

Arden Shay shifted on her upturned box. She looked apologetically towards the Celestian general. 'Ellisior is wrong. It can be hurt. I saw it hurt. A hit from a demi-cannon, right here in the chest.' Her right shoulder tensed. A painful half-second later and she hesitantly lifted her left hand to her breast. 'It felt it. I saw its skin bruise and heard its pain. It's like anything else in the realms. Hit it hard enough, fast enough, and it can be hurt. It can be killed.'

Vagria raised her empty hands to the others, entreating. 'All I am asking from you is a few minutes. Pin the orruks long enough for Brendel and I' – she nodded to the monkishly silent Knight-Venator – 'and the full strength of the Farstrike Hunters to destroy this godbeast once and for all.'

'We waited for you already,' said Lisandr quietly. 'You did not come.'

'I am here now,' said Vagria. 'And I need your faith. In me, as well as in each other, and in Sigmar. For just a few minutes.'

Braun and Lisandr shared a look, one cagey, one fundamentally broken in spirit, as though to gauge which of them would break first.

'Can you give me that much?' said Vagria.

Lisandr sighed and lowered her head. 'When Sigmar commands, the First Age Celestians are always ready. Whatever you ask for is yours, Lord-Aquilor.'

Braun shrugged. 'When?'

Vagria smiled behind her mask. Somewhere, wherever their souls now flew, she knew that Horac Long-Winter and the Heavenscar would be proud.

'Right now.'

CHAPTER TWELVE

The Accari Hounds advanced across the Eaten Plain by starlight and, for Braun at least, with no little déjà vu. The once familiar landscape had been transformed by the passage of the godbeast. A great trail of broken earth led all the way from the Mesas to the gate like a duardin highway, the complete destruction of Goreham and Honoria creating a fog of talc that turned everything the colour of bone. Before, they had charged across this plain in a fury. Now they skulked. Like dogs. Drawn by the collar to have their noses rubbed in their mistake.

Braun coughed, tightening the silk kerchief he'd borrowed from Lisandr around his face, and continued on. It had belonged to somebody called Aubreitn. Giving it up had seemed to mean something to Lisandr. He coughed again, in spite of the kerchief, squinting towards the play of dust and starlight on the plains. The knot of anticipation grew heavier in his stomach. Was that movement ahead of them? Or just the wind, blowing dust across the rocks?

Braun hated this plan. The Hounds were a light infantry regiment, and they had been decimated already. The Dozen had been reduced to six, including himself, and barely a quarter of the eleven thousand men he had led in defence of the city were marching with him. Rukka's Big Rukk, on the other hand, even without the megaboss himself to lead them, assuming his fall with Mother Thassily had slain him, were some of the heaviest troops in Ghur. Worse still was the gut-knowledge that something far worse was out there, in the city, hidden in the gloom and the dust, ready to destroy them all should Vagria fail.

He closed his eyes and looked up, still walking ahead, uttering a silent prayer of forgiveness for his lack of faith. Vagria would not fail.

Braun had turned to the God-King after the destruction of the Wildmen by Rukka's Ironjawz, and Sigmar had never failed him. No, Sigmar had chastened him with the taking of Jenk and Kanta and Murdo and Slayk and Kemrit and Ferrgin. As he had done before with the taking of his regiment, and his failure to kill Rukka at the first attempt. As Taal was always reminding him, the Azyrites always forgot that Sigmar was a barbarous god, the warrior-king who'd fought the greenskin god to a standstill, and then celebrated his brother god's feats in a month-long debauch from which parts of the Ghurish Heartlands still bore the scars. He was not a gentle god.

The God-King had roughed Braun over. He had bloodied his lip, blackened his eye, broken a bone or two, no worse than he had given his own Dozen over the years. And now he watched.

Would Braun take his beating lying down? Or would he stand up and give some of it back? Would he aid the God-King's champion in the beating of this pretender to his Ghurite crown?

Braun hated this plan, but he'd do it, for Sigmar, and resolved to thrash any man who did not profess to love it.

And at least this time Rukka was truly dead. Even that brute could not cheat the God-King a second time. Could he? But then, if the vision of his fight with Rukka had not been of Goreham and Honoria, and there were too many differences for him to hold onto the belief that it was, then surely he was destined to fight the megaboss a third time. Perhaps here? He resisted the urge to put his hand in his pocket and find the answer in prophecy. He could not afford the distraction, and the purity of prophecy that he would have needed just wasn't there.

And, in truth, he didn't want to know.

'Sigmar,' he muttered, advancing through the fog at a steady run that any Accari could keep up for hours. 'The god who bettered all gods. Lend me strength.'

The muted sound of approaching cavalry came up from behind, and he turned his head, privately hoping for a glimpse of the Lord-Aquilor to raise his Hounds' spirits before the fight. But it was only Lisandr with a half-strength unit of demigryph knights. Their silver harnesses and claws had been bound in cloth to muffle the sound they made on the rock.

The majority of the Freeguild who had escaped the destruction of the city had done so through the gnoblar tunnels, which meant that most of the surviving Celestians had been forced to execute their warbeasts rather than leave them behind. Half-strength units were all Lisandr could muster now.

The Celestian general brought her column to a slow walk to match the Accari infantry's pace. She had obtained a new set of weapons, and a shield, but wielded neither, her broken arm stiffly packed into a herbal cast of Taal's recipe. It reeked, but it worked.

'Here we go again,' she said. She smiled, but there was something broken behind her eyes.

They'd had their disagreements, more than they'd had agreements, but Braun knew the pain of losing a regiment, losing a battle, and it wasn't one he'd wish on anyone. Not even Azyrite royalty. The priests instructed that a man's defeats taught him more than his victories, and as one who'd tasted plenty of both he could say with certainty that it was true, but he wondered if it wasn't beholden on the priests then to come up with something better.

What else were priests good for?

'One last time,' said Braun, signing the hammer in the dark. 'For the God-King.'

Lisandr nodded, saying nothing either way, then clicked her tongue and pulled her heavy knights back into a canter.

'One last time,' he muttered.

If he survived this battle and made it home to Accar, then he swore he was going to retire.

Rukka kicked at a wall. His foot went through it, cracks spidering through the plaster as if to get ahead of his mashing toe. Rukka bared his fangs at the pattern it made, thinking of the clever omens that Weird Wurgbuz or the Shady King would see in it. Here was an omen for it…

Spittle flecking the inside of his grille, he kicked it again. The wall fell in, then the roof, wooden beams clattering over Rukka's shoulders, and he grunted in the warmth of a job well done.

The other bosses just didn't get it. The Godboss wasn't here to conquer. He was here to trample and stomp, to smash everything he found into its littlest bits until there was nothing of the man-god and his Order left in the Heartlands. And then smash it a bit more. For the fun of it. Aside from Rukka's Ironjawz, it was only the Bonesplitterz who seemed to properly 'get it'. The savage loons capered around the Godboss' enormous hooves, offering up the hardest bits of their biggest kills and the amberbone they'd dug up from the old Butchers' pits, both of which seemed to please him greatly. The Big Rukk, meanwhile, the green of their tough hides turned white from brawling in the dust, fought each other and broke stuff for his approval.

Rukka went looking for a bigger building to kick in. He'd ape the Godboss, do as the Godboss did, become as big as the Godboss had got by doing it, and then he'd hit the Godboss in the face and *be* the Godboss. It all made for a perfect kind of logic in his mind.

It was why they called him the Bosskilla.

Growling instinctively, he turned his face towards the wind that blew in off the dust-fogged darkness of the plain. Weird shapes seemed to be riding on it, the hint of a flash boss in purple and gold armour, riding on a wingless bird. It passed through him, spook-like, and disappeared, just a wind again, and then even that died away to a limp breeze and the scent of fresh rain. His nose wrinkled, a fizz of little lightning bolts frolicking like drunken loons between the iron bars of his grille and snapping at his tusks. He bit for one and missed.

'Wozzat?' Guntstag sniffed, jutting his helmeted face belligerently towards the Mesas.

'Gork,' Rukka growled.

'Gork,' said Guntstag, tasting his boss' reasoning and finding it good.

Rukka banged his armour with the flat bit of his choppa. 'Gork!'

'*Gork! Gork! Gork!*' the boyz roared approvingly.

Rukka lifted his pug nose to better taste the breeze. It smelled like fighting. It smelled Gorky. He gripped his choppa fiercely.

Now the Godboss would get to see how someone properly green got things done.

Vagria gusted out her last breath from the Eaten Plain… and sent it billowing through the chalky fog of the Butchers' Quarter. Starsid gave a quiet, stalking chirrup, the residual lightning of the winds aetheric rippling through his plumage. Answering calls, sounding like the vulcharcs and ghyrlacs on which the wild chargers preyed, sounded from the haze. The occasional glint of gold barding or bared starmetal, the match-strike of lightning from white feathers, was all she had to pinpoint her brothers and sisters in the night-time darkness and murk.

She gave a soft cry of her own, announcing herself and her position to the chamber while simultaneously spurring Starsid to keep up his pace. Bits of rock hit her at the relative speed of a bullet from a handgun, pinging loudly off her armour. She squinted so as to better shield her eyes behind the slit-holes of her Mask Impassive, loosening her figure on the trigger of her boltstorm pistol.

Still nothing.

Lisandr and Shay had described the layout of the city for her. Braun had been equally willing, but less certain of his details. Vagria found that her subconscious was more than able to fill in those details for itself. The feeling of familiarity that she had experienced while looking down upon the city from the Cuspid Mesas, she felt again severalfold now that she was here. It was as though she were returning home.

The Accari had constructed their settlements in the wards to the south, the Azyrites to the north. The gated entrance faced east, with the entirety of the city backing onto the Gnarlfast, to the west. The Butchers' Quarter sat in the middle, a hole in the ground like an open quarry, devoid of buildings except for a handful of rusty, half-ruined cookhouses left behind by the ogors themselves. The earth there was cracked open, just like the ground outside had been, glowering masses of amberbone thrown up by the old Butchers' pits winking like cats' eyes in the murk.

The occasional orruk grew out of the fog, cloaked in so much powdered gypsum that only their unsubtle physiques gave them away as orruks rather than Accari survivors lost in the devastation. They seemed to be gathering up the crumbs of amberbone that

Horac had left behind and paid little attention to the Farstrike Hunters until it was too late. The muffled crack of boltstorm pistols sounded against the haze, splashes of green soaked up by the dusty white, and the Vanguard-Palladors thundered past, unchallenged.

A shape began to emerge out of the distance. Bigger than an orruk. Much bigger. Vagria's first thought was that she had arrived at the Gnarlfast. Nothing living could be so huge.

Her first thought was wrong.

The bull-like giant loomed over the Butchers' pits, resting in a bed of fragmented amberbone in the lee of the mountain. A mane of earthy red hair cascaded down its broad trunk to splay across the verdigrised bronze armour of its hindquarters. In one fist it gripped a mace around which the air itself appeared to thicken, the dust drawn into the shape of a mouth and consumed. In the other was a tooth-rimmed buckler that Vagria would have struggled to reach across with her arms fully spread. The godbeast smelled of wet fur, of sweat, of panting breaths after a long chase, so primal and powerful that Vagria felt an uncomfortable shiver down her back and knew for a certainty that there had once been a time when she had known what it was to be hunted.

It was larger than the mega-gargant who had dispatched Kildabrae in the Morruk Hills. The power it exuded as effortlessly as a pheromone scent surpassed altogether the spirit of the Serpent River. The only comparisons she could draw on in her mind came from stories. Tarsus Bull-Heart and his battle with Nagash. Gardus Steel Soul and his embassy with a wrathful Everqueen. Thostos Bladestorm and his fateful duel with Archaon the Everchosen.

Vagria knew how those epics ended.

She pushed away the faintest, novel tremor of doubt. She was Vagria Farstrike, the foremost hunter in a host of storied hunters. If she was going to die then she could think of no better time or place.

The god gave a rumble as Vagria and her Palladors charged towards him in a wave moving at the speed of sound. His antlers scraped the dusty ceiling of the Butchers' Quarter as he rose from rest, his beard flaring around a bestial mouth.

'I smell the breath of Dracothion in you.'

His voice was the tectonic growl of continents, his words the collapse of cities and the sinking of mountains. The ground shook, and it seemed to Vagria the least that such words might do.

'He it was who led the Seraphon against me, he whose coils held me fast while the slann raised the Twinhorn to contain me.' His nostrils flared. 'I smell the breath of Dracothion in you.'

For the final seconds of her approach, Vagria found herself speechless. The beast was all the more loathsome for its eloquence.

'For Sigmar!' she roared at the last, loosing a flurry of lightning-charged shot towards the Titan's breast. Her Vanguard-Palladors followed her lead, forty pistols rapid-firing at close range and pummelling the thick fog with noise.

The god reared onto hind legs, ignoring the nuisance bites of the Stormcast Eternals' guns, and delivered a bellow that split the ground. 'Who is this Sigmar?' Shrugging off the bullet storm he swung his mace, smashing like a comet into the earth, and forcing a dozen Palladors into breakneck turns to avoid being crushed. One did not succeed, his mangled armour breaking up into motes before it struck the wall. 'I know him not.' The ground opened up underneath a Pallador named Brida and she screamed as she and her mount tumbled into its newly gaping mouth. 'I am Kragnos of the Drogrukh. I am the End of Empires. My hooves will trample your Sigmar's works. My roar will cast down his walls and my teeth will grind his people's bones.'

Vagria galloped towards him, firing upwards as the distance between them closed to nothing. Her bolts sparked across his lower body. She drew her sword from its sheath.

'Scatter!' she cried, drawing the god's ire from her hunters with her own flashing blade. 'Widen the snare!' Her sword rebounded from the creature's fetlocks as though she were striking at a granite pillar. His leg alone was taller and broader than she was.

Kragnos raised a hoof and stamped it on the ground. The earth shook as if from a duardin mining charge, the rock under Starsid exploding and flying full into his face. She heard warriors cry out as they were battered by rocks. The gryph-charger warbled, blood pouring across his muzzle. For what felt like an eternity spent teetering over the edge of an abyss, Vagria could not see for the rubble stuck in the holes of her mask.

With a frustrated cry, she pulled it off and hurled it up at the god. It bounced off his hip. Vagria immediately felt less of herself without it. Smaller.

The god looked down at her from his immense height. 'I see you. Human.'

Vagria gave Starsid her heels and, though blinded, half-maddened by pain, the celestial creature obeyed, turning out from under Kragnos as the god's hoof came down and shattered the earth where they had been. She turned in the saddle and emptied her boltstorm pistol into the god's flank, whacking her sword ineffectually across his haunches a second time as she cantered away.

A dancing mote through the fog caught her eye. Eliara swooped in from on high, followed by the lightning-snap hum of Brendel Starsighted as the Knight-Venator and his Prosecutor retinue finally caught up to the Palladors. Vagria had never been so pleased to see another person, nor so sanguine about sharing a kill.

'You need me again, Lord-Aquilor?' he called. 'This is getting embarrassing for you.'

'Take the shot, Starsighted!' she yelled up, in no mood for the usual jokes with a dozen of her hunters fallen already. 'Kill it now.'

The Knight-Venator was little more than a bright-winged

silhouette, but Vagria could still make out the star-bright flare of the fated arrow as he drew it from his quiver, nocked it to the taut electrical thread of his bowstring. It took time and energy for one of those arrows to manifest within the Knight-Venator, but it had been weeks since their battle in the Morruk Hills. He drew the bowstring tight and, with a *snap* of energy, loosed.

The arrow crackled unerringly towards Kragnos' eye. The god saw it and lifted his shield, but a star-fated arrow could not be avoided once its target had been chosen. It always found its mark. The arrow smacked into the god's eyelid and pierced the soft-jellied eye beneath, pinning it closed and dragging a roar of pain from the beast's throat. Kragnos swung his mace in a blind fury, bringing a cascade of rubble from the Gnarlfast.

Vagria pumped the air with her fist, and the Farstrike Hunters responded with a tumult chorus of catcalls and jeers. No foe was so mighty that it could not be mocked in defeat.

'Finish it!' Vagria yelled, as the wounded god scraped his hooves through the earth and clawed at his bleeding eye. 'For Sigmar and the Storm Eternal, and the tale we will tell of this day to our absent cousins in the feast halls of the Consecralium.'

Kragnos' roar deepened. He did not sound hurt any more. He sounded furious.

As though worlds should crumble.

'Ghur belongs to the Drogrukh,' he thundered. 'Your days in my realm are done.'

With a howl and a savage twist of the body, Kragnos sent his buckler smashing across Brendel Starsighted. The blow travelled too quickly for the winged warrior to avoid it. Sigmarite armour crumpled like dough around whatever metal the god's shield was made from, leaving the Knight-Venator hopelessly broken, even before his body flew into one of the Butchers' pits and punched into the side wall. Eliara's peal of grief was confirmation that no one needed, a moment before his remains exploded back from the pit in a shower of grit and bone.

The lightning bolt sprayed rock over Kragnos' startled bulk as it leapt upwards, zigzagging, lost, through the Cursed Skies. The god lifted his mace and bellowed after the departed Stormcast, as though sensing a challenge in the rolling thunder, or in the greater might displayed by Be'lakor in denying the immortal soul, where the best he could accomplish here was to obliterate the mortal remains.

Vagria felt the Titan's wrath shake her to her bones. Starsid mewled, blood streaming from his ruined eyes and into the fine white plumage and golden harness of his neck, as Kragnos scraped the ground with his hoof and snorted.

Vagria readied her pistol. It occurred to her that Lisandr may have been right all along.

It would not die easily.

Lisandr stared listlessly over the battle raging across the dust-swaddled plain.

The Freeguild's initial charge, by night, through a fog of pulverised stone, had caught the battle-drunk greenskins unprepared and out of position, and with the Celestians at the point of the wedge, they had pushed all the way to what was left of the east wall. But Ironjawz fought hard, and to the death. Each one that wasn't finished quickly slowed the push a little more and brought more of the hollering brutes from the city. It came as little consolation to her that that was the intention. The Accari on their flanks fought like dogs tearing at gristle. Their tenacity was commendable, so similar in end result to true courage that Lisandr would not quibble with them over the distinction, but against the Ironjawz their strength and savagery was quite outmatched.

Mestrade – Field Marshal Mestrade now, a brevet promotion

after the death of her former second, Jayko, in the defence of Honoria – pointed at something she had no interest in looking at, said something she did not hear. A Celestian of the First Age did not plan for defeat. It was simply not done, and so Lisandr had been thoroughly unprepared for it when it came, both mentally and practically. They had brought no supplies from the city when they had fled it. Everything had been left behind.

She looked up, over the bobbing plumes of the Celestian infantry, neat blocks of half-pikes in a cloud screen of wild Accari, towards the silhouette of the Gnarlfast. She thought of the priceless Ohlicoatl Jewel, irreplaceable, left in a box in her tent for any grot to find. Tears tracked down her face, half hidden by the cheek-guards of her tall helmet, hidden the rest of the way by the madness around her.

'Honoria…' she whispered.

'Sir!' Mestrade yelled, and Lisandr turned, blinking. The field marshal was sitting straight-backed on his demigryph, utilising the warbeast's great height to command the battlefield as best he could. 'The Hounds are close to breaking. The Lord-Aquilor should have returned by now. Something has gone wrong.'

Lisandr bit her lip and thought. She wondered what Lord-Castellant Orin Goldspear, whose biannual lectures in Stormhost strategy had thrilled her as a young woman, would have made of this. *Preparation and patience*, he was wont to say. *Every blow has its right moment. Strike late or strike early and you won't get another. Hit it true and you will only need the one.*

But it was not her place to question a lord of the Astral Templars. Braun had harboured no doubts and she found that she trusted his judgement more than she trusted her own. Worse, that did not seem to shock her.

Turning her restricted view to look over her shoulder, she took in the half a dozen knights mustered alongside her. The Big Rukk possessed no cavalry of their own, the few boar-riders they had seen belonging to the Bonesplitterz tribes who had largely abandoned the plain already to pursue the survivors into the Mesas and had been crushed piecemeal by Vagria's Stormcasts. According to Braun, the late Rukka Bosskilla had a pet hatred of anything bigger or faster than him and had never permitted them in his warclan.

'What should we do, sir?' asked Mestrade.

A brilliant flash of lightning lit up the swell of pig iron and starmetal, followed by another, then another, a rolling squall that silhouetted the Gnarlfast, a storm that raged not from the sky towards the ground but from the ground towards the sky. There, the bolts forked and split across one another, turning the sky from overcast white to the brown of overdone meat. Lisandr watched the breaking storm. Mestrade had understated. Something was *very* wrong.

'Sir?'

To her surprise there was no panic in Mestrade's voice. If anything, the twitch of his moustache as he turned towards her was almost laconic, as if there were a fine joke or a short poem just on the tip of the tongue, which would leaven the horror of the moment. For some reason, simply imagining that it was forthcoming was reassuring. Whatever the trial, whatever the great foe of the age, the Celestians of the First Age would be there, and they would rise to it.

She took a deep breath.

'Withdraw,' she said.

'Sir?'

She took a last look over the battlefield. Large swathes of the Accari line were already starting to break off and flee for the Mesas. Sigmarite discipline alone was keeping the Celestians in the fight. Her orders at this point, she felt, were entirely for show.

'Withdraw!'

She hauled her reins around. Mortal soldiers had done all they could. Vagria would need Sigmar with her from here.

The god thundered into a gallop.

There had been the briefest of opportunities for Vagria to stop him, and that had been while he had still lain entombed in the north. To defy him now, this god that predated Sigmar, who had battled Dracothion and endured, felt like madness equivalent to raising one's sword to confront a tsunami, or blocking the path of an avalanche with a shield wall.

Faith would not stall him. Sigmarite would not hold him. Courage would not defeat him.

These were the thoughts in Vagria's mind as the first of her Palladors went down under Kragnos' hooves, two more then mangled in a wild sweep of his antlers and flung to the winds. Pallador Oldro, the rider directly behind Vagria, as always, was crushed by the god's mace. Lightning sprayed from the warrior's crumpled armour with enough violence to flay his steed to the bones and throw a second rider from her saddle.

'Fall back!' Vagria screamed.

Not a rout, she assured her pride, but a withdrawal. The god was too powerful to be matched head-on. They had to bleed him until he weakened, then circle back for the kill. If she allowed Kragnos to drive this battle then it would end in a slaughter in moments.

Dragging hard on Starsid's reins she swung back into the path of Kragnos' stampede. If nothing else she would buy her brothers time for another volley.

Kragnos stamped on a Pallador as she attempted to crawl out from under her stricken mount. His mace, easily large enough to hit rider and mount in a single blow, lifted another Pallador and her gryph-charger into the air, whereupon the former broke apart into her component storm, leaving the latter to skid across the ground alone. The lightning circled the god for several increasingly furious orbits, as though confused by his power, before striking out in wild jumps towards the storm-wracked sky.

Vagria swung up her boltstorm pistol.

'You do not know Sigmar yet. But you will.'

The weapon roared in her fist, blasting Heavenly shot into the Titan's belly too rapidly for the arcana of the firing chamber to replenish. Kragnos roared, his stomach decidedly bruised. Vagria followed through with her off-hand, slashing her starbound blade across the monster's thigh before peeling away with a ringing hand and an overriding sense of despair.

'Ghur is mine to dominate,' the god bellowed after her, shaking the earth beneath her mount as though to drag her back to him with his words. 'It is mine to ravage.' He swung his mace.

The fog of the Butchers' Quarter became febrile with light. Stormcasts were dying, powerful souls shedding broken bodies with nowhere to go and nothing else to do but announce their parting with light and noise. Her heart pounded against the weight of her breastplate as though to call them back, or perhaps for them to wait and take her with them. *Fool-fool, Fool-fool*, it seemed to taunt with every strident beat.

She should have heeded Lisandr. Kragnos was every bit as potent as the mortal general had tried to warn her.

'Fall back!' she yelled, battling to be heard over the creaking of stone and the rolling, repetitive *booms* of brothers and sisters gone to the storm. The one attribute they all possessed to surpass even the god was speed. 'Draw him out!'

Kragnos responded with an ear-rupturing bellow. Cracks split through the ground. Iron ruins collapsed into newly opened holes in the earth. The entire city seemed to groan around them.

'My flesh is stone,' he spoke. 'I am Ghur.'

'Prosecutors!' Vagria cried, waving furiously as she urged her blind charger into a gallop, just to stay ahead of the stampeding god. 'From above!'

The Prosecutors, led now by Prime Artros, returned for a second pass. Javelins crackled to life in their gauntlets. Half a dozen bolts skewered Kragnos' immense torso, the god arching his back, red mane flaring as they dumped pure energies into his chest.

'Palladors–' Vagria began.

Kragnos gave vent to a colossal roar.

It rippled the dense air like the shockwaves of an earthquake, punching three Prosecutors straight out of the sky. Their wings winked out, doused, javelins vanishing from their grasp. Prime Artros himself hit the ground like an inert lump of sigmarite with a body trapped inside.

Eliara, circling above, the star-eagle still incandescent with grief for the Starsighted, feathers fringed with lightning, shrieked and swooped at Kragnos' chest as though to dive into the god's body and claw out his heart. Kragnos raised his shield and, incorporeal as she was, Eliara thumped into it like a bird hitting glass. The god shook her off as one would mud from their boot, not so much as a burn mark on his shield.

A moan went up from the remaining Stormcast Eternals.

'Keep your distance,' she cried, with a rising pitch of hysteria that she had never heard from her own voice before. She was losing, her warriors were dying. It was a situation that she had never confronted before and she did not know what to do. 'Short… short bursts.' Her voice dropped to a murmur, realising, for itself it seemed, that no one but Starsid was left who could still hear her, and the gryph-charger was too wild with pain to care. 'Keep firing. Keep your distance and… and… keep firing.'

Kragnos bellowed. His mace destroyed another rider. Everything was coming apart. Kragnos was too powerful.

He was a god.

She heard Prime Columna's voice, calling out through the bedlam, but couldn't see her or make out what she was shouting. She saw Raukos' surviving retinue scattering from the Titan's rampage, firing back over their shoulders. She watched them overrun and slain, their deaths lighting up the fog with lightning flashes and the abused nobility of their souls, blasting the eye with after-images that would live forever in Vagria's memory, even if the warriors themselves never found their way back to the Forge Eternal.

Anguish transformed itself into something she barely recognised in herself. The hunt was over. She had failed. Ghur was doomed. The people of the realm had put their hopes in Vagria Farstrike and she had taken them onto herself, because it had never, for one moment, occurred to her that she could fail.

A notion came to her then, so outrageous it made her dizzy just to think it. If everything was lost, then there was nothing left for it but to...

'Run?' she murmured.

No sooner had she uttered the word than Starsid, blinded and in agony though he was, gave an outraged shriek, sensing the moment of cowardice in his rider's mind. Vagria knew how fast the gryph-charger could be, better than anyone, but even she was caught unawares as he bucked and threw her. She was in the air before she realised it, grasping at a wavering blur that was already a hundred miles hence on the winds aetheric. She fell back through the clear air that had formerly contained her one constant companion in the realms and landed in a heavy clatter of plate and a dose of remorse. Her unmasked forehead cracked on the rock, twelve coloured stars bursting across her vision, mingling there with the livid memories of her fallen brothers.

She wiped the blood from her eyes and got up. The ground was shaking. The Gnarlfast itself was coming down. Starsid was gone.

Vagria wasn't nearly so fast on her own feet, but animal panic overtook her. She forgot about shame. And somewhere, deep within her original, human soul she remembered what it was to be hunted.

Without once looking back, she spun on her heel and ran.

CHAPTER THIRTEEN

Braun's breath came in chesty, wheezing gulps that made his ribs shudder like the keel of a ship, exiting again in uncontrollable huffs that rippled his cheeks and sprayed his chin with spit. The landscape, low hills swathed in jungle, the outskirts of the Accari's home, wobbled even more than was usual with his tired eyes and increasingly ropey stride. This wasn't the steady run that any Accari could keep up for hours. This was a madcap dash through country that, after several long centuries of restless slumber, was just starting to wake up and realise that it was hungry. A desperate and probably futile bid to keep the handful of miles between them and the pursuing Spiderfang to a handful of miles.

'I… could… eat… a… Stormcast,' said Altin, between gasps, sweat causing his kohl to run in long black streaks down his cheeks.

The Izalmaw Cannibal dragged his feet, a yard behind, Olgar and Woan at either shoulder, trailed finally by Ragn. The hardest head in Accar, the Hounds were calling him now, having been hit over it by both Grob Bloodgullet and Rukka Bosskilla, and suffering no more for it than a face that even Sigmar wouldn't recognise. His cheeks were red and he was blowing, thin hair stuck to his head. His muscular frame wasn't made for running, but he was too tough and stubborn to slack further off the pace. The boneheaded pride of an elite.

With a pang of hurt, something like nostalgia but more painfully *present*, Braun realised that, with the exception of Taal – who just couldn't run so fast with his gut in stitches and so had been put with the rearguard – this was the last of the Dozen. He should probably stop thinking of them by that name. It felt like an insult to the God-King, who'd preserved them in his service so long. He'd surely broken them for a reason, and it wasn't for Braun to second-guess.

He concentrated on breathing, on putting one foot before the other.

And again.

And again.

Two thousand men and women, give or take, straggled out through the clutching, knee-high vegetation, a ragged front about a mile across. The gap between the fittest and fastest at the leading edge of the crescent and those trailing behind was several orders greater, and growing with every stride. From the front, Braun could only wonder at how many had fallen away and been left behind, swallowed up by mouths that opened up under the ground cover to claim fighters by the score, or picked off by the pterosaurs that circled like the gulls around Excelsis Harbour, awaiting scraps. If it was fewer than the Ironjawz had claimed on the Eaten Plain, then he would have taken that and called it relatively bloodless by Ghurish standards.

The Celestians, to his surprise, clattered alongside the Accari at a reasonable pace. Their dark, patrician faces shimmered with sweat, their heavy clothes steaming. They weren't accustomed to the heat, to the exertion, to terrain that actively sought to eat them. They weren't dressed for the humidity. The warriors had been resting, by turns, using the few demigryphs still at their disposal, which the Hounds had initially laughed off as typical Azyrite cheating. No one was joking now though. About anything. They didn't have the breath for it. But the hateful glares they spared for the armoured knights, fast asleep on their cantering warbeasts, cost them nothing.

The Ironweld, lugging their heavy guns on limbers without roads or horses, arguably had more to complain about than the Accari, and the fact that they weren't was impressing nobody. The Accari were passionate complainers. They did it loudly and under the flimsiest of outrages, and could neither understand nor respect a person who'd suffer silently by choice.

Of the Celestians, the only one who'd thus far refused her turn in the saddle was Lisandr. She slogged determinedly alongside Braun and the Dozen, her helmet banging a marching rhythm against her thigh as it swung on its silver wire. Her face was drawn with the titanic effort of breathing and moving at the same time. Her long white hair, streaky with blood that was green as well as red, had fallen loose of its braids about four days ago, flittering as far down as to where her left arm hung in its cast, twitching with every stride.

Whether she was looking to prove something to the Hounds, the Celestians, or to herself, Braun didn't know, but he understood a fellow general's need for penance, and approved. Nor did he seem to be the only one. More than once since their rout from the Gnarlfast he'd seen one of his fighters running alongside to whisper encouragements in her ear, to help her upright as she stumbled, or to nudge her forwards as she slowed.

The Accari might have given stoicism short shrift, but there was nothing more likely than an empty, pig-headed gesture to win their hearts. She looked as bad as Braun felt, only worse for trying so hard not to show it.

A tremor passed under their feet, shaking foliage, shaking mail. They wracked the landscape every hour or so, sometimes more frequently, rarely less, often rolling straight into the quake that had come before, as though they were all just shivers from the same hideously abused fault line that the godbeast had driven into the bedrock of the Gnarlfast.

The subsurface shaking built towards a rumbling, wrenching roar, mud sliding down the hill to Braun's right. The trees groaned, then released a brown cloud of soil, followed by insects, birds and flying reptiles, like game beaten from the brush to be shot. And if any of the Accari had the strength in them to balance a javelin then they would have been. Braun smiled feebly, grimly, as he heard Blind Lusten cursing Ghur for taunting him so with such ample game, before losing it again under the rasping of his own breathing.

The godbeast had done all this, and it had done it alone.

For now, it seemed, the behemoth rested, intent on devouring the spoils of the Butchers' Quarter back in Goreham. From the Mesas, a day or so ago, Braun had seen that the city they'd sought to build was already gone, the earthquakes and ground slips driving those greenskins who'd not already been crushed by their own god to pursue the escaping Freeguild onto Ymnog's Trample.

Fingers shaking with exhaustion, Braun touched the cardinals of the hammer tattooed across his face. To think that just a week ago his greatest fear had been having to fight Rukka Bosskilla a second time. Rukka had cost him his regiment, left him with just eleven men, but he'd come out of it a hero, and he doubted the godbeast was going to let him off so lightly. He was either going to be annihilated, utterly, along with everything else in the

Heartlands, or he was going to be lucky again and come away with at least his skin to show for it. Taal had been right. Prophecy was a most imperfect guide to the future.

He watched for a time, his head set in a direction it would take more effort to change, as the pieces of rubble dislodged by the slide began to pick themselves up and totter back uphill, butting one another with nub-horns of rock. Loud *clacks* rang off the hills. Something metallic glinted amongst the foliage. Purple. A hint of gold. He stared at it, eyes too worn out to focus properly, but it did not come back.

'We are not going to make it to Accar,' Lisandr panted, swatting tiredly at an insect that had been drawn to the sweat on her forehead and missing it.

'Have to,' Braun answered. Hateful glares were cheap, but words were expensive.

'We should go to ground. These hills… these hills could be defensible.'

Braun gave the slowest headshake in the Ghurish Heartlands. 'Eat us alive. Need walls. Make a stand. Greenskins always scared of Primeval Jungle. Seraphon. They'll back off. Or we make them pay.'

'And the godbeast?'

There was a moment's quiet, or close to quiet, ignoring the grunting of their breaths, the scuff of their boots on the ground, the drag of their shins through the undergrowth. Neither of them had come out and explicitly said that Vagria Farstrike had failed, or what that meant for the rest of them. Perhaps because it was so obvious that it didn't need saying aloud. They could all sense it, the excited rumbling of the earth, the call to Waaagh! that even the Celestians could not deny they were now starting to feel. Also, the souls of the Stormcast Eternals, half a week on, continued to wrack the sky with amethyst lightning. Braun wondered if the

Farstrike herself was up there. Was she conscious of it? Did she suffer? Was she looking down on them in some way, as Sigmar clearly hadn't been looking down on her?

And if he'd not been watching over *her*…

'We have to find a way to kill that thing,' Lisandr breathed, breaking his reverie.

'Listening.'

'We could be the only soldiers west of Excelsis.'

Braun didn't waste his strength answering.

'Excelsis… needs us. If we can't… make it back, then… then we have a duty to stop it.' She gasped for air. 'Or die trying.'

Braun didn't disagree, but he'd seen the Titan brush aside an entire chamber of Stormcast Eternals and demolish a city. It had taken some of the mountain with it. Braun was stronger than Lisandr. He was uninjured and he commanded more fighters. By the straightforward rules of Ghur, that put him in charge. The written instructions of a distant commander meant little to him, and less, he knew, to his Hounds. But just then he didn't care, and he wasn't sure he wanted the responsibility of getting this lot back to Accar, or of stopping the godbeast, anyway. He felt guilty about burdening Lisandr with the task, but not so guilty that he wasn't prepared to do so.

'Listening,' he said again.

Lisandr had no answer to give, and so for a while they ran on without speaking. The thudding of their feet on the ground and the rasping of their lungs marked time, but too monotonously to be counted. Progress, Braun measured by the dragging of the hills, the thickening of the jungle, and of the air.

'Have you considered… replacements… for the Dozen?' she asked, at length. 'Continuity is important. For morale. It is why I promoted Mestrade.'

Braun thought back, to the battle on the frozen Izal, and almost shivered in spite of everything.

The Dozen were more than just an elite company. They were a blessed company, the only twelve to have survived that battle. It wasn't Braun's place to promote new members, any more than it had been his place to kick anyone out, as spiteful and as irritating a bastard as Ferrgin could be. They'd been bonded by something thicker than blood. Until the day when they weren't. It reminded him of something Vagria had said to them, about not knowing if Sigmar chose his Stormcast Eternals, or if they somehow chose themselves.

'Think about it,' he said, sparing himself the trouble of having to explain it, and looked away, catching again that flicker of purple amidst the slowly encroaching jungle.

By the time he noticed it, it was already gone.

Her pursuers could not quite believe that she was running from them. Vagria did not know what to believe any more. Her flight from Kragnos had broken something in her. She was no longer sure who she was, or what she was supposed to be, or if Vagria was even her given name at all. She was small and scared and half-feral, full of wounded rage and the spark of *something* that the God-King saw in her as good.

Ten years old, she was, half-clothed in skins and filth, armed with a spear of Rûfhal flint that had cost her warlord father the rights to his favourite battling grounds. But her father was dead, slain by the bloodreavers who had come over the Krondspine to burn her hall in the Gnarlfast. Her life was ash. She should be dead. She felt it in her marrow and in her soul, slain ten times over for a god whose name she had forgotten.

The eager yips and shrieks of her pursuers told her that she was, somehow, still alive. And so she ran. It was the only thing that she knew with absolute certainty that she could do.

She knew, because she was sure that she had done it before.

Grint got up, ran forward a dozen paces through the chest-high grass, then knelt back down again. Insects droned around him, unable to tell the difference between his head and the flowers that bobbed around him, flesh-coloured and inflamed with human-like blood to lure in their prey. Ignoring the occasional bite, he made quick cuts with his spice knife, roughly shaving away enough thorns to create two handholds in a length of creeper.

He pushed the short blade into the dirt, easier than sheathing it properly when he'd have to draw it again soon, and pulled the vine taut, looping it into a snare and pegging it down with a Y-shaped stick. Drawing the knife from the dirt, he hammered in the peg with the pommel, then brushed dried insect husks and soil over the loop to conceal it.

He took a moment to admire his handiwork. The vine ran up into the branches of a lifeleach palm. The tree was short and broad, with a partial canopy of sticky green-brown leaves that would trap insects, birds, wind-blown seeds, or even a human if they were foolish enough to try and touch one. The lifeleach was a hardy pioneer. It dotted the borders of the Primeval Jungle where larger species of plant hadn't yet managed to invade. Some said those broad leaves could even sustain the tree on Hysh-light alone, without needing to drain sustenance from living prey. Grint found that hard to imagine. Everything in the Heartlands survived by consuming something. Grint's snare was taut enough to yank up whatever stepped into the loop, with enough rubbery strength to drag even a giant spider into its canopy and hold it there long enough for the mouths on the underside of those leaves to do their work.

The surrounding undergrowth rustled with movement. Accari scouts, spaced out every ten to twenty yards and bent like rice farmers in the skingrasses and sharp ferns, setting traps or fashioning them from the flora, a few bolder veterans stringing tripwires and firebombs between the stems. The terrain might not slow the Spiderfang. But this sure as damn would.

On a deep breath, Grint pushed himself up again, lurching onto a leg that had taken the opportunity to cramp, and then hobble-ran through the grass like a sixty-year-old man. He kneaded the offending muscle as he ran. It felt like a Fyreslayer's, studded with molten gold. The chiefs up at the front were having it easy. All they had to do was run in a straight line. He'd like to see how Braun and the Dozen coped with zigzagging, squatting back down again every twelve yards, and being constantly alert to wandering across Debrevn or Mikali's paths and stepping in their traps.

He grunted, the pain in his thigh flaring up rather than settling down, and stumbled to his knees as though shot in the back.

'Gah! Damn it.'

Dragging himself on, he slid a hand into his knee-pit and manually dragged his cramped leg up, positioning the foot flat on the ground in front of him. The Spiderfang were ten, maybe even five minutes behind. The last thing he wanted was to fall back and be left behind now.

A weight landed on his shoulder. He cried out and flicked at it, and fell sideways into the undergrowth. Angellin looked down on him. She was unhelmed, her mail coif pulled out so that her neck could breathe. Her silver-blonde hair had been drawn into a ponytail, which looped down over her breastplate.

'Are you all right?' she asked. Her hand, hovering where it had been laid on his shoulder, turned to help him up.

Grint blew out through his lips, relieved. Better than a winged bloodsucker or a grot spear. Days spent without sleep. Days of living in terror. Those wants and worries of the last few months seemed so petty to him now that he gave a tired laugh.

Angellin looked at him as though he'd gone mad.

'Just a cramp,' he said, before she could think about leaving him. He wouldn't have been the first Accari to find escape in insanity. His cousin, Petrec, had left them that way. Taal had ordered him a Ghurish burial: tied up and gagged for the beasts to tear apart.

'I'll be fine,' he added.

'Keep moving,' said Angellin. 'I thought you Heartlanders could run all day.'

'We can.' Grint offered up his hand and winced as Angellin pulled him back up onto his cramped leg. He leant into her. 'It's the stopping that's killing me.'

'Do you hear anyone else complaining?'

'You Azyrites have no heart,' said Grint as she led him on, his weight across her shoulder.

'You Ghurites have altogether too much.'

'It's all right for you. All you've had to do is keep watch.'

There was the hint of a smile on her face, sparkling with reflected sunlight and pooled sweat. 'It is fascinating to see you Accari here in your element. This is why I always wanted to leave Azyr and travel, to see the Mortal Realms beyond my home. Maybe it is because my family was never all that noble, but I never had any interest in glory. I wanted to see Ghur. I wanted to live it. I wanted to see how people like you survived for so long without us.'

Grint intended to reply with an incredulous *people like me*, but he found that he was staring mutely into her dark blue eyes, overcome by the artless melancholy of not having much of a tomorrow to worry about. He let his breath out. It didn't seem very important now.

His whole spirit felt numb, and he didn't quite notice at first that he was smiling. As though his face was openly mocking his heart. It was the smile of someone who'd risked death on a foolish dare and broken an unreasonable number of bones but come through it all alive. He felt as though he'd shed a burden. Regardless of what his future might have been, he found he was glad to be spending his last few hours without having to worry about it.

'All right then.'

Angellin looked at him again, as though debating whether she'd been too hasty in judging him sane. She shook her head and looked away. 'You Ghurites are very strange.'

The undergrowth ahead of them rustled.

Grint felt Angellin's body tense against his, but he knew the different sounds that creatures made when moving through jungle. This was a man: a man, moreover, walking with a pronounced limp and a stick. Angellin relaxed as Efrim Taal pushed his way through the curtain of palm fronds. The shaman's amber skin was waxen, the faint gangrenous reek of his wound smothered by the heavy odour of the jungle. In spite of all that, however, he didn't look in the least bit out of breath.

'The realm has come to something,' he said, 'when *I* need to come back for *you*.' His eyes narrowed as they focused on Angellin. 'I've been hearing things about you, Celestian. I didn't think you'd be the one to lag behind.'

'We will catch up,' she said smartly.

'Good,' said Taal, as though praise was a diseased bit of fingernail to be peeled off and tossed away for his pets to gnaw on and fight over.

'It's my fault,' said Grint. 'She only stopped to help me.' He eased himself off Angellin's shoulder and took his weight on his own leg. The muscle gave a little flutter, but it didn't hurt too much. 'I'm fine now.' He started to move.

Taal put his staff across his path, knuckles whitening, eyes still fixed on Angellin. Grint swallowed and looked up. The saurus head mounted at the top of the staff looked back down. It was twice the size and weight of a human skull, thick with bony frills and ridges. Grint barely had to work his mind at all to imagine its power.

What blessings did the Heavens pass on to the Accari war-priest through the relic? he wondered. Or was it just an imposing piece of bone, as genuinely threatening as the earrings his mother had made from the teeth of her dead husbands? Were the powers of Azyr as ambivalent towards Accar as their mortal lords in Excelsis?

With a dry mouth, Grint looked back down.

'I've been hearing things all right, Ilsbet Angellin.' Taal spat the name as though it were poison drawn from his foot. 'The Azyrite who killed my nephew.'

Grint glanced at Angellin, his fear of Taal's ire turning a shade to awe. Sigmar, he was hopeless. He thought he fell in love with her just a little bit more.

'*You* killed Ferrgin?'

The Celestian wasn't holding him any more. He couldn't feel her body against his as her muscles prepared themselves to fight. Nor could he see the change in her, but that was another demonstration of how good she was. Every sense that Grint had screamed to him that she was a coiled adder, ready to lunge.

He threw an urgent look over his shoulder. The jungle behind them buzzed and droned, and wafted in a scant breeze. There was no sign at all that the Spiderfang were minutes behind, but he knew that they were.

'We don't have time for this,' he thought, and surprised himself by muttering it aloud.

For the first time in about half a minute, Taal broke his stare and looked at Grint. Malec was two inches taller than the shaman, broad with youth, but Taal somehow made it appear as though he was looking at a fly that had just landed on his boot. The shaman eased his grip on his staff, and dragged the ferrule back through the undergrowth from Grint's feet.

'Ferrgin fought and he lost. That is the way of things.' He glared hard at Angellin. 'But when the wound that your general gave me is healed, and we survive the battle that is coming, then you and I are going to fight.'

The Celestian looked puzzled. 'But you said–'

'That, too, is the way of things.'

Angellin looked to Grint, as though for a translation.

'You were the one who wanted to see Ghur,' he said sourly.

'If you were wise,' said Taal, leaning against his staff, a hard glint in his eye. 'Then you'd kill me now, while I'm still weak.'

'The spiders are coming!'

The shout, coming from further back in the jungle, startled Grint, as he'd thought that he and Angellin were the last. Everyone looked back to see Bad Luck Mikali tearing out of the jungle, waving her arms above her head and kicking through tall grass, stumbling from side to side around more aggressive-looking plants and, in so doing, unerringly avoiding every snare, mantrap and tripwire that Grint had spent the last painstaking half hour laying. His relief at not seeing her strung up or with her leg broken was tempered by some annoyance.

'One of Altin's girls, isn't she?' Taal grunted.

'A... grand-niece, I think,' said Grint. After their escape from Goreham and Honoria had showed him how little he knew about his apparently closest friend, he had done some asking around. She held all of Taal's attention now. It almost made Grint hope that the Spiderfang caught her first.

'I wonder if there's some old Accari blood in her family,' Taal mused. 'I'll have to talk with the old cannibal when this is done.'

Angellin, meanwhile, had run back to get her, catching the other woman in her arms just as she tripped on a root and, Grint noticed, right over his last concealed snare. Casting fearful looks over her shoulder, she leant into the Celestian and stumbled the final yards towards Grint and Taal. Grint bent down to take Mikali's other arm over his shoulder, his thigh muscle twanging painfully one more time, just as an explosion ripped through the jungle about half a mile behind. Screams pierced the tree cover, accompanied by the pitter-pattering of spider-legs raining on the canopy above their heads. Taal cackled as they smelt the first spiders burn.

Grint swore, dragging Mikali up and turning to flee, as the jungle came alive with squeals of outrage. And the chittering movement of many, many sets of legs.

When Vagria had been a mortal girl, long before the Bloodgullet had moved into the abandoned Gnarlfast and devoured the verdant plains that had once supported her people, trees had roved Ymnog's Trample in predatory, migrating packs and the Primeval Jungle – the power of Mekitopsar and Koatl's Gullet at its apogee – had been ten times its current size. New vistas had erupted every day, chasms opening under long-settled and dormant landscapes to swallow the ruins of ancient civilisations. Mountains had hurled rocks at one another, crushing unwary nomads thousands of miles from the Nautil Peaks, while the continents of Thondia, Andtor and Gallet had butted and fought. Rivers overran their banks and multiplied. Orruks had marched on every city, grots and trogg-herds emerging, blinking, from every dank and mildewy hole, while every frigid breeze from the Brokenjarl and Thunderbellow Mawpaths had portended ogors and their hunger.

And increasingly, as the months following her flight from her defiled hall had turned into years, there had been the dark things that had hunted *them*.

The parallels around her were everywhere. They were the bulwarks, safeguarding the barriers her traumatised immortal mind had built around itself and ensuring they did not fall. An old god had returned to claim its due. Then it had been the Blood God, Khorne. Now it was another.

Kragnos. God of Earthquakes. End of Empires.

She shook her head, refusing to acknowledge his name in her head, and fled, unwittingly tracing the exact same path from which she had fled the bloodreavers. In her mind she was that child again, but her body was that of a sigmarite-clad warrior goddess, and she bulldozed her way through trees, old walls, and even small hillocks, covering twenty times the ground in half the time that she had in ages past.

She exited the Trample by a ravine that had been at the far eastern boundary of her savage people's known world. It had changed over the centuries, as the landscapes of Ghur were wont to do, but not by much. Called Thordar's Gap, after one of the eldest sons of the World Titan, it extended from the Slannstongue River to the Nautilor Mountains. According to legend, Thordar had become so inspired after drinking from the Slannstongue that he had taken to lying on his back and gazing up at the stars. He had remained so many aeons unmoving that his body had sunk into the earth, creating the Gap, and providing fodder for the civilisations that would follow. It was a parable to warn against the danger of spending too long with one's mind in the Heavens.

The Gap's wide basin was dotted with small hills of its own that were, in fact, the barrows of a race of gargants who had fallen to primitivism thousands of years before the others of their kin, in the cataclysms following the sinking of the continent of Donse. The Slannstongue wound far to the south, concealed from view behind jungle and wildlife.

This was where the bloodreavers had run her down. She had slain six of them before fleeing into the jungle, hoping to find sanctuary in the legendary star-city of Mekitopsar. Now, as then, grots in glossy armour and stalkspider webbing swarmed the old mounds of the Gap. The sunken vale rang with the shrill cries of pack hunters cornering large prey. The scuttlemobz had been stalking her for days, but had decided to make an end of it here. Caught in the centre of the Gap there could be no escape, and nor could the hurtful eye of Hysh intrude on them between the high ridges and the jungle canopy. They were eager, keen to spill blood and take skulls for the Green God of the hunt.

But their ambush had not gone entirely according to plan, or to the girl Vagria's mortal recollections.

The Spiderfang rode wide circles around the walls of the Gap, screeching at her and shaking their totem-crowned banners as if to draw their prey into leaving the valley and attacking them. It might, a small, safe part of her mind reasoned, be because she was that much greater than the girl she remembered. But they also outnumbered the bloodreavers of old by many hundreds of times, and their god was so very much more *present* than the Blood God had ever been in Ghur. He was so close to her that she could feel his breath on the back of her head, hear the thunder of his hooves beneath her breast.

If she allowed herself.

She blinked quickly, seeing for the first time what her mind had chosen to overlook before.

The mega-gargant simply did not fit with her blurring of present and past. It was limping towards her, crossing the Gap in the opposite direction in answer to Kragnos' call, leaning into a huge splintered tree that it was using as a crutch and dragging a crushed leg behind it. Its bulk was clad in a crudely stitched leather jerkin, its downcast features withdrawn behind a scruff of bear, as though a creature so immense could make itself small enough to be overlooked by the predators of Ghur. Even hunched over its improvised crunch it towered over the dotted features and vine-strangled Seraphon ruins of the Gap, every crutch-stab and foot-drag of its awkward gait passing over as much ground as a troop of light horsemen could cover in the time.

Vagria closed her eyes, as if to buttress the walls around her mind from the reality of what they witnessed.

The gargant race, as it had existed in her mortal childhood, had not yet grown so massive. That transformation had only begun in recent times with the slaying of Behemat, the World Titan, at the hands of the Celestant-Prime. But she also recognised this one: the torn clothing, the bruised arms and face, the crushed leg. The sight of it was a battering ram to her mind's defences.

She mouthed a word, a name that was most precious to her.

'Heavenscar...'

Here was the same brute that her Knight-Vexillor, Kildabrae Heavenscar, had died fighting. She felt her walls crumble. Pain, but also light, forced the breach. She looked down at her hands, giant things clad in blood and sigmarite. She was that girl – that frightened, feral child – and she always would be. But she was also a warrior goddess in amethyst and gold, beloved of Sigmar, in spite of her many flaws, and reforged into a brotherhood of souls in his mighty image and martial purpose.

Venting her sudden mix of emotions in a wordless scream, she ran at the mega-gargant. Her boltstorm pistol was in its holster, her starbound blade clotted to its scabbard by greenskin gore, but she did not pause long enough to draw either of them.

She was so small, relative to the immensity of the mega-gargant that it did not, initially, notice her coming. If it heard her cry at all then it dismissed it amongst the hollering of the Spiderfang all around it. Though mighty, the mega-gargant was no match, in its wounded state, for so many, and knew that they would come to the same realisation eventually if it could not first clear the Gap before they did. Similarly, one unarmed, unprepared Stormcast Eternal was insignificant enough to be overlooked, either as a threat or as a meal.

Her boots tearing through the orchids and vines that strangled the undergrowth, she charged headlong at the mega-gargant, aiming herself for the monster's wooden crutch. The trunk was wider across than the span of her outspread arms, but splintered from heavy use, particularly at the base, where she struck it. The impact with her body obliterated it.

Like a great tower, undermined from below, the mega-gargant fell.

The legs went over first, then the hips, then the upper body and head, then the flailing arms, and the mega-gargant face ploughed into the ground in a blow that reverberated through the Gap and shook roosting reptiles from their treetops. Vagria leapt onto its back, filled with pain, filled with fury, suffused with the spitting wrath of the storm, and drew her pistol. She did it without thinking, a Stormcast Eternal again, without yet consciously realising or acknowledging the fact.

An Astral Templar: born, not made.

The mega-gargant shook its head and groaned, outraged and confused at finding itself face down in the soil and under attack by something it had not yet noticed. It spat a mudslide from its mouth, uprooting whole copses of trees as it drew in its fingers in preparation for pushing itself back up.

It was wounded, but still an almighty brute, a match for any Stormcast Eternal unless put down hard.

Vagria aimed her pistol at the back of its skull. The mega-gargant's head was massive, larger in diameter and volume than her entire torso and with a thick skull to protect its diminished brain, but relative to the size of its gargantuan form it was small and vulnerable. Its main protection, ordinarily, lay in being a hundred feet above any potential harm.

She emptied the chamber into it, drilling into the monster's skull and spraying her greaves with its brains.

The Spiderfang around the valley sides shrieked as they fought to flee the Gap, startled by her killing of the mega-gargant and her refulgent fury. Ripping her starbound blade from its sheath, she hacked at the gargant's stump of a head with it, the starmetal sword rising and falling, rising and falling, striking with a strength, a speed and a killing zeal that would have been beyond the powers of any mortal hero. Let alone a desperate, half-starved girl of ten.

Wiping a loose strand of hair from a face that still felt strangely numb to the touch, she stumbled back from the wreckage of her foe. She looked up. The clash of steel and the boom of gunpowder could just about be heard above the rustle of Spiderfang fleeing through the trees.

A sound, a dolorous *THUD*, rang through her chest.

Holstering her pistol and taking up her starbound blade, she set off away from the sounds of battle. Something in the jungle called to her.

Her last mortal journey had not yet been completed.

Braun sprinted downhill. The irony of how much sweat he'd shed running up the thinly jungled incline didn't escape him. About a mile below, already abundantly visible through the sparse jungle at the base of the rise, an avalanche of yellow-and-black chitin, bright feathers and vivid warpaint swept through the trees. Hundreds of Accari fighters were still coming uphill, the rearguard and the stragglers, running scared, some of them too exhausted to run any more and dragging themselves on all fours to keep ahead of the spiders on their tails.

Hearing the tramp of something heavy closing on him from behind, Braun threw a look over his shoulder and swallowed a curse. He threw himself to one side as a pair of demigryph knights thundered past, clawing up great clods of undergrowth as they built up towards a gallop. Braun spat grass from his teeth as the two Celestians scattered another group of fleeing soldiers further down the hill. He recognised Gorman, and Varden, from Blind Lusten's mob, as they patted themselves down and hurried back to drag a grizzly-haired older fighter from the churned-up jungle floor. Braun slid down to help them, getting his hands under the third man's arms and pulling him up.

The old man looked up at Braun, then turned and spat over his shoulders. 'D'you have a javelin spare, chief? I left all mine in the Spiderfang and these two *babies* here want me to run and get more.'

Braun grinned. He liked Lusten. Even the Celestians seemed to like Lusten. His hair was short and grey, his beard a saw-edge across his chin. Braun remembered him as the street-corner beggar with a wealth of outrageous stories, a knife-juggler and a lizard-charmer and now, who would've thought it, the best shot in the Hounds. But then a Heartlander didn't get to see fifty-five without some nails.

Bran shook his head. 'I never had much of a throwing arm.'

'The general throws like a troggoth,' Gorman said with a laugh.

Lusten cuffed him. 'Take me with you, general.' He drew his spice knife, forcing Varden to veer out of the way of his swing. 'Hunting with a knife's the same as hunting with a javelin, just closer.'

Braun laughed, and gestured to the two men either side. 'Get him out of here. Come back when you've got your javelins.'

'General,' said Varden.

'General,' said Gorman, with a finger-tap to the forehead by way of a salute, and the two men returned to dragging their protesting chief uphill.

Braun sighed. Blind Lusten was born to be in a company like the Dozen. In another time, perhaps, or another realm. If Sigmar gave him the sign.

Thunder rolled from the top of the vine-strangled rise that

Braun had just been trying to climb. He looked up, a wail passing over his head, followed by an explosion that flung mud and sap and bits of spider high into the air.

'No!' he roared, turning and waving furiously towards the gunners on the hilltop. A second cannon boomed, muffled and far away, the wrath of a distant iron god, and a geyser of wood pulp erupted from a shredded palm. 'Move the guns on to Accar! The city needs them more than we do.'

Ignoring him, or unable to hear over their own noise, the guns continued to bark from the jungle slope, laying fire into the oncoming horde.

The Spiderfang swarmed under the bombardment. They moved like a mudslide, never slowing, never going around what could be ridden over, an eager, uphill avalanche of clashing colours and chittering teeth. The Ironjawz and the majority of the other greenskins seemed content to wait on the godbeast to emerge from the ruins of Goreham, but the Spiderfang, for reasons of their own, had pursued the Freeguild in strength. There must have been hundreds of them pouring out of the trees. Thousands. Braun wasn't certain he could even slow them down.

He resolved that he would either drive them off, break them before they could sweep through to Accar, or make a massive dent in their numbers trying.

Hurdling the shrapnel-riddled corpse of a giant spider, Braun skidded into the rear ranks of what even a Ghurish general would hesitate to call a 'line'. The last of his downhill momentum he spent on an overhead swing that ended with a spider's carapace splintering under his hammer. The pony-sized monster squealed and rolled away, taking its luckless rider down with it.

A small riot of cheers greeted his return.

Braun acknowledged it with a wave of his chipped hammer. 'I heard there were fighters here who needed help killing grots!'

The Hounds yelled back that this was lies.

Braun mashed in a spider's head with a blow from his left-hand hammer. He wasn't one for big speeches.

Off to his flank, he saw the pair of demigryph knights that had almost trampled him earlier wheeling together through the mass of spiders, crushing spindly legs under their heavier bodies and thundering free. They dragged a ragged wedge of pursuing spiders uphill, and straight into the fire of the Ironweld handgunners lining up on the hill to defend the artillery.

The panicked grots fled downhill.

A low growl, like a large bear in a deep cave, rumbled out of the jungle to the far left of the line, as though roused by the guns and raising its voice in challenge. The trees noticeably swayed and thrashed, and several grots in the close vicinity turned and fled from it. But it was too far ahead of the Freeguild line to be of any concern to Braun. The jungle was full of beasts and this was Ghur: there weren't many that would turn their noses up at a grot if it was offered on a plate.

There was a shout in his ear and Lisandr ran to join him in the front rank, thrusting ahead with her half-pike, the blade-tip going in low and neat and killing the monster instantly by piercing its heart. The grot rider was sent flying towards Braun and met an altogether messier end on Braun's off-hand.

Braun raised the weapon in salute and saw that the woman was grinning.

Ghur would make savages of them all yet.

Flushed with exertion, Lisandr twisted her spear and drew it from the spider's thorax. She lowered the spearhead and set herself behind her shield, wincing as she handled it with her splinted arm. She thrust her weapon over the top. Another spider squirmed on its tip and died. Braun held another at arm's length while he bludgeoned it to death with his hammer. The Celestian jabbed her spear a dozen times in quick succession, overcoming a spider's attempts at batting the shaft away on its forelimbs and stabbing it through the mouth.

Braun held his hammer aloft and roared. This was how all defeats should be.

An answering rumble echoed from that same bit of jungle to the left, twinkling lights playing through the gaps between the trees. It was bright and hard, that light, no warmth in it at all. A frightened murmur passed through the Freeguild as they watched it, but its effect on the Spiderfang was more pronounced. The local panic became contagious as the starlight grew brighter and more widespread and, without any obvious order being given, the horde that had previously looked unstoppable was turning around and fleeing, north-west, back towards Ymnog's Trample and the Eaten Plain.

'It is the Seraphon,' announced Taal, holding his staff aloft a few ranks back, quiet as a gnoblar in a Butcher's pantry when he'd a mind to be, the light show from the trees flickering across his upraised face. 'The lords of Mekitopsar march to do battle. In Sigmar's name!'

'*SIGMAR!*' the Hounds cheered.

But listening to the roaring and thrashing, spying that glint of gold that he was certain he'd glimpsed before, Braun of all people found himself uneasy in assigning the credit to the God-King. If the Seraphon had decided to fight, then it was to defend their borders, and not to aid the human 'friends' that they had never aided nor acknowledged in the fifty years that Accar had existed.

Waving his arms towards the Ironweld batteries on the hill, he yelled for a retreat.

The Primeval Jungle and its environs had been a protectorate of the Seraphon for as long as the earliest legends of her people could speak of it. The fortress at the eastern end of Thordar's Gap had been a ruin when the girl Vagria had first stumbled across it. It looked exactly the same now, the span of her immortal years an inconsequential blink of the eye relative to the cosmic *age* of this place. Once an outpost of Mekitopsar, it had been so long neglected that the jungle had scrambled over every lump of masonry that remained, knotting tight like the fibres of a rope, and adding a fringe of monkey vine to every crumbling arch and freestanding column of wall.

She saw a mound of white stones, once part of a greater structure but now rubble cloaked in moss, and in her mind's eye she saw upon it the heavy skull of a saurus warrior. It rested upon the pedestal, waiting to be claimed by a young Accari mage who lifted it with reverence. The mortal's face lit up with rapture as he raised the skull to his ear and turned away into the jungle. The vision faded as she laid her own hand to the pedestal. Her fingers made ripples in the freshwater puddle that, over the centuries, had eroded a shallow bowl from the stone. As the ripples dispersed and the clear water again became still, she caught a glimpse of her own, unmasked reflection. She touched her face, as if to be certain that the reflection she was seeing was hers.

Memories, as clear in front of her as her own likeness, appeared in the reflection. Behind her, she saw the Eternity Warden whose skull the Accari mage would come to claim centuries later. It stood over her, a piece of living statuary, an ancient thing of celemnite and starmetal scales, disgorged into the Age of Chaos by the upheavals of the realm. Its scales were so hard that light itself rebounded off them. Golden cladding blurred the lines between armour and adornment. Numerous plates and piercings adorned its skull, a necklace of weighty glyphs in gold, obsidian and coloured gems layering its broad chest. The saurus might have remained in aetheric hibernation throughout the long aeons, slowly fading along with the ruined fortress to which it had been geased as castellan, if not for Vagria's incursion.

She had invaded the sovereign realm of Mekitopsar, and the Warden had made no discrimination between this feral child and the bloodreavers that pursued her. It had slain her.

Or had sought to.

She remembered, watching the reflection play out, seeing the mortal girl she had been spreading her arms, head bowed, waiting for the slow-thinking warrior to administer the death blow. The Warden looked down at Vagria. Deep, slow thoughts, thoughts that had originated in the heads of godlike creatures, spawned in pools aeons before the second dawn of creation, moved with the grace of constellations through its eyes. It raised its gold-spiked stone club.

And held the blow.

Vagria watched as the girl's body disintegrated before her eyes, claimed by the God-King for his own. She closed her eyes and let the tears run. She had been so young, and yet so ready to die. Sigmar had seen her hunger for it and made it into a tool of his own, needful of a mortal favour that she had failed to return in her battle with Kragnos.

Her heart hardening, she sniffed back her tears, wiping them from the cheeks that she now realised were not hers, but wholly Sigmar's. This was the reason for the dysmorphia that had always left her uncomfortable with her own face and body. They were not hers. She had been a child still when Sigmar had taken her up to be reforged. She had never been an adult, never grown into a body of her own. All she was, was that which the God-King had made of her.

She did not wear a mask. She *was* the mask.

A birdlike chirrup sounded from the thicker vegetation amongst the ruined Seraphon fortress. Vagria turned from the reflecting pool, eyes still raw, wondering if the Eternity Warden from the reflection might, in fact, have been behind her all along. The Seraphon were slow to embrace change. To many, the Stormcasts remained new and strange, as threatening to their perfect order and the great plan of their masters as the Slaves to Darkness.

There was nothing there. Just a single, sparkling white feather lying on the ground, tugging at the jungle floor in a sudden, clear-scented breeze. She looked up, aware of something beyond her perceptions moving uncannily fast, deeper into the jungle. Picking up the feather, she bowed her head to it and smiled.

'I understand,' she whispered.

She was alive, and so long as that was true then all past sins could yet be forgiven. She had the opportunity, yet, to throw that life away, in whatever manner she, or Sigmar, deemed needful.

One warrior of the Farstrike Hunters still remained. And her hunt was not yet over.

Accar.

Thirty years after its Free Charter had been filed in the Great Library of Azyrheim, fifty-five after the jungle tribesmen who had claimed the Primeval Jungle for their own had been killed, bribed or set to work putting down its first walls, Accar was a city under constant siege from the jungle that surrounded it. Giants armoured in rugged bark crowded its timber stockades, undermined their pilings, threw explosions of brilliant green foliage and poisonous flowers over their parapet. The hoots, shrieks, caws and wails of reptilian fauna assailed it day and night, oppressive heat and beating rains working the long battle on the Accari's resolve.

For fifty-five years it had squatted, a toad of decaying wood and human dreams, under mists so thick that there were days when the entire city simply faded into the jungle. It had weathered the arch ambivalence of the Seraphon of Mekitopsar. The sorcerer-priests who ruled from the lost city could have wiped Accar from their domain with a wave of their cold-blooded hands. They hadn't. Yet. Nor had the lizard-folk ever left their hidden ziggurat to aid the humans on their doorstep either, until today, and Braun wasn't wholly convinced about that either.

The wisest amongst the Accari, those elderly survivors of the original tribal populations subjugated by Azyr, of whom the Taal clan were the most powerful, claimed that it was because fifty-five years was not nearly long enough for the slann to have noticed their presence, much less come to a decision regarding what to do about it.

The purpose of the city's founding a half century ago had been this: to put the stamp of Order on the Primeval Jungle; to extend Excelsis' influence westward, inland, and to one day connect it by trade and common governance to the Templia Beasthall and the old cities of the Mawbight. The jungle, as was Ghur's way, had thus far resisted ordering. Now, Braun got the distinct impression that it was pushing back.

When Accar's overgrown, vine-strangled walls appeared through the mists, Braun let out a cry that had two thousand road-weary, battle-hardened fighters looking to him in dismay.

The Freeguild had been gone for almost four months. Accar was isolated, but word would have reached them of the onslaught of destruction throughout the Coast of Tusks. The arbiter, her city not yet mature enough to have earned its governor the appellation *high*, had extended the defences, raised the north-west wall, built casemates for artillery that positively bristled with greatcannons and mortars. She had even fixed the door, which had never properly closed in Braun's lifetime. He barely recognised his home city, but it was also horribly familiar.

It was the gate he had seen in his prophecy. This was where he and Lisandr would fight Rukka Bosskilla.

He barely noticed as Altin, Ragn, Olgar and Woan dragged him, still wailing, through the gates, and to the most resigned of homecomings that any of the Hounds could have imagined.

The Ironjawz megaboss was alive.

Their final battle would be fought here.

CHAPTER FOURTEEN

'Make way!' Malec Grint pounded the spongy boards that snaked through Accar with a tight-rolled lizardskin sheet in his hand. Parchment or paper, though Excelsian merchants could get it for you, was hardly ever used, except for when the high likelihood of the writing material breaking down before it got to its recipient was considered part of the appeal. 'A message for the general!' He winced as his heel turned over a canted board, hobbled a few paces along the boardwalk before deciding he was unhurt after all, and sped back to a sprint. 'Make way!'

The boardwalks were quieter than he remembered. A lot of the local populace had fled already, heading towards Excelsis, hunting lodges in the deeper jungle or even the semi-mythical sanctuary of Mekitopsar or Koatl's Gullet. Most of those still left had been press-ganged to bring the decimated Hounds back to something resembling strength. The Dozen had needed to make a few examples first. Nobody forced an Accari to do anything they didn't want to do, not unless they were prepared to back it up with force.

Despite the calm of the deserted streets, the jungle was a constant clamour. Trees grew everywhere, walking pines straddling the narrow boardwalks, monstrous rubber trees erupting right through the middle of mud-and-timber stilt huts and bursting from their roofs, strung with bird nets and dreamcatchers like extensions of the home. Creeping bromeliads and towering heliconias scrambled up every upright surface and hummed with insects. Reptiles chirped, croaked and cawed from every conceivable niche and scurried semi-wild between grassy hummocks and the boardwalks.

The few Accari he saw, tanned, shaven-headed and wearing bitter looks, crowded the balconies of the still-houses and arraca-dens and onto the boardwalks. They bared mouths full of pitted teeth, slumped in chairs, and slurred unintelligible insults as Grint rattled the boards beneath them. Grint wondered if his home had always felt so joyless and so hard, so predisposed towards summary violence. Had the godbeast's awakening stirred something in the Accari as it had in the greenskins of the Heartlands? Or was it the doom that the Hounds had brought with them that drove them so hard to nihilism?

Or was it, more simply, that Grint had left Accar as a boy and was seeing it now with the eyes of a stranger?

Braun's hut was in one of the better parts of the city. The spice barons who'd helped found the city and sponsored the raising of the Hounds had built their walled estates on artificial hillocks, where temperate microclimates could be engineered through the cunning use of fans, mechanised water features and screening ferns. The less extravagantly wealthy, the merchants, the gang bosses, the more successful moonshiners, and even renowned Freeguild generals like Braun, had stout wooden homes in the centre of the city. It was muggy, overgrown and as uncomfortable as anywhere in Accar – arguably more so – but there was a status to being able to say that you'd fought your way to the middle of the herd and stayed there.

The hut's legs were thick, and wound with poisonous creepers that had the look of deliberate cultivation rather than the unhealthy parasitism that killed off most Accari houses after a decade or two. A high parapet ringed a deck where potted trees burst with bright foliage and insectivorous flowers, shading the greater bulk of the house behind a curtain of green. A grating reptilian song chirped from the canopy. It smelled of stagnant water, fruit decaying on the vine, and breathing plants.

A wooden spur, like a jetty, stuck out over the boardwalk. A rope ladder hung from it. Puffing out his cheeks, Grint stuffed the lizardskin under the waistband of his shorts and climbed. It was only eight or nine feet, but he was gasping by the time he collapsed on the deck. The air cloyed. The jungle heat sapped a man's strength. The Accari reputation for belligerent laziness was well earned, but it was an honest adaptation to their jungle home.

He palmed aside a hanging frond and called out.

'General?'

The windows were enormous, the heavy wooden shutters thrown open for ventilation. A smoke that looked like arraca coiled over the sill, but the distinctively bitter odour was absent amongst the mass of flowers.

'A message for you, general!'

He stepped through the open door and coughed. The air was thick and lazy. Too listless even to push its way out through those huge windows or the open door. It just lay there, getting fat and heavy. Where it brushed his lips or singed the hairs of his nostrils he finally caught the taste of burnt arraca, as well as more exotic, prophetic, odours that he'd become painfully acquainted with during his time in Goreham.

He sighed, then pinched his eyes and willed the prophecy to get out of his head.

When he opened them again, he took in the brawny figure sprawled across a mattress in the middle of the floor and swore.

'Not again.'

Efrim Taal was sitting cross-legged on the floor by the general's side, wrapped up in his thick robe in spite of the heat and smoking an arraca stem as long as his forearm. Bad Luck Mikali sat next to him, legs folded under her, apparently killing time with a game of maws and crosses. Taal scratched an *X* into the mat of vegetation covering the floorboards. Mikali pursed her lips as she studied the game board, looking up and giving Grint a shrug that might have been apologetic.

He supposed being apprenticed to Efrim Taal was better than going back to running suicide missions and errands. With Kanta Grint gone, that seemed to be Grint's lot again.

Sagging in his shoulders, Grint turned back around. Out on the deck he looked down at the lizardskin in his hand. He held it for a while, shaded by the general's canopy, and then unrolled it. What was the worst that could happen now?

The leather was scratched with the old letter forms common to Accar, used by human nomads in Gallet since long before Sigmar's return to the Heartlands. The angular characters were easy to cut into leather, or carve into stone, and many a witch hunter and warrior-priest from Excelsis had remarked on the similarities between it and the basic greenskin alphabet.

He squinted at them, but he was no more literate in the local alphabet than he was in that of Azyr. He doubted the message held any great revelation. The godbeast was coming. Everyone and their dog knew that already. It was what they were going to do about it that Grint wanted to know.

There was a time when he would've sat on the deck and waited as long as it took for Braun to pull his head back together. Either that or run around Accar like a headless gnoblar looking for the next chief in line. But he couldn't find it in himself to care that much about it.

There weren't enough hours left.

He stuffed the lizardskin back down his shorts, wishing he could dispose of the godbeast and his armies as easily, and climbed back down the ladder to the boardwalk.

He was surprised to find Celestian Angellin waiting at the bottom. She'd cut her hair short, as several of the Celestians had done since arriving in Accar, to better cope with the heat and the pests. Grint hated to think it, but it didn't suit her at all. Unlike the Ghurites she was emulating, she was so thin in the arms and upper body that it made her look like a child. She'd also foregone her uniform cloak and long-sleeved silk undershirt, but was otherwise fully armoured as her regiment's traditions required.

'Are you following me?' he asked.

Angellin laughed. Uniquely amongst the few Celestians that he'd spoken to, she didn't appear to have decided to blame the destruction of her regiment and stranding in Ghur squarely on the Accari. 'General Lisandr *was* curious about your movements and whereabouts, Malec, I will grant. But before I attended to that she asked that I deliver this message for General Braun.' She indicated the lizardskin that she, too, was carrying, tucked into her weapon belt.

Grint shrugged. 'Don't bother.'

The Celestian raised an eyebrow, but didn't ask. After a while, her expression turned into a concerned frown.

'What is it?' she asked.

Grint's face went blank. 'What's what?'

'You were staring.'

'I…'

Grint coughed, pulling on his tunic collar. It felt very warm all of a sudden. Probably because it had felt so cool on Braun's balcony. Yes, that was probably it.

Before he could say anything though, Angellin cursed and swatted the back of her neck. She drew her gauntlet fingers away and looked at them, disappointed. 'I swear the bugs here favour Celestian blood over Accari.'

'They'll get bored of it eventually.'

The smile drained from the woman's face. Grint frowned. He'd meant it to be flippant. It wasn't quite so funny when you expected to be dead in the next day or so.

'What's the message?' Grint asked, changing the subject. 'From Lisandr?'

'The message...' Angellin surfaced from her thoughts. She put her hand on the lizardskin roll, as she might seek the reassurance of a sword hilt. 'It is not for me to share. I should probably find Chief Ragn or that degenerate, Altin, and deliver it to them.'

Grint shrugged as though it didn't matter. Which it didn't. He jabbed his thumb back towards the house. 'Taal's up there, but don't expect him to be helpful.'

Angellin smiled again. 'General Lisándr has forbidden us from passing any messages for Braun through Chief Taal in any case. After last time.' The Celestian sighed. 'I suppose it is harder to keep a secret in a city like this than it was in Fort Honoria. General Lisandr was simply hoping for Braun's assistance with the evacuation. The Spiderfang continue to prowl the jungle, and the general believes we have only a matter of days before the rest of the godbeast's horde arrives to reinforce them.'

In the half-day since their return to Accar, Lisandr and Shay had been attempting to organise the city's evacuation. Despite the evidence of recent fortification, however, they found a city stubbornly unprepared to be organised. The spice barons had already gone, as had the merchants, the bureaucrats. Even the priests had departed for Excelsis weeks earlier. Discontent had been rumbling through the city for months since, even while the Hounds had been trapped in Goreham, but it had worsened with the immediate danger. Violence that went beyond the usual thuggery. Godhead glyphs and crude maws scrawled on walls.

Some of the older citizens, the last elders of the native tribes, had even begun to agitate for overthrowing the new order and casting in with the new god in the Heartlands. Only by throwing down their false walls and joining him, as their ancestors had followed the Green God on his Great Waaagh! to Realms' Edge, they argued, could they hope to mete out destruction rather than suffer it. Altin had personally strung up eleven elderly men and had their corpses delivered to his hut, which had put a stop to that kind of talk for a while.

But at least Lisandr was trying. It was more than Braun had done.

He sighed, and looked up. The sky was darkening, thickening with cloud as though tensing its stomach for a blow. When the attack came, it would come by night.

'What now?' he said.

'Now…' Angellin shrugged. 'Now, I suppose I look for Ragn or Altin.' She nodded towards the lizardskin that was sticking up from the waistband of Grint's shorts. 'Come with me?'

Grint let out a deep breath, then nodded. There were worse ways to spend your last day.

There were worse ways to spend your last day, but Efrim Taal couldn't seem to think of any. He was sitting cross-legged on Braun's floor, idly turning his staff clockwise and then counterclockwise between the palms of his hands. The various fetishes and charms strung from it tinkled. The skull of the great saurus mounted on top shook its head, as though in grave disappointment in his choices, that he would spend his final hours in such fashion.

He would do one great deed in his life, it had told him. He would save the people of the Heartlands from the tyranny of the Returned God.

Since his return from his Mekitopsar pilgrimage and his acceptance into the shamanic tradition of his forefathers, he'd thought that the voice of Sigmar had been referring to the Azyrites of Excelsis. All his adult life, he'd been working towards that goal, to throwing off their tyranny and finding a new home for the Accar beyond the reach of their civilisation.

But now a new god had arisen in the Heartlands and he'd been forced to think again. Only now, for example, was it occurring to him that perhaps Lisandr and her Celestians were not his enemies after all. He was starting to feel actual *guilt* for the desecration of their temple in Honoria, and for the sacrilege of his behaviour towards the late Mother Thassily, honourably fallen in battle with Rukka Bosskilla.

Taal believed in Sigmar. Fiercely. The God-King was powerful enough to fight his own battles, but spread too thinly across the Mortal Realms to concern himself with the affairs of Efrim Taal and his old ways. He had immortal heroes to aid, and epic crusades to conduct. He would be looking at Excelsis now, as all the gods surely were, and the only way Taal could hope, or even pray, to avoid the fate that was heading for Accar was to be quicker, faster, tougher, more cunning.

The Ghurish way.

His eye caught movement and his gaze flicked down. Mikali scratched a maw into the undergrowth with her spice knife.

'Three in a row, you win,' she said boredly. 'This is a rubbish game.'

'It is a very ancient game.'

'Whoever goes first always wins.'

'This is true.'

'And you always go first.'

Taal felt a grin pulling up the corner of his mouth. *Bad Luck* they called her, but Taal felt fortunate indeed to have found a talent to replace Ferrgin at this late hour. Her knack for bending the aether to her advantage was obvious, if one was looking for it, if untrained. With a little schooling, she might learn to become more powerful than Ferrgin, always so lazy, had ever been. Perhaps, one day, more powerful even than Taal.

Was this his *one great deed?* He was doubtful. Even with training, no mortal sorcerer, however gifted or mighty, could hope to defeat the godbeast, not where all the might of an Astral Templars chamber had failed. And nor did he have the time to train her fully. That was a commitment of years. Of lifetimes. They had days, and had so far spent it playing children's games on the floor and smoking arraca.

'Another round?' said Mikali

Taal frowned, looking sage, and nodded.

The young woman sighed and set about cutting another four-by-four grid out of the grass. Taal rolled his eyes up to the saurus on his staff. Mikali caught the direction of his gaze and looked up.

'I'd always thought the Seraphon went back to the stars when they were killed.'

'Many will,' said Taal. 'But those who live in the Lower Realms and call themselves the Coalesced are flesh and bone, like you and I.'

'Like those in Mekitopsar.'

'They've been here so long that the essence of Ghur has become a part of what they are. As it has for us as well.'

He glanced towards Braun. The general was spread out over the mattress like somebody's favourite drunk. He was huge, massive with muscle, but he wasn't getting younger and his belly, his brow, were already succumbing to the mercies of middle age. Glasslike splinters of low-grade prophecy littered the bedside and twinkled from his big chest, returning the little bit of light that made it past the screening vegetation and the arraca fog.

Taal had never taken prophecy. He'd always preferred to scry the future in other ways. Older ways.

And he'd seen how it had ruined Braun.

Casius Braun had been a great man once. He had been the sort of man who would face down a brute like Rukka Bosskilla, and who, by example alone, could convince ten thousand raw troops to charge right behind him. He had been a man that Efrim Taal, one who had little respect for any citizen of the civilised coast, had been proud to follow.

Look at him now. Hiding under his bed from the monsters, hoping to find a solution to their plight in prophecy.

The muscles of Taal's jaw twitched as he realised he didn't have much choice. He gestured for Mikali to stop what she was doing.

'Gather up the general's prophecy. Anything that's not totally dark will have some power left in it.' Positioning himself so that his back was to the wall, he propped his staff up beside him where it could stand unsupported, and then sat back. He loosened the collar of his robes. 'Then bring it to me.'

Whatever future Braun was delving into, it was time for Efrim Taal to hurry things along.

The First Age Starhold Celestians, the few hundred of them that were left, had garrisoned the grand half-timber folly that had formerly housed Accar's Grand Conclave.

The building's stone foundations rose to become mouldy timber, something of a high watermark of Excelsian ambition for the place, whereafter their architects had accepted the logic of building cheaply and replacing what the jungle destroyed rather than attempting to defeat it with imported stone. Compared to most Accari architecture the structure was relatively sound, the various privy chambers were well suited as officers' quarters, and the main auditorium provided excellent stabling for the demigryphs.

Lisandr had taken the arbiter's study as her headquarters. The accommodations were more rustic than she was accustomed to, when she and civilisation met in passing, but she hardly noticed. There had barely been time to sit down. There had been supply chains to organise, goods to pack, spicing gangs to round up, bodies to arm and armour and jungle to clear. Added to that, everything that could not find its way to Braun managed to get itself diverted to her.

She sighed, wondering if Braun had had the right idea of it, and took a sip of the former arbiter's wine. She took it unwatered, a hit of undiluted alcohol straight from the bottle to the back of the throat and the front of her brain. As the harsh buzz of the inferior quality wine passed, she found herself thinking of young Lydia Victoria Aubreitn and felt an unexpected stab of real grief. Her squire had come from an excellent family. She would have *insisted* that Lisandr dine properly and at the appointed time. She looked down the wine-stained sash sticking to her grimy breastplate. Lydia would have ensured that she was properly dressed and presentable. She would certainly never have allowed her to receive her officers while slumped at her desk and questionably sober.

Lisandr considered commending the girl for a posthumous honour. But she did not have the time. None of them had enough time.

There was a knock at the door. Lisandr set the bottle down, a makeshift paperweight on a sheaf of order papers that might or might not ever get delivered, and wiped her mouth on the silk cuff of her long sleeve as Field Marshal Mestrade marched in.

The officer saluted and stood to attention at the other side of the desk. Lisandr gestured for him to sit. He relaxed, slightly, and pulled back the chair, respectfully removing his helmet and setting it neatly on his lap as he sat.

Lisandr felt that she ought to like Mestrade more than she did. He was dutiful, respectful of rank, performed his orders promptly and without complaint, and boasted a repertoire of inspiring verse unequalled in the regiment. He was, in every sense, a testament to the higher virtues of Azyr. And yet…

She found herself wishing for Braun. Somehow, the two of them had managed to lead their respective regiments to this point in, arguably, better shape than either of them would have achieved with unchallenged authority resting in one set of hands alone. She pinched the bridge of her nose and gave a quiet groan. Obviously, she needed more sleep than she had allowed herself to take.

The field marshal cleared his throat and began his report. It made for grim listening.

The Accari Hounds stood at close to their full strength of twenty-five thousand for the first time since the launch of the Bloodgullet Crusade, but most were untried conscripts, those too old, young, sick or stupid to have fled with the city's worthies, and painfully undisciplined. There was no way of recruiting more Celestians without returning to Azyrheim, and so the hundred or so knights that she had were all she could reliably command to hold a city or marshal one final retreat.

The walls were her one bit of good news, recently refurbished and cleared of vegetation, but she did not expect them to withstand a serious assault. Regardless of what the former arbiter had done to improve them before she had fled, they remained weaker and less high than those Lisandr had been forced to abandon at Fort Honoria. They did not have half of the arsenal that Shay had commanded there. And they were without the Stormcast Eternals.

According to Altin's scouts, the so-called cannibal having taken charge of the Accari contingent in Braun's absence, the enemy's outriders were two to three days away and had replenished most of the strength lost during the sack of Honoria. The scouts that Lisandr had ordered south, tentatively exploring the possibility of seeking out and beseeching aid from the Seraphon, had returned with hints of a second, even larger greenskin force that they expected to pass the jungle from the south-east, and which was presumably also on its way to Excelsis. They claimed to have seen banners proving that the horde was led by none other than Skaggrot the Loonking, *and* by the dreaded Fist of Gork, Gordrakk, himself.

The scouts had, of course, found no trace of the legendary Mekitopsar.

In her heart, Lisandr knew that Accar did not have the means to defeat a god, but nor could they hope to outrun it and make it to Excelsis. The news of that second horde only convinced her of the necessity of their sacrifice. Accar would stall the god here, for as long as was mortally possible. They would weaken him if they could, and if nothing else they would buy Excelsis however much time their lives were worth by preventing his union with that second horde.

And if they could fight long enough that a few more fighting Accari could reach the coast intact, then that was a sacrifice worth any true soldier's while.

Mestrade concluded his report and cleared his throat. Lisandr was about to dismiss him when a thought occurred.

'What time is it?'

'Mid-afternoon, sir. The squires have just been preparing lunch.'

With a sigh, Lisandr sat back in her chair and flicked through the stack of undelivered orders. 'Let the warriors have their meal. It may be their last. Then have the squires sent here to deliver these final orders to the evacuees.'

'Yes, sir.'

Lisandr put her hands flat to the desk and pushed herself up from her chair. Her head spun and she staggered half a step sideways, rattling the drawers. She gave her head a vigorous shake. She had not realised quite how long she had been sitting there. She glanced at the bottle sitting on top of her papers. She had not realised quite how much of the arbiter's wine she had put away either.

May as well live a little now.

She took up the three-quarters empty bottle and downed the rest. Mestrade had already risen from his chair opposite her and thrown a salute. If his eyebrows climbed any higher they would have been above his head.

'To the gate,' she said.

'Yes, sir.'

Efrim Taal knew that he was dreaming. He knew because he'd had this dream, or dreams like it, so many times before. The place was the Izalmaw. The time was ten years ago, the last decisive battle against Waaagh! Bosskilla before it had grown large enough to threaten the cities of Izalend or Bilgeport.

Or at least, that was what it was supposed to look like. That was how his biased mind had chosen to represent the prophecy.

Orruks bellowed, brawling with one another in the snow whilst fighters in the red and tan of the Accari fled towards a gleaming city on the distant coast. The heavy tread of troggoths and warbeasts reverberated through the deep drifts, lowing as they killed one another.

THUD.

Taal shook his head. This was a vision, not a memory.

He looked up. It wasn't snowing. It was raining amber.

'You shouldn't be here,' said Braun.

The general was standing beside him, where he had conspicuously not been before, but Taal did not find his appearance there surprising. He was clad in maw-krusha leathers with red epaulettes in the shape of the Arrow stitched into the sleeves. In his hand was a spear. Its glowing head was amberbone, as his ancestors had used to make them, before the coming of Azyr and its laws. His bald head was smeared green with orruk blood, obscuring parts of the Shatterer tattoo across his face in ways that Taal imagined were meaningful, but the battlefield was too full of imagery and noise for him to focus on any one detail. He found that he had some sympathy for the Prophesiers' Guild of Excelsis, who foretold a new doom for every season, whilst somehow always missing the crucial facts of the omen.

'Why not?' he said. 'It's my future too.'

Braun looked at him, *really* looked. 'Taal?'

'Who do I look like?'

'Like you, only… this is the real you, isn't it? How're you here in my vision?'

'I've a few tricks of my own, you know. And there's no point looking to the future if the future catches up to you first.' He folded his arms over his chest, shivering in the not-quite-cold of the not-quite-snow. 'They're all killing each other.'

'I noticed that too,' said Braun.

'Why?'

Braun looked up at the glowing point of his spear.

THUD.

'Braun…'

They both turned.

Rukka Bosskilla, a mass of spikes and iron, stomped towards them up a slope made of dead orruks blanketed in snow. He was wearing a crown of arm-length yellow teeth that Taal did not remember him possessing before, and which seemed to have swelled his head to the point that his tusks were buckling the grille of his helmet. Taal hadn't seen him at Goreham. He'd only heard. He'd forgotten just how big the megaboss was. His gauntlets alone looked big enough to swallow a man and crush him out of hand.

How Braun had fought him once, he'd never know. And that he'd fought him twice…

Perhaps he'd been as unfair on Braun as he'd been on Thassily and Lisandr. He'd earned his vices and the degradations of middle age, as surely as any man ever had.

Rukka looked at Taal. 'Who's dis?'

Taal took an instinctive step back. Prophecy, he knew, could be as dangerous as any lived reality, if the participants were powerful enough. Braun, however, levelled his spear as though to fight.

The Ironjawz boss shook like a bag of change as he laughed. 'Nah. I's only lookin' to fight the best. And dat ain't you any more.' He turned around.

Braun had eyes only for his old foe, but Taal obliged and looked up.

THUD.

Amber, or was it snow, swirled around a colossal figure, so huge that its antlers interfered with the Heavens, its bloody mane orbited by a rogue moon with a hateful face. Wherever that spiteful satellite flew it pronounced doom simply by being, bowling through constellations, knocking aside stars, breaking orbits. Portents that had been millennia in the making unravelled in the cackling of an evil moon, new ones falling randomly together with a mischievous disregard for godly schemes and mortal destinies. Taal observed the formation of the Constellation of the One-Eyed Troggoth, the Loonboss, the Eating Hand. The blizzard started to fall faster. Faster. As though the godbeast and its Bad Moon were pulling the stuff out of the sky, slaughtering the clouds they came from like defenceless beasts and ensuring that there would never be more.

From way up high, the light of amber burned through the snow. The glare of a volcano.

'I am Kragnos,' it declared. 'And I am the end.'

Taal quailed, although Braun, somehow, remained oblivious to it through his fixation on the Bosskilla.

He'd heard that name, as he'd dimly recognised his appearance outside of Goreham. Kragnos was a monster from a children's story. A god of earthquakes and the violent earth. Worshipped by both the humans and the orruks of the Heartlands long before Sigmar had found his way through the Realmgates to the Realm of Beasts. In the legends, he had been captured by Dracothion, the Great Drake, and caged under Ursricht's Kill as a demonstration of the God-King's power.

The moral of the parable had been to warn against dangerous boasts. Dracothion had not been able to slay Kragnos, and in the end both he and Sigmar had been left looking weak, while Gorkamorka had returned to rule in Ghur.

THUD.

'Anyfin' still around when he gets 'ere is gettin' krumped,' Rukka growled, and Taal watched with dawning realisation as the megaboss turned from Braun and stomped back through the snow towards the oncoming godbeast. 'But I want wot's mine.'

There was a reason that the prophecy consistently brought Braun back to the Bosskilla. He was the answer that the general was seeking. Braun's focus was just too narrow for him to see it.

'The future is not for you, little man,' Kragnos' voice boomed. 'Be patient. Your doom will come for you in time.'

'How–?'

'Begone!' the godbeast roared.

Everything ended.

Taal awoke doused in sweat, but shivering as though buried to his neck in snow. His abrupt return sent splinters of exhausted prophecy twinkling off his bare chest and to the grass-carpeted floor like droplets of smoke. He looked around, startled by the chirp of reptiles and the low hum of insects and the sawing of the wind through the jungle outside Braun's window.

Surely none of those things could share a realm with the Avatar of Destruction.

Mikali rushed to him, face worried, rooting in her pockets for an arraca stem which she then lit and pushed into Taal's trembling fingers. As every Accari in the Hounds had learned about four months ago, arraca smoke was the cleanest comedown from a prophetic high.

Never again. Never *ever* again.

Sitting up, breathing deep and coughing up the bitter fumes, Taal crossed his arms over his knees and glanced towards Braun's mattress. The general was just waking up too, and looking far worse for it than Taal. He scratched his bald head, opening his hand and looking at the palm as though expecting to see a magic spear.

'That was some vision. Every time I think I'm gonna quit...'

'Don't expect another one like that again,' Taal snapped, then turned to Mikali. 'I need you to go and get Lisandr. Shay too. Have them go through the baggage that the Astral Templars left with the Ironweld. They'll know what they're looking for when they find it.'

'What's this?' Braun grunted softly.

'I've got a plan,' said Taal.

Braun sat up, wincing at the soreness in his head, and flicked his fingers out towards Taal. 'I hope you're gonna share that stem with me while we wait.'

'The humans make their plans to destroy me.'

The Godboss galloped over the vast flats of Ymnog's Trample, the ground breaking under his hooves to leave a crevasse a thousand miles long. It stretched way back, to what was left of the Bloodgullet gluthold and even further. Earbug looked back mournfully, watching the landscape shaking itself apart as far away as both horizons. He'd really fancied that gluthold.

'Before, I could smell only their despair at my coming,' the Godboss went on. 'Now, I sense an eagerness to fight. It is an affront to my power.'

A wild carnival of destruction whirled abreast of the Godboss. Grots bounded giddily along on rabid cave squigs, or on garishly coloured spiders, their mounts scuttling easily up and over the clefts that the Godboss had foisted on the poor earth. Ogors bludgeoned their own way through the defiles, mournfangs and stonehorn keeping dogged pace through brute stamina rather than any spectacular gift or turn of speed. Orruks kicked their boars and gruntas until all but the strongest were dead already. Gargants strode alongside lazily with a league-swallowing gait.

'The gargant stomps are much diminished from the days when Behemat and his father walked amongst them.' The Godboss issued a grumbling sound that might have been a sigh. 'I remember Ymnog.'

By virtue of his mighty know-wotz, innate Morkiness and the immense stamina of the Glossom Queen, Earbug had been allowed to ride right up front with the Godboss. The war-spider's rickety howdah rattled with war trophies and fetishes, a lot of which he'd had his boys surreptitiously take the knife to, converting the eight-legged god into ones with four. It had all been quite the honour, especially with Rukka slogging along at the back. It hadn't occurred to him that he'd have to make conversation with a god.

What did you even *say* to a comment like *I remember Ymnog*?

'The Father of Gargants was so vast that, with his arm, he could reach across the aetheric gulfs and in one hand shake a Realmsphere.' The god gave a snort, hot with rampant animal temper.

'But Ymnog was slain by this Sigmar. Behemat was beaten and caged. Only I am still here.'

'Er, yeah, boss,' Earbug piped in, as he did from time to time when it felt appropriate. 'What d'you wan' us to do about 'em?'

The god turned his head towards him, peering down with weighty eyes.

'The humies, I mean,' Earbug explained. 'Not… er… Ymnog… er…' Mork, he was pathetic.

'Their plans are irrelevant to me. It is their fate to fall beneath my hooves.'

Earbug fiddled with the dangly bits on his staff, hoarding his scraps of courage like a starving little yoof gathering up shrooms. 'Does we… um… does we have to trample *absolutely* everyfing?'

The Godboss did not have the face for smiling. His heavy mouth broadened, baring huge, blunt teeth. His eyes flattened and widened. His mammoth body gave off an energy that had the Bonesplitterz around them careening after him on their boars like the tail of a psychedelic comet and hollering up at him with glee.

'Yes,' was all he said.

Earbug looked crestfallen, but at least he hadn't been krumped on for his impertinence.

'But,' the Godboss went on, and Earbug's flappy ears pricked up. 'When that is done, I will raise a new empire. One made in my image, and that I will rule, and that you, perhaps, and others like you, shall rule under me.'

Earbug stood gangly tall on his rocking howdah, all dagger teeth from ear to ear. 'Yes, Boss Trampla!'

'The greenskins were a plague upon the Drogrukh, even in my time, a warlike and unruly menace even to the great empire, which I would have ruled, had I not chosen exile.' Again, that horrible not-grin. 'Before they pledged their strength to me, and I turned them upon my people's enemies.' The Godboss turned away, towards the green fuzz of the Primeval Jungle on the horizon, and sniffed the air.

His nostrils flared, and his eyes burned with sudden anger.

'Boss?'

'Stardust and lizard musk,' the Godboss growled. 'A city of the slann. Here in Ghur.'

'Yeah, it's been dere forevver. No one mess wiv dem star lizzies. Not even da Chaos ladz.'

'Not forever,' the Godboss answered.

Earbug looked towards the jungle. The smallest fear that the Trampla was about to turn them round and order him to lead an assault on the Seraphon fortress made his lip tremble.

'It was their sorcery that had me within the Twinhorn while the Zodiacal Dragon held me in his coils. When my vengeance falls it will fall hardest on Kroak and his descendants.' He grumbled. 'Their annihilation is millennia overdue, but it must wait. I would see first to the fate of my homeland, in Donse, and discover for myself if any of the Drogrukh yet live.' His monstrous visage became a snarl. 'It irks me that these humans believe they can stall me.'

'Let me take 'em, boss,' said Earbug. With the threat of the Seraphon taken off the table, anything felt possible. He was still picturing himself in the biggest bosshat of them all, Earbug Glibspittle, Da Shady King, Regent of Ghur. It had a nice shine to it. 'Let me and my lot do this fing for you. It'll be all nice and trampled before you's even there to bovver wiv it.'

Kragnos considered, then dipped his antlered head in regal assent.

'Destroy them in my name, Earbug of the Deepenglade. And when I have the need, I will remember yours.'

Once Braun was up and clothed, he gathered the others in his dining room, one of the larger and less-used rooms in the house.

Braun pulled a dust sheet off the table, leaving everyone in the room coughing. In addition to Lisandr and Shay, whom he'd actually called for, Mestrade was there, dressed for battle and looking impatient, along with Taal and Kanta's boy, Grint, in case of an urgent need to call in somebody else. Bad Luck Mikali and a Celestian named Carnelian stood guard on the deck outside the back door.

Once they'd all arranged themselves and been seated and Taal, at Braun's insistence, had spoken a short prayer, they began.

Shay set a fleece-wrapped bundle on the table. Taking her time over it, working with just one hand, the gunnery-professor unwrapped it. An amber glow painted the six tired faces that surrounded it, throwing gnarly man-shaped shadows across the timber walls.

Braun leant over the table as though drawn in by the hairs of his nostrils. His prophecy headache ebbed, displaced by an urgent throb in his temples, fierce hunger pangs and an ache in his mouth, like ulcers all over, as though it was eating itself.

He forced his fists to unclench.

'Amberbone,' said Shay. 'There's a ton of the stuff where this piece came from.' She looked at Braun. 'How did you know that it would be there?'

Braun scratched his head. 'It came to me in a vision. Or rather, the vision reminded me of something that Horac and Vagria both said. They told us that they unearthed the amberbone from under the Morruk Hills and must have brought it with them when they found us on the Cuspid Mesas. And if they'd had it with them, then they must've left it behind when they rode into Goreham to slay Kragnos.'

'Kragnos?' Lisandr raised an eyebrow.

'The godbeast's name.'

'And you–'

'Saw that in a vision,' Taal confirmed, with a smile that held too many teeth and too little humour. 'He did. Kragnos. The God of Earthquakes and the End of Empires. The Avatar of Destruction. Captured and bound by Dracothion in the Age of Myth, long before the God-King himself had ever come to the Mortal Realms.'

Mestrade smiled ruefully. 'Where is Dracothion when one needs him?'

Braun glanced up through the web of fingers that his face had sunk into. He flashed his teeth, and made the sign of the hammer. 'Gods make examples and mortals follow.'

'Children, please,' said Shay. The loss of her arm had made her short-tempered. She reached across the table and closed the fleece over the amberbone. It was as though a menacing drunk had just been thrown out of the room.

Braun put his throbbing head back into his hands.

'This would all make for a fascinating lesson in history,' said Shay. 'But is there a plan somewhere in our near future?'

'We turn Rukka, and the rest of Kragnos' horde, against him,' said Taal, making a fist of his hand and tapping it meaningfully on the tabletop. 'And Kragnos against his horde.'

'Using this?' Lisandr inclined her head towards the fleece-wrapped bundle.

The table beneath it seemed to be shaking, although Braun, his thighs pushed up against the underside, felt nothing. It was only after a moment's attention that he saw through the illusion. The table wasn't shaking. It was millions of mites, worms and beetles, many too tiny to be seen had they not been part of a greater swarm, burrowing upwards through the table's expensive veneer, drawn to the realmstone as powerfully as Braun had felt himself be. Once there, however, repelled by whatever celestial magic imbued the fleece, the creatures instead turned on one another, and already a dust layer of microscopic insects a quarter of an inch thick had built up around the bottom of the fleece.

Ghur consumed all. Even itself. Thus did amberbone always return itself to the earth in the end.

'I have read that amberbone needs to be worked properly in order to produce a reliable effect,' said Lisandr.

'And the lore required to shape amberbone is very rare,' said Shay.

'I can help with that,' said Taal. 'The old lore might've been driven out of Thondia, but here in Gallet you'll find it alive yet.'

'I like this plan,' said Shay. 'I do.' She looked around the table. 'But can it work?'

'We all felt the effect of this one piece.' Taal licked his teeth. 'Now *imagine* what it will do to an orruk.'

'We have a matter of days,' said Lisandr.

'Then we had best get started,' the shaman replied.

Shay gave a spluttering laugh. 'I have worked with celestium in purpose-designed and rune-warded forges. I have experimented with Aqshian brightstone in my gunpowder mixes before abandoning the work as too dangerous. Amberbone is...' She glanced apologetically at Lisandr and Mestrade. 'I have read every word that has been recorded on the subject. Scholarly interest. The Artillery School is more permissive towards that sort of thing than the rest of Excelsis these days.' She cleared her throat. 'But anyway. *Days?*'

'You will have the entirety of my clan to aid you,' said Taal.

Shay drummed her fingers on the table as she thought. 'Days. Maybe less. So we shouldn't forge anything too complicated. No swords. No axes.'

'Spears,' Braun interrupted.

Shay paused, and considered. 'Yes. Yes, spears would work. We would only need to fashion the heads, and as many as we can put out in the time we have. They wouldn't have to be works of art.'

'I'd rather have a javelin,' Grint put in, in a small voice from the far end of the table.

Braun glared at the boy, who shrank back into his seat. 'And javelins,' he grunted.

'What is it, Casius?' Lisandr leant across the table. 'I know when you are holding something back. You are not very good at it.'

Braun lifted his head, as heavy as it felt on the end of his neck, and through bloodshot eyes looked directly at Lisandr. 'I saw myself in a prophecy with an amberbone spear. You and me, in front of these walls with amberbone spears, are going to fight Rukka Bosskilla.'

'While Kragnos turns on his horde,' Taal added.

Braun felt a shiver as his shaman spoke. As though, together, they were hammering a shape onto something that, up until then, had been ephemeral and vague. As though they'd just made it real.

'And do we win?' asked Shay.

Braun shifted uncomfortably on his seat. 'I don't know.' He glanced at Taal, but there was no help there. The shaman's face was etched with deep frown lines that gave away nothing.

'I have never seen you so reluctant for a fight,' said Lisandr. Braun gave an empty bark, what a laugh would sound like from a person incapable of joy. 'After the loss of Fort Honoria *you* were the one who had to push *me*.'

'I don't need pushing, Ellisior. I called you all here, remember? This is my plan.'

Taal coughed at him.

'*Our* plan.'

Lisandr leant an elbow on the table, resting her narrow chin on the knuckles. 'I have spoken with Stormcast Eternals who have fallen in combat with Ironjawz megabosses. How did you ever beat Rukka Bosskilla the first time?'

'I poisoned his maw-krusha,' said Braun. Beside him, Taal appeared to be grinning, reminded of simpler days, although he doubted somehow they had felt so simple at the time. 'Two days before the battle I sent Woan out with a group of scouts to throw poisoned meat into the monster's pen. Most of the gore-gruntas died before the horde reached the Izal, but Facekikker, tough creature that it was, made it all the way to the battle.'

'Already, Sigmar was showing his smile to Braun and the Dozen,' said Taal.

'The maw-krusha died right under the megaboss,' Braun went on. 'Fell out of the sky and almost drowned him in the river. Rukka managed to get his head through the ice, and all I had to do…' He mimed a hammer-stroke. 'He went back under. We never found the body. We searched for him afterwards, the Dozen, all of us who were left after the battle, but we never found him. We assumed he'd sunk to the bottom, cut the head off the next biggest orruk we could find and took it to be paraded around Izalend.'

'Sigmar praises cunning as much as he admires brute strength,' said Taal.

'Then…' Lisandr sat back. She looked as though she was debating something with herself. 'I believe that Sigmar would find favour with this plan.' She produced a narrow smile. 'Let us outwit the Ironjaw one last time. With his pretender-god here with him, and with Sigmar watching from afar. I will hold an amberbone spear if that is what it takes. Let us do this. Let us go to our deaths in a manner becoming an Azyrite *and* a Ghurite.'

'It's been prophesied,' said Taal. 'It's going to happen. Everything we've done has brought us here and everything you try to do now will only get you the rest of the way. We may as well go along with it now.'

Braun glanced across. 'What if I'd never taken prophecy in the first place?'

Taal produced a nasty smile. 'The God-King may have an answer, but I'll bet that question drives the prophesiers crazy.'

'Fine, then,' said Braun, less than happy. 'Good.'

'He'll come right at us,' said Shay. 'Kragnos, I mean. He'll come straight through the wall, just like he did at Goreham and Honoria. If we put every gunner, javelin-armed Accari and grenadier on the north-west wall, then *maybe* we can slow him down long enough for your amberbone weapons to do the rest.'

Braun grinned in spite of the doubts he had in his shaman's plan. One almighty punch to the face, everything they could throw. What could be more righteous?

Mestrade cleared his throat. 'We should also consider accelerating the evacuation.'

'We'll need everyone who can fight on the walls if we're going to hold Kragnos at bay,' said Shay.

'We are not going to hold Kragnos at bay,' said Mestrade. 'And if I understand this plan then it is to enrage the greenskins enough that they turn on one other, and on Kragnos. It would seem wise then that we have as few of our people in the way as possible?'

'There is a logic to it,' said Lisandr. 'All right then. Anyone that Arden can spare, or that Casius does not feel he needs, is to be evacuated through the south gate along with the remaining civilians. With enough prayers, they might make it to Excelsis.'

'Do you honestly believe they can keep ahead of Kragnos?' asked Taal.

'Maybe Excelsis isn't his goal,' said Braun.

'It'll be his goal.' Taal smiled, although, as usual, there was little warmth in it. 'Excelsis is always in peril.'

For all Sigmar's efforts, the Ghurish Heartlands remained untamed and unsettled, except by greenskins, and by human tribes who were little better. Excelsis was the only city of consequence in the entire Heartlands with the exception, perhaps, of the ziggurat at Mekitopsar, which wasn't entirely a part of the Mortal Realms at all.

It was the only city across four continents that was worth the attention of a god.

'They can make it,' said Lisandr, sounding confident. 'If we can hold Kragnos here for long enough. If we can cull enough of his horde. We know where he is coming from. We know the path he's taking.' She turned from Braun, splitting her attention between Taal and Shay. 'We have more amberbone than we could ever make into weapons in the time we have. What if we were to mine the path they will take through the jungle? They might tear one another apart before they even come near to the walls. If nothing else, they will be primed to turn once they arrive.'

'Maybe,' said Shay. 'With realmstone, nothing is predictable.'

'And it would be dangerous,' said Mestrade. 'The jungle is already infested with spiders.'

'Nothing that follows from now is going to be safe,' said Taal. 'I'll go.'

Braun blinked. 'You're injured, and Shay may have need of your lore.'

Taal waved his concern away on both counts. 'There are others in my clan who can be more helpful, but none who can fight a god or who know the jungle as well. I should be the one to go.'

Braun could see that he was set. 'But why?'

The shaman sat back. He looked up at the staff that he was holding lightly in one partially open hand, as though it were standing on its own while he merely advised. 'I don't feel as though I have given Sigmar all he expects of me yet.'

'Regardless, you cannot mine a whole jungle on your own,' said Lisandr.

'That's what the make-up mobs are for,' said Taal. 'And the

conscripts. They'll be useless for anything else. And I'll take Mikali with me.'

'*Bad Luck* Mikali?' said Braun.

Taal grinned sharply. 'Depends who you ask.'

Braun puffed out his cheeks, and then shrugged. He was out of arguments, and he was starting to get a headache, and the shaman seemed stubbornly determined. 'All right then.'

'I do not have many warriors left to spare,' said Lisandr. 'But I will ask for volunteers to escort you there and, Sigmar willing, back.'

With that, and without further ado, the Celestian general rose. They all had work to do.

CHAPTER FIFTEEN

Efrim Taal left straight for the wall from Braun's home, but it was still well over an hour later by the time that he, Mikali, Grint, Angellin, a laden demigryph and two-score Accari conscripts passed through the north-west gate.

A sense of common purpose seemed to have burnt through Accar like a tropical fever. Arden Shay, with the aid of Taal's many cousins and brothers, had already crafted spearheads that Celestian squires had, albeit grudgingly, fitted to their mistress' spear. They'd made javelins, which were eagerly taken up by Accari Hounds. The walls were crowded with defenders, and Taal could still hear their cheers and their songs, even after dusk fell and the city returned to the mist.

He looked around. The darkness of the jungle closed around his mob, as if sewn together with thorns. Lips moving soundlessly, he invoked a spell of protection that was as much prayer as sorcery. A prayer to whom, exactly, he didn't know any more. If Braun had been there to ask him then he would have said that it was to Sigmar, but the words long predated the God-King's worship in the Heartlands.

It occurred to him, and not for the first time, that if things had been just a little different then he and his family might have been fighting on Kragnos' side right now. If he had not followed Braun to Izalend. If Kragnos had not struck at *him* first. Pulling down Azyrheim's order and returning the Heartlands to the old ways: these had always been Taal's dreams, but a mortal did not get to choose their enemies. They could only fight what was in front of them, or else they died.

That was the oldest of ways. The Ghurish way. Taal would have this Kragnos' respect for that, even if his ultimate fate was to die under the godbeast's hooves today.

And perhaps Sigmar, too, would see his courage and reward it.

He snorted to himself. Perhaps. He nudged aside an aggressively leafy strangler fig on the head of his staff and peered into the moon- and starlit gloom of the jungle ahead, waving Angellin and the others to wait behind him.

Taal had grown up in the jungle. It had never frightened him until now. It was too quiet. He missed the cacophony of cold-blooded monsters. In its place, the scrape of leaves across bark sounded ominous and hungry, like a knife across a fork. The swaying of the trees admitted the occasional chink of starlight, a knowing wink almost, as though ever-watchful Azyr knew what was coming, how this day of destiny would end, and would have let Taal in on the secret if it had thought for one second that he would have wanted to know.

It had taken them half the night to get this far. Kragnos' vanguard might be on top of them already. He looked up.

Nothing there.

'Better do this now or not bother.'

He turned and waved to the others to spread out, just enough starlight falling through the canopy for him to see the glint of teeth, eyes, tattoos and blades separating out into the jungle. Fifty paces off and to the left, lost in the tangle of vines and darkness, Bad Luck Mikali hammered a shard of amberbone into the bole of a rubber tree. The sound ricocheted around the silent gloom, a discontented rumour shared between trunk, branch and leaf. Taal closed his eyes and listened to them speak.

The undergrowth to his right thrashed. He whirled towards it, hand on his knife belt.

Grint put his hands up, eyes going towards the demigryph to indicate that he was coming for more amberbone.

Taal let go of his knife. 'Call out next time. You're not in temple.'

Grint nodded, giving Taal a nervous look and a wide berth as he circled around him towards Angellin.

The Celestian was several yards behind, leading the – to Taal's eye, subdued – demigryph by the reins. The beast was unarmoured, but didn't look any smaller for it, half again as big as the most magnificent horse, its pale feathers glittering faintly under even the tiny amount of starlight they could catch. A pannier loaded with unprocessed amberbone, each piece carefully wrapped in the calming fleece left behind by the Astral Templars, lay over its broad shoulders. Angellin smiled at Grint as the boy collected a new piece, his hands bound with leather to be doubly sure that bare skin never touched unwrapped amberbone. Then Grint was thrashing his way back into the jungle and the Celestian returned her attention forward.

The Azyrites didn't understand the jungle the way the Accari did, but Angellin did appear to have superior night vision to any other warrior at his disposal, and Taal had had no qualms about putting her up front. And if an attack were to come, who better than her nephew's killer to meet it first.

'How long do you think we have?' she murmured.

'What makes you think me wiser in that than you?'

'This is your jungle. It would be foolish of me to think that you do not know it better than I.'

'I don't know about foolish. But it would make you pretty damned unique amongst First Age Celestians.'

The woman laughed lightly. Taal could almost be led to believe that she wanted to be here, fighting for this barely habitable jungle so incalculably far from her home and family.

He breathed out slowly, peering around in the dark. The jungle was alive now. The Accari knew how to move silently through jungle, but the secret tended to involve not travelling in a fifty-strong party, by night, and throwing chunks of amberbone into the foliage as you went. Shortening his stride, he dropped back until Angellin and her demigryph caught up.

'We need to move faster,' Taal returned, sticking his hand into one of the demigryph's swaying baskets.

'Do you know something?'

'I don't know. Just a feeling that we are not alone.'

He drew a piece of warm-to-the-touch amberbone from the basket and removed the fleece. Leaning his staff against a tree, he took the unbound realmstone in his other hand to hurl it overarm into the jungle, when a sharp pain shot through his palm to the back of his hand and he dropped the arm to his side. He swore and looked down at it.

'Ravenak's teeth,' he swore. 'It *bit* me.'

'Are you all right?' said Angellin, appearing at his shoulder.

'Fine,' he snarled.

'Are you sure?'

With a growl, Taal took the amberbone overarm again and hurled it into the trees. It hummed like a dragonfly as it flew, swatting aside the intervening branches before slapping into clutching undergrowth somewhere far from sight. 'This is what happens when you try to eat Efrim Taal,' he spat after it. 'Bastard.'

'Sir?' said Angellin.

He turned back to her, panting. 'Don't call me that. I'm not your chief.' He opened up his hand in front of his face. A hundred tiny pricks dotted the palm, wide and deep enough that blood was trickling down his wrist. Little flecks of amber travelled down his arm on the flow.

Swearing again, he wiped his hand on his robes, leaving a series of long red smears over the woven patterns. At the sound of a faint rustling in the jungle ahead, he glanced up, and then to Angellin, trusting himself to her sharper eyes. She seemed unalarmed, and so he picked up his staff from the tree where it was still resting, turning only when another of his returning fighters opened his mouth to say something.

'*Gungh.*'

'What?'

Taal looked at the conscript impatiently as he stumbled to the ground. A black-fletched arrow with a wonky shaft stuck out of his neck.

'Spiderfang!' he roared, as more arrows zipped through the leaves, murderous laughter ringing from the canopy. Men and women wearing precious little armour dropped to the ground, clutching at arrows. 'They're here. Drop whatever you're carrying and run for Accar!'

Angellin let go of the demigryph to take her spear two-handed, pivoting to put herself between Taal and the majority of the arrows.

'It could just be a few scouts. We know that the Spiderfang have been in the jungle for several days.'

'We will find out soon enough. And if it is, then you and I can continue on alone.' He spat on the ground and clutched his staff tight. 'I can't run fast with this wound in my gut anyway.'

Before Angellin had the chance to argue with him, the jungle rustled. This time it was directly above them.

Taal and Angellin both looked up.

The spider was near invisible in the meagre light with its moonless-night carapace, its grot rider striped head to toe with black camouflage paint. It dropped from the branches before either Taal or Angellin had the chance to react, landing between them and on the demigryph's unarmoured back.

The Azyrite warbeast reared, trying to throw the spider off, twisting its neck to dig its beak into the creature's head. But the spider clung on, sinking its own mandibles into the warbeast's neck while the grot gibbered something shrill, stabbing its short spear in through the demigryph's ribs.

Angellin spun with a cry, wielding the butt of her spear like a quarterstaff to crack the grot's skull, then twirled the weapon, reversed, adjusted her footing while she reclaimed the spear in both hands and thrust its amberbone tip straight forward, through the spider's eyes.

She was good.

Taal's knife-hand – his torn, bleeding, amber-flecked hand – itched with the notion of killing her while her back was turned. Get out of Accar, away from suspicious eyes like Braun and Lisandr, steal a few hours alone in the dark with Ilsbet Glorica Angellin. That was why he'd suggested this. Wasn't it? It surely wasn't to make offering to a god whose children had done nothing but encroach on his lands and persecute his ways. No. It was to murder the Azyrite who'd killed Ferrgin Taal. His nephew. His successor. To kill her and–

He shook out his aching hand, and gritted his teeth. No. He had Mikali now. The tradition would live on. Vengeance could wait.

He watched as the spider that Angellin had just killed curled up on itself and died. He didn't know what he'd been expecting the amberbone to do, but something more than that.

The spider stayed dead.

He drew his knife, brandished his staff, turning back to back with the Celestian as more dark-patterned spiders came scuttling down the broad trunks and wriggling through breaks in the trees.

'It's more than just a few scouts,' he barked. 'This is the first wave of the horde.'

More arrows rained out of the canopy. It was a monsoon. Accari scrambled to take cover under exposed roots and thick leaves. Taal watched an Accari conscript pierced by half a dozen arrows at once as she fled, pinning her to a tree trunk. She squirmed, still alive. Another arrow hit her in the back of the head. Hidden grots cackled as if this was greater entertainment even than they'd been promised.

Mikali ran back towards them, keeping as close as she could to the leaves and holding a gigantic rubbery palm frond over her head like a shield, but Taal suspected she could have run in a straight line naked and not been hit.

'We've got to get out of here,' she said.

'I already said that. Go!'

Mikali was fumbling with his arm to pull him back, as if he were an old man rather than a veteran twice her weight and three times her strength, and he was shrugging her off in turn when a terrific, splintering *crunch* caused them all to pause and turn.

A colossus of a spider, yellow-bodied and slapped with black paint, was forcing a path between two protesting trees, eschewing the path taken by its lesser kin in favour of bulldozing its way through the jungle directly. Its low-slung body carried a howdah crowded with wildly decorated and heavily intoxicated grots. Rickety ramparts and turrets were strung with little flags and chemical lanterns that punched multicoloured lights like spikes into the jungle floor. The trees went down under it with a crunch and a manic, drunken cheer from the grots on board.

Taal grunted, feeling a painful pull on his stomach, and sagg into his staff. Angellin and Grint rushed towards him, but he was barely able to acknowledge them. His mind reeled from the insane power that was building up amongst those cheering grots. There was a powerful sorcerer mounted on that arachnarok. More powerful than Weird Wurgbuz, against whom Ferrgin and he had matched spells across the Izal. The most powerful he'd ever felt, in fact, which he'd not left Accar expecting to encounter. Grot mages were better known for their enthusiasm than their aetheric might.

Mad laughter pealed through the aether as whoever it was prodded at his mind with a finger that, even in its astral, projected form, felt bony and clawed. Taal groaned under its investigations. The laughter went on. Arising from the spirit rather than the body and without any need to pause for breath, it could have gone on forever, although Taal felt sure that it would've driven him mad long before then.

The flickering of a conjuration appeared within the crush of scrawny revellers on the arachnarok's back.

Taal raised his hand, though it weighed a ton, and waved a counterspell.

The summoning dispersed back into the aether and Taal breathed a sigh of relief. He gripped his staff tight enough to make the totemic saurus tremble, fingernails digging into the meat of his palm and drawing blood as he prepared a powerful spell of his own. It would have caused the grots' clothing to moult from their backs, transforming into a swarm of ravenous insects to strip their flesh, but the words ran ahead of him, untameable, as the grot sorcerer worked a countermeasure of his own and the casting unravelled.

Taal gasped, knuckles whitening around his staff.

'Is dat all you has, humie?' a shrill voice called out from the back of the arachnarok. 'Good. I hates it when peoples fight back.'

'Is the amberbone affecting them?' Angellin cried.

'Oh yes,' Taal managed to grind out. 'It's affecting them.'

It was exciting the grot fighters beyond even their usual warlike degree, and swelling the sorcerer's power in turn. They'd made a terrible mistake.

'Run,' he panted. 'Really, this time.'

A spider the size of a large pony scuttled out from the trees and stabbed the hook-barbed foot of its front leg at Taal. He moved his staff across his body to block, but he was weary, sluggish after his contest of wills with the Webspinner, and the impact knocked the staff from his hand. The spider barrelled into him. He caught it by the sharp hairs of its head and fought to hold it off as its mandibles snapped for his face.

The spider was as stocky as a beast of burden, but Taal was an Accari and he had some strength in reserve yet. With the spider practically on top of him, he rammed his spice knife up, under its hard carapace and into its soft underbelly. He gritted his teeth in disgust at the rancid effluent that gushed over his upper body and stabbed it a second time. The curved blade required a jiggling, sawing action to pull back out, opening up the spider's thorax and unravelling the creature's innards. It collapsed on top of him.

Wheezing, he pushed it off and sat back. His head spun.

Not far behind him, Angellin was busily engaged with four more. Or maybe eight. Everything was spinning and blurring, an amber hue bleeding into his vision. *Let the murderer fight them all.* He tasted blood and brought his hand to his mouth, unwittingly smearing his lips with the cut on his palm that must have reopened in his duel with the Webspinner. Flecks of amberbone glittered on his fingertips. Pain suddenly wracked his skull, and he folded back over.

He heard another crunch, followed by whooping cheers, as the arachnarok forced over another tree. He shook his head to clear it, his spine tingling with the build-up of aetheric power. The grot mage was preparing another spell, but he'd lost his staff, and he couldn't concentrate hard enough to even try to stop it. All he could think about was his injured hand. It was throbbing.

He squeezed it into a fist but it didn't help at all. It made it worse, but once clenched he did not seem able to unclench it. The pain goaded him to anger. It urged him to lash out, to make it better, told him that it did not matter who or what.

He looked up. Saw Angellin's back.

Struggled furiously to get up.

'Chief!'

Mikali caught up to him and made a grab for his arm. This time, Taal wrenched his arm away from her and threw the elbow back into her face. There was a *crunch* of bone and the woman reeled back with a look of shock, her cheek smashed, blood smearing half of her face. Taal bared his teeth, half-turning to finish what he'd started, but with a tremendous effort he forced his aching fist back down to his side.

No. Not Mikali.

She was his legacy. If she survived then the old ways might still have a future. 'Run, I said,' he snarled over his shoulder, and limped back towards the Spiderfang. He didn't see if she obeyed, knowing only that she did not come back.

Angellin was kneeling by her dying warbeast, her immediate adversaries dispatched, soothing the huge creature with gentle words. The rest of the skittermob was hooting and jeering, loosing arrows after the routed Accari. The arachnarok was minutes from crushing her, assuming a grot spell didn't obliterate them both first, but she clearly felt she had the time to honour a proud animal of Azyr.

Her back was to him.

'I never took you for a hero,' she said quietly, without looking up.

Taal didn't know what to say. He hesitated a moment, his Sigmarite faith warring silently with the amberbone in his blood that demanded he take *exactly* what he want and not wait a second longer.

With a grunt, he turned the spicing knife over, striking her on the back of the head with its heavy pommel. The blow stunned her, the meteoric iron of the helmet taking the full force of the blow. The Celestian staggered around, dropped her spear, and fumbled dazedly for her sword grip, a look of shock on her face and a slurred question on her lips.

Curse Sigmar and all his children. Curse them, curse them, curse them.

Taal struck her a second blow. The pommel cracked the bridge of her nose. Blood spurted up Taal's arm and splattered his robes, and this time she crumpled.

He eased her silently down to the jungle floor and hid with her amongst the waist-high ferns, holding his breath as the immense weight of the arachnarok spider and its cargo uprooted a rubber tree mere yards from where he lay.

He flexed his hand. It still ached. It hungered.

'I'm a Ghurish kind of hero,' he muttered, dragging Angellin's unconscious body further into the jungle.

Earbug Glibspittle, Shady King of Da Little Kingdom, felt *spectacular*.

The humies were legging it into the jungle in terror of his awesome sorcerous might and, he conceded, just maybe, in fear of the Glossom Queen. The boingrot boyz that he'd 'borrowed' from the Moonclan were already crashing on ahead, flattening a great swathe of jungle that his skittermobz were easily scuttling over. The squigs might almost be at the walls already. The thought made him giddy. The Bonesplitterz boarboyz meanwhile, not nearly bright enough to ride on spiders like properly right-thinking greenskins, blundered way back, struggling gamely on through the dense jungle.

They were all so geed up that Earbug's head was spinning,

spinning so hard he had to hold onto it in case it flew right off his neck and into the canopy.

He looked up and cackled.

'Look at me!' he whooped, careful to keep a hold of his head. 'I ain't scared o' no lizzies!'

Seriously powerful thoughts exploded inside his brain like fungus fireworks, colouring the battle for him, such as it was, in mad and hilarious colours. He peered down from the toppest tier of the Queen's howdah for the humie wizard who'd had the snotty gumption to challenge him in a contest of spells. But he was gone. Probably got his head exploded from the effort. Like what happened to Scuzzdrip that time he'd decided to scoff a plate full of madcap and 'see what happens.' And good riddance! He unpeeled his long-fingered hands from the sides of his head and spread his arms to the Bad Moon.

Who needed the Boss Trampla to be king of all the clammy places in Ghur? Not the Shady King, that was for damn sure.

And now it was raining *orange*.

'I sees...' he muttered in a portentous slur, a terrible weight pushing against his skull, and raised one very long, very glowy finger to the sky. 'An awesome sign.'

The Glossom Queen made a kind of moan that he'd never heard her make before. It sounded almost frightened. He decided it was probably awe.

Yeah. Totally awe.

Fifty generations of Shady Kings she'd carried since Grublang the Git had first fed her and worshipped her and got up on her back without getting eaten, but never one that was going to the places that Earbug Glibspittle was going.

He peered down from his howdah, annoyed to see a scuttle-mob of grots taking advantage of his moment of supreme glory to shiv one another in the backs.

'Oi!' he yelled, his words so ripe with power that they crackled into life as tiny green spiders that then crawled out of his open mouth and stung his eyeballs. 'Cut it out!' He scrunched his eyes and waved vaguely towards where the squig-riders had gone. 'Da fightin's gonna be over that way.'

None of them listened.

Earbug shook his head. The worthless ingrates never listened. He laced the long fingers of his bony hands and cracked his knuckles.

'If a job's worth zoggin' doin'...' He took a deep breath, drawing in enough Waaagh! power that his eyeballs felt as though they might pop out of his head and his ears bleed. His teeth hummed and he almost giggled.

He'd never felt so *drunk*.

'Boss...' Goonsplat complained, leaning over the wonky wooden rail of the lower deck as though he was about to puke over the sides, and holding his face in his hands. 'I don't... I don't feel... so good.'

Earbug opened his mouth to offer the perfectly reasonable suggestion that Goonsplat was a wimp and a disgrace when Goonsplat's head exploded, splattering the surrounding shamans with blood and a surprisingly copious amount of brains. A besmeared Webspinner wiped his face on his hand, grunted in annoyance, and then laughed so hard that his head exploded too.

'I sees...' Earbug muttered. 'I sees...'

Now that he thought about it, he didn't feel so great either. There was a swelling under his forehead, a terrible pressure building behind his eyes. His entire face was tingling.

He saw his future, and it was up there in the trees.

'Zog,' he drooled, and wished he was still holding onto his head.

Braun sat up and stared as the explosion lifted the roof off the jungle. It was about half a mile out from the gate, mushrooming as it climbed into the sky, the green cap swelling in size and adopting a cruel face that leered over Accar as it grew. The torches set above the walls guttered and pulled, as though in fright, curses drifting off the casemates as the Ironweld gunners found their chemical wands snuffed out.

Braun blinked and rubbed his eyes, but he wasn't asleep. He picked up the hammer he'd been polishing. One of the reasons he'd been an early adopter of the hammer was to spare himself the arm-ache of sharpening an axe, but it did take regular cleaning to get orruk blood out of the grooves in the enamelling.

He made the sign of the Shatterer.

'What in Sigmar's name was that?'

'They're here,' said Ragn, in the same conversational but disinterested tone with which he might comment on his chief's new boots.

'Thanks for that, Ragn,' he scowled.

'Any time.'

Braun snorted and looked to his men, but everything about him was already up and in motion. Men and women gathered up their gear and got themselves into ranks. Celestians mounted up, taking plumed helmets and lances bedecked with fluttering pennons from squires who then drew swords and shields and took their places with the Hounds. In their blued mail and silk surplices, even the servants looked like princes and princesses amongst the barbarous Accari. Altin moved casually about the more seasoned Hounds, fighters for whom the ability to sleep through any battle was a hard-earned skill, singing a lullaby in his uniquely terrifying voice and kicking them awake. Olgar reluctantly spat out his arraca stem. Woan leant back against the half-opened gate with his eyes closed, his lips moving as he prayed.

There weren't many of them. The make-up mobs had gone out with Taal. The unconscripted civilians had been sent ahead into the jungle and would, hopefully, make it to Excelsis before this storm hit there.

Only the very best had been left behind.

A Celestian war-hymn drifted off the walls. It was soft, lilting, measured, like most Azyrite music, but like most Azyrite music it stirred something in the soul. Braun felt his bare arms goose-bump as Lisandr lifted her own voice to join in.

'Starlit soldier, Sigendil unwaning,
Mail clad and faith girt
Sigmar our hammer,
But the gate is shut.
Our light is unwaning,
But the gate is shut.
The skies are brass, the plains are claws,
This realm hungers, its waters run red
A throne of gold for one of skulls.
Starlit soldier, Sigendil unwaning,
We fight here forever, 'ere his return.
My home is the Heavens…'

'But the gate is shut,' Braun growled, having no talent at all for singing.

He turned to Lisandr, who he found was in the process of donning her helmet and looking at him in surprise.

'What?' said Braun, unexpectedly defensive. 'I went to school.'

'I didn't take you for a student of Theraclese.'

'Mine was the best school in Excelsis. The best that took the children of Reclaimed, anyway.'

'I had always wondered what an unreformed Ghurish savage was doing with an Azyrite forename.'

Braun sighed. 'My parents wanted better for me, and they started with my name. They had hoped I'd practise celestial law.'

Lisandr laughed. Braun gave her a dangerous look.

She shook her head, clamping her lips shut, fighting to hold onto a straight face. 'What happened?'

'Ghur,' he said. 'For some of us, it's just in our blood.' They were silent a moment while he prepared his weapons and an Accari Greathammerer helped Lisandr into the saddle of her demigryph. At length, he frowned, and said, 'But if you breathe a word to *anyone* that I've read Theraclese then I'll kill you. I'll kill you and I'll eat your body. Your daughter won't even get your bones.'

'I promise.'

'I'm not joking.'

Lisandr lifted her hands from the reins and displayed her palms. 'I know.'

'Then why're you still smiling, dammit?'

The Celestian turned away and, with the back of her head to him, said, 'You know, Field Marshal Mestrade leads a recital group every Moonday.'

'Chief.' Altin intercepted his general's retort, gesturing with his butcher's cleaver towards the treeline, across the painfully narrow killing ground that the Accari cleared in bi-annual celebrations with hand-axes and duardin fire. A horn sounded its warning from the battlements, and Braun turned his face towards the Heavens.

'Thank the gods for that.'

The squig hoppers were the first into the killing ground, black-robed grots clinging on tight and giggling madly as their semi-wild mounts came crashing out of the jungle canopy and *boinged* in scattershot fashion towards Accar. The wall crackled with gunfire, like the paper-dry skin of a serpent made sluggish by night-time, and grots and squigs rained out of the sky. Next came the spiders, scuttling over dead stumps and fallen branches, glossy black carapaces winking as the light from the city caught their armour and was turned aside. And then the orruks, but not the Bosskilla's Big Rukk, to Braun's relief. Bonesplitterz emerged, mounted on boars, their tattoos glowing evilly in the dark.

The Ironweld's artillery woke and barked, and explosive spouts of greenskin blood, spider ichor and chips of amberbone erupted from the field and geysered high into the air. Shay, trusting the dangerous task to no other, had personally packed the offcuts of her spear-making into grapeshot bags for the demi-cannons and filled rockets with shavings. The old gunnery-professor had marshalled her cobbled-together battery of temperamental Excelsian guns and bronze-barrelled Accari pieces with bird's nests in the bores, with authority and skill. It was hard to believe that it was the same woman who had complained so wholeheartedly throughout the Bloodgullet Crusade. Her mortars, rockets and culverins kept up a rate of fire that was, frankly, staggering, and deafening to those below.

'We fight for Sigmar,' yelled Lisandr, fighting and largely succeeding in being heard over the barrage. 'Though we know that we may well die, we fight for the honour of Azyr, and so that others who will fight for her might live to fight another day.' Her fearsome mount bridled at the cacophony of the guns, armoured plates glinting by torchlight and muzzle flash, clawing at the earth with one monstrously heavy paw. 'One last battle!' She tore the hood from her spear, unmasking the crude amberbone head, little more than a lump with a point, and let the fleece rag flutter to the ground. 'For Azyr!'

'*FOR AZYR!*' the Celestians and Accari roared as one.

At a more conversational volume that would never be heard above the guns, she turned to Braun. 'We should sally now, and break the greenskins while Arden's guns have them pinned.'

'Not yet.' Braun slid his hammers into their sheaths, and picked up the spear that he'd left resting against the inside of the gate. He rolled his neck and snapped the crick in his spine. He couldn't remember the last time he'd been this tense. Probably never. 'Not until Rukka's here. It's him we fought, in the prophecy.'

'And what if your vision of the future was not a prophecy of what must be, but a warning of what might be avoided? If we were to shatter the Gloomspite grots and the Bonesplitterz now, before their heavier allies have time to catch up, then our chances of delaying Kragnos here that little bit longer will be much improved.'

Braun bit his bottom lip as he tried to think that one through, then shook his head. Who could think with those guns pounding in his ears anyway? 'No,' he said, trying to sound sure. 'The prophecy showed me what it showed me. There's a reason, there's always a reason.' However violent, petty or irrational it looked to mortal eyes. 'Trust in Sigmar.'

Lisandr looked uncomfortable, but held her tongue and relaxed back into her saddle. 'It is not as though either of us has very much to lose by getting this wrong.'

From the casemates and battlements of the city walls Arden Shay herself led the cheer as the last randomly bouncing squig was punched out of the sky, pierced cleanly through, or so it looked at a glance, by an amberbone-tipped javelin hurled by Blind Lusten. The small chief stood up on the parapet, sinewy chest bared, milking the accolades and the applause with a typical lack of modesty. If just the two of them survived this then Braun resolved he would promote the man to his Dozen. He'd take *that* as his sign.

'Look!' Lisandr suddenly yelled, an excited pitch to her voice that immediately had Braun following her gaze to where her finger was pointing.

The squig that Lusten had felled wasn't yet entirely dead. Rather, it was charging along the ground on its tiny legs, in spite of its fatal wound, and proceeded to chomp the front legs and mandibles from a giant spider. The Spiderfang creature shrieked and bit the cave squig's rubbery face. Its grot rider stabbed it in its huge mouth, but not before losing a stirrup and the foot that'd been in it. He squealed, reaching over to staunch the flow of blood pumping from his torn ankle, and in so doing inadvertently tipped himself into the squig's bloody mouth. The squig spent its last moments furiously chewing as the spider tore its body to pieces, before succumbing to its own fatal mauling and collapsing in an exhausted, chitin-strewn heap.

Everywhere Braun looked now, it seemed, any greenskin or beast with so much as a flesh wound was turning on their kin. Moonclan grots murdered Spiderfang grots. Spiderfang grots spitefully fell on Bonesplitterz orruks. Bonesplitterz orruks happily butchered *each other*.

And in the meantime, every greenskin with a feather-topped staff or a head of mushrooms or the mad-eyed stare of a prophet of the Great Green God was detonating themselves in dazzling displays of wild magic, as the sheer enormity of greenskin energy poured into heads that had never been exactly stable.

Braun whooped. It was working. His plan, the plan that Sigmar had put into his mind through prophecy, and with a little help from Efrim Taal, was actually working.

'A cheer for Vagria Farstrike and the Farstrike Hunters!' he roared. The Astral Templars might not have been there to fight alongside the Accari in person, but in leaving the Ironweld with the Morruk Hills amberbone, they might have done as much as they ever could have in the flesh. They might have just saved them all, and Excelsis as well. 'The saviours of Accar! May they ride back to Sigmaron avenged!'

A roar sounded from the jungle as though in mocking answer.

It was deep, deeper than that of any beast that walked or flew in Gallet, and every beast native to Accar had fled its territory hours before this beast's coming.

Braun lowered his spear. Before, it had been a trophy, the

instrument of their triumph. Now it looked like what it was. A crude weapon for a mortal to range against a god.

The galloping hooves drew nearer, the thrashing, crashing of trees. The earth under Braun's feet trembled and he threw his arms wide for balance, catching hold of Lisandr's mount, whose barding rattled in the earthquake. The fighters ranked up around him murmured their unease as they struggled to hold their formation and the very walls behind them shook.

He felt his guts tying themselves into ever tighter knots as though to hide themselves from his fear, escaping his surely doomed lips in an unedifying moan as the god Kragnos burst free of the jungle and showed his face at last.

Giant kapok trees, their trunks twenty feet wide at the base, shook themselves to wood pulp and toppled into the fissure that Kragnos' hooves had left of the jungle floor. He barged aside the last of the trees still attempting to slow his passage and trampled their bark to sawdust. His red mane blazed about his monstrous head, like fire flaring off a descending comet, while the shape of reality itself seemed to bend around the substance of his mace-head and then break with spasms of green fire.

Slamming his forward hooves into the shaken earth, his headlong charge slewed to a stop, driving the rock ahead of him to rear up and roll across the killing ground towards Accar, tossing aside grot and orruk alike as it went.

With outrage and mirth locked in constant conflict across the features of his savage face, Kragnos took in the anarchy.

Braun and Lisandr, directly before the god's charge, found themselves speechless. Arden Shay, however, up on the battlements, was yelling until she was hoarse. Braun couldn't help but wonder if more had come of the professor's work with the amberbone than a few hundred spearheads and some shot. Even in the thrall of godly dread, Braun was approving of the change.

'I want every gun,' she yelled, stalking the battlement walk with a bulky, steam-powered repeating revolver in her one hand in place of the book that Braun was more accustomed to seeing there. 'Every cannon, every rifle, every damned *pistol*. If it shoots, load it, and make it ready.' She aimed her own multi-barrelled contraption towards the ruined treeline and the snarling god that waited there. 'The realms have moved on since you last walked, Kragnos! Come and face the Ironweld.'

True to Shay's intention, the Ironweld had positioned every gun in the city on that wall, and at her command its entire length lit up, the reports of a hundred pieces, great and small, rolling off the battlements like a tsunami of stone. Kragnos watched it from the treeline, unperturbed. Perhaps confused. And a second later the bombardment fell.

Braun heard a distant *crack* as a mortar shell, exquisitely aimed, exploded in Kragnos' face. The blast staggered the god, showering him in shrapnel and rinsing his bearded face in heat. Answering pain with pain, Kragnos delivered a roar that knocked cannon and musket balls from the air, split every tree trunk within a hundred yards and turned every leaf and frond into an explosion of green pulp.

The god tensed his hugely muscled torso, dug hooves into the ground, locked knees, and held himself square-on as a cannonball thumped into his stomach. He grunted as it bounced off, leaving an ugly black ring and, Braun hoped, some pain. Another hit his shoulder. Braun heard it wrench the joint.

A rocket wailed over Kragnos' head. It burst in the air, showering a mob of orruks – Mug Fisteater's Shinner Mob, if Braun recognised their flags correctly – with amberbone as they picked their way out of the quake-stricken jungle. The orruks immediately stumbled to a halt and started to hack at one another. A pack of mournfang-mounted ogors, who until then had been angling to go around, decided instead to plough right through the brawling Shinners and hack them to bits with their heavy cleavers. A mega-gargant who was wearing a whale as a cloak and wielding an entire shipwreck as a club paused as he too emerged from the jungle to stomp on the ogor skalg and his mount, apparently on purpose, before striding on towards the walls. The now leaderless Beastclaw ogors gave up on the orruks to fire their crude ironlock pistols at the behemoth's calves.

The god laughed. Though bruised and reeling, he laughed, and his laughter shook what the barrage had left of the jungle.

'Ignorant mortal fools! The orruks of my time plied me with amberbone from all over the realm to raise me above them into a god. There is more of the Ghurstone in my bones than there is in the Heartlands today.'

He beat his mace against his shield, the collision of the unstoppable and the unbreakable unleashing a shockwave that went as far as the wall, disintegrated every missile it touched, and obliterated the ridges that he himself had raised up out of the earth with his arrival.

And then he came galloping through the dust. Straight at Accar.

'We cannot wait a moment longer,' Lisandr screamed. The ground was shaking. Her voice was shaking. *She* was shaking.

'Not yet,' Braun cried back, unable to tear his eyes from the avalanche stampeding towards them. 'Rukka isn't here.'

'The prophecy is wrong.'

'Prophecy is never wrong.'

'I am sorry.' Lisandr firmed her grip on her spear, sliding incrementally forward in the saddle and bringing a chirp from her demigryph. 'Do what you feel you must, Casius, I am sure that Sigmar will judge you fairly. But I will not allow Kragnos to slaughter us all on the basis of your prophecy, or condemn those who are counting on us to hold the godbeast here. Not while a Celestian of the First Age still breathes to defy him.'

She gave the demigryph its spurs. The rest of her knights, all seven of them, streamed after her, an all-too-brief clattering that thundered through the barbican tunnel as the warbeasts picked up speed and swept towards the oncoming god.

Braun felt eyes on his back. Ragn was looking at him thoughtfully.

'You've something bad in your mouth, Ragn, then spit it out. Don't stand there chewing on it looking all sour.'

The ugly fighter looked away.

'Yeah, I thought so.' Braun frowned into the future. There was nothing good there. 'Fine.'

He drew his spice knife in his left hand to complement the amberbone spear in his right. He couldn't make himself choose between his beloved hammers. The God-King had blessed both equally. He spat on the ground. What was left of his Dozen formed up around him. Intent. Resigned.

'Let's go do Sigmar's work.'

CHAPTER SIXTEEN

Casius Braun and his Dozen led the Accari Greathammerers out onto the killing ground, jogging over corpses and craters and the splintered stumps of obliterated trees. A number of the bodies, and no few of the stumps and craters too, were still alive and trying to eat one another. It made for slower going than Braun would've liked. Several Accari lost feet, or were forced to fall back to bludgeon a half-dead Spiderfang or Moonclan clinging on to their clothing. If you were going to run straight at death, then better to do it as though you meant it.

With yips and calls, Lisandr and her knights veered away. The demigryphs barged through the crumpled-up bodies of dead spiders, moving in formation in an arc to hit the god from the side. They expected to die today, but they might as well do all they could to make it interesting.

Braun grunted and ran on. He wasn't built for speed, but this was terrain that needed power, and he stole a yard on his warriors, forcing the Greathammerers to huff to catch up.

The Accari weren't manoeuvrable enough to flank Kragnos like the Celestian cavalry. If they were to try it, then the god would be past them and on top of the gates before they could get back into place. A tempting thought, but he decided against it. Not today. Today was a day for heroes to be made.

They would hit Kragnos head-on – hopefully, if they could time each other's charges just right, at exactly the same time as Lisandr's heavy cavalry came in from the flanks. Otherwise, regardless of whatever else this day was going to be, it would be short.

Breathing hard already, he looked up. Across the mile and a half or so of cleared jungle, a kraken-eater mega-gargant, a city-killing behemoth of the sort that plagued shipping up and down the coasts and rivers of Izalend, was laying into a pack of mournfang riders and a mob of armoured orruks that were still looking to push on out of the treeline. Braun's grim smile at the bloodshed froze as he spotted the cuffed blue and white checks marking the orruks' huge armour. His stride faltered, only decades of experience of pursuing dangerous prey on foot preventing him from tripping and ending his battle there under Kragnos' hooves.

They were the Ironjawz of Da Choppas. Rukka Bosskilla's Big Rukk.

Brutes climbed up the mega-gargant's shins using their choppas like climbing pitons, hacking boisterously at the monster's knees. Warchanters with pig-skin drums lashed across their midriffs egged them on with a furious, anarchic rhythm, as though they didn't care who their mates were fighting provided they were winning, and probably not even caring whether or not they were winning so long as they were fighting. The mega-gargant grasped helplessly with a hand the size of a Scourge pirate schooner as the mass of Ironjawz pulled it down and hacked it to death. A warchanter, a conductor of sorts, stood on the felled gargant's shoulders. His face was painted with blue and white squares, and he stuck out a tongue that had been painted in the same, eyes closed in deep concentration or in ecstasy as he furiously pounded out the march on his drums.

Wheezing over the earthquake-shattered field, Rukka Bosskilla led them out.

The Ironjawz moved like drunken flathorns across the broken ground, stumbling in their massive armour over exposed roots and craters, but physically heavy and powerful enough otherwise to simply walk through most of the obstacles in front of them.

'Braun!'

The Bosskilla's voice was deep enough for a realm's worth of hate. He beat on his chest with his giant choppa, spraying the twisted iron bars of his helmet grille with his spit. Braun couldn't tell if the amberbone with which Taal and his mob had mined the jungle was exerting its effect on the megaboss or if this was simply Rukka Bosskilla as he'd always been.

He felt a thrill of fear, but it was passing. This was it. His moment. For the first time in a long, long time, Casius Braun knew exactly what he was supposed to be doing.

'Rukka!' he roared, adjusting his angle by the slightest degree to carry him wide of Kragnos' charge, and dragged his Dozen with him.

He'd lived this moment. From here, it was just repetition.

He was the warchanter, standing on a gargant's back, his heart a drum that pounded for Sigmar in his chest. His face was glowing, the great tattoo of the Shatterer, he could almost believe, blazing with the might and faith of Azyr.

And why not?

If the crude prints and primal markings of the Bonesplitterz worked to channel the blessings of the Green God then why not Casius Braun and the God-King?

'SIGMAR!'

With a roar he scaled a crest, forced up out of level ground by Kragnos' power, and leapt, already thrusting with his spear.

The God-King was watching.

The amberbone point banged against Rukka's chestplate. The megaboss grunted and staggered. He was bigger than Braun. Half again as tall. Twice as strong. Ten times heavier.

He didn't stagger for long.

Rukka retaliated with a kick that would have buckled the front plate of a steam tank, but Braun was marginally the quicker of the two and bent around the megaboss' shin. Dropping to one knee, he caught a ding from the spiked knee joint and was sent sprawling. The tough plate of maw-krusha leather took the brunt of it and Braun leapt back up. His off-hand spice knife scraped Rukka's armour.

The megaboss' choppa descended like a guillotine.

Braun rolled aside. He'd seen every move ahead of time, but now that he was here it didn't feel like someone acting out a part. Living it for real was a different thing, performing the actions, *feeling* the consequences. There was no time to think about what he'd already seen and then afterwards put it into action. Only instinct was fast enough to keep up with Rukka's fury, and it was only afterwards, in brief moments of hindsight, that he was able to note that every move had been exactly as he'd foreseen it.

From prone, he thrust upwards with his spear. It hit the sweet spot of bare green throat, between the bullish thrust of the megaboss' iron gorget and his chin spike. The amberbone tip pierced the Ironjaw's throat and Braun roared in triumph, but Rukka's hide was tougher than leather and it took all of Braun's strength just to break the skin. Braun bared his teeth, leveraged the spear against the ground, and managed to drive the point a quarter of an inch into the muscle of Rukka's neck.

The megaboss swatted the ironoak shaft contemptuously aside

on the back of his gauntlet. The wound wasn't bleeding. He leered between the thick bars of his helmet grille.

'Next time you wants to skin somefing for yer armour, skin me instead.'

The Ironjaw punched him in the chest.

Braun flew back, into the lee of the ridge he'd just charged over, and lost the contents of his lungs. Head spinning, he fell to his knees, bringing the spear up defensively as, with a great roar, the Accari came charging over the hill.

The megaboss bellowed in frustration as the Greathammerers piled into his Big Rukk and separated him from his rival. Altin staved in an orruk's helmet with a looping swing of his cleaver. Ragn took three quick punches from a pig-iron gauntlet to the face, but Grob Bloodgullet and the Bosskilla himself had already done their worst to that skull and the old fighter merely spat out a tooth and knifed the brute in the eye. Woan was grappling with a warchanter for his drumsticks. Olgar smashed an orruk's grille in with a blow from his axe.

For a moment, it almost looked as though they were winning, but then an unholy roar shook through the earth, the ridge at Braun's back showering him with grit, and he remembered that his was not the only battle being fought. He looked back, over the ridge.

Kragnos loomed over the battlefield, haloed in fire and shrapnel as Shay continued to bend the firepower of an entire city to the goal of holding a god at bay. Braun was no artillerist, but he could see that it wasn't going to be enough. Mortal hands just couldn't be made to work that quickly. No gun could take it. Even now, the entire wall ranged against him and blooming with gunfire, the god ground forward under the shelter of his buckler, which responded in kind with periodic lashes of power that sundered the earth beneath his hooves. Lisandr's wedge of knights, their charge unsupported and already broken, were streaming back across the shifting ground, glittering cairns of magnificently armoured dead left to mark their wake.

Faith, Braun told himself. Sigmar desired Kragnos' humbling more than he wished for Braun's insignificant death at the hands of an Ironjawz megaboss. Why else would he have manipulated the fates to give Braun the best glimpse of a future in which to do his work?

With a scowl ten years deep etched into his brutish face, piggish red eyes glaring through the warped metal of his grille, Rukka waded back towards him. Accari Greathammerers went flying as he shoved his way through the press.

'What's it... like?' Braun panted, as Rukka flung Olgar bodily out of his way and swung his choppa. Braun sidestepped. The crude blade smashed into the face of the ridge and showered them both with pebbles. 'The... great... Bosskilla.'

Braun's spear-point glanced across the Ironjaw's armour. Rukka stepped into the thrust, inside Braun's weak guard, and beat him back into the rock wall with a frenzy of blows.

'Being... a... minion?'

The megaboss murdered rock and air with absolute abandon. His attacks were unaimed but each one so ludicrously powerful that a glancing hit from any one would have crippled a man forever. Braun snuck another blow through the onslaught of pig iron, banging the spearhead off Rukka's grille.

The megaboss grunted and went briefly cross-eyed. It bought Braun a moment's respite.

'Orruks follow da biggest and da hardest.'

With a growl, Rukka swung. Braun ducked, but the Ironjaw hadn't been aiming for him. The choppa dug into the rock at head-height, deep enough to stay put when the megaboss removed his hand from the grip and, instead, closed the enormous gauntlet around the middle shaft of Braun's spear.

'Even if he ain't all that green.'

Braun braced himself for a tug of war, but as muscular as he was, the Ironjaw's strength was monstrous. He yanked Braun towards him with the spear, and threw a punch designed to hit the point where Braun's head would've been had he not let go. The megaboss' knuckle spikes raked his cheek, spun him one and a half times around and planted him face down on the broken ground.

Rukka snapped the spear across his knee, and tossed the two halves aside. Stumbling dustily to his feet, Braun brandished his knife. Rukka flexed the muscles of his chest, brought his gauntlets together in a *thump* that raised a plume of dust from the ground, and bared his yellow tusks.

It was hopeless. The megaboss was getting stronger and angrier even as they fought. The long march in pursuit of Kragnos and the mounted tribes had tired him a little, but he was working himself back up to it. Braun hadn't felt his full strength yet. He couldn't beat him. They both knew it.

'I's been around a long, long time, Braun. I's had uvver bosses, and I followed 'em all, untils I got da chance to kill 'em in a fair scrap. And den I was da boss.'

The Ironjaw threw a succession of one-two punches. Braun parried with his knife, sparks flying off the metal. The pulverising strength in the megaboss' fists forced him to switch hands, the onslaught breaking bones one by one by one until simply gritting his teeth and taking his punishment was no longer within his power and he had to watch the knife go flying from his grip. He fell on his back with a scream.

Rukka ground his knuckles into the palm of his hand. 'I'll be da boss again in da end. Dat's just da way of fings. I's always da boss in da end.'

Braun looked up from the ground, no weapon, both hands

broken. The ground underneath him was trembling. It dawned on him that there was something he'd overlooked.

The Celestians hadn't been fleeing *towards* Accar.

'Celestians of the First Age! For Azyr!'

Lisandr and the last of her demigryph knights slammed into the Ironjawz's flank with a sound like a foundry press designed for turning blocks of iron into flattened sheets. Rukka bellowed and turned towards this new outrage, offended not so much by the gall of the Celestians themselves as the magnificent beasts they rode. His nostrils flared and, for that split second only, he entirely forgot his enmity towards Casius Braun.

Braun rolled onto his belly and scrambled, lizard-like, to where the top half of his amberbone spear lay discarded on the ground. He screamed and almost passed out as he tried to get his broken hands to close around the shaft, lifting it at the fourth attempt by pressing it between the flats of his palms. There, he wedged the split end to the ground and turned the point towards Rukka, shoving it at the megaboss' groin and howling, in pain on top of frustration, that he had no strength left with which to push.

Rukka's gorget squealed as the megaboss turned his head and looked down with contempt. And worse: with pity.

It was the look he was still wearing as Ellisior Seraphine Lisandr, sitting on top of three tons of demigryph and coming in at fifty miles per hour, hit him. Her spear punched through Rukka's backplate, but not quite with force enough to break through the breastplate. At the same time, however, the collision forced the megaboss onto his leading foot, turning his body and driving it forwards and pushing his groin onto Braun's broken spear.

Braun howled in pain, and toppled backwards.

Lisandr circled her mount around Rukka's twitching, cross-sectioned hulk to draw in alongside him. Locking her boots in the stirrups, she reached down for his wrist, ignoring his whimper of agony, and hauled him to sit behind her in the saddle.

The megaboss wasn't dead. As Braun had learned, and then been made to learn again, it was almost impossible to kill an Ironjaw. Not without taking off heads or dealing the sort of damage that only a Stormcast Eternal or a direct hit from an Ironweld greatcannon could hope to deliver on the battlefield. But he was skewered between two ironoak shafts, jaw working a wordless apoplexy. His eyes, red before, Braun was certain, burned the colour of molten amber, and his muscles bulged as though something titanic was welling up inside.

With a furious growl, he tightened his grip around the spear embedded in his groin and *pulled*.

'Run,' Braun managed to whisper.

'Run!' Lisandr agreed.

Rukka Bosskilla was incandescent.

He'd been left behind, forced to slog it with the troggherds and the Shinners and all the grunta-scrapings of the Godboss' horde for *miles* while Earbug got to ride up ahead with the Trampla. He was knackered, he was stiff, and he was angry. Not even the sight of several thousand greenskins and ogors scrapping in a great split in the ground could take the edge off his rage. He was sick to the zogging death of the sight of great splits in the ground.

He took a short, bad-tempered breather as his boyz clanked up to him. Guntstag looked at the spear sticking out of his back, impressed.

'*Gork!*' he roared, looking to get some enthusiasm going.

Rukka punched him in the gob. The boss went down like a bucket of scrap.

'I's heard *enough* outta you.' He'd thought he'd been angry before. He hadn't known what angry was.

Hot breath rasped through the bars of his grille as he drew the Celestian's spear slowly from his chest. It clanged around inside his armour. It didn't seem to want to come out, which, given that Rukka wanted it out, meant at least one of them had a problem. He growled and pulled, tearing out the shaft but accidentally snapping off the head and leaving it stuck somewhere inside him. He held the stick up, like a paintbrush coming out of a pot marked 'Boss Green', knotty lumps of Rukka Bosskilla stringing their way back to his insides.

He glared at it and then, half a broken spear dripping in his fist, he surveyed the battlefield with the air of one who sees a lot of very complicated things at fault with the realms but nothing that couldn't get fixed with a great deal of smashing.

The spear-point in his guts felt… *funny*.

By all that was green and Gorky, he was mad. He scowled after the fleeing humies. Rukka was fed up with running. He looked for something slower.

He found it.

'Look at 'im,' he thought aloud. 'Walkin' through the 'umies' big gunz like he's 'ard as all that.' Licking the meat off the snapped-off spear end, he set off with an unhurried, unceasingly belligerent pig-iron clank.

Another orruk might have wondered why his own boyz had decided to peg it back to the jungle at the same moment as the humans had fled for their city. He might have wondered at the aggressive tingle reaching into his muscles from the awkward knot of pain around the spearhead in his belly.

But he was only this orruk. The Bosskilla.

And he could use a decent scrap.

Ilsbet Angellin opened her eyes. The jungle was quiet. Leaves scratched overhead and something rumbled in the distance, sending faint tremors under the ground and through the tree that she appeared to be sitting up against. She felt shaky, but did not seem to have been tied up or injured. Her forehead was wet. She lifted her hand to wipe the sweat away, then stared at her palm for a minute or more while her thoughts struggled to bring her memory up to speed.

Not sweat. Sweat was not red.

'Huh…?' she managed to say.

'You're awake. Good.'

Efrim Taal was crouched a few yards away, sharpening the long crescent edge of his spicer with an oilstone and a rag. The repetition rolled his massive shoulders side to side, side to side, the motion hypnotic, and Angellin felt herself begin to drift back out of consciousness.

'No, you don't.'

The Accari shaman pinched her lolling head by the chin, tightly enough to bring her back awake with a gasp. She reacted to the pain as she had been trained to do. Her hand shot up, coming inside Taal's wrist and *twisting* it. Her reward was a snarl of pain, then a punch to the face that jumbled the fragments of her broken nose and cracked the back of her head against the tree.

She sank into a pillow of epiphytic ferns. She fell unconscious again. She had no idea for how long.

When her eyes fluttered open a second time, Taal was back where he had begun, sharpening his knife, as though giving her the opportunity to try this one more time. Her memory ebbed, high tide in a sea of treacle.

'The arachnarok…' she murmured. 'The Spiderfang. What happened?'

Nodding to himself, as though this was better, Taal wrapped the oilstone in the cloth and tucked it away.

For the longest while Angellin had shared her comrades' view on the Accari livery as quaintly barbaric. With time, however, she had come to appreciate that it was versatile, efficient, breathable and perfectly adapted to jungle warfare, less an outfit than a harness for the pockets, sheaths and pouches in which a human body could carry everything it might need to protect and sustain it through one of the most hostile planes in all the Mortal Realms. And none, she had come to realise, were more skilled survivors than Braun's Dozen.

'I took you away from them. Kept you safe.' Taal raised the sharpened knife, apparently testing its edge against the starlight. His face contorted, the knife wobbling as though he was fighting something inside and it was unsteadying his hands. 'No quick or easy death for my nephew's killer.' He squatted down beside her. 'Ghur has an older god than Sigmar. We worshipped him before, I think, my ancestors, before Dracothion bound him. Drawings of him are all over the Heartlands. His name is a legend. And now he's *here*.' His face became a snarl. 'Where is Sigmar now?'

Angellin was just starting to feel lucid enough to be afraid. 'You're *a priest*.'

Taal laughed. It came out less of a human sound than that of an animal panting. The sort of noise that a bestigor would make while smelling meat.

'He's not trying to shape this realm into something it's not. He's not Khorne, or Nagash, or Sigmar. He just wants to *be*. Isn't that all any of us want?'

Angellin forced her mind to think. Taal had sent Mikali and the others back to Accar. Coincidence, or was that too convenient? Had he planned for this from his first suggestion of the plan to Lisandr and Braun as a means to avenging the death of Ferrgin? Or had something happened to him in the jungle that she had not seen? Was even this a trick somehow, to confuse the Spiderfang and their master?

She wondered how long she had spent unconscious. From the redness of dawn that was even now creeping through the trees and the deep rumble of battle in the distance, she suspected that it had been hours rather than minutes. Would Grint and the others think to come back for her when they discovered that she was no longer with them? More likely, they would assume they had been overrun by the Spiderfang, grieve for her in their own Ghurish way, and run on.

She could not wait for help. If she wanted to fight another day, then she would have to ensure it herself.

Taal brandished his spice knife, and Angellin marked the drip of blood that ran down from his clenched fist towards the pommel, the telltale glimmer of amber.

Gods of Heaven, she thought.

'A beautiful weapon, isn't it?' he said, misinterpreting her horrified appraisal of his knife-hand, and turned the crescent blade under the starlight to show it to her. 'The long edge is always kept sharp. See? It's for cutting vines. Or predators. This curve here is to shield the fist from whatever you're cutting.' He reversed his grip as he spoke, switching the knife to be point down in his fist, with the inside-curve pointed towards Angellin. 'This edge though… this edge is blunt by design, a rough finish, like a grater, for stripping bark.'

He leant forwards, his breath wet and hot against her face. The point of the knife was a perfectly adapted glint of metalwork half an inch from Angellin's left eyeball.

'You don't want to know about this edge.'

Angellin tried to turn her head aside. Taal pinned it to the tree with his other hand. She struggled, but he was much too strong.

'If you wanted to kill me then why aren't I dead already?'

Taal gave another laugh-bark, another shake of the head as though ridding himself of an unwanted voice. 'I don't want to kill you. Don't you remember? Yes, yes, that's it. I told you that when my wound was healed, you and I would fight.'

Angellin looked down to the shaman's waist. Blood was oozing through the maw-krusha plates of Taal's girdle padding and staining his robes black.

'I do not think it has completely healed.'

'I feel fine,' Taal snarled. 'Stronger than ever.'

'I… I would not want to take advantage of an unfair match.'

Taal backed up, spreading his hands in invitation, knife held in the open palm with a killer's lightness of touch. 'Get up. Draw your sword.'

Angellin looked down to her sword belt. Taal had not bothered to disarm her, or to tie her up. More proof, if she needed any, that the Accari war-priest was not in his right mind.

'It is the amberbone making you act this way, Chief Taal. Look at your hand, and see that I am right.'

'Get up!' Flecks of amber decorated his spit, the light of madness in his eyes.

'No!'

For a moment, he looked stunned by her refusal, uncertain what to do next, and Angellin dared to hope that she had reached him.

He tossed the knife aside and advanced towards her. 'Of course, we'll settle this like animals in the dirt.'

She drew her sword awkwardly, pushing herself backwards on the heel of her foot, off the tree and flat onto her back amidst the ground litter to give herself the draw-length to get the thing out of its scabbard. Taal punched the tree, leaving the skin of his knuckles and a lot of blood over the bark. He did not seem to feel it. The shaman loomed over her. She stabbed up with her sword, into the chest, right in the heart. But he was too close. The tip scuffed right along his armour and grazed the bare skin of his arm.

Taal growled in anger, lips drawing back over his teeth, and this time Angellin *saw* the swirling amber in the whites of his eyes. No Hound had ever looked so massive as their shaman did just then. His barrel chest heaved with pain and fury. His mouth drooled with hunger, his robes clinging wetly to the outline of muscle. It was hard not to believe that she was not looking at an orruk that had somehow disguised itself as a man. It would have been easier to believe that. Killing a human being had not turned out to be as easy or as glorious as her tutors at the War College had led her to believe.

'Fight me properly,' he managed to snarl through a jaw that no longer seemed to be working properly. 'Kill me. Cut out my heart and eat it.' He beat savagely on his chest. 'This is Ghur!'

She kicked him in the kneecap. He grunted, leg bowing in, and dropped a clenched fist towards her face. She swung a knee, knocked the other leg out. His punch hit the ground and he fell on top of her. She bit his ear. Blood and something that tasted of teeth and claws and wild fear filled her mouth while she worked and chewed, cartilage loosening, and all the while Taal howled in pain he was laughing, laughing higher and madder until the ear came away from the side of his head and he staggered back towards the tree without it.

Angellin spat the ear out, and kept on spitting as if she could rid her mouth of even the memory of the taste of it. Taal touched the bloody side of his head, laughing breathlessly, and then kicked her in the side. Angellin heard the *crunch* of his breaking toe against the meteoric metals of her plate, but the blow winded her just the same.

Taking the opportunity, she pushed herself back through the undergrowth, turning her back on the war-priest just for a moment to roll herself onto her front and push herself up. She whirled around, dizzy, swaying, and brought her sword into a proper guard.

Unless Taal resorted to spellcraft, she could beat him. She had sparred with Azyr's most celebrated tutors, aelves and humans and Stormcast Eternals, and with a sword in her hand she knew she could beat almost anybody. And she had the feeling that Taal was too far gone into madness to remember that he could use magic. Or to want to.

A glimmer passed across her eyes, and she blinked it away, putting it down to another symptom of being hit across the head. But rather than disappear, the glimmer moved, picking up and gleaming from another spot amongst the trees closer to her. It reminded her of the odd light that she had seen, and that many of the Accari had reported following them across the Trample.

What was more, Taal appeared to see it too.

'Azyr,' he breathed.

His face went through a number of expressions, the cold light coming closer than any of Angellin's words to shaking him from his madness. But this was not simple madness. He was corrupted by realmstone. This was not an affliction that could be shaken off with a sufficient application of will.

He growled, turning his back on the light and rounding on Angellin again. She brandished her sword threateningly.

The jungle issued a warning chirp.

Angellin and Taal both turned their heads. The light had reappeared right beside them. Arm's length. Angellin's mouth dropped open. It was not Seraphon.

The gryph-charger's feathers were the white of fresh snow and flecked with gold, its armour and raiment bearing the colours of the Astral Templars. Its size, so deceptive from afar, with the beasts being so much thinner and leaner than a demigryph, was absolutely shocking up close. It was all power, as flawless as a moonbeam. A demigryph might have been heavier with muscle, with powerful jaws and a beak that could crush invictunite, but here was a nobler beast, one that would strike faster and truer than any flesh-and-blood creature could equal. And in the grey scars that marked the position of its eyes, she sensed a wisdom that transcended her own, never mind that of any beast that had ever borne her to battle.

She could not imagine herself ever presuming to master such a beast as this. Even if it were to offer itself to her, she did not think that she would ride it.

It chirped again, and turned its blind eyes towards Taal. The shaman bared his teeth and, with Angellin distracted, took a step towards her.

He halted suddenly and gave a cough. His eyes widened.

Angellin almost mirrored the expression as she noticed the purple-armoured fist erupting from the man's chest.

Without a word of apology, explanation or regret, Vagria Farstrike, Lord-Aquilor of the Farstrike Hunters, put her hand on the back of Taal's head and pulled her hand out of his chest. She did it as though the Accari war-priest was something unpleasant that her fingers had got stuck in.

Angellin stumbled back from her, sword still en garde, horrified by the Stormcast's terrible strength, and the callousness with which she would employ it towards ending a human life.

'Starsid,' she said, in a voice that ground on the ears like a passing storm.

The gryph-charger crowed and clawed at the ground as though in welcome. Ignoring Angellin completely, the Stormcast brought her bloodied gauntlet to the gryph-charger's head, scratching behind the scarred holes of his eyes.

'I remember now. I remember how I offered up my life to Sigmar, and how he took it, so that he could better spend it some other time. I believe that time is now.'

The animal clacked his golden beak and cawed.

'Thank you for reminding me. You are a true friend.'

Starsid lifted his long neck and gave an ululating hoot that sounded joyous. The Stormcast mounted, and in doing so appeared to notice Angellin for the first time. All the distinguishing features of her raiment had been scratched away with blades and claws, caked in mud, or lay hidden behind an unkempt mane of blue-black hair. Her eyes were haunted and distant. The bags beneath them were heavy.

There was nothing human left in that face.

'Go,' she said. 'This hunt is mine.'

'But–'

Angellin finally remembered the sword, and lowered it, but – as though the movement had tripped some kind of illusion – both Vagria and Starsid wavered before her eyes and promptly vanished. She stared, shocked, but there was nothing left of the Stormcast Eternal but the scent of fresh snow and a cold wind against her face.

And the faint rustling of disturbed undergrowth, racing in the direction of Accar.

'Oi! Trampla!'

The Godboss turned from the city as Rukka clanked angrily across the killing ground towards him, his gargantuan turning circle breaking the earth in a wide fan beneath his hooves. A shell that had been bound for his chest whistled over his shoulder, bursting a way distant in a gob of fire. Orruks flailed around as they burned, painting the Godboss' hide in bloody red writhing with rotten-tooth black. Rukka shoved through the heaped dead like a snowplough.

'It's da Bosskilla's turn now.'

By any greenskin measure, and most especially by his own, Rukka was a giant. The Godboss, though, was huge. Rukka stood no higher than his haunches. The Trampla was *mocking* him with his size.

'Da Bosskilla's da biggest,' he grumbled, and threw a punch that crunched the knee joint of the Godboss' foreleg.

The god sucked in a hot breath and roared, tearing up a tsunami wall of earth that pummelled Rukka with grit and stones. He stumbled, waving his hands in front of his face, the stuff still managing to clog up his grille, and went in hard.

He was an Ironjaw. When an Ironjaw stumbled, he stumbled *forwards*.

Bellowing as though, in his own head, he could match the Godboss for volume as well as strength, he pummelled the Trampla's breast and forelegs with his iron knuckles. He wasn't armed, unless he counted the spear sticking out of his back that he hadn't been able to reach, but the blows came too low for the Godboss to stoop and block with his shield.

The Trampla roared in pain. Rukka grinned.

A rocket launched from the city exploded against the Godboss' back. The explosion staggered him, opening him up for a free punch that Rukka used to twist his ankle. He laughed, mad with it, almost blind with the grit in his grille and the burning amber in his eyes. The spear in his guts burned horribly, as though he'd swallowed a hot stone, but it didn't hurt. It didn't hurt at all. It made him want to hurt others instead, and the Godboss most of all.

'The Drogrukh were a civilisation of intellect, temperance and wisdom.' The Trampla reared up onto his hind legs, fore-hooves flailing and showering Rukka with mud. 'But it was my temper that led me to choose exile. It was my rage that shook the earth and made me a god.'

His fore-hooves slammed back down. The ground around him sank six feet as the bedrock crumbled. Rukka struggled to keep his balance, a challenge made all the more difficult by the muck and madness in his eyes. The Godboss rammed him before he had the chance. Rukka back-pedalled, massive enough, just, to resist being thrown down and trampled out of hand, but lining himself up just perfectly for the underarm upswing that followed.

The Trampla had broken the mile-thick walls of his prison in the Twinhorn. He'd broken the skulls of the Seven Serpents with it, breached the walls of Ur-Harracho, shattered the Great Temple of Dracothion in Vexothskul, and smashed Grob Bloodgullet's gate. The last one he knew. The rest were stories the Wurrgogs and Weirdnobz were telling one another. They said that all the strength and savagery of Ghur itself went through the almighty lodestone at its head.

Rukka's armour folded like wet clay, the Bosskilla winging back like a stone kicked by Ymnog across the realms. He punched through ridge after ridge after ridge, finally losing enough of his momentum to skid to a stop at the foot of a smouldering troggoth between the annihilated stumps of what used to be a stand of trees at the treeline.

The Trampla cleared the distance between them in a single earth-shattering leap.

Rukka tried to fight his way back up, but he was too heavy, his armour fused together in unhelpful ways. There was still mud clogging his grille and he snorted blindly as he felt the *THUD* of Kragnos' landing shudder through his plate.

'I admire your stamina,' the Godboss said. 'Perhaps the long dominion of Chaos has not been wholly to Ghur's detriment, if it has bred orruks as warlike as you.'

Rukka spat. 'You're... tough... but you ain't... so green.'

'I subjugated the orruks of my time. I bent their battle-lust to my will and I broke them. I will do the same again.'

'Get... down 'ere... and say... dat.'

The last thing Rukka saw was the Boss Trampla's hoof coming down.

Vagria Farstrike had never been to Accar. The lords of Mekitopsar kept their jungles in order without recourse to the services of the Templia Beasthall and the human city had not existed the last time she had hunted in this part of Gallet. But it was not difficult to find. Her path through the jungle was paved with cracked and fissured earth, her approach to the city signposted for her with the broken remains of grot, orruk and ogor dead. It was unmissable. More a geological feature akin to a mountain at the end of a flat plain than a trail for a hunter of Vagria's skill to follow. Kragnos had carved an almost straight line from Ursricht's Kill, via the Gnarlfast, to the gates of Accar. Vagria had been unconsciously shadowing his trail for days.

Starsid, in spite of his recent blindness, tackled the broken ground with agility and focus, flying along an almost-even path that only the keen senses of a gryph-charger could pick out. He travelled at an easy canter. Even so, his speed felt glorious.

The jungle fell away beside her. The walls of Accar came into view.

They were wooden stockades, with the occasional stone buttress or tower, the entire city strangled with vines and plant life like a small brown mammal in the coils of a serpent. The defences had been sundered in many places, but through siege craft, valour and monumental good fortune, they had not yet been breached. Nevertheless, human fighters were fleeing the parapet, even as she watched, even as the greenskins and their monstrous kin turned their backs on them in favour of waging war on each other. There was a *hum* and a *snap* in the air that she had not felt since the Morruk Hills. It tasted of amberbone. Puddles of burning pitch and the occasional spontaneously combusting greenskin lit up the night.

Vagria applauded the mortal generals' recklessness. To use amberbone as a defensive weapon. And on this scale. It smacked of courage. It was only their sanity she doubted.

And she could think of no higher praise than that.

The god, Kragnos, was halfway across the killing ground, but already facing towards her. His eyes were bloodshot, his nostrils flared. Sickle-shaped bruises lacerated the humanoid reaches of his upper body, while powder burns and ash coated the tawny fur of his lower quarters and mane. He stood with one foreleg lifted, as though it had been broken.

There was no shame in picking off the wounded. It was what any good hunter would do in her place.

'Let us aid the Accari, Starsid. While one mortal yet prays to the God-King for their deliverance, let us aid them.'

Grinning fiercely, her spirits lifted by the sensation of wind and debris on her face, she spurred Starsid to run.

Every fraction of a second in which Starsid shot towards him, the god seemed to grow, as though he towered over the city behind him. It was a trick of perspective, arising from the fact that he was monstrously huge, yes, and so very much closer to her, but it gave Vagria's heart a nervous flutter to see it nonetheless. Starsid chirped an anxious question, to which Vagria's answer was a reassuring squeeze on his neck feathers.

'I am not afraid, my good friend. Not any more.'

Hatred, perhaps, came the closest. Not for who he was, but for *what* he was. The power he represented. If allowed to roam free and unchallenged, Kragnos would break all the God-King had fought so hard to build. As he had broken her.

With a roar louder than all the war-horns of Azyrheim, Kragnos welcomed her challenge. He stamped the hoof of his good leg, shook out his mane in a sweeping display of antlers, and then, too ill-tempered to wait, thundered into a charge of his own. Those creatures in his path, whether grots or gargants, whether they saw him coming or not, were trampled or thrown aside.

'You come alone!' he bellowed. 'After I slew so many!'

'However many you slay, I will always come.'

Vagria felt a smile on the face that was not hers, a savage whimsy that was her birthright as an Astral Templar, and as a daughter of Ursricht the Great Bear. She leant forward, chest down to the hard-racing muscles of her mount, as Kragnos thundered furiously towards them both.

'We are not the hunter here, Starsid. Today we are the prey. Do as prey does.'

She gripped his reins tight in readiness as, from a running start, the gryph-charger took the winds aetheric.

The city disappeared. The jungle became a blur. Only Kragnos, cosmically massive, remained of the exact same dimensions as he had occupied in the flesh. Worse even than the god himself was his mace. In the aetheric it resembled a black and spinning void, an eclipsed sun, haloed by a toothed rim of boiling amber.

Here, Vagria decided, was one object she dared not ride through. She bade Starsid to go around, bursting anew into the smoke and fray of the battlefield half a second ahead of her own peal of thunder.

Vagria blew out a breath. The detour had cost her in terms of effort, but Starsid had still managed to carry her several hundred yards, circling the perimeter wall while maintaining a distance from it and running *through* thousands of orruks too intent on killing each other to notice the snowy gust of Azyrite wind through their armour.

Vagria wheeled Starsid back around as, behind her, Kragnos slammed to a stop with a bellow of such rage that, even half a mile away, Vagria's armour groaned and twisted. She raised her hand and waved cheerfully.

'That's right,' she said through smiling teeth. 'Your prey tweaks your nose. What do you intend to do about it?'

His mane flaring, Kragnos gave a trumpeting bellow as he swung around and surged back into a gallop, heedlessly flattening the orruk mobs that Vagria had passed through on his way. He drew back his mace, intending to smash Vagria from the saddle, and again, Vagria laughed and spurred Starsid onto aetheric winds the moment he came near.

Twice more Kragnos came for her. Twice more she fled, merrily pulling the god backwards and forwards across the battle line, slaying thousands of the greenskins without ever once drawing her sword. She hoped that would be enough to buy the mortals of Accar the chance to strike whatever blow they intended to deliver.

When Starsid emerged from the winds aetheric it was at a speed that Vagria herself would not have been too hard-pressed to outdo alone, his long neck hanging low to the ground. He was not alone in his suffering. Vagria's eyes stung from the battering winds, and from the constant lurches in speed and perspective, while her hands were so stiff they had almost locked around the gryph-charger's reins.

He would not run much further without a chance to rest.

She turned to face Accar. Most of the city's defenders had already abandoned the wall. Presumably Lisandr and Braun, knowing as well as she did by now that Kragnos would not easily be stopped, had only ever intended to delay and perhaps injure him, holding him here while the city was emptied and as many lives as possible spared.

Vagria approved. Had she been there to advise them, she would have probably recommended a similar course. With luck, her actions here in diminishing Kragnos' horde and distracting the deity a little longer could have only aided them in that plan. Silently, she saluted the courage of those who had agreed, or volunteered, to remain behind while others fled, and commended their souls to Sigmaron.

The God-King could do far worse.

Vagria glanced over her shoulder. Kragnos drove towards her like an avalanche.

'One more ride,' she leant forwards and whispered in Starsid's ear. 'For Sigmar.'

Starsid gave an exhausted crow, but sprang once more.

Kragnos' howl of frustrated fury broke across and burst around them. The winds aetheric eddied and pulled, making it less like riding a river of wind than galloping headlong into a storm. The gryph-charger shrieked in pain. Vagria simply closed her eyes and willed him ahead of the god.

There was a flash of golden light, a *bang* of displaced air, and Vagria Farstrike and Starsid burst limply back into the Realm of Beasts. Starsid's talons clattered over spongy wooden boards, the gryph-charger having sprinted clear through the walls of Accar as well. But now he was spent.

As he plodded to a standstill, Vagria shifted in the saddle, looking back just in time to hear the *crack* of sturdy timbers and watch as Kragnos, antlers down, drove through the stockade and trampled it under his hooves. Then, he threw the wreckage off his mane and roared.

Tough-looking wooden buildings, built to survive in a place where humanity had always been ill-advised to try and build, split at the joins and came apart. Boardwalks ruptured underfoot, trapped gases geysering up between them. Trees fell. Vast, overlapping sheets of insect netting collapsed as though the sky itself was coming down at Kragnos' cry.

But no people came running onto the streets. They were already gone.

Good.

'Toy with a god at your peril, Stormcast,' Kragnos snorted. He looked around, marking, as Vagria had, the abandoned streets and emptied homes. 'Do you think to slow me? Injure me? I will heal.

To cull my followers? As long as the amber wind blows there will be more. My last true companions fell in battle with the draconith and to the treacheries of the slann. I have lost nothing here that could not be replaced. Fight me or do not, but this game you play will tire you before it tires me.'

Patting Starsid's trembling neck, Vagria leant forward and whispered in his pinhole ear. 'Take me to Sigmar, brother. As he took me all those years ago.'

The gryph-charger warbled its understanding back at her, high and mournful. Unlike the Stormcast Eternals, the gryph-chargers were not immortal. But then, thanks to Be'lakor and his Cursed Skies, neither was Vagria. They rode together now as equals.

'Let us chase down our brothers and sisters, Starsid. Let us carry them back with us to Sigmaron.' She held her sword aloft, and thunder rumbled in answer across the almost-dawn sky. Sigmar's gaze was never as far away as it could at times appear. In spite of his weariness, Starsid lifted his neck proudly and cawed.

'You are not wrong, Kragnos. I do grow tired of playing.'

Finding his last sparks of strength, the gryph-charger turned.

Vagria grinned. Even as a mortal child, she remembered now, she had been possessed of a reckless streak and a powerful attraction to death. In every hunt, everywhere, this moment always came. The moment when the prey gives up running and fights back.

Starsid flashed into a short charge. Vagria struck overhand with her starbound blade, using Starsid's incredible burst of speed to forge a god-killing stroke. It scraped useless sparks across Kragnos' buckler, leaving no mark at all on the uncanny metal but chipping the sigmarite blade. Starsid sidestepped, smoothly manoeuvring her out of the arc of Kragnos' mace. The gryph-charger was as fast as a change in the wind, light on his taloned feet as cirrus cloud. He was also beyond exhausted. Vagria delivered two fierce cuts towards Kragnos' belly, both of which were solidly turned on the god's shield.

She howled. Not in frustration, but in a savage, long-awaited joy. In every hunt, everywhere, this moment always came.

And afterwards the prey always lost.

Starsid sidestepped a second time, continuing to keep Kragnos' own body between Vagria and the god's mace until, with a petulant roar, the god snapped and simply punched her with sigmarite-breaking force with his buckler.

Vagria cried out as she slipped out of the saddle. Not screaming but laughing. Not falling, but *flying*, soaring on electric wings and rising on aetheric currents. Her body was breaking apart, her senses overwhelmed by joy. Eight times she had fallen in Sigmar's service. Never once had she been afraid. It had never hurt.

Nor had it ever felt so satisfying.

She had played her part, and if this was to be the last verse in the song of Vagria Farstrike then let it be sung in the Heldenhall by tear-eyed warriors with the same gusto as the sagas of the Bull-Heart and the Bladestorm, forever remembered as the warrior who had fought the impossible and bravely lost. But Vagria knew that she had gone one better and achieved something that those legends never had.

She had come back and fought again.

Her last sight before the lightning took her senses completely was of Sigendil. The beacon lit the Heavens, shining eternally bright.

Vagria Farstrike did not believe that this was to be her end. She was a hunter. The greatest of hunters. It would take more than Be'lakor and his Cursed Skies to keep her from finding her way back to her master's hand.

It would be a new challenge, if nothing else.

'One last adventure!' she screamed as she flashed, faster even than Starsid could have ever carried her, far further than the fury of Kragnos could follow, towards the Heavens.

EPILOGUE

The ground next to the Great Trade Road climbed on its way to the sea. Huge, chalky white cliffs two miles high overlooked the outlet of the Serpent River and the Bay of Mallus. A lighthouse stood on the promontory. It was more like a castle. The high tower was ringed by concentric walls, in the classic dodecahedral plan of Azyr, with casemates for fixed artillery positions built into the basic architecture. Lisandr remembered passing it on her way west, to Accar. The garrison had been put out in their parade best to wave off the First Age Starhold Celestians on their crusade. Their success had been assumed, not merely because it was the Celestians who conducted it, but because the march of Order across the Mortal Realms was inexorable. Who would not desire the civilisation and prosperity enjoyed by the citizens of Excelsis?

The outpost was in ruins now, pulled down from within. The lighthouse itself was still mostly whole, although the cupola had been smashed and the beacon doused, but the defences had been ransacked. The walls had been scrawled with graffiti that seemed to be demanding a purging of the aristocracy, the murder or exile of the aelves, and the outlawing of all magic, with an especial ire reserved for the practitioners of prophecy. Someone had scrawled *Nullstone Brotherhood* in ten-foot-high letters across the gatehouse.

Lisandr spurred her tired mount up the rise, raising her hand to brace herself against the sudden onslaught of the sea wind, and to shield her eyes from the great reopening of the horizon. She saw ships burning on the water, others wrecked on the cliffs below. The aelven fleet was gone.

Feeling cold, Lisandr turned and looked back down to the road. Several thousand Accari marched below, snaking between the burnt-out roadside villages and trading posts. Celestians, standing out in their glittering armour and tall helmets, marched to one side of them every two hundredth or so, like training sergeants drilling their raw recruits in marching order. The sea wind, lesser down there, blocked by the mighty cliffs, lightly rumpled their banners. The croak of seabirds and the rusty murmur of distant bells welcomed the conquering heroes to the coast.

She saw Grint and Angellin as they marched below her, amused by the brief snatch of their bickering that came to her as they passed. It was something to do with a thus-far-fruitless pursuit of a certain 'Bad Luck' Mikali, niece of Altin the Cannibal, heir to the late Efrim Taal and newly promoted to Braun's Dozen. It seemed to be amusing young Ilsbet greatly.

Watching them brought Lisandr a dull ache of pride. She had led twenty thousand men and women across a turbulent realm and to the threshold of safety, ready to fight and bleed together for Excelsis. The thought brought her out in a rare smile. Barely seven months earlier, she had marched in the opposite direction with two thousand of Azyr's finest to plant Heaven's flag in the Ghurish Heartlands. She had done battle with a god.

How her ambitions had diminished.

She glanced over her shoulder to the ruined lighthouse. All of their ambitions.

'All the years I spent as a boy, spoiling my life chances to get away from this place. I never thought I'd be this glad to see it again.'

Casius Braun trudged wearily up the hill to where her demigryph tore suspiciously at the grass. Demigryphs were carnivorous by choice, but they would eat anything if they were hungry enough. If not for Lisandr's soothing presence then the beast would undoubtedly have made an attempt on the Accari general before trying the grass.

'It's like a stain I can't seem to wash out.'

'Azyr will always be home to me,' said Lisandr. 'However far I travel, whatever happens to me while I am here, it is a comfort to know that Sigmar will always hold that realm safe.' She turned to Braun. 'Perhaps you feel the same for Excelsis.'

Braun shrugged, neither agreeing nor exactly arguing, and turned to behold the city of his birth.

A thousand domes, spires and minarets rose from behind alabaster walls ten times higher than those of Goreham and Honoria. Every brick had been hardened with protective sigils in celestite and electrum and individually blessed by one of the twelve Grand Theogonists of Azyr. Lightning flickered across the battlements, making the city's towers waver and dance as though in a haze. The power was generated by the six occulum fulgurest engines, huge machines housed in brass-plated onion domes that had been built into the curtain walls at intervals, and which siphoned storm energy direct from the Spear of Mallus to power the city's arcane defences. A hundred thousand soldiers in a score of liveries watched the Accari warily from the walls. Five times that number would be garrisoned elsewhere, keeping the unstable peace in that vast city of millions.

If she squinted, catching the spark and lull of fulgurest energies just right, then Lisandr could almost make out the turrets of the Consecralium that stood watch over the bay, and the upper tiers of the Seraphon embassy-ziggurat of Serpentanis.

And then there was the Spear of Mallus itself. A billion tons of pulsing rock, hovering impossibly above the bay, surrounded by a spiderweb of mining platforms, gantries, Swifthawk eyries, Collegiate observatories, and the Warscryer Citadel of Lord-Ordinator Dolus of the Knights-Excelsior. It looked invulnerable.

But Lisandr knew better.

Kragnos was coming.

'They aren't opening the gates,' grunted Braun, peering belligerently towards the God-King's capital in Ghur.

Lisandr cast a last look over her shoulder, because Kragnos was coming, and then turned back to the Trade Road. She took a deep breath, and spurred her demigryph onwards.

'Let's see about that.'

ABOUT THE AUTHOR

David Guymer's work for Warhammer Age of Sigmar includes the novels *Hamilcar: Champion of the Gods* and *The Court of the Blind King*, the novella *Bonereapers*, and several audio dramas including *Realmslayer* and *Realmslayer: Blood of the Old World*. He is also the author of the Gotrek & Felix novels *Slayer*, *Kinslayer* and *City of the Damned*. For The Horus Heresy he has written the novella *Dreadwing*, and the Primarchs novels *Ferrus Manus: Gorgon of Medusa* and *Lion El'Jonson: Lord of the First*. For Warhammer 40,000 he has written *The Eye of Medusa*, *The Voice of Mars* and the two Beast Arises novels *Echoes of the Long War* and *The Last Son of Dorn*. He is a freelance writer and occasional scientist based in the East Riding, and was a finalist in the 2014 David Gemmell Awards for his novel *Headtaker*.

YOUR NEXT READ

HARROWDEEP
by various authors

Adventurers brave the sunken hell of Harrowdeep, each with a different mission to fulfil. From questing Stormcasts to rival pirate captains, every one of them must fight to preserve their sanity, or risk being buried forever. This collection contains the novellas *Knives in the Deep*, *Nadir* and *The Tale of Priests*.

For these stories and more, go to **blacklibrary.com**, **games-workshop.com**, Games Workshop and Warhammer stores, all good book stores or visit one of the thousands of independent retailers worldwide, which can be found at **games-workshop.com/storefinder**

YOUR NEXT READ

GHOULSLAYER
by Darius Hinks

Gotrek Gurnisson, last survivor of the world-that-was, seeks the Undying King himself amidst the bleak underworlds of Shyish. Surrounded by the ghosts of the past, can Gotrek achieve his goal, or will his soul be forfeit?

For these stories and more, go to **blacklibrary.com**, **games-workshop.com**, Games Workshop and Warhammer stores, all good book stores or visit one of the thousands of independent retailers worldwide, which can be found at **games-workshop.com/storefinder**

YOUR NEXT READ

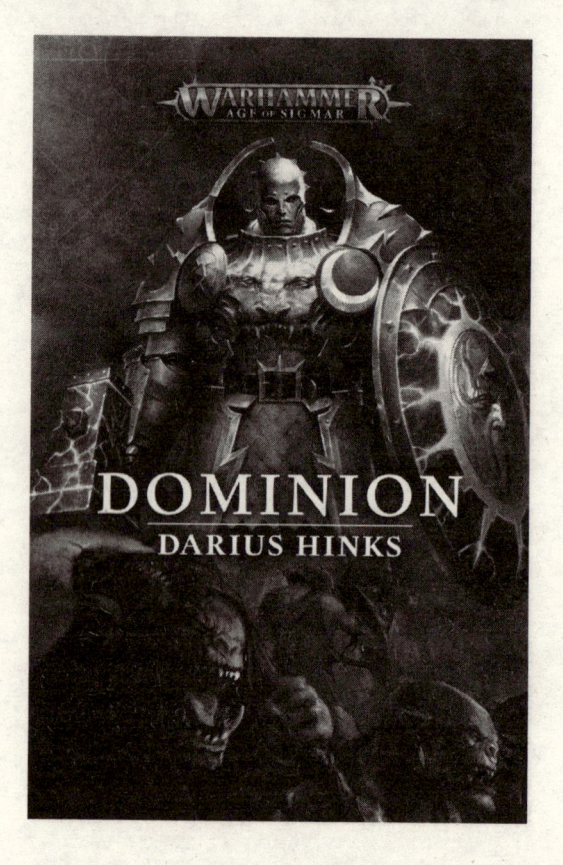

DOMINION
by Darius Hinks

Witness the destructive forces that are on the rise in the Realm of Beasts first-hand, and see the indomitable defences of Excelsis tested like never before.

For these stories and more, go to blacklibrary.com, games-workshop.com, Games Workshop and Warhammer stores, all good book stores or visit one of the thousands of independent retailers worldwide, which can be found at games-workshop.com/storefinder

An extract from
Dominion
by Darius Hinks

The city grumbled and lurched, almost hurling Niksar from the wall. He was perched on a broken lintel, looking down over one of Excelsis' most unwelcoming streets – a rain-lashed warren of lean-tos and hovels that looked discarded rather than built. The Veins had always been one of the poorest parts of the city and, during the tremors of recent months, several streets had caved in, opening craters and revealing the coiled horrors that wormed through the city's foundations.

Excelsis was besieged. Not just by tribes of greenskins but by the land itself. Walls groaned as grubs devoured the mortar. Sewers flooded as lizards spilled from drains. Slates tumbled from roofs, hurled by screeching, feathered rodents. Nothing was stable. The ground stirred, constantly, and every shattered flagstone revealed something repulsive. It was like being on the deck of a sinking ship. And this close to the city walls, the tremors were even more violent.

Niksar looked over at Ocella, hoping she was nearly finished. Ocella was only standing a dozen feet away but he could barely make her out through the mounds of rubbish and debris. He was sure it must be dawn by now, but the light clearly had better places to be. Niksar could sympathise.

As far as he could tell, the exchange was going as planned. The street was deserted and Ocella was talking eagerly to her contact, showing no signs of alarm. She had promised Niksar this would be an easy job. She was meeting a dockhand to buy information, tipped off by one of her pets, and as usual she wanted Niksar on hand in case there was a disagreement. Niksar almost wished there would be so he could shift into a different position, but it all seemed to be going swimmingly. The dockhand was a weaselly old salt Ocella had met on several previous occasions. He was hunched and wizened but Niksar guessed he was probably no older than thirty. Life beyond the city walls was brutal. It took its toll on everyone who sailed the Coast of Tusks.

The dockhand kept glancing up and down the rubble-strewn alley, peering through the rain, clearly nervous. Niksar could see why Ocella had asked him to hide himself up on the wall.

Ocella twitched and threw back her head. Then she laughed. Her laugh was peculiar, a kind of 'haw haw' that reminded Niksar of a coughing dog. The more he worked with her, the stranger he found her. He knew she was wealthy, but she wore filthy animal skins and a tattered cloak of greasy feathers. She looked like she had never slept under a roof. She wore a crooked feather headdress and had dozens of tiny bird skulls plaited into her hair that clattered as she moved. And she moved constantly. It was hard to be sure of her age, covered as she was in muck and feathers, but Niksar guessed she was around twenty years old. Despite that, she held herself like a palsied crone, always flinching, spitting and scratching. She leant constantly on a staff carved from a wing bone. The bone was taller than she was and as she talked it juddered in her hands, shaking rain from the beak at its head.

The meeting continued to be uneventful and Niksar's attention wandered. He had never mentioned it to Ocella, but the role of lookout did not really play to his strengths. He thought about the deal they were hoping to make tomorrow with an armourer over on Quadi Street, then his thoughts ranged into the distant future as he returned to his favourite fantasy. He pictured himself rising from the squalor he had endured for the first twenty years of his life. The city was on the verge of collapse, but his own fortunes had never been better. He was close, this time. Close to really becoming someone of importance – someone who did not have to scrape by to survive. So many of his schemes had come to nothing, but working with Ocella had gained him an incredible collection of artefacts. Strange as she was, he had to agree they were a good team. And, because Ocella thought everyone else in the city was trying to kill her, Niksar could not see their lucrative relationship ending soon. Visions of opulence and power filled his head.

His daydreams were interrupted by movement near his hand. A beetle wriggled from beneath a stone and pounced on a plump, slow-moving grub. The beetle locked its mandibles around its prey and swallowed it whole. Once it had finished eating, the beetle took a few steps, then paused, as though remembering something. Niksar leant closer, fascinated, knowing what would come next. Sure enough, the insect juddered and fell onto its side, twitching and trying to stand, then its carapace burst, revealing a mass of teeming larvae. Mature burrow grubs sacrificed themselves so that their young could start life with a hearty banquet. Niksar grimaced as the larvae devoured their host. There were so many it only took a few seconds.

The land is always hungry, thought Niksar, remembering the words of an old Thondian song.

A loud bang echoed down the alleyway, followed by the acrid

smell of gunpowder. Niksar cursed in surprise and leapt from the wall, drawing his sabre and pointing the blade into the rain.

Ocella stumbled away, and for a moment Niksar thought that his golden goose had been shot. Animals shifted under her furs and glossy eyes stared out at the drizzle, panicked by the noise. Then he noticed that the docker had a hole in his forehead. The man wheezed quietly and crumpled to the ground.

'Sigmar's teeth,' muttered Niksar. In all the times he had worked with Ocella, his presence had been a formality. She was crippled by paranoia but there had never actually been any need for a bodyguard.

The alleyway was empty, but the sound of the gunshot would have carried to all the nearby streets. Passers-by might come to investigate. Or even the city watch.

'Niksar!' cried Ocella, staggering away from the corpse, hysterical, waving her staff at the shadows.

'Damn!' he spat, rushing to her side and staring at the dead body.

Ocella looked everywhere but at him, her eyes rolling loosely in sunken sockets. 'Why weren't you looking?' She laughed, making the haw haw sound again. 'The lookout who doesn't look!' Her straining eyes made it clear that she did not really find the situation amusing. She reached under her furs, trying to calm her rodents and birds.

Footsteps echoed towards them and Niksar hauled Ocella behind a lean-to.

'It came from that direction,' he muttered, peering through the shadows. He tried to shove her further back but she gripped him like a terrified child.

'I told you,' she whispered. 'They're after me.'

'Who?' demanded Niksar, but before she could answer a figure strode into view, splashing through puddles, silhouetted by the dawn. 'It's a guardsman,' muttered Niksar as he saw a Freeguild uniform replete with a polished breastplate and a broad, feather-plumed hat.

'A soldier?' Ocella wiped drool-sodden hair away from her mouth and tucked it behind her ears. She tried to look less panicked but her mouth refused to stop twitching. 'Here? No one comes here. That's specifically why I chose here. Here is where people aren't. If you ask anyone about here, they will–'

'Niksar!' cried a familiar voice.

Ocella gasped and stared at Niksar. 'Did you sell me out?' Her eyes filled with tears. 'You? I thought I could trust you.'

Anger pounded in his temples. 'Of course I didn't sell you out. Just because I fight for glimmerings doesn't mean I'm a–'

'Niksar!' cried the soldier again, pointing a pistol his way and stepping close enough for Niksar to make out a face. It was a young woman in her mid-twenties with an angular, proud face and large, dark eyes. She was tall, broad-shouldered and powerful looking.

Niksar lowered his sword in shock. 'Zagora?'

'Who is it?' hissed Ocella, swaying and stumbling as she tried to look.

'My sister. She won't hurt…' Niksar's words trailed off as he looked at the docker's corpse. 'Zagora,' he demanded, striding out of his hiding place. 'What are you doing here?'

'Saving your life.' She was reloading her pistol as she strode past him towards the docker.

Niksar's rage was starting to be replaced by concern. His sister had forged an impressive career in one of the city's Freeguild regiments. She was risking a lot by coming here and associating with the likes of him and Ocella – never mind shooting dockworkers.

'What are you talking about?' he asked, following her over to the body.

Zagora dropped to one knee beside the corpse, avoiding the quickly spreading pool of blood, and ripped the man's doublet open. Then she stepped back, bumping into Niksar.

'What?' He pointed his sword at the corpse, expecting something to leap at him. His pulse quickened as he saw the tattoos that covered the dead man's chest.

'The Dark Gods.' Zagora made the sign of the hammer across her chest as she stared at the crudely inked symbols. She turned to Niksar, her expression neutral. 'What have you got yourself mixed up in, little brother?'

Niksar shook his head. 'That can't be right. I was just here as a–'

'There are purges happening today. Did you know? This morning. Right across the city.' She pointed at the dead man. 'Because of this. Because of him.'

There was a clattering sound behind them followed by the splash of running feet. Niksar whirled around to see Ocella weaving off through the darkness with surprising speed, her head held low. Niksar considered chasing her but his sister shook her head.

'You really don't want to be seen with that woman.' She nodded in the opposite direction, to the other end of the alley. 'This way.'

Niksar hesitated, looking at the crumpled corpse. 'My fee.'

'Do you realise how bad this is? Even for you?' Zagora waved at the crumbling buildings. 'The city is falling apart. This really is not the time to be seen with cultists. Can't you see what's on his chest? The man's a heretic. If you so much as touch him you'll be strung up outside the White Angels' tower, feeding gulls with your innards.'

Niksar stared at the corpse again. The tattoo was so repulsive it was hard to look at. The shape was simple enough – a fish-like swirl with a circle in its lower half, but it was the details that made his head hurt. The design was covered in intricately inked flames and scales that were morphing into screaming faces. The faces were partly human, but partly something else, something that Niksar could not quite explain but that filled him with inexplicable terror.

He nodded weakly and let his sister lead him away. As soon as they emerged onto one of the wider streets, Zagora stopped running and adopted a confident, nonchalant stride, ignoring the glances that came her way. She was dressed in the gold and red of the Phoenix Company, one of the regiments formed in the wake of the city's recent hardships. She cut an impressive figure and people scattered at her approach, ducking back through the doors of their crooked, tiny shacks.

'I had no idea.' Niksar's pulse was still hammering at the memory of the tattoos. People had been put in the gallows just for looking at symbols like that. 'How did you know? Ocella has always seemed like a reputable–'

Zagora glanced at him. 'Reputable?'

Niksar licked his lips. 'Reputable might not be the right word. But I'd never have dreamt she was involved in anything to do with... I can't believe she would knowingly involve herself with cultists. I didn't think–'

'You didn't think at all. You rarely do. Did you ask her where she met that docker?'

'There's not much point asking her anything, to be honest. She generally just–'

'You could end up swinging from a rope.' Zagora glanced around and lowered her voice. 'Me too, if anyone saw what happened back there. Or if that witch decides to talk.'

'She won't.' Niksar spoke with more confidence than he felt. 'And she's a fool, not a witch. And I'm the only person in the city she trusts. She won't want anything to happen to me.'

Zagora shook her head and continued down the street. 'I heard about this from someone in my regiment, Niksar. I dread to think who else has heard about it. That docker's linked to a cult called the Mirrored Blade. And then, when I heard he was selling things to someone called Ocella I remembered that *you* worked with someone called Ocella. Aren't you two partners?'

Niksar took a deep breath, trying to calm himself. 'Not partners, exactly. That's not the word I would use. I'm just her muscle, really.' Niksar was slender and wiry, but he was good with a sword and he had grown up on the streets, so what he lacked in bulk, he more than made up for in speed and nerve. 'Look,' he said, 'there's no real harm done. Thanks to you. You've got me out of a mess, Zagora. I won't forget it.'

They turned onto one of the city's main thoroughfares leading towards a large market square. The city was as unsteady as Ocella, but life continued. Lots of the traders were already setting up whalebone awnings and unloading their wares, attracting a crowd of peevish-sounding gulls that battled against the rain.

'You might not be out of the mess yet,' said Zagora. 'This morning's purges are being organised by witch hunters.'

'The Order?' Niksar stumbled to a halt.

Zagora waved him on. 'We need to put some distance between us and that body.'

Niksar shook his head as he stumbled across the square. The Order of Azyr were hard-line zealots, killers who hunted down anyone considered a threat to the Sigmarite faith. Their methods of extracting information were famously inventive and as the assaults on the city grew worse, the fanatics gained even more power, striking without censure at anyone they deemed suspect.

'And you need to stay away from that woman,' said Zagora.

They left the square and hurried through the growing light to the edge of the Veins. Finally, after walking in silence for half an hour, they left the slum stacks behind and headed out into the wider, cleaner streets of the Temple Quarter with its grand stormstone facades. The buildings here were sturdy and well-made, and they were still mostly intact. Even here, though, there were cracks in the road that revealed ominous, sinuous shapes beneath. As they wound higher, up through the levels of the city, they began to catch glimpses of the bay and the city's hulking bastion walls, lined with garrisons and siege cannons. Beyond the rain-whipped harbour and the bobbing masts of the ships, Niksar saw the Consecralium: the forbidding keep of the White Angels. It was probably the city's last hope of survival. But it might also be his final resting place if this ever got out.

Zagora saw his troubled glance and paused. They both leant against a wall to catch their breath.

'Look,' she said. 'There's so much going on at the moment that your idiocy will probably go overlooked. You've promised me you'll have nothing more to do with her. And I killed the dockhand. So he's not likely to talk. And I'm sure you weren't so stupid as to be seen in Ocella's company. As long as there's nothing linking you to either of them the Order won't come looking for you.'

Niksar frowned.

She studied him. '*Is* there something linking you to them?'

He looked at the Consecralium again, imagining the White Angels spilling from its depths, nailing the faithless to walls. 'There... Well... Possibly.'

She closed her eyes and let her head fall back against the wall.

'Ocella didn't usually pay me with glimmerings,' he said, referring to the prophetic stones used as currency in Excelsis. 'We had an arrangement. I kept her safe and then we shared the objects she... procured.'

Zagora looked amused. 'You kept her safe?'

'She's still alive.'

She laughed. 'How you've made a career as a hired sword is

beyond me. I saw you up on that wall. You were looking off into nowhere when I shot the docker. Lost in a daydream. Like always.'

'I'm not the dreamer.'

She ignored the jibe. 'Did you keep all the "objects" Ocella gave you?'

'Why wouldn't I? I knew she was odd but I had no idea she was a cultist.'

'I don't know if she's a cultist. But she certainly doesn't worry about whose company she keeps. I'll be amazed if she survives the day. This is not the time to be involved with dubious societies. Did you keep *everything* she gave you?'

'Yes. My plan was to sell them as a collection. I need to raise a lot of glimmerings, you see. I have a problem with–'

Zagora held up a hand. 'One problem's enough for now. I can imagine how many other disasters you're working on.' She looked out at the harbour and the churning clouds. 'Everything might still be fine. If you'd sold any of those things people would be talking about them. But if you've still got them stashed away, no one knows you have them. You have to get back to your rooms. Destroy everything that connects you to Ocella. What are we talking about? A couple of weapons? Some jewellery?'

Niksar massaged his temples, avoiding her gaze. 'It might be easier if I show you.'